last
Bride
standing

D0834458

last
Bride
standing

NEW YORK TIMES BESTSELLING AUTHOR
GINNY BAIRD

Entangled Publishing, LLC
644 Shrewsbury Commons Ave., STE 181
Shrewsbury, PA 17361
Visit our website at www.entangledpublishing.com.

Amara is an imprint of Entangled Publishing, LLC.

Edited by Lydia Sharp
Cover design by Bree Archer
Stock art by VitalikRadko/Shutterstock,
demianchuk.photo/Shutterstock
Interior design by Toni Kerr

Print ISBN 978-1-64937-372-4
ebook ISBN 978-1-64937-416-5

Manufactured in the United States of America

First Edition July 2023

AMARA

ALSO BY GINNY BAIRD

MAJESTIC MAINE

First Bride to Fall
Second Bride Down
Last Bride Standing

BLUE HILL BRIDES

The Duplicate Bride
The Matchmaker Bride

THE HOLIDAY BRIDES SERIES

The Christmas Catch
The Holiday Bride
Mistletoe in Maine
Beach Blanket Santa

To Jill Marsal,
for being the best agent an author could hope for.

CHAPTER ONE

Charlotte Delaney paused outside the airport terminal, scanning the crowd. Throngs of arriving passengers swarmed past her, grasping their shoulder bags and pulling rolling suitcases behind them. Most people were dressed for the mild September weather, in sweaters and light jackets. Others wore flipflops and shorts, like they'd just arrived in Maine from Miami.

Her sisters, Nell and Misty, stood close by, as did Nell's fiancé, Grant, and his best friend, Jordan. The guys had followed Nell's car in Jordan's SUV, coming along "for protection." As if Charlotte needed protecting from anyone but herself.

What on earth am I doing?

Oh yeah, marrying my dad's archenemy's son to save the family business.

Didn't help that she'd lost that bet with her sisters, landing her in this position—as the only one of them not to have found her own true love.

"There!" Nell said, pointing. "I think that's them!"

A tallish guy in a dark blue suit sauntered onto the sidewalk, holding a backpack over one shoulder. His starched white button-down shirt was open at the collar—no tie. Everything about him screamed *upscale*. Even his brown lace-up shoes appeared expensive. He looked like he'd walked straight out of a fancy boardroom meeting, the kind held in London skyscrapers with views of Big Ben and the Thames.

The curvy brunette beside him dragged along a suitcase pasted over with psychedelic decals and travel stickers. She wore a canary-yellow jumpsuit with retro bellbottom pants. Enormous sunglasses shielded her eyes, and her layered hair bounced against her shoulders. From the text Aidan had sent, Charlotte and her sisters knew the woman's name was Trudy.

Misty shouted and waved. "Aidan! Trudy! Yoo-hoo!"

The pair spun in their direction, then Aidan's gaze flitted over the group, landing on Charlotte. Her breath hitched. Aidan Strong was *not* what she expected.

This grown-up version of the nerdy adolescent she'd known as a child wasn't geeky or gangly. He was model-like handsome and carried himself with confidence and style. He strode toward them, the expert drape of his suit jacket and slacks showing off his lean frame. Every. Single. *Ounce* of him was toned to perfection.

"OMG," Nell whispered. "He's—"

"—*hot*," Misty finished for her, speaking in hushed tones.

Charlotte's mouth went dry and she swallowed hard. Looks certainly weren't everything, but he'd come out better than she'd imagined. About a *billion* times better. And it was his billionaire status she needed to focus on, and nothing else.

Her intended marriage to him was in name only and for strategic purposes. He'd agreed to keep her parents' café from going under by subsidizing their outstanding bank loan, and—at the end of five years—she'd own one half of Bearberry Coffee. The half that should have rightfully belonged to her father, if Aidan's dad hadn't cheated him out of it years ago.

So the fact that Aidan was handsome didn't matter one bit.

Still. Her pulse fluttered as he snaked through the crowd with his assistant trailing him.

His short brown hair was cropped closer at the sides, and a portion on top dipped down across his forehead in a sexy swag that seemed purposely casual. His trimmed mustache and beard delineated his sturdy cheekbones and jaw.

Charlotte's heart pounded.

No, no, and no.

But yeah.

If she didn't mistrust him already for agreeing to this business marriage in the first place, she might find herself the slightest bit attracted to him. Assuming he was a stranger and they had no history together. Or a future, either. And, boy oh boy, did they have one of those.

Aidan drew nearer, with Trudy on his heels.

Okay—here we go.

And here he comes.

Looking so much like a dream that Charlotte had to blink. Twice. She stroked the power crystal pendant dangling from her neck when her nerves hummed. Maybe the platonic part of their arrangement wasn't really necessary?

Stop it, Charlotte.

She couldn't muddy the waters by actually

becoming involved with Aidan. That would make things extra messy when dissolving their deal later. Besides, he was probably a jerk. But—*oooh*—his lopsided grin made her knees melt.

She was such a sucker for great-looking men. Unfortunately.

Aidan smiled at her sisters and the guys, then settled his gaze on her. "Hello, Charlotte."

His chestnut-colored eyes twinkled below straight dark eyebrows, and a delighted shiver tore through her. She shook it off, maintaining her cool, although her face burned hot.

"Aidan." She hated that she'd gone a little breathy. "Hi."

"Misty?" Aidan said, observing her sister's shorter stature. "And Nell?" He'd recognized each of them at once.

Then again, Nell's princess hair was pretty hard to mistake. She'd basically been styling it the same since she was younger. He was clearly calculating how grown up they all were, and Charlotte had no doubt her sisters were thinking the same about him.

Nell flipped her long curls back over her shoulder. "Aidan." She grinned and fiddled with a button on her knitted cardigan sweater. Grant wore a matching one. "This is, uh, my fiancé, Grant, and his good friend Jordan."

"Lovely to meet you," Aidan said, before introducing the woman beside him. "This is my assistant, Trudy Steele."

Trudy pushed back her sunglasses, and they formed a headband for her wavy, dark tresses. She kept her gaze on Jordan for an extra beat, then said with a tired smile, "Any chance of a cuppa and a biscuit 'round here? Bloody long flight. I'm knackered."

Her British accent was definitely heavier than Aidan's. Then again, he'd spent his childhood years in America.

Jordan grinned at Trudy. "I'm sure Mr. Mulroney will fix you right up," he said, referring to the owner of the Majestic B&B where they were staying.

"Brilliant," Trudy said. "Can't wait to get there."

"Jordan and I can give you a lift," Grant said, and glanced at Aidan. "Then maybe you can meet up with Charlotte in town?"

Nell grimaced. "My car is small—"

"Right." Aidan nodded. "You're in the saloon."

"Saloon?" Misty wrinkled up her nose, and Aidan chuckled.

"Sorry. I've been in the UK a long while. Saloons are what we call sedans over there."

Misty laughed. "For a minute I thought you were ready to hit the bars."

"Not a ton of those in Majestic," Grant quipped.

Jordan smiled at Trudy. "But the ones that we've got here *are* pretty good."

Charlotte remembered some of that vehicle terminology from the semester she'd studied in Scotland. She was counting on more colloquial tidbits coming back to her once she moved to London. She'd do all right. Maybe not blend in, but get by.

Jordon lifted Trudy's suitcase. "Should I toss this in the *boot* then?" he asked.

Everybody laughed, and Charlotte was glad to feel the tension easing. Good. This was good. The sooner they got this done, the better.

Aidan glanced at her, and his eyes sparkled. Her stomach did a tiny twirl. *Darn it.*

Was she more than he expected? Less?

At least he appeared pleased rather than petrified. He was also incredibly nonplussed for a man about to marry a relative stranger as the result of a remarkable bet. Although they weren't strangers, really. More like long-lost frenemies.

Jordan was absorbed in talking with Trudy, and Grant nudged him then spoke to Nell. "See you back at the ranch?"

By that he meant Nell's cottage by the cranberry bog, because he'd practically moved in there, and this was Nell's day off. It was clear they were going to spend it together. Probably playing Scrabble and kissing.

"Yep." Nell's cheeks turned pink beneath her freckles. "See you there!"

What an exhausting month this had been. First, Nell and Grant had become last-minute engaged, and then so had Misty and Lucas. Charlotte was almost relieved to have their race against each other to find husbands first drawing to a close. Even though she was the designated loser of their bet, at least she was doing something for the greater good of her family.

She stole a glimpse of Aidan's gorgeous profile. Maybe short-term marrying him wouldn't be *too bad*. Assuming he'd outgrown his incredibly annoying one-upmanship habit. For some reason, he'd mostly pulled that with *her* when they were kids and not with her sisters.

Misty glanced at Nell's car, and her brown-with-green-highlights ponytail swung sideways. "Looks like we'd better get going," she said to Nell, who took out her keys.

Wait. Misty's hair had been highlighted pink before, and then purple. Now, suddenly, it was green? How had Charlotte missed that? Maybe because Misty had been riding behind her in the back seat? The color had to be brand new. Like, since yesterday. But that was Misty, always changing her hair, especially when something new happened in her life. Green probably had something to do with her engagement to Lucas.

Aidan tossed his backpack into Jordan's trunk beside Trudy's suitcase. From the size of it, he wasn't planning to stay in Majestic long. Probably just long enough for their rushed nuptials, which meant they needed to get the formalities over with now. Charlotte had agreed to make an appointment at the courthouse for their civil ceremony, but she'd been waiting until he actually showed and made this real.

And boy did it feel real now. Too real.

Charlotte waved at Aidan as Jordan shut his trunk, and his gaze fell on her.

"So…you *did* bring a ring?" She was dying to see it, expecting a huge diamond, one that shouted "I'm engaged to someone filthy rich!" Aidan definitely wouldn't pass up a chance to flaunt his wealth. She'd half expected him to exit the airport holding out a ring box and flipping it open. Which was overly dramatic. She got that. But if they were going to marry for convenience, they could at least pretend to do it right.

Aidan's eyebrows rose. "Ring?"

He was joking, right? He would laugh any moment now and say, "Of course, here it is." But he didn't, and her stomach dropped. Aidan just stood there with a confused look in his eyes, like giving your fiancée a ring was some sort of new idea that hadn't occurred to him.

Seriously?

Airport security guards blew their whistles, motioning vehicles forward. But Charlotte wasn't going anywhere. Not until she knew—for sure—that Aidan was here to uphold his end of the bargain.

She forced her left hand up in the air, even though it felt like it was set in cement, and pointed to her ring finger. Aidan peered at Trudy, and Charlotte's pulse spiked. Maybe he was rethinking things? Having second thoughts? He couldn't do that—not now.

"I'm afraid rings won't be necessary," he said.

Indignance burned through her at his superior tone. If Charlotte could tough out this arrangement and put on a happily married glow in public, then so could he.

"Oh?" she asked. "Why not?" It wasn't like he didn't have the money, and Charlotte would *not* be left out or left behind by her sisters this time.

Nell had a gigantic rock on her hand, thanks to Grant. And Misty and Lucas had exchanged promise rings. Charlotte didn't need much. Just some kind of token. A symbol that Aidan was actually going through with their plans. And since he could afford high-end jewelry, it would have been considerate of him to think of giving some to her.

Trudy pulled a face. "There's not going to be any wedding, ducky."

Charlotte blanched. She could actually feel all the blood draining from her face.

He *wouldn't*—

Nell gawked at Aidan. "You're backing out on our deal?"

Misty set her chin, looking bullish. "You might have said something sooner."

Aidan's left eyebrow arched at Charlotte. "I thought you'd be pleased."

He thought *what*?

She gritted her teeth and tried not to scream. After the utter panic she'd been through? The manhunting, the machinations, the making her sisters believe she might actually win their bet when she'd always known in her heart that she'd be the last bride standing. To what? Get rewarded with a runaway groom?

"You think I'm pleased that you're bailing?" Her temper flared. "Yes, Aidan, I'm thrilled. This is exactly what I wanted—to lose everything."

"Hang on!" Aidan held up his hands. "Nobody's bailing. That's not how this is."

Charlotte glowered at him. "Then how is it?"

His stare back at her was formidable, too. He evidently wasn't apologizing or backing down, no matter what she thought of him.

"Are you saying you put us through that bet for nothing?" Charlotte fumed, running a hand through her hair. "It's been murder in Majestic these past three weeks."

Now, it was September twentieth. Just ten days

before her parents' bank loan came due and they risked losing their café *and* their house.

"Not *totally* murder, though," Nell gushed quietly.

Grant shot her a lovesick grin, which looked a little off on such a tough outdoorsman. "Yeah," he crooned, taking her hand. "Some things have worked out."

"Agreed." Misty sighed, with stars in her eyes.

Charlotte was happy for her sisters—she honestly was—but extremely put out for herself. Not to mention her parents and their family café. She glared at Aidan. The absolute *nerve* of this man. "So all of this has been for nothing?"

"Nothing's been for nothing, Charlotte." He gave her a smug grin. The same know-it-all look he used to get when they were kids that drove her completely over the edge. He'd tended to use it before lowering the boom about something, proving he was right. And Aidan loved being right. All the stinking time.

"What's that mean?" she asked him. Her heart skipped a beat and then it hammered harder. It seemed like the rug was going to get yanked out from under her, and Aidan was going to do the yanking.

Trudy removed a folder from her over-the-shoulder purse and handed it to her. "We're only staying in Majestic long enough to execute our agreement."

Charlotte felt like she'd missed a step and stumbled on some stairs. She wheeled on Aidan. "What's she talking about?"

He cocked his head. "I've no interest in marrying

you, Charlotte. Not here, not now. Not in England later." He frowned. "Pretty much not ever."

The words landed on her like an avalanche, and for a moment she couldn't breathe. Nell steadied her arm, and Misty's eyes widened with fear.

No interest?

Of course he didn't. Charlotte wasn't his sort of woman.

She was a small-town girl who wore flouncy peasant skirts, and he was a world-class bigshot who thought quite a lot of himself. Obviously. Maybe she should have expected his last-minute trick maneuvering. Should have known better than to think he'd honor their arrangement. Or that he'd be honorable at all.

He calmly folded his arms in front of him, like it had all been settled. Like he wasn't just dropping a bomb on all of them.

And with his next words, the bomb exploded, leaving her dazed.

"I'm *giving* you your half of Bearberry Coffee," he said. "Free and clear."

CHAPTER TWO

"What? Why?" Charlotte pressed the folder to her frilly white blouse and pinned Aidan with a hard stare. For a moment, he stared right back, distracted by her eyes. He'd never forgotten their unique color, almost cobalt blue, but seeing it in his memory did no justice to seeing the real thing.

"Because," he said, shaking himself out of his trance before anyone noticed, "your family needs it more than I do."

She wrinkled up her forehead, her dark hair framing her face. It was a nice face, attractive. No. More than that, very lovely actually. But he wasn't interested in Charlotte in that way. He'd been over his boyhood crush on her for ages.

"I don't understand. The agreement was supposed to be for five years, right? And there was something about legalities and splitting the estate?"

"Only in the case of a divorce," he said. "No sense divorcing when this can be settled much more easily."

Her eyebrows twitched. "You mean as a gift?"

"Precisely."

He could sense her mental wheels turning as she chewed on her lip.

"So," she said. "There'll be no marriage?"

He leaned toward her and whispered, "I hardly think we need to do that twice."

Charlotte's face went beet red. Ah, so she did

remember. He'd been wondering about that since Saturday, when he'd learned Charlotte was his appointed "bride."

She stepped closer and hissed, "That was decades ago. We were kids."

True. And Nell had officiated, while Misty had served as the flower girl, but it was doubtful that anyone but him and Charlotte remembered.

It was hard to say whether it had been before or after their pretend nuptials that he'd started thinking of her as alluring and far too sassy for her own good.

But then he'd moved to London and had forgotten all about her for a while. Until his mum and Mrs. Delaney renewed their friendship after his dad died.

Then, lo and behold, his mum announced her plan—he would marry one of the Delaney sisters to save their family business. He'd been more than a little shocked when the three of them had actually gone along with such a ridiculous idea. But he had no intention of ever seeing it through. What was the point?

Charlotte opened the folder and scanned the paperwork, flipping through the pages. "This goes on forever," she said, looking up. "How do I know you're not tricking us somehow?"

"Charlotte, Charlotte," he tsked. "Always the mistrustful one."

That seemed to get her dander up, because she straightened on her…*very nice* cowgirl boots with heels. They suited her and showed off her shapely legs in that short, swishy skirt.

Aidan's chin jerked up. *Stop getting distracted.*

"Mistrustful's not the word I'd choose," she told him. "I'd say careful."

"And caution's a good thing," Nell said, stepping forward.

Misty flanked her other side, surveying the group. "But this is good, right? Bearberry Brews will be saved, and nobody has to go to London. Yay!" She shrunk back and looked at Trudy and then Aidan. "Except for you guys."

Charlotte slapped the folder against her palm, thinking. "I'll need to look this over."

"Of course." Aidan nodded. "Take all the time you need."

"Well," Trudy said. "Not *all* the time. The agreement will need to be executed by close of business on September thirtieth."

"But no reason we can't get it done sooner than that," Aidan said. Much sooner. By late tomorrow morning, he hoped. Then he and Trudy could be on their way.

Charlotte nodded. "Okay. I'll take a look. We all will," she clarified with a glance at her sisters. "Can you send this to me electronically, too?"

Trudy efficiently took out her phone, tapping with her thumbs on the keypad. "Sent!"

A few seconds later Charlotte's cell dinged. "Um, thanks, Trudy," she said, appearing a bit stunned.

Charlotte Delaney had grown into a beautiful woman. But she wasn't the woman for him. A marriage of convenience in the modern age? No. That would do a huge injustice to both of them, and enough hurts had already been heaped on the Delaney family by the Strongs. Aidan wasn't going to add insult to injury by including one more.

"Brilliant. Looks like you're off the hook, then."
He grinned, leaning toward her. "And so am I."

• • •

Aidan turned to Trudy in the back of Jordan's SUV.
"Well, that went swimmingly, don't you think?"

"Erm. I wouldn't say Charlotte was chuffed to
bits. I think she was a touch thrown. Maybe all of
them were?"

Jordan smiled at Aidan through his rearview mirror. "Generous offer, though!"

Grant cleared his throat and mumbled something
about too little too late.

When Trudy raised her eyebrows at Aidan, he
whispered, "Better late than never."

She nodded in her professional way. Trudy was so
on point with everything. He'd never get along without her. She'd been the one hounding the attorneys
about the corporate division while he'd been busy
running the business. There were a number of things
he'd needed to set in place before taking this trip to
America.

Ahh, Maine.

He settled back in his seat, enjoying the view. The
rugged coastline lay beneath the highway, white-
capped waves battering the shore. It was quiet here.
Scenic. And the farther they got from the airport,
the more serene the ocean's panorama became. The
sun was halfway down in the west, and a purple-and-
orange haze stretched across the water, traveling out
to sea.

So far from home now, and yet he was also coming home. Back to the place where he'd lived as a boy. When he saw the town with fresh eyes, would Majestic look the same? He had so many happy memories of this place—he tugged at his too-tight seat belt—but also a few really awkward ones.

Though the Delaney sisters had all matured physically, he still spied glimpses of the girls he'd known in their personalities. Tender, mother-henish Nell. Sweet, wide-eyed Misty. Headstrong, spunky Charlotte.

There was still something about her. Something slightly unnerving. Maybe even exciting…

But no. He wouldn't let his mind go there.

Not even for a minute.

"Penny for your thoughts?" Trudy whispered, and he realized he'd missed a bit of conversation. Jordan had been asking Trudy if she'd been stateside before and telling her about fun things to do in and around Majestic, but Aidan's mind had been elsewhere.

And it kept flipping back to Charlotte.

He'd guessed that the Delaney girls would all turn into attractive women, but he hadn't pegged Charlotte for the stunner she'd become. She was also the marketing muscle behind Bearberry Brews, so she was clearly intelligent as well. And yet, when she'd needed to find a husband in thirty days, she hadn't.

"I'm just ready to get this over with," he said, answering Trudy. "The sooner, the better." This drama between his family and the Delaneys had gone on long enough, and he was ready to put an end to it.

Then he could return to London and get back to the business of running one half of the company that should have been jointly owned with Charlotte's family from the start. Sure, there'd be adjustments to make, but righting past wrongs was never easy. Charlotte was just the sort of person to point that out to him, repeatedly, so he'd decided to nip that problem in the bud by proactively giving her what she wanted, rather than live with her reminders during the course of some insufferable fake marriage that was never meant to be.

He recalled Charlotte's deep-blue gaze washing over him, and he yanked at his open collar, cooling his suddenly warm neck. She'd had some sort of effect on him when they were kids, but that was ages ago, and now that they were grown, one thing was certain. Aidan wasn't letting Charlotte call the shots anymore. He was the one fully in command of this situation, and he was determined to hold his ground.

• • •

Misty leaned forward from the back seat of Nell's car. "So this is good, yeah? Aidan's giving us one half of Bearberry Coffee free and clear!"

Charlotte cracked open the folder. "Hmm. Maybe."

Nell shot her a glance from behind the steering wheel. "Charlotte," she said in lilting tones. "What's that sneaky gleam in your eyes?"

Charlotte dropped the folder to her lap. "It's not sneaky, Nell. I'm just thinking."

"What's there to think about?" Misty asked her.

She peered over her shoulder. "Oh. A lot."

Charlotte crossed her arms and stared out the window, still fuming. Aidan might have warned her that this was his plan instead of torturing her with the thought of marrying him until the very last minute. She couldn't help believing he'd dropped his bombshell the way he had on purpose. To somehow get the better of her and her sisters.

Maybe because he'd disapproved of their bet, so he had never been fully on board with the moms' proposed merger to begin with. But if that's how he'd felt, he could have stepped up and said so.

Thank goodness she wasn't marrying him. He *was* a jerk. The jerkiest kind of jerk. The sort who enjoyed jerking her chain, and she didn't like it. One bit.

"Oh. My. Gosh." Nell gasped. "You're insulted, aren't you?"

"Insulted?" she asked, probably sounding very insulted for sure. "No."

Misty laughed in disbelief then spoke to Nell. "It's true." Charlotte flipped down her vanity mirror, seeing Misty shake her head. "She's ticked."

"Why?" Nell turned to Charlotte. "Because he rejected you?"

Charlotte tsked. "Did you see that smug look of his? Like he'd planned this?"

"Well, he had to have planned it," Nell stated reasonably. "Gotten things in order."

"He could have let me know, too." Every word snapped like a rubber band. "Might have given me some warning. Warned all of us, Nell."

"Come on, Charlotte," Misty cajoled. "Lighten

up. It's not like you actually wanted to marry the man."

Nell playfully rolled her eyes. "Yeah, and he pretty clearly doesn't want to marry Charlotte."

A muscle in Charlotte's jaw tensed.

"At least she won't have to tell Mom and Dad about her sudden horrible marriage now," Misty went on in a gossipy fashion. "Although, to be fair"—she giggled—"Aidan doesn't seem so horrible after all. He's total man candy."

"No joke." Nell laughed. "Charlotte nearly swallowed her tongue!"

"You two can stop talking about me like I'm not here now."

"We weren't talking *about you*," Nell said.

"Yes, you were. You were doing that thing."

Misty's mouth fell open. "What thing?"

"*Oh, Charlotte knows everything*," she said, imitating Misty. "And, *leave it to the bossy one to be the boss*!" she finished, mimicking Nell. "You both do that, you know. Talk about me to my face behind my back."

Misty sighed. "That doesn't even make sense."

"She's just cranky," Nell said.

Charlotte groaned. "You're doing it again!"

"Yikes!" Misty said. Then she added more meekly, "Sorry, Charlotte."

Charlotte glared at Misty, but then she softened her stance. "What's with the hair, anyway?" She pointed at Misty's ponytail. "Why green?"

Misty grinned goofily. "Because of me and Lucas." She batted her eyelashes. "Our love is evergreen."

"That's sweet." Nell sighed, and Charlotte shook her head. Her two sisters were sappier than the sappiest Maine maple tree. Still, she loved them both dearly. They couldn't help who they were any more than she could.

Nell put on her soothing voice. "Honey, look at the bright side," she said to Charlotte. "This is a good thing."

Charlotte cocked her chin. Somehow she felt like Aidan owed them more. "Could be better, though, right?"

"Char-lotte," Nell said. "What are you thinking?"

She wasn't prepared to tell her sisters how it had stung when Aidan had practically scoffed at her about that ring. The imaginary ring that had only ever existed in Charlotte's head. But Misty was right. It wasn't like she actually ever wanted to marry Aidan.

"Better how?" Misty asked.

"He's already giving us half," Nell said.

"Yeah, but," Charlotte turned in her seat to look at Misty and then Nell, "more than half would make more sense, don't you think? Would better make amends."

Nell briefly took her eyes off the road. "More?"

"Think about it," Charlotte said, because her mind had been whirling ever since Aidan made his pronouncement. "Maybe fifty percent isn't good enough. It was Dad and Mom who came up with the whole berry-flavored coffee theme, not the Strongs. They're still innovating to this day, inventing more flavors, while Bearberry Coffee—the corporate deal—has stuck to a steady but limited brand."

"Their branding seems to be working," said Nell.

Yeah, Charlotte knew all about branding because she'd studied marketing in school. She also believed that Bearberry Coffee could have expanded its niche in the coffee industry even further if they'd been more innovative. By having her parents involved in product development, for example. But they hadn't.

"Our parents started the shop!" she contested hotly. "They only brought in John and Jane Strong as a favor, due to Dad and Mr. Strong's old friendship. Mr. Strong was out of work and Mrs. Strong had just had Aidan."

"It wasn't just on account of their friendship," Nell said. "Mr. Strong was very good at business and about seeing the big picture. Mom and Dad are creative and fun, but more focused on the smaller details."

"True," Misty chimed in. "Finances have never been Mom or Dad's strength." She paused. "Didn't Mrs. Strong used to keep the books for the shop?"

"She did," Nell said. "Then Mom handled that for a while, which honestly"—she shrugged—"might have helped land us in this financial mess. When I took over the bookkeeping after college, things were in a shambles. Dad had tried to help Mom, but he was more hopeless with numbers than she was. And the more they struggled, the less they could consider hiring outside help."

"Wait." Misty rubbed the side of her nose that didn't hold the silver stud. "Is that why you majored in accounting?"

Nell smiled at Misty in her rearview mirror.

"Somebody had to step in. And anyway." She flipped back her curls. "I'm good with math."

"Yeah," Misty said. "And Mr. Strong was great at business."

"Right." Charlotte frowned. "So great he cheated our dad—therefore our family—out of some pretty hefty profits. Profits that should have been *maybe even more than* fifty percent ours. Say, seventy-five percent." Her stomach churned. Somehow that number didn't seem high enough. Not considering the extra anxiety Aidan had put them all through without announcing his intentions honorably and from the start. "No, eighty percent."

Misty giggled behind her. "Wow, Charlotte. Why not go for a hundred percent while you're at it?"

Of course. Yeah, she should. Because, honestly? What did she have to lose? Aidan wouldn't pull back his offer now, but he could potentially make it sweeter. "Misty," she said. "You're a genius. I think we should."

"You want Aidan to give us a hundred percent interest in Bearberry Coffee?" Nell raised her eyebrows. "I don't think he'll go for that."

"He might." Charlotte stared back out her window. "When I appeal to his pride."

●●●

Jordan pulled his SUV up in front of an old wood-framed Victorian house. The brick-red paint that Aidan remembered had faded to a dusty rose, and spreading boxwoods partially obscured ground-floor windows.

"It's better on the inside," Jordan said, hopping out of the driver's seat.

Aidan nodded. "I'm sure it's fine."

Nothing could be too bad for just a day or two. He was bone-tired from his flight, so he would sleep well tonight regardless. Besides that, there was no other lodging in Majestic.

He stared at the house with its peeling white-painted railings, recalling the colorful gardens that had once hugged its wraparound porch. Mr. Mulroney had apparently struggled with running the place since losing his wife, although Jordan had said he'd recently hired an assistant.

Trudy and Aidan exited the vehicle, too, as Grant rolled down his passenger-side window.

"Have a great short stay in Majestic," Grant said.

"Will do, mate." As soon as he and Charlotte executed that paperwork, he'd be on the very next plane. Which was precisely what Aidan wanted. Any curiosity he had about the town and how it had—and hadn't—changed could be satisfied in a couple of hours. He'd already witnessed the transformation among the Delaney sisters.

Trudy smiled, her eyes masked by her sunglasses. "Nice meeting you, Grant."

"Yeah, Trudy. You too." He shot her a captain's salute, and Aidan grabbed his backpack.

Jordan reached for Trudy's bag. "Want me to take this in for you?"

"Why, thanks, Jordan." She lowered her sunglasses then removed them, dropping them in her purse. "I heard there were gentlemen in America."

Jordan laughed. "Yeah. One or two."

Aidan's cell phone buzzed, and he took it from his pocket.

Charlotte: *Coffee at Bearberry Brews?*

Aidan checked the time on his phone and the fading light in the sky. The café had to be closing soon. Charlotte's family owned the place, though, so she could stay as late as she wanted.

Aidan: *Be there shortly.*

She didn't have to tell him how to get there. He'd lived in this same part of town growing up, and the main drag facing the ocean was just three blocks from here.

Jordan paused by the inn's front door, holding it open for Trudy.

Trudy glanced at Aidan and he tucked his phone away. "Coming!"

The B&B had a musty aura, and heavy swagged curtains lined its windows. A posh parlor sat to the left, and a dining room with a long table and seating for twelve was situated on the right of them as they stood in the foyer. An old-fashioned registration desk lay straight ahead. An older woman with gray braids stood behind it.

"Welcome!" Her baby-blue eyes shone within her wrinkled face. "You must be our guests from London."

"We are." Aidan smiled. "Aidan Strong."

Jordan set down Trudy's bag beside her, and she smiled at the innkeeper. "Trudy Steele."

"Crystal." The elderly woman checked a hardcovered register, flipping forward and backward through its pages.

"Sorry," she groused, but her tone was cheery. "I

keep telling Matthew we need to automate." She ran a knotty finger down a page then grinned, looking up. "Here you are! In rooms three and four upstairs."

An older gentleman tapped his way toward them using a cane. His white beard and mustache matched his snowy hair. He grinned at Jordan. "I see you've made your special delivery."

"How ya doing, Mr. Mulroney?" Jordan asked.

"Can't complain." He grinned at Crystal. "And if I do, somebody here will scold me."

"Well, maybe you need scolding once in a while," she said with a hint of sass.

Mr. Mulroney shook his finger at her, but it was all in fun. "Second day on the job and she's already taking over."

Crystal passed Trudy and Aidan their keys. "If I'd taken over," she quipped, "we'd have online booking by now."

Mr. Mulroney play-shuddered. "She wants to get me on the internet."

Jordan's dark eyes sparkled. "Maybe that's not a bad thing?"

"Not teaching this old dog those new tricks." Mr. Mulroney motioned toward Aidan and Trudy. "Come with me. I'll show you around."

Jordan stopped him before he turned. "Ah. Once they're settled in, could you fix them up with some tea?"

Trudy flushed, her gaze traveling over Jordan. "Kind of you to remember."

Mr. Mulroney said, "Of course. Crystal"—he shot her a look—"can you put the kettle on?"

She rolled her eyes at the others. "No microwaves in this house."

"Who needs microwaves," Mr. Mulroney grumbled, "when we've got a perfectly good stove right there in the kitchen?"

The rest of them laughed at their mild banter.

"How do you take your tea?" Crystal asked Trudy and Aidan as they departed.

Trudy smiled. "One sugar and a spot of milk."

"I'll skip the tea for now," Aidan said. "But thank you. I'm meeting Charlotte for coffee in town."

Trudy's eyebrows arched. "Would you like me to come with you?"

Since he wasn't sure what Charlotte wanted, he decided to decline. Charlotte had been broadsided at the airport, unprepared for how to respond. Now that she'd had a few minutes to think on his offer, she was likely brimming with gratitude. It had taken a serious effort with his attorneys to find the best way to cede half his corporation to the Delaneys without saddling them with a huge tax burden and other headaches. All Charlotte had to do now was sign on the dotted line on behalf of her family—and before a notary public.

"No," he told Trudy. "Why don't you stay here and relax? Rest up for our flight back tomorrow."

"I can bring your tea up to your room if you'd like?" Crystal offered.

Trudy covered her mouth when she yawned. "That would be splendid, thanks." She smiled at Jordan. "Thanks again for the ride."

Jordan grinned and backed toward the front door. "Any time."

After Mr. Mulroney's brief tour of the downstairs, Aidan and Trudy headed to their rooms to settle in. They paused outside their doors, which were across the hall from each other.

Aidan took out his key. "Guess I'll see you back here in a bit."

Trudy nodded and unlocked her door. "Have a nice coffee with Charlotte."

He hoped it *would* be nice. Nice and short.

Though he was accustomed to being lauded professionally, he'd never handled personal praise very well. He didn't need to sit through a prolonged bout of Charlotte gushing out her thanks. Her simple acknowledgment of his very fair offer would do fine.

CHAPTER THREE

Charlotte fiddled with the coffee stirrer at her café table, unsure why she'd even grabbed one. She took her coffee black. After helping the others clean up, she'd left a few things on the coffee bar, including a carafe of home brew and a carafe of creamer, in case Aidan wanted some. She checked the time on her phone. He'd be here any minute.

Which was fine. Totally fine. Exactly what she wanted.

She needed to nail down her agreement with him, but not in the way he suspected.

Lucas passed through the room, jangling his keys. "Want me to leave these in the door?"

"Yeah, sure. I'll lock up."

"Good luck then. With Aidan." Lucas was so sweet and sincere. Thank goodness he and Misty had finally made things official. It had taken Misty forever to get it through her thick skull that their gray-eyed café manager was her *one*. Charlotte still didn't regret the "marry me" billboard. Not given the outcome in her little sister obtaining her happily ever after.

"Ready to go?" Misty asked, appearing from the kitchen. Lucas nodded, and she cast a glance at Charlotte. "If you want us to stay, though… While you and Aidan talk?"

Charlotte smiled. Kind of her to offer, but Charlotte operated better on her own, without her sisters' interference. "I've got this. Thanks."

"Well, I for one hope he goes for it," Lucas said.

Misty slipped into her denim jacket. "I for two!"

"Me for three," Mei-Lin announced, bouncing into the room and tucking her folded apron behind the counter.

She'd been in a great mood ever since she'd connected with Dusty. That had been on account of Charlotte's billboard as well. She had to take credit where credit was due.

Mei-Lin buttoned her coat then slid her frameless glasses back onto her nose where they immediately slipped. "One day I'm going to get these adjusted," she joked. "Or maybe…" She shrugged. "Make a bold move and get contacts."

"I like you in those glasses," Lucas said. "But I can see where contacts would work."

"Mei-Lin's always beautiful," Misty said. "No matter what she wears."

Mei-Lin rolled her eyes, but then she giggled. "Thanks, guys. I love you, too." She turned to Charlotte. "I can hang for a few, if you'd like." But Charlotte knew she had things to do. Mei-Lin had been invited to Wyoming to see Dusty's ranch, and she was bubbly excited about it.

"Don't you have packing to do?"

Mei-Lin grinned. "Yeah, I guess." Misty was driving her to the airport at the crack of dawn, so they had an early morning tomorrow.

Charlotte gestured toward the door, shooing them away. "Seriously, guys. I'll be fine."

Still, her hand shook when she laid it on the table. She wrapped her fingers around her ceramic coffee mug to steady them. Silly to be nervous. And she wasn't, really. All she was going to do was try to convince Aidan to give her family more than half his business. All of it, if things broke the way she hoped they would. This was her town after all. She knew it best and that would work to her advantage in what she had planned.

"So then," Misty said, following Mei-Lin and Lucas out the door. "Text me?"

Charlotte gave her a thumbs-up and waved to Mei-Lin. "Have a great trip!"

She heard them exchange greetings with some-one on the sidewalk. Seconds later, Aidan pushed open the café door. "Charlotte." He grinned and her heart gave a tiny thump.

She didn't need that.

Not today. Or any day.

And definitely not with Aidan.

She had a deal to strike with the man, who— *moved like poetry in motion. Everything about him flowed.* That careless sweep of hair… The contours of his beard… The subtle smile that said he knew how to take control.

Of about any situation except this one.

He took off his suit jacket, hanging it over the back of his chair, and taut muscles flexed below the fabric of his shirt.

She would *not* be swayed by a super-hot body and a handsome grin. She'd been down that road before, and it was a dead-end street.

Charlotte sat up straighter in her chair. "Coffee?"

"Sure." She stood to serve him a cup, but he held up his hand. "Stay where you are. I've got it." He winked and her skin tingled all over, darn it. "I've had a bit of practice."

"I'm sure you have." *Moving all that product after your family cheated mine.* But she needed to stay focused here and negative thoughts clouded her mind.

He poured himself a cup of coffee from the carafe and raised the cup to his nose. "Ahh. Caramel apple something." He glanced at her. "Am I right?"

"Cranberry," she said, naming the other prominent flavor.

He took a careful sip because it was piping hot. "Mmm. Delicious."

He walked toward her, and she tried hard not to think about how great he looked. She'd been out with dozens of nice-looking guys, but he put them all to shame. Still, that didn't mean she was interested in *him.* She was merely being observant.

He sat at the table across from her. "You wanted to see me?"

Charlotte gathered her nerve, focusing on her goals. And *not* on his chestnut-colored eyes. Or the little shimmer they held in the dim light. "Yes, I did."

"Because if you've brought me here to thank me, that's not really—"

"What?" She blinked. "I mean, yeah. No. Of course I'm sort of grateful—"

"Sort of?" His eyebrows knitted together, and she blew out a breath.

"Listen, Aidan. It's not what you think."

"No?"

"No. This conversation's not about me accepting

your offer." She licked her lips. "I want you to reimagine it."

He leaned back in his chair. "Reimagine it how?"

Charlotte's heart pounded. "By making it fairer."
She tucked a lock of her hair behind one ear. "More
fair."

He appeared amused, then drank from his coffee
cup before saying, "Look, Charlotte. What I'm offering is more than fair."

"We Delaneys don't take handouts," she said
proudly. "We work for what we get, even though
sometimes we don't get all that we've worked for."

He set down his cup, waiting for her to continue.
"I'm listening."

It's now or never, so here goes.

"Okay," she said. "Your offer is generous, yes. But
maybe not generous enough, given the financial
strain my family endured when you guys went off to
England to lead your ritzy lifestyle."

"Wasn't always so ritzy."

"What? No gigantic estate? Fancy cars?"

"All right," he conceded. "There might have been
a flash car or two."

"Two?" Charlotte's blood boiled, but she found
her anger helpful. Far better to become incensed
than attracted. Too much was at stake here. "Misty
still doesn't even own one."

"She's the youngest of you three."

"She's twenty-six, Aidan." Charlotte clicked her
tongue. "How old were you when you got your first
'flash' whatever."

"Sixteen."

"Make?"

"BMW." He sank down in his chair. "So, okay. My family came out better than yours. You might even call them minted—"

"Minted?" She squared her shoulders and leaned forward.

"Loaded, fine. However you say it, rolling in the dough, and I'm sorry, Charlotte. Really, I am. That's why I want to make things right."

"By giving us half of Bearberry Coffee?"

He smiled. "That was the deal."

"That was the *initial deal* our two moms concocted," she noted, "but maybe my mom wasn't thinking big enough." She thought of her parents and her heart ached. "You were gone these past twenty years, so you don't know what it's been like around here. Dad was never the same after that sneaky trick your dad pulled about distribution rights."

"Look. I know that wasn't cool. But I didn't even understand what had gone down until after my dad died and I took over the business."

Her eyes grew hot, but she held in her tears. "My dad never even got my mom an engagement ring. Did you know that?"

His face fell. "No, I… I didn't know."

"In the early days, none of them had money. Your folks were broke and unemployed and my folks were dirt poor after they'd used the last of their savings to open this shop. In spite of that, my parents took pity on yours and brought them into the business. Even though they could barely rub two dimes together themselves, that's just how they were. Are. No matter how small the meal is on the stove, they always make more room at their table. My sisters and I saw that time and again growing up, and they're still like that today. So good-hearted.

"Dad proposed to Mom saying someday he was going to make Bearberry Brews really special. Something bigtime in Majestic, maybe even the world." Hurt bubbled up inside her, burning her throat. "And the moment he did, he was going to buy her the largest, most glamorous diamond money could buy."

Aidan frowned. "But that never happened."

"Today's their thirty-fifth wedding anniversary," Charlotte said. "After all these years, Dad decided to finally go for it. Since he's cash-poor, he made an arrangement with a local jeweler. Paid on a ring on lay-away for nearly a year. Mom didn't know anything about it, but maybe she does by now. He'd planned to surprise her with the ring today."

Gentle creases formed around his mustache and beard. "That's sweet."

"Yes, but so unnecessary. Dad shouldn't have had to go through that, or the threat of losing their house. The café's been hurting financially more and more, and now we're on the brink of—" She pressed her lips together because she couldn't bear to say *closing permanently*.

He reached across the table and touched her arm.

Charlotte's nerves skittered when warmth pooled in her belly.

"Listen," he said, his voice all husky in a way that made her skin tingle. "I'm sorry. So sorry about everything your family's been through. That's why I'm here with Trudy and the paperwork. I'm not sure what else I can do."

"I want all of it," she blurted out before losing her nerve.

He pulled back his hand as if she'd slapped it. "All?"

"Yes, Aidan. Everything. One hundred percent interest in Bearberry Coffee. My parents came up with the concept and the coffee blends that made it a success."

"Maybe that's true, but— "

"One hundred percent. I won't settle for less."

He laughed. "You can't be serious."

She bristled. "Oh, yes, I am. After everything you've put us through, you and your parents too. We deserve it. You could have told us, Aidan. Told me and my sisters about your intentions from the start. That you wanted to give us our share outright with no kind of marriage involved. Instead you led us on about the bet, wreaking havoc in our lives."

"No, Charlotte. You did that. That bet was all on you three. I had nothing to do with it."

"I beg your pardon, you had everything to do with it. We were all in a race not to marry you!"

"In that case." He smirked. "Congratulations to Misty and Nell for taking the Silver and Gold."

"Very funny."

He slowly clapped his hands. "And you're the 'loser.'"

"I only 'lost' because I wanted to," she claimed, growing irritated. "I threw it."

While that wasn't technically true, because she hadn't given up until the end, who was she to argue with Nell's and Misty's newfound happiness? It wasn't like she had a *happily ever after* in store for herself anytime soon. And she might *never*, as far as she knew.

"Threw the bet?" He set his elbows on the table. "Interesting. Why?"

"Because I knew it was for the best for Nell and Misty. And just look at them. I was right. They've found their perfect guys."

"I'm sorry I'm such a disappointment." His lips twitched. "That must have been hell, believing you had to marry me."

"Oh, stop."

"A young, single billionaire who runs his own corporation. No doubt enough to send most women fleeing from that consolation prize." She could tell he was trying not to chuckle. "I'm surprised you never asked for a photo."

"Would you have sent one?"

He shrugged. "I had no trouble tracking yours down."

Charlotte gasped. "What? Where?"

"On social media," he said. "You're all over the place."

"That's promo for the café."

"Looked more like promo for yourself. Except for that one interesting shot of the billboard saying 'Marry Me: Misty.' That was clearly for her."

Charlotte didn't know whether to be creeped out or flattered that he'd cyber-stalked her. "What were you looking me up for anyway?"

"I guess I was curious about the woman who'd throw all caution to the wind and get on a plane to

London to marry some fellow she hadn't seen in twenty years."

"Well, I was never curious about you. Not even the tiniest bit," she lied. "Besides, Nell was willing to do it too. So was Misty. Any of us would have stepped forward to save the family business and our parents' home."

"Yes, but, ultimately, it was you who did." His eyes sparkled. "In a way, I'm glad."

"Why's that?"

"I couldn't imagine having as interesting a conversation with either Nell or Misty. I'm betting neither of them would have asked for one hundred percent interest in Bearberry Coffee, either. That kind of action takes balls."

She squared her shoulders. "Why didn't you tell us sooner? Huh? Tell us you never intended to follow through with the marriage of convenience with any of us?" She leaned toward him, and he angled forward too.

"Because," he said in a low tone, "I had no clue about what you ladies were up to over here. Honestly? I thought the three of you might be pranking me, like you used to do when we were kids. *'Hey, psst. Let's pick on Aidan. Let's tell him a big whale's washed up on the beach and watch him rush down there only to see that one hasn't.'*"

"Okay. But that only happened once."

"There were other things too," he said. "You three Delaney sisters were tricksters, and you, Charlotte, were the trickiest of all." He winked, and her face flushed in spite of herself.

"So what?" she asked. "Not telling us was

payback for all that childhood stuff? We were kids, Aidan. And you pranked us too."

"Payback?" He laughed. "You must be joking. Why would I go there?"

"I don't know. Why would you?"

"Why would you, Charlotte? Hmm?" He held her gaze, and her breath quickened. "You clearly want payback now, don't you? A hundred percent?" He scoffed but a smile tugged at his lips. "What do you expect me to do? Just hand over the whole company?"

"No," she said with an edge. "I intend to win it from you, fair and square." She expected him to mock her or make some glib comment about that never happening. Instead, he leaned back in his chair, waiting for her to continue.

"What do you have in mind?"

Okay then. It's go-time.

"I'm proposing a contest between the two of us."

He shook his head. "Competitive to a fault."

She ignored his comment and barreled ahead. "We have an annual festival coming up. Fall Fest. There are booths for food and drinks. Local artisans sell things. You probably remember it from when you lived here as a kid."

"Yeah. And?"

"And I was thinking we could sell things too."

"We?"

"You and me," she said, super proud of herself for arriving at the idea, since she was pretty much guaranteed to win. "But not together. Separately. We'll each man a booth selling our own brand of coffee. Whichever one of us sells the most cups of coffee wins."

He rubbed the side of his neck. "That's hardly a contest."

"It is when the stakes are high enough."

His eyebrows rose.

"Here's what I'm suggesting," she said. "If you win, you do exactly what you came to Majestic to do. Cede one half of the company to my family."

"And if I lose?"

"You give us everything."

His mouth dropped open, but then he closed it. "Everything? Meaning, I'll be out of a job?"

"Like my parents and my sisters and I have been teetering on the edge of losing ours?"

"Those stakes are awfully high, Charlotte."

She folded her arms across her chest. "I knew you'd be too chicken to do it."

His eyes flashed. "I'm not chicken."

"Oh yes you are." She flapped her arms like chicken wings and made squawking sounds.

His cheek flinched. "I'd have thought you would've given up on jeering by now."

"I am not jeering. I'm challenging."

"But doubting."

"What?"

He grinned. "You don't believe I'll do it, do you?"

Her heart beat double-time. "Will you?"

"All I have to do is outsell you with coffee?" he said. "Easy-peasy. Bearberry Coffee has been outselling Bearberry Brews for years."

"Underhandedly."

"Even so." He cocked his head. "By billions."

"Billions which should have been rightfully ours."

"So, it's winner takes all with you, is it?" He pursed his lips. "But only if you win?"

Charlotte's face steamed. "When I win."

"You seem very sure of yourself." Aidan stroked his beard. "How do I know you haven't got this contest all stitched up?"

As if she'd had time to arrange anything sneaky and dishonest. No. That wasn't her. "I'm affronted you'd even think that."

"I'm affronted you called me a chicken."

"Well, maybe you are a little chicken. Maybe that's what this trip is all about. Your chickening out of our marriage deal."

"So. Wait. You actually *wanted* to marry me?" He gawked in disbelief and she backtracked quickly.

"You know I didn't," she huffed.

He studied her a moment. "And yet you were prepared to go through with it."

"For the sake of the business and my family." She tried to turn the tables. "Don't tell me you wouldn't do anything for your mom. Isn't that why you agreed to the bet to begin with?"

"I never said that I agreed."

"I beg to differ. You most certainly did."

"No," he insisted. "You set up the wager with your sisters and sent me the particulars."

Charlotte got her guard up. "And you texted back *brilliant*."

"Because it was such a brilliant plan. In a nineteenth-century sort of way." His mouth twitched at the corners. "Who thought it up? You, Charlotte?"

"It wasn't anybody alone," she said defensively.

"It was the three of us together."

He whistled through his teeth. "Ace team. I suspect they're going to help you sell your coffees then? Misty and Nell." He grinned. "At the Fall Fest."

"Wait." She swallowed hard. "You mean you'll do it?"

"I can't see why not. If it makes you feel better about things, I'm all for it. So yeah, my dad was shite to yours, but now that's over, and my giving you one half of the company that my dad built with his business savvy seems more than fair. Since that's not good enough for you, I'm happy to up the ante, because I know one thing for certain."

"What's that?"

"I'm a far better businessperson than you are, so you'll never win." Those were fighting words. "Not in the way you're hoping you will."

Says who? She was good at business. No, *great*.

Okay. True. Her family business was failing, but she wasn't to blame for that. She'd been helping Bearberry Brews with her advertising—every chance she got.

He grabbed his jacket from the back of his chair and shook it out before sliding it on. "I'm willing to humor you, though."

Humor? She gritted her teeth.

"For old times' sake."

He stood and so did she, scraping back her chair.

"How good of you." Sarcasm dripped off her tongue, then she faked a British accent and said, "Brilliant."

"I am rather a brilliant fellow, aren't I?" He

stepped toward her. "Which is why I'm rising to your challenge and saying yes."

She couldn't decide if she wanted to smack him for his arrogance or hug him for agreeing to her contest. This could be huge for her and her family. Either way, it was a win. The only one with anything to lose was Aidan.

He not only stood to forfeit his entire business, he was blithely abandoning what was supposed to have been their arranged marriage. He clearly thought he could take her or leave her. That she wasn't worth considering in any sort of romantic way. Maybe he wouldn't have been so cavalier about canceling their personal merger if he'd understood what he was missing.

"And when you *lose* Bearberry Coffee," she asked him, "how will you support yourself?"

"I'm a trust fund baby." He smiled. "I'll land on my feet."

"How lucky for you."

"My dad set up separate nest eggs for both me and my mum."

His whole world could be turned upside down and he didn't care? Nice to be that comfortably taken care of that losing your job didn't matter. None of the Delaneys had ever known that luxury, but evidently the Strongs had.

"So you'll do it?" she asked.

"Under two conditions."

"And what are those?"

"One. We can't let on to the town what our bet's about. Not the stakes, I mean. That's tantamount to playing the sympathy card. If folks learn you're trying to better your family business, that might throw things in your favor."

"That's fair," she agreed. "And two?"

"Any discussion of marriage stays *off* the table."

Her jaw clenched involuntarily. So hard it ached. "Naturally."

He'd made his point profusely. She got it. Aidan Strong did *not* want to marry her. Fine. It was mutual. She'd never marry somebody as insulting and inconsiderate as him, no matter how gorgeous he was. Looks couldn't buy you everything, neither could money. Though she was determined to get a substantial financial settlement out of this good-looking guy.

His light-brown gaze washed over her, and for an instant she couldn't breathe. Probably from hyperventilating because he made her so flaming mad.

"So?" she asked him. "Do we have a deal?"

He stuck out his hand and firmly shook hers, wearing a lopsided grin. "Now, when is this Fall Fest of yours?"

CHAPTER FOUR

Aidan returned to the Majestic B&B as Trudy exited onto the porch, holding her purse. She'd changed into more seasonal clothing: slacks and a dark brown jumper over a crisp white blouse.

"Going somewhere?" he asked.

"I thought I'd nip down to the docks to grab some grub. American style." She grinned. "Burgers and beer."

Good, she needed to get out for a bit. She wasn't on his clock all the time and deserved her own space.

"Don't worry," she said. "I won't make it a late night. I know we've got work to do in the morning before catching our noontime flight."

"Yeah, Trudy. About that." He raked a hand through his hair. "I'll need you to change our tickets. We won't be leaving now until the first."

"Of October?" She gaped at him. "Why?"

He cleared his throat. "Charlotte and I have made a little wager."

She frowned, looking grumpy. "Is that bloody wedding wager back on? Because you know I was opposed from the start."

"Yes, and so was I. I'd never planned to go through with it."

She blew out a breath. "So then. What's this about?"

"Charlotte won't take what she calls 'charity'

outright, but she's fine with *winning* her business interests in Bearberry Coffee."

Trudy's eyes narrowed. "And how would she do that?"

"There's a festival here on September thirtieth called Fall Fest. It's been a Majestic tradition for a long time. I remember it being fun when I was a kid."

"Oh-kay…" she said, clearly not following.

"Charlotte has proposed a contest between us: Winner Takes All."

Trudy scrunched up her face. "I'm not liking the sound of the 'all' part."

"Don't worry about that," he said calmly. "She'll never win. Her idea is we each man a booth selling our unique coffees—a few signature flavors from Bearberry Brews versus some of Bearberry Coffee's classic brands. Whoever sells the most cups of coffee during the festival wins. If I win, I hand over half of Bearberry Coffee as we intended."

"And if she wins?" Trudy asked.

"She gets the whole thing."

"One hundred percent of the business?" Trudy scowled. "That's madness."

"Not when she can't possibly win."

Could Charlotte really snag all of Bearberry Coffee right out from under him? Not a chance. But he looked forward to watching her try. The thought of competing against her had him feeling light on his feet, charged, ready to sell the pants off her. Figuratively.

Maybe spending a few more days in Majestic wouldn't be so bad.

"How do you know she can't win?" Trudy pressed. "She's on her home turf. Lots of family and friends around to support her."

"Ah. But I've got my business sense—up here." He tapped his temple. "Plus, you're going to help me."

"Right, I gathered that. But help with what exactly?"

"The coffee sales, the contest, the logistics, all of it."

Her mouth was drawn, her eyes lost in thought. Aidan knew he could count on Trudy, though. She just needed a minute to sort it out in her head.

"That'll be a challenge on such short notice," she said.

"You're very good at challenges, Trudy," he assured her. "Besides, it's only straight-up coffee. Not super whips and fancy biscuits."

"All right." She waved, departing. "You've got it, boss!"

Aidan entered the B&B, catching Matthew and Crystal huddled together behind the reception desk, appearing chummy. She had her laptop propped open and seemed to be explaining something to him.

"Howdy," Matthew said, looking up. "How was your coffee?"

"Very nice, thanks," he said, still mulling over Charlotte's proposal. Did she actually believe she could top him at selling coffee? His whole livelihood was doing that on a global scale. And Charlotte did what? Advertise for her small family shop in the local papers? Post a few pics on social media for their dozens of followers? The businesses they each ran were so far apart they couldn't be compared.

Crystal smiled. "Well, if you decide you'd like more later, we've got plenty here. Decaf, too, and tea."

"Soon enough it will be self-serve," Mr. Mulroney said, sounding mildly befuddled. "We've just ordered ourselves a Care-rig."

"That's Keurig," Crystal said. "Next thing you know, we'll have online booking."

Matthew grumbled. "Not so sure about that."

Aidan guessed Crystal would bring Matthew up to speed before too long. With him dragging his heels the whole way.

"If you'd prefer something else to drink," Crystal said, "we have bottled water in the mini fridge in the butler's pantry, and sherry in the decanter in the parlor."

"A glass of sherry sounds grand. Sorry—great!" He laughed. "Been a Brit too long."

Crystal smiled. "I think your accent's charming."

He had an accent? He'd always believed his accent to be fairly neutral, owing to his intercontinental upbringing.

"Ha-ha. Cheers." Oof. "Thanks." He'd get the hang of his Americanisms again. Sweater not jumper. The restroom versus the loo. Not that he'd have to bother with those for too long, but when in Rome, and all that.

Aidan stared around the room. Some bed and breakfasts kept stacks of menus for nearby restaurants or takeout places on hand. He found a small stash on a coffee table, deciding to peruse them upstairs.

He poured himself a sherry, considering his eventful day. In a way, he was looking forward to becoming reacquainted with Majestic. It seemed different seeing it through a grown-up's eyes. More shopworn perhaps, but also quaint and homey. He hadn't noticed the stunning historic architecture of the older buildings downtown as a kid. Or appreciated the nuances of the cobblestone streets and old-fashioned streetlamps.

In some ways, the place he recalled had stood still in time. In others, it had moved forward by opening new restaurants and micropubs, a premier wine shop, and a juice bar. On his walk back here, he'd passed the Mermaid Tattoo shop and Dolphin Donuts, two businesses he recalled from back in the day.

Bearberry Brews had been here, too, and he was glad they'd kept their head above water financially, at least long enough to hold on until now. Though it seemed they were sinking fast. He'd arrived here with his offer just in time.

He passed through the foyer, holding his sherry glass and menus, on his way to the stairs. "I'll just take these up with me, if that's all right?"

"Of course," Crystal said. "Make yourself at home."

Matthew added, "Let us know if there's anything you need."

Aidan stopped at the bottom step. "I meant to mention this when I came in. Trudy and I will be staying for a few more days now. Until October first, if that's not inconvenient?"

"Nope." Matthew grinned. "Be our guests."

Crystal clapped her hands together. "So you'll be here for Fall Fest? Oh yay!"

"That's the plan." There was quite a lot of additional work he'd need to do in pulling things together, and most of their supplies would need to be laid in ahead of the fair. "Oh, say, one final thing. I don't suppose I can get a car hire 'round here?"

"In Majestic? No." Matthew rubbed his cheek. "They've got rentals back at the airport."

"No need for the airport," Crystal said brightly. "You can borrow my van." She nodded toward the dining room, and Aidan peeked out the window. An old green-and-white Volkswagen was parked there, covered with colorful daisy stickers.

"I'd hate to put you out…"

"Nonsense!" Crystal said. "My pleasure. Majestic is so walkable, I hardly ever use it."

Matthew leaned toward her using his cane. "Except for when you're driving those grandchildren of yours around."

Crystal smiled. "Yes, on the rare occasion. But they don't have any soccer games coming up for a while."

"Well then, thanks," Aidan said. "That's very kind."

Her eyes twinkled. "Just don't forget to top off the gas."

Matthew cleared his throat. "And the oil."

"Oh yeah." Her lips turned down. "There *is* a tiny leak."

Aidan was starting to wonder about the condition of this van. Then again, he and Trudy wouldn't be traveling far. "We'll be sure to mind both, thank you."

He retreated upstairs, deciding to order a pizza from Majestic Pies. He'd eat in and surf through some online mail-order catalogs. Since he was going to be here for ten days, he'd need more clothes, but he didn't need to get posh. He heaved a sigh. Majestic was very unlike London. But charming in its own way.

His room was nicely furnished with antiques, including a queen-size canopy bed and a mahogany dresser with a tilt mirror. There was no desk, per se, but the small table with two chairs could double as a work space. The window beyond the table overlooked the front yard, and he cracked it open, letting in a cool ocean breeze.

He'd missed the sound of the waves and the briny scent of the sea. And other things about Majestic. Its quaint storefronts hugging the cliffs. The vibrant dock area and its scenic lighthouse that had served as a beacon for ships since the 1800s. A small coffee shop named Bearberry Brews and the three old childhood mates called the Delaney sisters... While they'd had their moments, they'd generally gotten on.

A memory of Charlotte's determined gaze washed over him. She'd sounded so sure of herself when she'd proposed their contest, and her extreme confidence had given her a glow. Aidan had always been drawn to take-charge women.

He took a sip of sherry. But he was not letting Charlotte Delaney take charge of him. Didn't matter that she was smart. Or pretty. He was a business professional and all he wanted to accomplish was to do right by the Delaneys. If that meant going along with Charlotte's wishes for ten days, fine. He intended to do that on his own terms. He also planned to win.

• • •

Aidan arrived at Bearberry Brews at nine the next morning, and the place was humming. He'd arranged to meet Charlotte's parents here because he wanted to see for himself how they were faring. Hopefully not as horribly as Charlotte had intimated. Plus, he wanted to see Charlotte and get the lay of the land. Glean a few more details about the fair.

Customers in fall clothing crowded toward the counter and the line was deep, filing back toward the door in a zig-zag fashion, divided by the retractable belts anchored on stands. If these were hard times for the Delaneys, good times must be outstanding.

He squeezed past a couple at the end of the line, stepping into an open area filled with quaint tables. The bay window overlooking the ocean formed a cozy backdrop to a small sofa and grouping of plush chairs.

In many ways, the café was just like he remembered with its exposed wood-beam ceiling and white stucco walls. When he'd come here last night to meet Charlotte, he'd felt like he'd entered a time warp. Only the black-and-white photography on the walls was new. The beachy scenes in and around Majestic had been captured by a sharp eye that appeared to belong to the same photographer.

Aidan spied a chalkboard on the wall behind the pastry case, listing their daily specials, including bagel sandwiches and breakfast croissants. Misty was so busy at the register she likely hadn't seen him come in. Another fellow worked with her, taking orders and filling each one with admirable efficiency, while Misty rang people up and bagged pastries to go.

The scents of fresh-roasted coffee filled the air and his mouth watered. He detected cherry and dark chocolate. Caramel and coconut, with hints of cinnamon and vanilla. This coffee shop was no cookie-cutter replica of hundreds more like it. The vibe was unique and homey. One of a kind.

Everywhere he looked people were laughing and chatting while enjoying their beverages and food, except for the few earnest-looking types hunkered down with their electronic devices.

"Aidan Strong!" A woman with graying hair approached him with open arms. Though her face had aged, her welcoming smile was just the same. She hugged him then stood back to appreciate his height while holding on to his shoulders. "Aren't you a sight?"

He'd gone casual today in a sweater and jeans, since Majestic was a low-key kind of town.

"Your mom didn't lie." She glanced at the stocky man beside her with thick gray hair, then back at Aidan. "You came out *very* handsome."

His neck warmed. "Good to see you, Mrs. Delaney."

"You're looking well after all this time." Mr. Delaney held out his hand, and Aidan shook it. He'd expected a cool reception from the couple, but he was glad to be wrong.

"So are the two of you," he said.

"We're looking older." Mrs. Delaney waved her hand, and he noticed the shiny new ring on it.

"But we don't mind it," Mr. Delaney said. He cast a fond look at his wife. "At least we're in this together."

"Neither of you has aged one bit," Aidan said graciously, and they laughed. He glanced around. "Good to see business is booming."

"We've seen a definite uptick since that billboard of Charlotte's," Mr. Delaney said.

"Not that we approved of it." His wife frowned. "Still hasn't been enough to bail us out of this fix we're in. If we'd been doing this well all along, maybe."

Mr. Delaney nudged her. "No need to weigh Aidan down with all the family business."

Like he wasn't weighed down already. Aidan had stepped off that plane and into a quagmire of Delaney troubles, but by the time he left here, he'd have set everything right.

"Charlotte told us about your offer," Mr. Delaney said. "Very decent of you."

"Superbly kind." Mrs. Delaney's hazel eyes sparkled. "But did you really mean it? About the contest to sell the most coffee?"

"I did mean it, and still do."

"We couldn't ask you to hand over everything," Mr. Delaney said. "That wouldn't be right."

"No one's going to be giving anything away," Charlotte said, striding up beside her parents with a confident grin. "I'm going to win it. For all of us."

Her blue eyes held a determined cast, and Aidan

tried not to be swayed by their sparkle. He and Charlotte were competing against each other now, and she was not getting the better of him this time.

Mr. Delaney held up his hands. "I have nothing against a wager. I mean, most of them."

"Right," Mrs. Delaney agreed. "We're very relieved that marriage bet is off the table."

Aidan laughed. "Yeah, me too."

"My sisters and I are all very glad," Charlotte said.

"Now, Charlotte," her mom said in embarrassed tones.

"It's all right, Mrs. Delaney," Aidan said. "I can't blame your daughters for being happy they're off the hook. Nobody enjoys being roped into a marriage of convenience these days."

Mrs. Delaney's face reddened, reminding him that the idea had been hers to begin with. Hers and his mum's.

Charlotte changed the subject. "Where's Trudy?"

"She's gone to the bank to get the notary public appointment set up for the afternoon of the thirtieth. She's also drawing up a second set of paperwork, in the event there's a different outcome than the one I first planned for."

"Meaning, in the event you lose?"

Aidan grinned, and this seemed to unnerve her. "Ah, but I don't intend to."

"Nobody intends to come out a loser, Aidan."

He met her stare. "With the exception of the occasional odd duck who throws a contest."

She smirked. "I won't be throwing this one. Believe me."

"Where will you get your coffee to sell?" Mrs. Delaney asked, diverting his attention from Charlotte's shimmering blue gaze. She almost looked more beautiful when she was proving difficult, in some strange way.

"We have plenty of business offices stateside," he answered. "Shops in the geographical region too. Trudy will bring all of that together by running some inquiries."

"We can't wait to meet this Trudy of yours," Mrs. Delaney said. "She sounds like a phenomenon."

"She is," Aidan agreed. "Top notch."

Mr. Delaney considered him a moment. "I'm guessing you'll need someplace in town to run your operations. Set everything up for the fair."

"The Majestic B&B's just a stone's throw away," Charlotte pointed out.

"Yes," her mom said. "But the Fall Fest takes place right here on Kittery Street." She grinned at Aidan like she was arriving at a new idea. "Which is why you should use our office."

"What?" Nell asked, stepping up to them and taking the word right out of Aidan's head. She gaped at Charlotte then turned to her parents. "But Charlotte's going to be working in there, and so am I. It's not a huge space."

"Not tiny either." Mr. Delaney tapped his chin. "Come to think of it, that's perfect. Aidan will need a place where he can manage the logistics. You can't possibly have all your coffee deliveries made to the B&B. I imagine you'll truck in large urns and such."

"Yes, sir. That's my plan."

"Well then, truck them in here!"

Charlotte's eyes went wide. "*Dad.*"

Mr. Delaney sank his hands in his pockets. "Why not? We've got a gravel parking area out back that Aidan's trucks can pull into. Access to Kittery Street will be difficult the day of, since the road will be blocked off."

"Other vendors set up on the day, no problem," Charlotte argued.

"Yes," her mom said. "That's true. But those other vendors aren't selling hot beverages in volume."

"We do," Nell put in.

Her dad shook his head. "We set up our booth right out front. Aidan can do the same."

Charlotte buried her face in her hands. "Mom. Dad. You can't be serious?"

"Think of it, Charlotte," her mom said. "This contest of yours will be good for business. Our business eventually. The more people who see the Bearberry Coffee name around here, the better, don't you think?" She preened in expectation. "Sounds like we'll be owning part of that business one day very soon. Besides that, you're in marketing. What better marketing opportunity is there than for folks to see Bearberry Brews and Bearberry Coffee working side by side?"

Mr. Delaney grinned. "In harmony!"

Oh, now this will be fun. Head-to-head combat over coffee sales against Charlotte? It would be so sweet and easy to gather intel on her pricing, and a simple matter to outsell her. He almost felt sorry for Charlotte. Winning this contest was going to be like taking candy from a baby. A very spoiled and misguided one. "I think that's a brilliant plan."

"Naturally you do," Charlotte said, like she had this covered.

And she did, for her fifty percent.

His gaze snagged on another picture on the wall of stone steps leading down to the beach from Kittery Street. "Lovely photos," he said. "Who's the photographer?"

"I took them," Mrs. Delaney said. She blushed. "Some time ago."

"Then you should definitely take more."

"Don't think that will work, Aidan," Charlotte sniped. "Buttering up the parents."

"It was an honest compliment, Charlotte."

She frowned like she didn't believe it, but Aidan didn't care. He was more concerned with organizing this coffee contest so he could win.

"I'd love to see that office space," he said, smiling all around. His gaze settled on Mr. and Mrs. Delaney. "If the offer's still good?"

CHAPTER FIVE

By the time Aidan and Trudy arrived at the coffee shop the next day, Charlotte had been there nearly two hours working on her newsletter. With Fall Fest just one week from tomorrow, there was no time to spare, and she wanted to get the word out to all their regulars about their special deal.

Nell was pitching in as a barista to cover for Mei-Lin, who'd left for Wyoming this morning, but Charlotte wasn't using her desk. She sat at one of the long collapsible tables they used in their booths at fairs. Lucas had set up two of them.

The second table was across from Charlotte's, facing the window. So when Aidan and Trudy sat in their folding chairs, they'd be able to see the ocean. It was a small concession and Charlotte didn't mind making it, because Aidan was bound to lose. Might as well leave him with some lasting images of Majestic, since he'd made it clear he wouldn't be thinking about her.

"Morning," Trudy said in a brisk voice. She grinned and surveyed the cramped room. Nell's desk sat off to one side and her inbox was cluttered. Her laptop rested in the carrying case she'd deposited in her swivel chair. The worn armchair that typically sat in front of it had been moved into the kitchen to make more space.

Aidan peeked out the window, where rough winds tussled the waves. "Nice view."

Charlotte gave them a polite smile. "Hi, Trudy. Aidan."

Aidan nodded. "Charlotte."

He was dressed in his same sweater and jeans from yesterday, and Trudy had dressed casually too. But it didn't so much matter what Aidan wore. He still looked dynamite at eight in the morning.

"Did you get breakfast at the inn?" she asked them.

"Oh yes," Trudy said. "Matthew and Crystal fixed us right up."

"Very posh," Aidan added. "Ham and egg souffle with sausages and pineapple compote."

"Compote?" Charlotte asked. "What's that?"

Trudy set her purse on the table. "Broiled pineapple rings covered in toasted coconut with some kind of cherry glaze reduction."

"Mr. Mulroney's upped his game." Crystal was maybe a part of that. The Majestic B&B had never done elaborate breakfasts before.

Aidan met her eyes and her pulse fluttered. Darn it.

Charlotte tugged away her gaze to find Trudy watching her. Hopefully, she hadn't noticed Charlotte's appreciative stare. Trudy was probably used to women ogling her boss anyway. Not that Charlotte had ogled. Not since yesterday, and that had been purely due to the shock over how handsome Aidan had become. Now that this was a known fact, she didn't need to feel caught off guard by that sexy grin every time he flashed it.

She steeled herself for the mission at hand. She had to finish this newsletter and design the coupon she wanted to include. "Have a seat," she said, gesturing to the folding chairs.

They'd both brought their super thin laptops and paperwork. Aidan also had a tablet, which he removed from his backpack and set on the table. He pulled something up on his screen and tapped it, speaking to Trudy. "I guess we should start with this vendor list here, like we discussed at breakfast."

Trudy took her phone from her purse. "I can make some calls and do site visits."

Aidan and Trudy yammered on, discussing minute points about coffee freshness relative to the grinding time of the beans, while Charlotte pretended not to listen. They were casting their net wide, gathering resources. Given Bearberry Coffee's vast number of outlets, they'd have no problem there, whereas Charlotte was constrained by her budget. Something Aidan wouldn't know anything about, being *minted*. She was betting he'd never pinched a penny in his life.

Reflected sunlight glimmered in his eyes, and Charlotte's heart caught in her throat. Their light brown color dazzled beneath his dark eyebrows and that dip of hair falling forward. She hadn't realized he'd been staring at her and had no idea for how long.

"How many would you say attend this annual fair, Charlotte?" Aidan asked.

She had her laptop in front of her and a legal pad with a few pens off to the side. She shrugged, reluctant to give too much information away. She was in this to win, not help him. "Majestic's small and not everyone shows up for this."

Aidan nodded. "Rough numbers?"

Charlotte scowled, begrudgingly giving her answer. He could easily look it up. "A few thousand maybe."

Aidan took notes on his tablet while Trudy did the same on her phone. "How many vendors?"

What did he think? That *she* was another assistant?

"I'm not exactly sure," she said. "Probably dozens."

Aidan stopped typing, and his eyebrows arched. "Only dozens? Not more?"

Charlotte fumed and then grumbled, "Do your own darn research."

He was the one with the high-speed internet operation while she was figuratively stuck with dial-up. Bearberry Brews hadn't even been brought into the twenty-first century technology-wise until Lucas had updated their internet during Charlotte's senior year in high school. She could still hear the annoying echo in her ears of the crackly-sounding line dialing through. Aidan made her feel like that now, old-school and grumpy.

But he was certainly no Mr. Sunshine.

Trudy pulled her attention from her cell phone screen. She'd been busy scribbling stuff in a small spiral notebook with zebra stripes on its cover. "Can you at least hint at what these vendors sell?"

Charlotte sighed. This was all pretty standard stuff. They'd probably guess it anyway or could ask anyone around town. "Produce from local farms. Apple butter and jams. Goat cheeses. One guy always sells hot fish and chips. A few other businesses have fresh-shucked oysters, and of course there's oyster stew. There are craftspeople too, selling artwork and ceramics, hand-carved walking sticks, knitted items."

"Sounds like all sorts." Trudy smiled. "I love a good market. Grew up with quite a few of them around home in Wetherby."

This pulled Charlotte out of her gloom. When she'd lived abroad, she'd loved venturing to local markets in the UK. "You're not from London?"

Trudy shook her head. "West Yorkshire, about four hours north."

Charlotte grinned. "Closer to Scotland, then?"

Trudy laughed. "Closer, but not quite there."

"I studied in Glasgow for a semester," Charlotte said, reflecting on her happy memories. She'd won a scholarship to go overseas. Those were good times. "I loved it."

Aidan's face registered surprise. "I had no idea you'd crossed the pond."

Charlotte's face heated. "Our families weren't exactly on speaking terms then."

"No." He frowned. "Shame, too. I love Glasgow. I'm often there on business."

"What was your favorite part?" Trudy asked Charlotte.

She sighed, recalling the glamour of being swept away in a foreign country. How could she choose just one favorite?

Trudy giggled. "I mean aside from the 'men wearing kilts' part."

Kilts weren't a daily thing, but the guys did don the traditional outfits for special celebrations. And yes, the better-looking ones were every bit as hot as those models on the covers of the books Nell and Mei-Lin read.

Charlotte laughed, too, warming to Trudy. "Yeah. There was that."

Aidan raised his eyebrows. "I'm part Scot, you know. On my mum's side."

"You do *not* have a kilt," Charlotte joked, trying hard not to let her mind go there. Because, honestly, it painted a very sexy picture.

Aidan pursed his lips. "Not saying."

Trudy gasped. "Do you?"

It was Aidan's turn to laugh now. "Maybe it's something I keep locked away."

Charlotte was dying to know if he was serious, but she'd never in a million years ask.

Trudy startled when she glanced at her phone. "Oh! Seems I missed a text coming in." She gathered her things and stood. "I'd better go and phone that vendor—"

"But can't you call from in—" Aidan started, but she was already halfway out the door. She shut it, leaving Charlotte and Aidan alone. Awkward. Although it shouldn't have been.

It wasn't like there was anything untoward going on between them. In fact there was nothing between them at all except for a healthy dose of competition. And, okay, maybe a small smidgen of animosity. *His fault.*

"Well. I'd best run some calculations."

"Right," Charlotte said, avoiding his eyes and staring at her computer. "Me too."

An image of him in a kilt flashed through her

mind—and he wore it *really* well…

Charlotte rammed on the mental brakes. She was *not* letting her mind go there. The last thing that would be happening was "her and Aidan." He'd made that perfectly clear.

And that was 100 percent fine by her.

• • •

While Trudy was away, Aidan fielded text messages and emails from London that had come in over the past few days. None of them was urgent, but there were items that needed addressing, like a minor distribution hiccup concerning their Paris stores.

The chit-chat in the café spilled in through the closed office door, as did the occasional clattering of dishes in the kitchen. The coffee roaster's whirring had been the most distracting sound of all, but it made up for any auditory annoyance with the tantalizing aromas it put forth.

Maybe Charlotte was right about Bearberry Coffee not being innovative enough. But no. Innovating was risky, and Bearberry Coffee had built its brand by playing it safe. The company's growth had been slow and steady, and their marketing spot-on.

The door opened, and Nell poked her head in, holding two steaming mugs. "Coffee, anyone?"

"Thanks," he said to Nell. "I think I will."

Charlotte looked up from her computer and smiled. "Me too. Thank you!"

Nell walked toward Aidan's table. "How's it going back here?"

"Making progress," he said when she handed him a mug. "Thanks."

"Need cream and sugar?" Nell glanced over her shoulder. "Because I can—"

"No, no." He bowed his head. "Black is fine." Same old nurturing Nell, always taking care of other people. In the love department, it seemed she'd recently taken care of herself. Aidan had read all about her and Grant's quickie engagement in *The Seaside Daily*'s online edition. Even though he'd guessed it was coming, he was still stunned by the announcement. The Delaney women were fast movers. Now Misty was engaged as well.

With their marriage of convenience no longer happening, would Charlotte be next?

In answer to Nell's earlier question, Charlotte nodded toward her table, since she was busily typing. "Lots of progress! Loads and loads."

Nell set Charlotte's coffee down beside her and surveyed the room. "I guess I'll leave you guys to it." She flipped back her hair and strolled out of the office in her silky red flats.

Charlotte was wearing her sexy cowgirl boots, the ones with the heels and turquoise stitching. Their rise was low enough to show off her shapely legs beneath the hem of her flowery skirt.

"You okay over there?" she said.

Busted.

His neck warmed and he rubbed the side of it. "Um-hm, fine."

Aidan took a sip of coffee and locked his gaze on his computer. He needed to focus on his spreadsheet and calculations for amounts of supplies he'd need for the fair and not on Charlotte's physical attributes. As enticing as she was, he wasn't in the market for a girlfriend. And he would never entertain the idea of dating Charlotte anyway. He'd had the opportunity to marry her, of all things, and had rightly passed up that chance.

Marriage? Him and Charlotte? As much as they got on each other's every last nerve? Not happening. Good thing he'd called that off.

Charlotte hummed a short tune to herself while resting one hand on her coffee mug. Her eyes stayed glued to her screen, and she wore a perky smile as she browsed through something while periodically clicking her trackpad.

Aidan held in a chuckle. For the love of him, that sounded an awful lot like "Jingle Bells" and here they were in September. He recalled Charlotte singing as a kid. She'd had a nice voice and probably could have done something with it. Joined a choir, or perhaps even sung professionally.

"Getting in the holiday spirit already?" he said.

She glanced up from her computer with her stunning eyes, which were even bigger and bluer than ever. A jolt of attraction shot through him and his heart gave a little start.

What was *that* all about?

He needed to stop thinking about her eyes, and her smile, and *those legs*—heaven help him—and start remembering his mission to cede half his corporation to her and get the heck out of Majestic before he did something reckless. Like lose control of his emotions and his heart. A critical thing he prided himself on was his ability to remain in control of virtually any situation, and *distance* always served him well.

"Oh… Was I singing out loud?" She shrank back in her chair, unbearably cute in her embarrassment. It was pretty impossible *not* to be charmed by her.

"Only humming." He smiled, noting her nose had gone bright red, an endearing quirk she'd had since they were kids. "Why 'Jingle Bells'?"

"Because I was dreaming of Christmas."

Intriguing. "Why?"

She sipped her coffee, appearing distant for a moment. "I was thinking of all the great presents I could buy once I'm the full owner of the company."

Charlotte, Charlotte. Always so sure of yourself.

"Careful there." He smirked. "You won't want to bust the bank all in one day."

She tucked a lock of her dark hair behind one ear, showing off the gentle curve of her cheek and her creamy skin. She had the faintest smattering of freckles across her nose, which had turned light pink now. Her freckles weren't really visible from afar. Nothing like Nell's mask of many, or Misty's pronounced few. That was the Irish in them, as was the reddish sheen to their hair. Nell was full-on auburn and Misty a burnt brown. Charlotte's dark tresses captured the sunlight with crimson-colored hues.

"I wouldn't really let all that money burn a hole in my pocket," she said, laughing. "But it's fun to think about not being so cash-strapped for once."

He frowned. "Yeah. I'm sure that's been hard."

Guilt coursed through him because of the underhanded way in which his dad had treated the Delaneys. He wasn't sure how his dad had been able to live with himself, but the man had never seemed to experience a shred of remorse over his business dealings. Probably thanks to his incredible ability to compartmentalize.

Charlotte studied him a moment. "Hasn't been for you, I'm sure." She crossed her arms. "You've probably always pretty much gotten what you've wanted."

"Pretty much," he said, because he had been blessed with many privileges.

Interestingly, Charlotte hadn't been thinking of splurging on herself. He'd taken careful note of her words. She'd mentioned buying presents for others.

"So what would you buy," he asked. "And who would you give it to?"

"Well, for starters, I'd like to send my folks on a big trip. Maybe to Ireland. They've never been there." She grinned, and warmth spread through his chest. Again. She really was a kind person, way down deep on the inside—when she wasn't sniping at him.

He dragged a hand across his sweater to quell the unwelcome flurry of emotion. "That's a nice thought. Anything else?"

Her smile grew even brighter. "I'd love to buy Misty a car."

He shut his laptop, considering her goal. "That's thinking big."

"Misty deserves big. She's earned it. She just won a scholarship to RISD." Charlotte closed her laptop, too, like this was something she'd firmly decided on.

"What's that?"

"An art school in Rhode Island and an excellent one. Top tier."

That sounded great for Misty. "So she and

Lucas—?"

"Have worked things out. He's going to keep working here while renovating the property he's buying, with plans to turn it into a book café."

"Nice." It was really good for people to follow their ambitions.

"Yeah." Her smile revealed she thought of Lucas fondly. "It's always been his dream."

"And Misty's dream has been art school?"

"Yes." She picked up her coffee mug, taking another sip. "And now the two of them have each other. After Misty starts school next fall, they'll see each other on breaks. I have faith they'll make it as a couple. They're so totally meant for each other."

"So, Misty will need a car then," he said, putting things together. "To get back and forth to Majestic?"

"Exactly. She's gotten by without one until now and doesn't really have the funds to change that. But if I could help." She shrugged happily. "Wouldn't that be amazing?"

"It would," he said.

Charlotte was pretty amazing as well. He'd never had brothers or sisters, or anyone else to rely on apart from his mum and dad. And his dad's availability had been spotty. He'd spent more time in airports than at home.

Anxiety churned in Aidan's gut. He didn't want to be like that if he could help it.

"Who's next on your list?" he asked.

She rolled her eyes toward the ceiling in an adorable way. "Hmm. I'd say Nell. Maybe she and Grant would appreciate a little nest egg of some sort when they start their family."

"What? Are they talking about that already?"

"Not yet." Charlotte giggled. "But I wouldn't be surprised to catch Nell knitting baby booties soon."

His eyebrows rose, then he recalled their coupley matching jumpers. "She's the knitter then?" He stopped, wanting to be fair. "And not him?"

Charlotte laughed. "Grant's good at tying off climbing ropes for rappelling and that kind of thing. Nell's the handy one with the knitting needles."

"I see." Sunlight shone all around her, making her appear effervescent in the window. Or maybe it was just her smile that had her all lit up from the inside. Their conversation was remarkably going so well, he couldn't help wanting to banter some more.

"Things must have been fairly hectic around here, huh?" he teased. "With the three of you trying to outwit each other—all on account of me."

She shook her finger in a scolding fashion. "Yeah. Thanks a lot."

Aidan pushed back in his chair and grinned. "But, like you said, it's all worked out beautifully."

"In two cases out of three." She cocked her head. "And now maybe in the third case—my case—things will work out, too." She bit her lip and narrowed her eyes. "You're not going to beat me in any contest in Majestic, Aidan. This is my hometown."

Aidan set his elbows on the table. So much for their easygoing vibe. "Mine, too."

"Maybe *was*," she said smugly, "but hasn't been for years."

"Doesn't matter." He clicked his tongue. "I was born here."

She pouty-frowned. "Then you left."

"Involuntarily."

She sighed. "Come on, Aidan. No one here will probably even remember you."

"Nonsense. I ran into Mary Beth Blakely this morning on the way here."

Her face paled. "What?"

"You know, the girl from grade school? She recognized me at once."

"Oh. Well." Charlotte licked her lips, like she hadn't expected this.

"Truth be told." He studied the ceiling a lingering moment then met her eyes. "I think she's always fancied me."

Charlotte's mouth dropped open. "Has not."

"No?" he asked with a self-assured edge. "Then why'd she ask me 'round to the pub?"

Charlotte blinked. "Did she?"

He detected a nervous tremor in her voice. But no. She couldn't be jealous.

"Not straightaway," he said. "She wanted to verify who Trudy was first. Once she learned Trudy was my assistant, Mary Beth mentioned catching up over beers. Said…what was it now?" He pretended to search his memory. "Ah, yes. That the years have been good to me."

"Huh. Well." Charlotte scoffed. "I'd watch it with her. Mary Beth is always between boyfriends."

"She can't *always* be between," he countered. "She has to be dating some of them sometime."

Her cheeks colored. "Why are you arguing with me?"

"I'm not arguing, Charlotte. Just sharing some facts. If Mary Beth knew who I was, in spite of the years, others might too. And it's hard to believe that anyone here would hold my father's sins against me. Majestic is a friendly and forgiving town."

She moved her computer aside and leaned forward. "Yeah, with a very gossipy dating blogger and a super nosy reporter. That's probably why Mary Beth guessed who you were. Our story was all written up in the local paper and online. Everyone knew you were coming."

"Lucky me." He smiled. "Nothing like advance publicity."

"The publicity was not *for* you, Aidan. It was *about* you and our whole marriage deal, which you shirked."

He shrugged. "With good reason." He scanned the room, eager to change the subject. Leave it to Charlotte to upend an easygoing chat by tossing in a few barbs. "Where has my stellar assistant run off to?"

"Trudy *has* been gone a while. She can't still be making those calls?" Charlotte stared at Aidan and his heart thumped. On account of his "missing in action" assistant, and not because of Charlotte and her unnerving blue gaze. Or the way she was so cocksure of everything, including herself, and in her belief that she'd win their contest.

Okay, so Charlotte was a beautiful woman. Didn't mean that she was the woman for him. He'd yet to meet the woman who was. With good reason.

Relationships required investment, and Aidan didn't do emotional investments.

He'd already sunk all of the emotional stock he had into Bearberry Coffee.

CHAPTER SIX

Aidan entered the kitchen and waved to Mr. and Mrs. Delaney, who were seated at the table with Lucas, discussing something. Charlotte was beside him.

"Have you seen Trudy?" Aidan asked.

Lucas pointed to the door. "She left some time ago. Said something about taking a short road trip."

Aidan shook his head. "She might have said something to me."

"She's probably going to meet up with those shop managers she wanted to talk to," Charlotte said. "But how will she get there? Did you guys rent a car?"

"Didn't have to," Aidan said. "Crystal offered to lend us hers."

"Crystal did?" Mr. Delaney said. "That was nice of her."

"Yes." Mrs. Delaney's eyes twinkled. "How are she and Matthew getting along?"

Aidan shifted on his feet. "Very well from the looks of things."

"Isn't that sweet?" Lucas grinned. "Love at any age."

"Well," Aidan said. "I don't know about love." Because he didn't, not on behalf of the old-timers or himself. He'd never extended his heart in that way because it had always been too risky. And, in every case in which he'd exhibited caution, he'd been absolutely right. "But they certainly seem to be getting on—in a friendly way."

Mrs. Delaney clasped her hands together. "Friendly's good." Her gaze lingered on Aidan and then on Charlotte, and he got a funny feeling. As though Charlotte's mom was wondering about how friendly he and Charlotte were becoming, which was...not at all. Apart from the necessary camaraderie good manners dictated when two young professionals were forced to share a confined working space.

Aidan turned back toward the office—and Charlotte did too, at exactly the same time. He nearly bumped into her crossing the threshold, and she almost stepped on his toes.

She jumped back, and so did he.

They both froze in place.

"Oh!" He raised his arms. "Sorry!"

"No, no." She flushed and straightened her skirt. "It was me."

Aidan shrugged. "Or maybe just the two of us being clumsy?"

She raised her chin, bringing her mouth dangerously close to his. "I've never been clumsy, Aidan," she said in low tones. "That's you."

"Maybe it's catching," he whispered back.

She narrowed her eyes and electricity crackled between them, humming through his veins. "Don't count on it."

Her fiercely bright spirit beckoned him forward. Her full and kissable lips called him like a siren's song, pulling him into her depths.

No. This was wrong. So wrong.

He peered back out the door. Especially with her folks and Lucas looking on while pretending to focus on their coffees.

Aidan blinked and squeezed past Charlotte the rest of the way, his neck and ears burning hot. He needed to get out of here and clear his head. The sooner the better.

He strode over to his table and gathered his things.

"Wait," Charlotte said, following him. "Where are you going?"

He answered without meeting her gaze, because he was too afraid of what she might see in his eyes. His highly inconvenient interest in her. "I've got some business to attend to at the inn. But thanks for all of this." He swept a hand around the room and walked toward the door. "I'll be back in the morning."

"Aidan."

He stopped and turned around, taking one deep breath. "Yes?"

Her eyebrows knitted together. "Did something happen just now?"

"Not for me it didn't." His heart hammered. "You?"

Emotion flickered in her eyes. Maybe she thought he was lying?

But then she shook her head, and the tightness in his chest eased.

"Didn't notice a thing."

He hoped that was true, because the last thing in the world he needed right now was an involvement with Charlotte Delaney.

Aidan nodded. "Right," he lied. "Me, either." He slid his backpack over one shoulder and glanced at her—very briefly. "So. See you tomorrow?"

"Yep." She grinned tightly. "See ya then."

As headstrong as she was, it was going to be hard enough having to work with Charlotte. Becoming involved with her romantically would just add one more heaping load of trouble onto his already brimming plate. He did *not* need to go skewing his rational judgment by allowing another person into his personal sphere. His parents had warned him of the dangers of relying on anyone other than himself. Moreso with their actions than their words.

It was an enduring lesson.

• • •

Charlotte's heart hammered so hard she could scarcely hear herself think. What had just happened with Aidan? Not what she thought. No way. There'd been no shock of current between them. No spark. She'd just been thrown by that earlier conversation involving Scotland and kilts.

"What's going on?" Misty asked, walking through the door. "I saw Aidan leave. Trudy's disappeared on us, too."

"Yeah, uh." Charlotte sat in the folding chair at her table. "He had something to do. A video conference with his execs over in London."

Misty set Nell's bag on the floor and dropped down into her swivel chair, propping her ankle boots on Nell's desk, with one leg crossed over the other. "But everything's okay?"

"Yeah. We were just each doing our own thing, working on logistics, then we noticed Trudy had been gone a while. I guess she went off to talk to some of the shop people she hopes will help them."

Misty grimaced. "You mean help them *lose* the contest?"

"Yes," Charlotte said firmly. "Definitely. We've got this in the bag."

Misty's gaze darted to the doorway. "Is that why he went scampering out of here so—?"

Charlotte's cheeks burned hot, and Misty's eyes widened. "Wait. Did something happen?"

Charlotte pressed her lips together. "Nuh-uh."

Misty surveyed her with a knowing air. "Come to think of it, his ears did look a little red. His whole face, too."

"That's probably due to his coloring," Charlotte retorted. "He's fair."

"Not that fair."

Ooh, it was so hard to keep things from her sisters.

Charlotte caved. "Okay, if you *must know*," she whispered. "Shut the door."

Misty squealed quietly and did as she was told, hopping out of Nell's chair. "Okay," she said when the door was shut behind her. "*What* happened?" Her eyes twinkled. "You can tell me."

Charlotte hid her face in her hands and groaned. "I'm not sure."

Misty gasped. "Wait. What? You're attracted?"

Charlotte looked up. "No."

Misty set one hand on her hip. "Look me in the eye and say that."

But Charlotte honestly couldn't. Even though she wasn't.

Of course not. That would be silly.

She pulled herself together and met Misty's gaze. "We just had a moment. That's all."

Misty set her chin. "Define moment."

"When we passed each other in the doorway. Quarters got a little tight and...gosh, Misty." Charlotte's whole face burned hot. "He smells like summer rain."

"What?"

"All fresh and outdoorsy."

"No, that's Grant."

"No. Not like Grant."

Misty leveled her a look, and Charlotte held up her hands.

"Or Lucas either. Hey! Aidan is his own man with his own scent, okay?" She licked her lips. "Not that I'd noticed any of the others."

"Good," Misty teased. "Because I don't want you getting *that close* to my guy."

"Mist-y."

Misty laughed. "Okay. All right. So, summer rain?" She studied the ceiling. "That's very vague."

"Not to me it's not." It made her think of walking outdoors on the beach when it was windy. Just when it was starting to sprinkle. Each tiny pinprick of rain making her aware of her surroundings. Energized. Alive.

"Uh-oh," Misty said.

"Uh-oh, what?"

"Your nose has turned red."

Charlotte rubbed it and it felt warm. "Has not."

"Yes it has. And it's a foolproof sign." Misty's face lit up. "You're just like Rudolf the Red-Nosed Reindeer."

"Hilarious, Misty." She hated the fact that it was true. Where other women blushed evenly, Charlotte bloomed brightest right across her schnoz. It was embarrassing and made her faint freckles pop out even though she tried to cover them with concealer.

Misty sat back behind the desk. "Well, I think it's cute that you're sweet on Aidan."

"I am not—"

"Does he feel the same, do you think?"

"Misty, shush. It's not like that. Like I said, we just had a moment."

"Who had a moment?" Nell asked, prancing in the door. She covered her mouth with her hands and squealed, then whispered, "You and Aidan?"

"No," Misty said, deadpan. "Her and Trudy."

Nell blinked and shut the door. "Oh. Well. This is new." She shot Charlotte an encouraging smile. "Honey, that's great!"

Charlotte rubbed her temples. Nell was so sweet, but gullible. "Thanks, Misty."

Nell twirled a lock of her hair around one finger. "That's not true?"

"It was probably nothing." Charlotte waved her hand. "I should never have shared."

"Of course you should have shared," Nell said. "That's why we're here. All of us for each other." She stared at Misty in her seat.

"Oh sorry," Misty said. "You weren't using it."

Nell shook her head. "No, no. It's fine."

Charlotte addressed Nell. "Slow out there?"

"Yeah, there's a lull. So I thought I'd pop back here to see what was going on." She giggled, glancing at Charlotte. "Nice to know you and Aidan are staying cordial."

Charlotte rolled her eyes. "Doesn't mean I'm not staying focused on the festival. I am."

"Good, that's good," said Nell. She spoke to Misty. "And anyway, sometimes you catch more flies with honey than vinegar. No sense in Aidan and Charlotte being at odds just because they're in a little contest."

"The contest is pretty huge from my view," Misty said. "It could decide everything."

"Do you honestly believe he'll do it?" Nell asked. "Turn over his whole corporation?"

"He said Trudy drew up the second set of paperwork."

"Yeah, but…" Nell pursed her lips. "Have you seen it?"

"Not yet." Charlotte scratched a note on her pad. "Good point. I'll ask."

Misty wrinkled up her nose. "I hope that's something you can manage, Charlotte. Running a global corporation is no small deal."

"Aidan has people in place to run things. No reason I can't keep them on."

"But you'll run things from here?" Nell asked with a worried expression.

"Of course," Charlotte said. "As much as possible, I mean. With cyber communications and the internet, I don't see why I can't do most of what needs to be done from Majestic."

"Apart from the travel," Nell added. "There's

bound to be some of that. Maybe lots."

Charlotte squared her shoulders. "I'll handle that." And she believed she could. While their parents had insisted that each of their daughters get passports, Charlotte was the only one of the three of them who had used hers. The allure of jet-setting a bit seemed glamorous, even if the main objective was work.

Misty crossed her arms. "I still find it hard to believe Aidan would give up everything. Where would he go? What would he do?"

Charlotte smiled. "I suppose we'll leave that up to him. When we talked about the wager, he mentioned he has a trust fund. His dad had set aside a bundle for him before his death. So I don't think he'll starve or anything."

Nell frowned. "We wouldn't want that. Not after how fair he's been."

"He has been fair, hasn't he?" Misty asked. "Aidan's turned out to be a good guy."

"Don't forget what he concealed from us, girls," Charlotte said sourly. "The fact that he'd never planned to marry any of us to begin with." Least of all her, apparently. The way he'd goaded her at the airport still got to her. *I've no interest in marrying you, Charlotte. Not here, not now. Not in England later. Pretty much not ever.*

"It might have been better if he'd been upfront about things," Nell agreed.

"True. But." Misty shrugged. "Just look where we've landed."

"And we're going to wind up even better off," Charlotte said. "Leave it to me." She dusted off her hands, trying to rid herself of that super-silly smidgen of attraction she'd felt to Aidan earlier. Which was *not* helpful in the least.

"Not *all* to you, Charlotte," Nell said. "Misty and I want to help you."

"Good. Because I've got some great ideas about how we can definitely sell the most cups of coffee at the fair."

Nell frowned. "We can't just outsell Aidan with coffees. We'll still have to turn a profit somehow, a pretty big one."

Charlotte grinned. "There's no bigger profit than 'winner takes all.' And we're going to grasp that golden ring. I feel it in my bones, ladies. In fact, I feel like celebrating already. Drinks after work at Mariner's?"

Misty perked up. "I'm game!"

Nell inserted a cautionary note. "We don't want to go counting any chickens before they hatch, Charlotte."

"Maybe not." Charlotte winked. "But we can toast to our futures."

CHAPTER SEVEN

Aidan completed his conference call at the dining room table at the inn. Matthew had been kind enough to close off the room for him, assuring him that he and Crystal would keep their voices down as they played cards in the parlor. There evidently weren't enough innkeeping tasks to fill their time. Though they seemed to enjoy being around each other.

Aidan packed away his laptop, glad to have his work issues settled. After a mild panic by their Paris rep about supply chain upsets, he'd been able to calm the waters by offering an alternate solution. Their Paris shops could get support from an affiliate in Provence. It was all in a day's work, thinking on his feet. He did enjoy problem solving. He was also ready to share the burden with Charlotte.

Things might be overwhelming for her at first, as it would be for anyone in her position, but she was bright enough to train up for their partnership quickly. In a way, it would be a relief not to have to shoulder the weight of the company all on his own.

A motor chugged in the driveway and he saw Trudy driving up in Crystal's van outside the window. He checked his watch. She'd been gone for hours without even bothering to return his texts. He opened the sliding dining room doors, greeting her in the hall when she entered the inn. "There you are."

"Oh, hi, Aidan!" Her cheeks were pink like she'd been outdoors in the cold.

"You had me worried. Where'd you run off to?"

"Dashed over to Belfast." She grinned. "You should see the van. It's *loaded.*"

"You got supplies? Bravo."

"Yes, I got some supplies, and I've scheduled to secure more tomorrow." She pouted. "I'm afraid it will mean another road trip."

"Sure, sure. Great going." He studied her. "How about the coffee?"

"I'm working on who can truck in urns. That part's a bit more tricky."

"At this late date, I guess so."

"I'm thinking the local caterers might help. There are a few of them around who do weddings. If we supply the brew, they might loan us their urns, or allow us to rent them for a fee. I was thinking of checking some area churches, too."

"Trudy, that's brilliant."

She grinned. "That's why you pay me the big bucks." She turned and he noticed some fall leaves stuck in her blonde hair.

"You've been out in the woods somewhere?"

Her eyebrows shot up. "No. Why?"

"You just…" He tapped the back of his head, and she patted hers.

"Blimey! Don't know how that happened. Must have been when I broke down."

"Broke down?"

"The engine ran hot. So I had to pull over."

The oil. "Maybe this loaner's not such a good idea."

"Oh no! The van's so cool. And fun to drive. Truly. I kept forgetting about staying on the right side of the road, but other drivers were happy to remind me."

Aidan rubbed his temples. "Let me go with you next time."

"Oh no. I'm good."

"So how did you fix the van?"

"I didn't. A good Samaritan happened along." Something in her expression read funny. Like she was concealing certain facts.

"A good Samaritan, huh? Anyone I know?"

"Oh! Will you look at the time." She stared down at her phone. "I've got to dash upstairs and change. Meeting a friend later."

"Friend?" he called after her as she hurried toward the stairs. "What friend?"

She waved him off. "Can't be late!"

Trudy was very close with her family in the UK and had often said she'd never leave England. Aidan worried that she was developing an infatuation here that might leave her heartbroken in the future. But he was her boss and not her parent. Plus, she was a grown woman who didn't need telling what to do. He could urge caution, though.

"Careful then."

She laughed. "Of course."

Aidan set his hands on his hips. Trudy appeared to be making the most of her time in Majestic. At least she hadn't skimped on work. They could take those supplies she'd gotten over to Bearberry Brews in the morning and store them there. In the meantime…

Hmm. He glanced around at the growing shadows. He supposed he could step out for a while, too. These walls were closing in on him and he'd done takeout last night. Maybe a sit-down meal was in order.

His phone dinged and he checked it. Charlotte.

For an instant he wondered if she might ask him to join her for a drink or a meal.

That would be civil. Gracious even. But no. She was all business, wanting him to text over the modified agreement so she could share it with her family's lawyer.

Aidan blew out a breath. Fine.

He pulled up the doc on his phone and sent it, understanding her desire to look it over. Even though they'd never actually employ the larger plan of him ceding the entire corporation to Charlotte, his legal team back in London had done a great job in putting the second set of papers in order. In record time as well.

His phone dinged again and his heart skipped a beat.

But it wasn't Charlotte this time. Probably a good thing, too. She'd spent too much time in his head today already.

Mary Beth: *Would love to catch up if tonight works?*

Mary Beth: *Six o'clock, Mariner's?*

Maybe eating with an old friend would be the distraction from Charlotte he needed.

· · ·

Charlotte was glad to have the day wrapped up. She'd ordered additional specialty cups with cute fall leaves forming a heart around the words "Fall Fest." The Bearberry Brews logo was on the other side of the cup. She decided to omit the date in case all of the cups didn't sell. That way, the shop could store them away for use the following year.

Next, she needed to step up her game with advertising. She was printing up flyers with her two-for-one coffee deal to post at the shop and put up around town. All people had to do was grab the QR code for the deal with their phone. She also had her newsletter ready to go with its additional 10 percent off coupon for loyal customers.

She shared these ideas with her sisters as they locked up the café. Night had fallen and shadows filled the street under the streetlamps, but Mariner's was just two doors down.

"Those plans sound great," Nell said. "But you'll practically be giving away our coffee."

"The coffee part is easy," Misty said. "It's the supply costs that will do us in."

"No," Charlotte corrected them. "I'm getting them extra cheap. Once I explained to our vendors how critical it is for us to move lots of product at a discount this year, with hopes of still turning a profit, they were glad to cut back on their margins as much as possible."

"Explained to them how?" Nell asked. "I thought you and Aidan agreed not to reveal anything about your bet."

"We agreed not to reveal what the outcome of the contest would be," Charlotte said slyly. "Not that we were in fact competing. I said it was all in good fun and for publicity. To gain even more exposure for Bearberry Coffee at large and also raise the profile of our shop."

"Wow, Charlotte," Misty said. "You're good."

Nell smiled at Misty. "She's always had that way about her. She could charm the skin off a snake."

"It's true." Misty laughed. "There's no resisting Charlotte."

Easy for them to say. Tell that to the snob from London.

Charlotte scowled. "Guys, you're doing it again!"

They stared at her blankly.

"Talking about me. Gee."

Nell laid a hand on her sweater sleeve. "We're sorry, Charlotte. We were trying to give you a compliment."

That might have been nice if it were true. But the truth was Charlotte couldn't charm every single person on this planet. She sure hadn't charmed Aidan into wanting to marry her.

Which was fine, really fine. It wasn't like she'd actually been trying. Because if she had, he wouldn't have stood a chance.

"What do you think of Mom's new ring?" Charlotte asked.

"Gorgeous." Nell sighed.

Misty giggled. "She's flashing it everywhere, too, hoping people will notice."

Charlotte's heart warmed because it was true, and it was very unlike their mom to show off. This present deserved showing off, though. What an amazing gift of the heart. So sweet of their dad.

"So." Misty got a wry twist to her lips. "Wonder when she's going to give him his?"

"Ring, Misty?" Nell laughed. "Come on. Not everyone's like you and Lucas with those promise rings of yours." She glanced at the silver band with roses on it that served as Misty's engagement ring. When she and Lucas married, he'd move it from her right hand to her left, and she'd do the same with the promise ring she'd given him, which was silver too but with a Celtic knot design. They were so made for each other.

"True," Charlotte said. "Mom and Dad are very old-fashioned."

"Wait!" Misty said abruptly.

Nell reached out and protectively placed an arm in front of Charlotte, stopping her in her tracks.

Charlotte stared at Nell, who was goggling at Mariner's. Misty was gawking at something in the restaurant's front window too.

It was Aidan! There with Mary Beth, laughing and joking on a bar stool and having a great old time by apparently captivating a crowd.

Misty narrowed her eyes and glanced at her sisters. "What on earth is he doing?"

Nell tugged at Charlotte's elbow, and they all inched closer, staying off to the side and out of view from the window.

"I think…" Misty craned her neck to peer past Nell. "He's getting reacquainted."

"Yeah," Nell said. "With the townsfolk. Look! Clive just reached across the bar to shake his hand," she said. Clive was their good-looking local bartender, and they'd all had remote crushes on him for years. But he'd been married for a while now and had kids.

Charlotte bit her lip. "Guess they were friends."

Nell gasped. "*Ages* ago!"

"Whoa," Misty said. "Mr. McIntyre just clapped him on the shoulder."

Nell nodded. "And Mrs. McIntyre's smiling awfully big."

"She's probably telling Aidan he turned out well," Nell answered.

How was Aidan all of a sudden getting cozy with the townsfolk? This was her town, not his. At least it was *more hers* than his. "He's just doing this to gain the advantage," she said with a bitter edge. "In the contest."

"He can't help being recognized," Nell said.

"Would you have recognized him?" Charlotte asked her. She turned to Misty. "Or you?"

"Oh ho!" Misty said. "Here's our answer."

Charlotte peeked back in the bar, seeing Darcy Fitzpatrick and Allison Highsmith approach Aidan to introduce themselves. Of course they would. Not only were they the most gossipy pair in town, rumor was they'd coupled up again—after years of being apart. They'd apparently dated in high school and never gotten over those early amorous feelings. Darcy wrote a "Local Scene" column for *The Seaside Daily* and Allison kept a romance blog online.

Misty was busy on her phone. "Knew it!"

"What?" Nell asked.

"Allison must have been hiding at the airport somewhere. Just look at this pic."

Charlotte stared at Misty's screen, seeing a very

handsome shot of Aidan with his backpack slung over one shoulder. A small swath of yellow indicated that Trudy had been cropped from the photo. The caption read: *London Heartthrob Comes to Claim His Bride.*

Charlotte's jaw tensed. "But if that's the case and everyone in Majestic believes he came to marry me, what's he doing going out with Mary Beth?"

Nell frowned. "Could be just a friend thing?"

Just as she said it, Mary Beth tossed back her head in an exaggerated laugh and collapsed in fake hilarity against Aidan's shoulder, almost spilling her beer. The little sneak.

"Er," Nell said, also spotting the flirtatious move. "Or maybe not."

Misty gasped. "Looks like she's trying to steal Aidan for herself."

Charlotte scowled. "Homewrecker."

What right did Mary Beth have? Oh yeah. Every right, really. Charlotte didn't own Aidan. She wasn't even going to marry him any longer, and he was so past wanting to marry her he'd never gotten there to begin with. Charlotte's cheeks steamed. It wasn't like she cared. It was more like she resented the fact that he didn't.

"Technically." Nell wrinkled up her nose. "There's no home to wreck if—"

"Got it, Nell," Charlotte snapped without meaning to. An instant later she felt rotten when Nell's eyes misted.

"Whoa there." Misty sent her a look.

"Sorry." Charlotte's shoulders sank. "Don't know why it bugs me, because it shouldn't."

"We understand," Nell said kindly. "Aidan should be crying his eyes out over losing you." She paused. "Assuming he's a weeper. Which, honestly? Given that he's lived in London all these years and become all British—"

"Point is!" Misty said, interceding. "This is his loss. Big time."

Except, to look at him now through Mariner's front window, Aidan didn't seem like any sort of loser. He appeared to be having the time of his life. A fun little vacation in America. Cajoling a room, attracting attention. More women than Mary Beth had their eyes on him.

Charlotte couldn't bear to watch. "I think I've changed my mind about that beer."

"Don't be silly," Misty said. "We can go some-place else."

"Yeah," Nell said brightly. "How about the Dockside?"

Charlotte nodded. Maybe hanging out a little longer with her sisters would be good. Then she wouldn't have to think about Aidan, who'd just spun around on his stool to talk to...

Grant, really? Ugh. Lucas was standing beside him, too, acting friendly.

Well, what did she expect? They'd all gone to-gether to get Aidan from the airport, and now those guys were bound to have heard from her sisters about Aidan staying longer and their coffee contest. That didn't mean they had to become best buds or anything.

Nell grimaced at Charlotte's reaction. "They're just being nice."

"Maybe we should get going," Misty said.

But before they turned, Aidan stared over Lucas's shoulder and straight out the bar's front window. *Noooo.*

"Eeep!" Misty cried. "He saw us."

Nell pushed Charlotte forward. "Go. Go."

But Charlotte's boots felt rooted in quicksand as Aidan lifted a hand and waved.

He thought she was spying on him. His self-assured grin said everything.

Charlotte mentally face-palmed. Aidan thought she had the hots for him.

Unbelievable. Egotistical. He was so full of himself it made her want to scream.

"You can just say tomorrow that the bar looked too crowded," Nell said, offering her a ready-made excuse.

Charlotte's blood boiled. He was not going to go assuming she was just another fawning female. In fact, she was going to turn the tables on the man. "No," she said. "Don't think I'll tell him that at all."

"Then what?" Misty asked as they started walking.

"Maybe I'll just say…" Charlotte clicked her tongue. "Looked like you were having fun in there." She adopted a saucy tone. "Why didn't you ask us to come inside and join you?"

Nell gasped. "You're going to *flirt* with him?"

"You evil woman," Misty said.

Charlotte swished her skirt. "It's not so evil to want a man's attention."

"It is when you're capturing it just to throw it away."

Charlotte's boots smacked the sidewalk pavement with a *clip-clop-clip* as the ocean down below Kittery Street tumbled and roared. Oh yeah, she could do this. She could win that coffee contest *and* Aidan's affection too. Then he'd know how it felt to *not* be wanted. If the man had a heart.

"He's a big boy," she said. "Head of an international corporation—for now. Maybe we should trust him to take care of himself?"

"O-kay." Nell heaved a breath and urged them along. "I'm buying."

Which was code for Nell saying she was going to try to talk Charlotte out of it.

"Great!" Misty said, always up for a freebie. She nudged Charlotte. "Then we'll discuss this."

Charlotte raised her eyebrows. "What's to discuss?"

Yeah. This was good. A total plan. She wasn't angling to have Aidan fall *in love* with her. Because she'd never go that far then intentionally hurt his feelings. All she meant to do was catch his eye to the extent he'd leave Majestic wondering about the opportunity he'd stupidly missed. That would give the smug guy a taste of his own medicine.

And based on his reaction this afternoon when they'd nearly bumped into each other in the office, she stood a fighting chance to pull this off.

"Maybe one of us can talk her down from that limb," Nell said to Misty.

"Hope so." Misty gave her the side-eye. "For Aidan's sake."

Now Misty was defending him? Seriously?

"Hope so for both their sakes," Nell answered.

Charlotte stomped up ahead of them, striding faster. "You can talk about me all you want like I'm not here, but I'm not listening." She plugged her ears with her fingers and took off running.

"Charlotte, wait!" Nell shouted.

She broke into a sprint, and they chased after her, but Charlotte maintained her lead.

"Charlotte Delaney!" Nell cried. "This is a bad idea!"

"Yeah!" Misty shouted. "Really bad!"

"Can't hear you!" Charlotte called over her shoulder. She picked up her pace, reliving their childhood races. Nell and Misty had never beaten her once. At least, not since she'd been in fourth grade. Charlotte had become the fastest of the three of them that year.

Misty lagged behind Nell, bringing up the rear, and Charlotte was way ahead of them, darting across the cobblestones and swooping down the steep slope to the docks.

She raced them all the way to the bar's front door.

By the time Nell and Misty caught up with her, they were in hysterics. Bursting into giggles and hoots and hollers, just like they'd done as kids.

"Oh my gosh!" Nell giggled. "We haven't done that in years."

Misty chortled, huffing and puffing. "Remember when we used to race each other home when we got off of the school bus?"

Nell held her sides. "Because whoever got home first got to eat the most cookies."

"That's right!" Misty laughed. "Mom would

always leave out a plate for us for when we got home from school."

Charlotte grinned, but she was wheezy. "I always won." She had to run faster. And it wasn't just for the cookies. If there was one thing she couldn't stand, it was being left in the dust by her sisters.

"You did win, didn't you?" Nell said.

Misty glanced at Nell. "She always grabbed all the best ones, too."

Nell cackled at a memory. "Remember that guy on the bus? Jeremy Jenkins?"

"Oh *yeah*." Misty hooted. "He called Charlotte a two-by-four and she popped him one!"

Charlotte laughed. "That's because it sounded like an insult."

"He probably meant it that way," Nell said, still chuckling. "He hadn't learned any curse words yet."

"That was not funny!" Charlotte cried. "I had to go see the principal."

"Sure." Nell smirked. "But he let you off."

"Too bad Aidan missed that," Misty joked.

Nell got a mischievous gleam in her eye. "Maybe we should warn him Charlotte's got a mean right hook. Then he'd know better than to mess with her."

Charlotte rolled her eyes and Misty doubled over laughing. Charlotte held her. Then Nell hugged her sisters, too, so they were all in one big giggly group.

A guy exited the bar and propped open the door. He gazed at them uncertainly. "Going in?"

The three of them gave embarrassed flushes and contained their snickers.

"Yeah," Charlotte said, leading the way. "Thanks."

"He probably thought we were drunk," Nell whispered behind her.

Misty shoved Nell along with a snort. "Yeah."

Charlotte entered the crowded bar, glad for its warmth and the company of her sisters. She'd funnily forgotten about the two-by-four boy and being sent to the principal. She'd never quite gotten over that inner panic of being left behind, though. She shook it off as they approached the bar, weaving through the chatty crowd.

"You're buying, right?" she said, glancing at Nell.

Nell smiled and took out her purse. "Right you are." She found a spot on a stool, and Misty and Charlotte squeezed in beside her. "First round's on me."

Charlotte was glad Nell was fussing with her wallet and paying. That bought her extra time to think about besting Aidan by making him become all enticed by her. Charlotte knew how to turn on the charm when she wanted to, and she was going to start by cranking it up tomorrow.

CHAPTER EIGHT

Aidan sat across from Trudy at one end of the long dining room table. Matthew carried in a bread basket covered with a cloth napkin, steadying himself on his cane with his other hand. "A little treat to make you feel at home," he said with a cajoling grin. "Crystal made you some fresh scones."

"Oh, how lovely," Trudy said. "Thank you."

Aidan nodded, taking in the light, spicy scent. "Is that cinnamon?"

Matthew grinned. "Cinnamon apple."

Crystal appeared next with a serving dish. "Hot sausage-and-egg casserole." She nodded to the full pitcher of juice on the table. "To go along with the OJ."

Trudy sipped from her tea. "I could get used to these big American breakfasts."

"Me too." Aidan laughed. "But then I'd have to go for extra runs."

"Saw you coming back in earlier," Matthew said. "Looked like you'd gotten a head start on your day."

"Right." Aidan smiled. "Lucas asked me to join him for his morning run, so we met up."

"Lucas? How about Misty?" asked Trudy.

"She was back at her place, sleeping in," Aidan answered. "Something about a late night with her sisters." He reflected on seeing them in the street all huddled together and staring at Mariner's. Charlotte had clearly spotted him, so why hadn't they come in?

Maybe because they'd been headed someplace different?

It was probably a bit much to think she'd been spying on him while he was at the bar. Although on the surface it had appeared that way. She and her sisters had acted surprised when he'd seen them watching him and had quickly scurried away.

Charlotte, Charlotte, Charlotte.

She couldn't really...? Didn't seriously have a thing for him?

That would be oddly...interesting.

He toyed with the idea abstractly. She was a beautiful woman. Intriguing.

And also incredibly distracting.

No. It could never work and she wasn't into him. He was inventing stories in his head. He could only hope she wasn't imagining similar absurdities about him. That would be a riot. And also dead-on wrong.

He'd scarcely thought about her at all since yesterday.

You big fat liar.

"Well, you two enjoy your breakfast," Crystal said, backing out of the room.

"Help yourselves to more coffee or tea from the sideboard," Matthew added, retreating as well. He and Crystal accidentally collided.

Matthew leaned against his cane, his face red beneath his snowy beard. "My dear!"

She blushed. "Oops! My bad."

"Are you all right?"

"Yes, yes. Just fine." She swallowed hard, her cheeks pink. "And dandy."

Trudy cast Aidan a knowing look, and he pursed

his lips. What was it Lucas had said? Love at any age? He was right. This was sweet. Whether or not Matthew and Crystal had acknowledged their interest in each other, it was blatantly there for others to see.

"So," Aidan asked Trudy once the older couple had left, "where'd you go last night?"

"Out to get pizza."

"At Majestic Pies?"

She nodded.

"Their pizza's really good." He removed the lid from the breakfast serving dish, offering her some casserole.

"Sure, thanks."

He fixed both their plates, his mind snagging on a detail. When he'd let himself into the B&B last night, Trudy's shoes had been beside the door. They'd also been coated in sand. "Go out for a walk on the beach?"

"What?" she asked, appearing called out.

"I saw your shoes in the hall."

"Oh that!" She laughed. "Yeah, for a bit."

"Look, I know Majestic is a generally safe town. But you might think twice about walking on the beach alone after dark."

She stared at him a long while then focused on her eggs. "I was fine," she said. "It was fine! Besides that, I took a torch."

He wondered where she'd gotten a flashlight. Maybe from Mr. Mulroney? He was about to ask, but she turned the conversation around before he could.

"So, where were *you* all night?" She took a bite

of cheesy sausages and eggs. "Mmm. Delicious."

"At Mariner's reconnecting with some old mates."

"Really? That's jolly."

"Yeah."

"People remember you here, then?"

"A few. But mainly"—he shrugged—"because I was written up in the press. With photos."

"Well, look at you. Already famous in Majestic."

"More like infamous," he said.

She eyed him carefully. "So then. You went there all alone? To this pub, Mariner's?"

He shifted in his seat. "No. I uh…went there with Mary Beth."

"Blimey!" Trudy paused and chewed on a scone. "Watch it there," she said with narrowed eyes. "She's after you."

So yeah. It was true Mary Beth had ended their evening saying, *"This was fun. We'll have to do it again sometime soon. But maybe, you know, go someplace quieter?"*

He hadn't minded the bar noise himself, or catching up with people he hadn't seen in years. He'd vaguely answered, *"Yeah, sure. Sometime."* Mary Beth was a nice enough woman, but no. He couldn't see things going there.

"Did you tell her?" Trudy asked. "Say that you weren't actually marrying Charlotte like the whole town thought?"

"I did." Aidan cleared his throat. "When she pressed me on it."

Her eyebrows rose. "And then you told everyone else?"

"It was all over the pub before I knew it," he admitted. He took a moment to savor his breakfast. "But I can't see how that matters. The truth is bound to come out now anyhow, since there are no wedding bells ringing. Besides that"—he set down his fork—"I've got no time for romance this trip, and I think everybody knows that."

A foggy memory of his mouth hovering above Charlotte's flashed through his mind and his neck warmed. But that was ridiculous. He was not interested in Charlotte, and she was not interested in him. He was good at reading signals.

At least he thought he was good.

Or used to be.

Trudy dabbed her mouth with her napkin. "We'll need to be ready. Fall Fest is not far off. Which is why…" She glanced out the window at Crystal's van. "I've set up another meeting this afternoon with a supplier."

"What? I thought you already bought a boatload of supplies."

"I did. But I'll have to arrange for delivery of the coffee. We can't count on getting that from Bearberry Brews. Not when we're competing against them."

"No, that's true. They'll be busy enough fixing their own." Aidan sipped his tea. "Maybe I'll work on advertising while you're gone."

"Splendid idea. We'll want to get the word out about our superior sale."

"I've already gotten started." Aidan grinned. "Last night, at the bar, I let everyone know I was giving old chums a friends' discount. Fifty percent."

Trudy gasped. "Fifty? That's giving half our coffee away."

"Precisely," he said, smiling into his cup. "I'd love to see Charlotte try to beat that."

• • •

A short time later, Trudy ripped a flyer off a lamppost. "Bloody hell."

They were halfway to the café, and these bright orange flyers were posted all over the place.

He read the copy. "'Two-for-One Coffees at Fall Fest from Bearberry Brews'?"

"That's the same as we're doing," Trudy grumbled. "Two for one is as good as half price." She glanced at him. "Charlotte might be better at this than you thought."

• • •

When Charlotte entered Bearberry Brews, Misty and Nell were busy getting ready for them to open.

"Morning!" Nell said from behind the counter, where she stocked pastries.

Misty smiled while loading the register. "Hi there."

Though she had marketing plans to tackle, Charlotte still felt guilty about skipping out on work for another whole day. She strode behind the counter and grabbed two napkin dispensers, planning to set them on the creamer station.

"Wait," Nell said. "What are you doing?"

"Helping set up."

"We don't need your help," Misty said. "Sean will be here shortly."

"Yeah." Nell laughed and shook her head. "Let's hope he stays for his whole shift today."

"Whole shift?" Charlotte asked. "What do you mean?"

"Yesterday," Misty said, "he took off around three and never came back."

Charlotte was ashamed she hadn't noticed. Then again, she'd been working in the office and had had her mind on other things. "That doesn't sound like Sean."

Misty rolled her eyes. "Oh yes it does," she said all knowledgeable-like, since she and Sean had dated off-and-on for a year. Misty'd commented on Sean's free-spirited—but somewhat unreliable—nature. He worked odd jobs but had ambitions of becoming a musician. He lived above his parents' small grocery store, McIntyre's Market, which was not far from here.

"Want me to say something?" Charlotte asked.

Nell shook her head. "Lucas is doing the honors."

Good old Lucas. Of course. He was firm but also had a soft touch, making him a good and steady café manager. Charlotte questioned Sean's ability to take over for Lucas later on if he was starting to flake out. But maybe it was just a one-time thing?

The coffee grinder whirred in the kitchen, and crackling and popping coffee beans filled the entire café with their aroma. Her parents were preparing two specialty varieties just for the festival: Cranberry-Apple Crunch and Toasted Blueberry-Almond. Both debut flavors would be a hit with their regulars and draw in new customers, Charlotte was sure.

But first, she had to entice them to show up at the fair. She wanted to work on a print ad to run in *The Seaside Daily* the Friday before, which was just six days away now. Good thing she had connections at the paper, like she did at just about every other place in town.

"Stop doing that," Nell scolded when Charlotte grabbed the carafes for the creamers. "Misty and I can manage. You head into the office and get to work."

"But don't work too hard," Misty teased as Charlotte approached the kitchen. "Maybe you and Aidan will have another *moment*?"

Nell winked. "Righto."

Misty's forehead creased. "Just don't go doing that thing where you're setting him up to break his heart."

"She's right, Charlotte." Nell frowned. "That's mean."

"Shush!" Charlotte hissed as Aidan barreled in the door with Trudy in tow. He looked like a prize fighter, his eyes gleaming fiercely. What on earth was his problem and what did he have in his hand?

Was that her flyer?

Yup. It was.

Aidan acknowledged Nell and Misty with a nod, then turned his gaze on Charlotte. "You're offering up twofers now, are you?" He didn't sound at all friendly. Didn't matter. She was *not* going to be derailed from her plan.

She smiled sweetly up at him then gave his

admittedly great bod an appreciative once-over. "You're looking dapper today." She stole a peek at his bum, and Trudy blinked. "New jeans?"

Aidan's neck reddened then he raked a hand through his hair. "Don't try to change the subject." He waved the flyer at Charlotte. "I was talking about this."

Charlotte pouty-frowned. "And I was talking about *you*. Trying to give you a compliment, actually."

Aidan's mouth fell open and then he closed it. Trudy pulled herself up on her boots, stepping in front of him to address Charlotte. "Very clever," she said, glancing at the flyer. She pushed her sunglasses up, sweeping back her hair. "But maybe not clever enough."

"Why's that?" Charlotte asked, doing her best to act guileless.

"We've got the friends' discount." Trudy's eyelashes fanned wide, and then she grinned. "Fifty percent."

Charlotte knew what that meant. It was basically a twofer-type deal. "How clever of *you*." She'd tried to say it nicely, but it came off a bit sarcastic.

Time to redirect and channel Siren's Song.

She craned her neck to speak to Aidan, whispering behind the back of her hand. "You really do look nice today. Extra handsome."

"What?" Aidan shut his eyes and covered them with one hand. His thumb and pinky each massaged a temple. He stopped doing that to gape at Trudy. "Where's this coming from?"

She shook her head, and Aidan pinned his gaze

on Nell, who quickly turned away. Where was Misty? Oh there. Ducking down and hiding behind the register.

Charlotte turned back toward Trudy. "And where will you announce this brand new discount of yours?"

"We already have." Trudy extracted a rolled-up newspaper from her shoulder bag and passed Charlotte the newest edition of *The Seaside Daily*. Charlotte grabbed it.

Her jaw dropped when she read their printed ad. "What? Already?"

She looked up at Aidan, who shrugged. "What's good for the goose is good for the gander, Charlotte." His face was still flushed, but he seemed to have recovered from his momentary embarrassment over being called handsome. He had to be used to that sort of attention, just not coming from her.

Charlotte swished her short skirt, calling attention to her legs. Aidan's gaze dropped to her cowgirl boots just as she'd hoped before he met her eyes. "All's fair!" she said in flirty tones. "As they say."

Nell scrubbed a hand across her face and Misty was still on the floor somewhere.

"Opening in ten!" her dad announced brightly. He walked past them, jangling his keys. "Aidan. Trudy. Top of the morning to you both." He smiled at Charlotte. "Nice to see you all working together so beautifully." He peered around the counter then asked Nell, "Where's Misty?"

"Here!" Misty popped up like a jack-in-the-box, holding a fistful of bills. "Just dropped something."

"Yes, well," Charlotte answered her dad with only a brief glance at Aidan. "We'll just keep at it!"

Her boot heels smacked the floor as she strode through the kitchen, following Trudy, who led the way. Aidan was not far behind them, likely gloating over his minor victory. That was so like Aidan. Always beating Charlotte to the punch.

While she'd put up her flyers, *The Seaside Daily* had a far wider circulation than eight-by-eleven-inch pieces of paper stapled to lampposts. That's why she'd planned to run her ad on Friday, the day before the festival, to get the most bang for her buck. People in Majestic sometimes had short memories. Other things made a huge impact, though.

Like billboards! Yes. Maybe she should put up another one of those.

"How did you get an ad to run so soon?" she asked Aidan once they'd entered the office.

He casually took his seat. "Darcy offered to pull a few strings when we chatted last night."

Charlotte's pulse pounded in her ears. "You told Darcy about our bet?"

A grin tugged at his lips. "Never said that I wouldn't."

Charlotte slid her computer bag onto her table and then said coolly, "I thought we agreed not to share any details around town about our little wager?"

Pleasant. Flirty.

Ugh. This was going to be harder than she thought.

"And he didn't," Trudy said.

Aidan shook his head. "Not a word about the outcome. Just said we're in this fun contest to increase visibility for our brands."

"And the paper's going to cover it!" Trudy said, settling into her spot next to Aidan.

Fine. The more publicity the better. She'd turn that to her advantage somehow. Maybe by talking to Darcy ahead of time, playing on his sympathies for small-town businesses. After all, Bearberry Brews was the David to Bearberry Coffee's Goliath.

Aidan set his elbows on the table. "How about you?" he asked. "Still honoring our deal?"

Charlotte gripped the rolled-up newspaper in her hand so tightly it crinkled. "Of course." She sat and unrolled the paper, thumbing through its pages. *Aha*. She located the piece so she could examine it more closely. The ad was basically a clippable coupon for a 50 percent discount on every cup of Bearberry Coffee sold at the fair.

"Kudos on your ingenuity!" Okay, that was a bit too saccharine to sound authentic. She'd have to employ more earnest tones. She twirled a lock of her hair with a finger. "So…"

Aidan watched with rapt attention while she licked her lips in extra-slow motion. Excellent. Trudy was engrossed on her laptop, checking something on her phone, while typing quickly on her keyboard. Also excellent.

Charlotte smiled coyly. "How long do you intend to run this ad?"

"Every day through Saturday."

Naturally, since he could afford it.

Charlotte concealed her irritation with an admiring grin. "Nice work."

Aidan rubbed his neck and stared at her.

"Thanks." His penetrating look said he was wondering about something. Maybe he was noticing her new lipstick shade—pumpkin spice—and considering her attractive for once. Good.

She started to fold up the paper when an article caught her eye, along with its big black-and-white photo of Aidan standing at the bar, with Mary Beth on one side and Grant and Lucas on the other. All wore very big grins and hoisted beers. The headline read: *Prodigal Son Returns Home to Cheer the Town*. Frustration trickled through her. Okay, this was too much. Now Aidan was being uniformly embraced by Majestic.

"Cheer the town?" Charlotte asked, forcing a grin. "What's that mean?"

"Bring good cheer to Majestic, naturally," Trudy answered, taking a short break from her typing. Which had to mean she'd been listening to every word. "By participating in the local fair. Being a sport by helping your shop, Bearberry Brews." Trudy smiled. "And we *are* helping your café. One way or another, you'll be far better off when we've left here than you were last week."

While that was true, Charlotte wished she could feel happy about it. Instead, she felt on guard. Like Aidan was trying to stay one step ahead of her, and she didn't know what sort of trick he'd pull out of his sleeve next. Him getting all buddy-buddy with folks at Mariner's was a very underhanded move.

Charlotte closed the newspaper and set it aside, and Aidan opened his laptop.

"I thought I saw you and your sisters outside of Mariner's last night," he remarked casually, with his eyes on his screen.

The way that he said it left a lot implied. Like maybe he suspected she'd been spying on him intentionally. And she hadn't been. The entire episode had been accidental. But if he *wanted* to think she'd been mooning after him, that could work in her favor.

Her nose burned hot and she rubbed it. Oh how she hated what she was about to say, but it was for a worthy cause: her pride. "We were headed to the Dockside and then"—Charlotte cleared her throat— "something in the window at Mariner's caught my eye."

Aidan's eyebrows rose.

Charlotte coquettishly tugged on her crystal necklace, lightly swinging the gem from side to side over her cleavage. He acted as if he didn't notice what she was doing. Still, she saw his eyes drop to her décolletage once or twice.

Aidan thumbed his chest, and she grinned, smiling the sweetest, prettiest smile she could muster under the situation: trying to entice your archenemy into a crush so that you could crush his ego just as soundly as he'd stomped on yours.

An instant later, his eyes narrowed in suspicion. "You're up to something, aren't you?"

What? He'd nailed her? So easily?

"Me?" She dropped her necklace and straightened her top. "No."

If he was onto her already, this flirty put-on clearly wasn't working. It was hard to keep it up, too, on top of her growing irritation about his advertising ploy. Calling in favors with Darcy? How could he? Aidan scarcely knew Darcy at all, while Charlotte and Darcy and Allison all went way back. All the way back to high school. So much for team loyalty. Rah-rah Mustangs! The only team those reporters seemed to be on was their own, given their blatant desire to break the biggest story.

Trudy abruptly flipped her laptop shut and stood. She darted a glance at Aidan. "That's it! Better run."

"What? Now?"

"Yes, now." She packed up her things. "I've got an appointment at ten and need to go back to the inn and grab the people carr—" She stopped herself and giggled. "Van, I mean."

"Shouldn't you bring it by here to unload what you picked up yesterday?" Aidan asked her.

"Ahh, nope! That can probably wait. That way, I can drop off the whole haul at once."

"Okay. If you think that's best."

She nodded and scooted out the door. "See ya!"

Aidan stroked his beard. "She was acting a little odd, don't you think?" he said to Charlotte.

Charlotte shrugged, still grousing over the whole Mariner's thing. And his ad—running day after day. "She's your assistant, not mine."

"Meaning?" he asked with a smug air that honest-to-goodness got the better of her. She closed her eyes and inhaled deeply before letting out a breath.

"Meaning," Charlotte said, opening her eyes. "You should know her better."

Just like he was getting to know Mary Beth, apparently. Not that this bothered Charlotte in the least. Okay, maybe it smarted just a little. Why Mary Beth? And why here and now?

Okay, fine. It smarted a lot. Charlotte was ticked

that Aidan so cavalierly throw *her* over and then go gallivanting around town with another woman. A serial-dater woman, who was probably only after Aidan's status and money. Unlike Charlotte. She only wanted the money part, and gobs of it. But only because it was legitimately the Delaneys' due.

"I do know her better. Which is why—"

Charlotte snapped. "Oh, stop it, Aidan." She jammed her fingers in her ears, unable to tolerate his enticing British accent one second longer. Mary Beth was sure to have swooned over that. Which was great. Let her. But not Charlotte, no.

His eyes went wide. "Stop what?"

Charlotte removed her fingers from her ears. "Being so intentionally irritating."

"I could say the same of you." He folded his arms.

Charlotte huffed. "You can get cozy with the locals all you like, Aidan. Even print two-for-one coffee coupons days in advance—and run your ad forever. But you're not going to win this contest."

Amazingly, he *chuckled*.

Charlotte gritted her teeth.

His lips twitched. "I'm pretty certain I am."

Charlotte's temper flared. How could she have believed she could flirt with the man? He drove her completely bananas! "You can't possibly know that."

He held up both hands. "How about we call a truce?"

"Truce?" She crossed her legs, and then her arms. Then she uncrossed her legs, but not her arms. Then she uncrossed her arms, using her hands to brace herself on the table as she leaned forward. "What on earth are you talking about?"

He jerked his gaze up from her low-cut blouse. Or maybe he'd been staring at her crystal. Good. She hoped he'd been blinded by its positive energy and light, because he sure didn't possess any.

"Just for the moment." He spread his hands out in the air in a placating fashion. "Without Trudy here to referee us, things could get dodgy." The sparkle in his eyes was meant to be playful, she guessed, but it merely provoked her further. Pretty much every-thing about Aidan provoked her. That much hadn't changed since they were kids.

"Ha-ha."

"I'm serious," he said, appearing very far from serious. "You could out-and-out charge me. Run me over in a headlong tackle like one of your American football players."

Now he was goading her. Unbelievable.

"In your dreams, maybe."

"I'd love to hear about yours." His eyebrows arched. "Don't think I don't know what you were doing, Charlotte."

She blinked. "What's that?"

He rubbed the side of his neck and said, "You were trying to butter me up with all that flirty talk earlier to appeal to my weaknesses."

She met his gaze straight-on, refusing to admit he was right. "I thought you didn't have any weakness-es?"

"Not many." Aidan raked a hand through his hair. "But I do have a few fantasies. You?"

She was *not* getting sucked in by the sparkle in

his light brown eyes, or his appealing British accent. Or fantasies of him wearing that sexy kilt. *No*. She was so not helping herself, or the situation. How had he figured out her flirting strategy and turned it back on her? She'd clearly not been subtle enough about it. *Fine. Let him think what he wants—for now.* Later, she'd figure something better out.

She yanked her laptop from her bag. "I've got work to do."

"Yeah," he said, extracting his tablet from his backpack. "Me, too."

Charlotte pulled up her advertising contact at the paper on her phone and sent him a text before dashing off another text to Grant about the billboard. Meanwhile, Aidan was immersed in his own bubble. Like he hadn't a care in the world. She was also fairly certain he didn't care for her, which was a major problem. She really had to fix that—and fast. Otherwise, how would he regret passing up the chance to marry her when he left Majestic?

CHAPTER NINE

Aidan reviewed the Bearberry Brews website on his tablet. One link directed him to "Sign Up for Our Newsletter: Bearberry News!" and he decided he'd better. That way he might keep abreast of any other marketing strategies Charlotte had planned. Assuming she shared those with their regular customers, and he suspected there'd be a tip-off somewhere. Like her announcing Bearberry Brews' twofer special.

Charlotte efficiently shut her laptop. "Well, that's done."

He didn't expect her to answer but decided to ask anyhow. "What is?"

"Ah-ah." She shook her head and her raven-colored tresses glimmered red in the sunlight. "Not telling."

He shrugged. "Fine by me. I'm not telling either."

"What about that truce?"

He couldn't help but grin. "Seems to me we're fencing peaceably."

"Hmm. Yeah." She studied him a moment. "You know, Aidan," she said gently. "I don't want to be at war with you."

"Then thank goodness we've laid down our arms." This elicited the laugh he'd hoped for. So he continued in smooth tones. "We both want the same thing here."

Her eyebrows arched, and warmth spread

through his chest. "Do we?" she asked.

In spite of himself, he wanted to help her. See her achieve the victory she was so sure that she'd gain. But by giving her everything? No. That amount of restitution was way too much.

"Yes," he said. "We both want to see Bearberry Brews financially sound and to have it flourish in the future." She couldn't very well fight with him on that.

She pursed her lips. "True."

"So in that way," he said with a grin, "win or lose, you'll have your happy outcome."

She turned to peer out the window at the rocky sea. Though the sun shone, rough autumn winds tossed it about. When she spun back around, she asked, "What about your outcome?"

The panorama through the window was stunning as seagulls soared through the bright and beautiful sky. Charlotte's eyes were nearly as blue, but their hue was a bit deeper. Entrancing in their own way. When she wasn't being difficult.

"If you're happy, I'm happy," he said blithely, though in an unexpected way he meant it.

She snickered. "Yeah, right."

He relaxed back in his chair. "It's true, Charlotte. Whether or not you believe that is up to you." The way she'd tried to dupe him with her flirtatious behavior had been almost charming. It might have been more so if it had been authentic.

She templed her fingers in front of her. "I don't trust in people easily."

"You don't say." He tried to conceal his smirk but failed. He didn't trust her either. Not as far as he could throw her. From her behavior earlier, it was clear she'd do or say anything to win this coffee contest. He didn't know what she thought she had to gain with her flirting. She'd probably been trying to throw him off guard by getting in his head—just so she could mess with it. But he was smart enough not to let *that* happen.

She grabbed a pen off her table and hurled it at him. He ducked, and the oncoming missile clanked against the wall before diving to the floor.

"Suppose that was better than a tackle," he said, amused by her small display of temper. He'd clearly unnerved her, just like he'd been able to do when they were kids.

She stood, placing her hands on her hips. "Does nothing ever get to you?"

"No," he said, standing as well. "Should it?"

She strode toward him, and he met her midway across the room. "Everyone has their weak spots, Aidan. Even people who claim they don't."

He held up his arms like he was inviting her to tickle him. "Want to try to find mine?"

She groaned, and he smirked. "Sorry," he said, but he wasn't.

Her nose turned bright red. "You think you're so cute."

Aidan shifted on his feet then said calmly, "I've heard that from women."

"Ooh, including Mary Beth?"

He stroked his beard. "You're not jealous, Charlotte?"

She gasped, although the shimmer in her eyes made her look like she'd been called out. "You must be joking."

"Because, you know…" He leaned toward her and whispered, "Our engagement's off." They stood very close now, only a few feet apart. She inched nearer to glower up at him.

"Thank goodness for that," she said crisply. "What a disaster that would have been."

He stared deeply into her eyes, trying desperately not to fall into the eddies of heat and attraction he found there. "Train wreck. Yes."

She shut her eyes and seemed to be counting to ten. "So, tell me about you, Mr. Perfect?" she asked hotly. "If you're such a catch, how come nobody's caught you?"

His heart raced, but he held his ground, refusing to become flustered. He was good at keeping his cool in tense situations. He cocked one eyebrow and said, "I could ask the same of you."

She let out a sound that was half yelp, half growl.

"Stop trying to toss the ball back in my court," she said, wide-eyed.

"All right," he said. "I'll give." Her scent wafted toward him, all springtime flowers on a sunny afternoon. But he was *not* attracted to Charlotte. No. No matter how pretty or smart she was. "Maybe I haven't been 'caught' because I never really got in the game."

She clicked her tongue. "By becoming entangled romantically, you mean?"

"Precisely." He cocked his head. "And you?"

"Let's just say I haven't met the right guy."

"Now, that's a shame." His words came out husky and she blushed. He sensed that pull again, tugging at him like the ocean, sweeping him up in her tide.

But he pushed back hard against it. He was *not* falling for Charlotte Delaney. Once in a lifetime was enough.

Aidan cleared his throat and she took a step back, and then another.

She released a small breath. "I think I'm done for the day."

Her eyes met his, and Aidan's pulse hummed. He was *not* going there. Not even toying with the thought of what it would be like to hold her.

"Yeah." He dragged a hand through his hair. "Me, too." He glanced out the window, getting the urge to be outdoors. Fresh air would do him good. Do both of them good, probably. He didn't want to become involved with Charlotte, but they could get along as friends.

There was an idea.

He could view her as a pal, a friendly foe of sorts, and nothing more. Aidan didn't do serious involvements and a casual one with Charlotte would be reckless. Assuming she'd even want one to begin with. He'd thought *absolutely not* before, but a few of their exchanges had given him pause. The ones where it *hadn't felt like* she'd been pretending on her part.

He sank his hands in his pockets, unsure of her response. He decided to risk it anyhow. "Would you like to take a walk?"

• • •

Charlotte decided to seize the moment. This was perfect. Aidan was playing right into her hands—finally. It was impossible to charm him when he was being impossible. With him actually trying to be nice now, it was going to be a whole heck of a lot easier.

"We're headed out for a walk," she told her folks as they passed through the kitchen.

"Cheerio!" her dad said.

Her mom grinned, lines forming around her mouth and eyes. "Have a nice time."

Trudy nearly bowled them over entering through the side door from the alley, carting in packaged paper cups, lids, and the like. Sean was behind her, carrying twice as much in his sinewy arms. Sean was tall, blond, and lithe, and not a bad-looking guy, but he'd never been right for Misty.

"Here," Aidan said, stepping toward Trudy. "Let's give you a hand."

She nodded, and he took some of her load while Charlotte plucked the top layer of shrink-wrapped paper napkins from his arms. All were plain brown and made from recycled materials. Same as the kind Bearberry Brews used.

"Where were you this morning?" Charlotte whispered to Sean as they all set things in the storeroom.

"I had a thing." He stared at her poker-faced, but his green eyes flickered. Sean was up to something.

Charlotte glanced at Aidan's assistant. With Trudy? "A thing?"

"That's right," Sean said in hushed tones. "But it's on the downlow for now."

"Ahh," Charlotte said.

"I cleared my absence with Lucas," Sean said. "If you must know." His brow furrowed, indicating he didn't appreciate her being in his business. Although Bearberry Brews was her business, in fact.

"Not everyone has to know everything!" Trudy laughed, and Aidan gave her the side-eye.

"In any case," Aidan said, "Charlotte and I were just on our way. Anything else we can help you with first?"

"Yes," Trudy said. "If you don't mind."

· · ·

Twenty minutes later, Aidan accompanied Charlotte down the stone steps to the beach.

"Wow, that was weird." He raked a hand through his hair. "You don't suppose that Trudy and Sean—?"

Charlotte guessed a relationship between the pair was possible. "They have been coincidentally gone at the same time—twice."

Winds blew up from the beach, combing over them. Charlotte's flouncy skirt fluttered in the breeze, and she pressed it down against her thighs to hold it steady.

If Aidan noticed, he didn't make it obvious. Still, she caught him stealing a glance at her legs. "Trudy has been taking outings," he said, his gaze now on his footing as they scooted down the stairs.

"Outings?" she asked. "What do you mean?"

Aidan paused, holding the railing. "Out to dinner. Out for a walk on the beach. At night." He waited a beat and then added, "Alone."

"That does sound mysterious," Charlotte agreed as they reached the sand. She took two steps forward before realizing it was useless. She'd never get far in these cowgirl boots.

Aidan stared down at her feet. "You should take them off."

She wasn't so sure about that. The sun was already setting and the temperature going down. "It's breezy out and cool."

He stooped low and stuck his hand in the sand, moving his fingers. "The sand's not too cold, though. Still warm from the midday sun."

She crossed her arms then issued her saucy challenge. "If I go barefoot, then so do you." Her gaze snagged on his loafers, and he laughed.

"You always were so bossy, Charlotte." The way he said it, though, was like he didn't mind being bossed around by her too terribly. At least, not at the moment.

They returned to the wooden railing by the base of the steps and held on while they removed their footwear. "I'm not bossy," she protested. "That's Nell."

"Nell's sweet." His eyes glimmered in the waning light. "She doesn't boss. She recommends."

Charlotte belly-laughed at his assertion because it was so true. She held up her hand. "In the most affectionate and caring way."

She tucked her boots beside the steps, and Aidan left his loafers there too. Charlotte looked one direction and then the other. "Which way should we go?"

"South toward the lighthouse," he suggested. "Lookout Point?"

She liked that plan and the view was spectacular. "All right."

The beach was rocky in places with sharp shells wedged in between, so they had to navigate their journey carefully. Still, Charlotte was having fun. She hadn't gone barefoot on the beach in autumn since…she didn't know when. A wave crashed near them and a chilly burst of water splashed over her toes. She yelped and jumped back, and Aidan chuckled.

"It's not that cold. Come on."

"Easy for you to say because you're not standing in it."

His eyebrows arched then he accepted her challenge, rolling up his pant legs one at a time while cuffing them.

"Aidan." She giggled. "What are you doing?"

He straightened and dusted a few grains of sand from his jeans. "Going wading."

He wasn't really, though. Was he? "You'll freeze your feet off!"

"Don't think so." He stepped forward into the foaming spray. Sea water washed up in eddies, surrounding his ankles on the rocky shore. He frowned thoughtfully. "Hmm. Not bad. You should try it."

She stared down at his feet, which were turning purple beneath the tide. "Stop that!" she scolded. "You're losing circulation."

He faked a frown. "You're being awfully dramatic."

"And you're being stubborn. Come on!" She reached for his arm to grab it, but he caught her hand in his. She tugged him toward the beach, but he pulled harder, yanking her toward the waves.

"Why don't you come this way instead? Hmm?"

He tightened his grasp and she yelped.

"Aidan, no!" She stumbled forward and icy water splashed up to her knees, hitting the hem of her skirt. A shiver tore through her. But she wasn't sure if it was from the sudden blast of cold or the heat in his eyes. This was soooo not good.

Or maybe it was perfect. The opportunity she'd hoped for. A chance to sway Aidan into thinking of her as an appealing woman.

"What are you afraid of?" He pulled her closer as icy water splashed up against her, chilling her legs and her knees.

"You! You big tease!" She lost her footing and fell forward.

Aidan caught her by her elbows in the shallows. "Charlotte!" His breathing was ragged and so was hers. "I'm sorry." His forehead wrinkled, and his gaze was utterly sincere. "I didn't mean—"

A huge wave crashed toward them, sending her off balance, and suddenly she was in his arms. Aidan tightened his embrace, holding her against him, and her heart hammered.

"Charlotte?" he rasped above the wind. "Are you all right?"

She nodded but honestly wasn't sure. This whole flirty game had seemed harmless enough, maybe even a bit sexy. And Aidan Strong was an undeniably sexy guy. But she was the one who was supposed to be appealing to him and not vice versa. But, ooh, he was very appealing, standing with her in the waves and holding her in his arms, his light-brown gaze washing over her like the warmest summer rain.

A strand of her hair whipped across her face, and he tenderly reached up and stroked it back, tucking it behind her ear. Her nose burned hot even though her toes were going numb.

"I didn't mean to hurt you." His touch lingered on her cheek, and a delighted tingle shimmied through her. He was so much stronger than she'd thought. Tall, lean, and steady. Though the ocean threatened to rock them, he served as a bulwark, anchoring them in place.

"I know," she said, as winds flitted past them, riffling their clothing in big billowy puffs. "You didn't." But he could hurt her—and would—if she let herself get too close.

"You're just like I remembered." He dove into her eyes. "No. Better." Her feet tingled from the sting of the chilly water, and the receding tide buried her toes in wet sand. But Aidan clearly wasn't worried about the water. His entire focus was on her.

He held her closer, and her body molded against him.

His chin dipped low as her mouth angled up.

Charlotte's heart skipped a beat when she realized what was happening…

He was about to kiss her.

CHAPTER TEN

Charlotte could *not* let that kiss happen.

She reached down into the water, surprising Aidan with a burst of chilly spray. It hit the side of his neck and beard, but his shocked look of surprise was priceless.

"Charlotte," he growled.

But she'd already broken free and raced back to the shore. Thank goodness she'd come to her senses! That had been a really close one. Too close. She could not become physical with Aidan then purposely dump him. All she'd meant to do was entice him a little. How had he turned that all around so that *he'd* been enticing *her*?

She kept running down the beach, and running and running, kicking up sand and spray until her sides hurt and she had to stop for a breather. He caught up with her and bent forward.

"Very funny," he said when she couldn't stop giggling.

She felt just like a kid. So wild and free. Just like she'd felt last night while racing toward the Dockside along with her sisters. She almost never experienced that kind of lighthearted fun anymore. She scarcely had the time. She had the café and her parents to worry about, and life demands to meet. Like paying rent.

Aidan set his hands on his knees, also winded. "You're still a fast runner," he said with an admiring grin.

She couldn't help but banter. "You're not as quick as you used to be."

He smirked. "And you're still just as tricky."

She stuck her tongue out at him. "You started it!"

"Yeah. I guess I did." Aidan stood up straighter. "Listen, Charlotte," he said, appearing abashed. "About what happened back there—" He glanced toward the waves.

"It's all right," she said, still a bit breathless. "Nothing happened." *Thank goodness*. Because the scariest part of all was that a very tiny part of her had wanted it to.

Aidan raked a hand through his hair and said, "Right," like he was really glad about that, too. Good. So they were both on the same page here. A little flirtation was fine, but actually becoming intimate with each other was a giant no-go.

Aidan nodded toward the lighthouse down the beach. "What do you think? Want to keep going?"

The sun sank lower in the west, casting an orange-and-purple haze across the sky. Up ahead of them, the lighthouse's beacon had turned on. There were only a few other people on the beach, folks walking dogs and so on.

Charlotte shrugged. "Sure."

They were already three quarters of the way there. Plus, focusing on that objective would take her mind off that almost kiss. *How* had she let that happen? Her and Aidan for real? No. She was supposed to be making him sorry about what he'd miss. Not handing herself to him on a platter. There'd been heat between them, though. So maybe she was on the right track, as long as she didn't slip and do something stupid.

They ambled along the beach at an easy pace.

"Charlotte," he said. "About earlier." He tossed a look over his shoulder toward the sea.

"We cleared that up, all right?" Even as she said it, her face burned hot. She tried to ignore the flutters in her belly. "We were just kidding around, that's all."

He looked unconvinced. "Yeah, sure."

"Besides which"—she put on a flirty manner, but this time it felt a lot more real—"one kiss in a lifetime is all that you'll get from me."

His ears turned pink. "That was hardly a kiss and you know it. We were just kids."

"Well it was my first one." She hugged her arms around herself for warmth and kept going. "You?"

He rubbed his cheek in an embarrassed fashion. "You can probably guess the answer to that." His gaze swept over the dunes. "Speaking of weddings past…" He pointed to a sandy knoll covered with sea grass. "There's the scene of the crime."

She flushed even though she shouldn't have. "That was kind of criminal, wasn't it?" she joked. "Nell forcing us all into it."

"As I recall, she didn't force anyone into anything," he said. "We all went along with it as just another one of her games."

"Or plays!" Charlotte said. She giggled at the memories. "Nell loved writing those and then casting us into roles. She was always the director."

"As the oldest, of course," Aidan added. "Misty sure seemed to love playing a flower girl."

Charlotte smiled. "Nell made us all bouquets."

"Not me," he countered. Aidan patted his chest on the left side. "I had my boutonniere."

"Oh yeah." Charlotte sighed wistfully.

As they approached the lighthouse, Charlotte noted a family playing a game nearby. They had two long, flat boards laid out on the sand several feet apart from each other. Each had a hole cut in its far end, and the kids and adults were chucking bean bags at them. The boys, meaning the dad and his son, appeared to be competing against the girls, a mom and her daughter. The children looked elementary age.

Aidan grinned. "They're playing cornhole."

Charlotte stared at him in surprise. "How do you know about cornhole?"

He laughed. "I've been living in London, Charlotte. Not in a cave."

She noticed the large pink-and-white panda bear propped into a sitting position in one of the family's beach chairs. "Wait," she said. "I think I know them."

"Afternoon," the dad said, stopping their game so Aidan and Charlotte could walk by.

"Beautiful day," Aidan said.

Charlotte smiled at the kids. "Who owns the panda?"

"Me!" The pigtailed little girl raced to it and gave the stuffed animal's belly a squeeze.

"Your bear looks very loved," Aidan commented.

"I've got Bruce!" the little boy with curly blond hair and chubby cheeks announced.

"Oh?" Aidan's eyebrows rose. "Who's Bruce?"

The mom laughed. "His pet turtle back at home."

Aidan nodded, pretending to be extremely impressed. "I see."

Charlotte motioned toward the cute panda bear and smiled at the girl. "My sister Misty's got one almost just like it. Only hers is purple."

The child's face lit up in a big toothy grin. "Your sister is 'Feeling the Wind Girl'?"

"Oh yes, yes," the dad said. "Misty."

"And Lucas." The mom grinned. "Sweet couple."

Charlotte recalled seeing the family in the movie theater when she'd been there on a date and Misty had been there with Lucas. The little girl had called Misty "Feeling the Wind Girl" then too. But when Charlotte had asked Misty later what the heck that meant, she'd never answered.

"Yeah, they are," Charlotte said. "How do you know them?"

"Oh," the mom said, "we've seen them around town." She glanced down the beach. "Met them at the lighthouse."

"Uh-huh," the children said. "Misty's cool."

Charlotte grinned proudly. "She is super cool, isn't she?"

"Looks like this group is super cool too," Aidan said, and every member of the family grinned.

"Well, have a nice time," Charlotte said. "Enjoy the cornhole."

"We will," the mom said. "Thanks!"

Once the family was several feet behind them, Aidan said, "Nice bunch. Cute kids."

"Yeah."

"But what was the deal with Misty feeling the wind?"

Charlotte laughed. "Honestly, I have no idea. She sometimes does woo-woo stuff. Like communing with nature."

"Doesn't sound so woo-woo to me."

They reached the lighthouse and observed it for a moment before turning around.

After a lull, he said, "She always was really creative. Misty. I'm not surprised about art school."

"Maybe I shouldn't have been either," Charlotte said. "But when Nell and I first learned about it, we were surprised. Pleasantly, though. Neither of us knew she'd harbored that dream. She hadn't told anyone in the family. Only Mei-Lin."

"Who's Mei-Lin?"

"She's Misty's bestie. Also works at the café while studying to teach English to English language learners. During the whole Marry-Me-Misty billboard thing she met this cowboy called Dusty from Wyoming. They fell kind of fast and hard."

"You don't say?"

"I do." She grinned, remembering Mei-Lin's happy face as she'd left the café for her trip. "She's out there, as we speak, seeing his ranch and meeting his family."

"Sounds serious."

"Could be."

They passed the spot where the family had been, but they'd packed up their cornhole and other beach items and gone in for the night. The rest of the beach was empty. It was only the two of them now leaving their footprints behind them. The sand had cooled down quite a bit and Charlotte's feet were getting chilly, but they'd be back in her boots soon enough.

"It's nice to have good mates," Aidan said as they strolled along. "I've got Tony back in London. He's like a brother in a way, but I didn't meet him until uni."

She knew he meant university from the time she'd spent in Scotland. Over there, college meant high school. "So tell me about this Tony," she said, enjoying learning more about Aidan.

Aidan smiled. "He's a jokester, he is. The first time I met him he told me that he had form." That was British speak for a police record.

She gasped. "Did he?"

"No. He was just trying to rattle me before our first face-off in rugby." He studied her a moment. "You'd like Tony, I think. He's outgoing and fun."

"What does Tony do?"

"He's a record producer."

"No way. Like a real one? Who has he produced? Would I know any names?"

He shot her the lopsided grin that made her heart flutter, even though she didn't want it to. "Perhaps a few." He named a couple of pop stars and Charlotte squealed.

"I can't wait to tell Nell and Misty." She wanted to know more. "Is he married?"

Aidan nodded. "He and Jill just had their first. Ellie, a little girl."

"How sweet." Charlotte had always believed she'd have kids, but the idea was still a vague notion. "Do you think they'll have more?"

"My guess is that's probably it for them. Jill is a barrister and Tony travels a lot. So their work keeps them busy."

Charlotte understood that everyone's choice about whether to have kids, and/or how many, was very personal. And for herself, she couldn't imagine having just one. Her mom liked to say she'd grown up with a built-in play group, and it was true. She and her sisters had always been fast friends and had totally gotten along. At her parents' insistence, they'd been made to treat each other kindly from the start.

She thought of goofy Aidan and how awkward he'd been as a kid. She was ashamed to admit that what he'd said was true. She and her sisters had picked on him some. Not routinely, but yeah, a few times. Maybe it was from all that pent-up energy they had from being forced to behave around one another at home all the time. He may have been annoying and ungainly, and probably had provoked them on purpose at times. But she still felt bad about them teasing him when he'd been so seriously outnumbered.

She frowned. "I'm sorry if we were less-than-stellar friends to you back when we were kids. My sisters and I."

His eyes glinted in the fading light. "You all weren't so bad."

"Nice of you to say so."

"I liked hanging out with you three, even though I didn't always act like it." He shrugged. "In a way, it was like having a family."

Her heart softened to him. "You had a family," she said gently.

"I had a mum and dad." He met her eyes as they walked along. "I didn't have what you had. What you and your sisters still have."

She always knew their bond was special, but she'd never valued it quite as much as she did now with Aidan pointing this out to her. "Yeah. I guess I've been very lucky."

"In a way, when we moved—" He pursed his lips and turned away, gazing out over the ocean. "It was like losing everything."

She'd never thought about it that way, from his perspective. The transition to a new country had to have been hard. "But you had your grandparents there."

"My dad's folks were in London and my mum's in Aberdeen, it's true. But up until that point, I'd only seen them once or twice a year, so."

"Are they still living?" she asked, aware of the huge knowledge gaps she had concerning his life growing up.

He shook his head no.

"I'm sorry," she said, meaning it. "We've lost our grandparents too."

"You've still got your parents, though, and they're grand." She smiled at how British he sounded, and he backpedaled quickly. "*Great.*"

"You don't have to change how you talk for me, you know. I do understand you."

"I've been working very hard to stay on track," he said.

"You're doing just fine."

Dusk cloaked the beach as they reached the stone steps.

"Thanks for the walk," she said, picking up her boots. "And the talk. Both were fun."

He shook the sand from his loafers and slid them on, then offered her a steadying hand while she got her boots on. "It was a good time. Refreshing."

"Yeah." She looked into his eyes and his smile took her breath away. Sadly. She had to stop going all gushy over Aidan and remember she was the one who was supposed to be getting him to be all gushy about *her*.

"Tomorrow's Sunday," he said casually. "So there's not a ton of work on the fair either of us can do." He hesitated before asking, "Want to hang out?"

He looked so hopeful, she hated to let him down. She also needed to keep up their interactions so she could capture his interest—before obliterating him in that coffee contest. He might be acting nice now, but after another seven days, he'd be boarding that plane to London. Unburdened by her presence and his corporation. A free man.

"That sounds really nice…" Her pulse skittered nervously because she did want to see him. So much. Still, something inside her kept sounding alarm bells. *Danger! Danger!* There was no question about it. This was tricky territory. He was a hard guy not to like when he stopped being so genuinely annoying. But she did not need to fall for him.

Luckily, she'd never really fallen for anyone, so she'd had ample practice at remaining distant. Maybe maintaining some distance between her and Aidan would be good. Just look at what had nearly happened on the beach when he'd pulled her into the waves. "I should probably help out at work, though," she hedged. "Lately, all of my focus has been on the fair."

He crossed his arms like he knew something. "Lucas said it's your day off."

"Lucas? What?"

"He and I went for a run this morning." Of course they did. Aidan was befriending everyone in town, so why not Lucas? Grant would be next. Then, who knows, maybe even Sean.

She thought of Mary Beth, and her stomach soured. If Charlotte turned Aidan down for tomorrow, would he seek out Mary Beth's company instead? For whatever reason, she didn't enjoy thinking about that. Not that she was jealous. She wasn't. It was more like Mary Beth didn't have the same kind of history with Aidan and his family that Charlotte did.

"He's your café manager, isn't he?" Aidan asked. "He makes the schedule."

"Yeah." She licked her lips, seriously tempted. Spending additional time with Aidan could only further her cause, couldn't it? If she carefully watched her step, and they kept things on friends-only terms.

"Come on, Charlotte." He grinned and—against her better judgment—her heart melted. Right into a throbbing, liquid puddle at her feet. "Just say yes."

Maybe this wasn't such a hot idea. He'd caused her and her sisters to suffer through three long weeks of chaos when he could have prevented that entirely. Then he'd shown up here acting like the thought of marrying her was beyond absurd. Now, though, things were different. She'd piqued his interest just enough that he wanted to spend more time with her. And she could do that in a way that aligned with her goals. Tomorrow, she'd be the most amazingly captivating person he'd ever known. And the next day, and the day after that...

Then, when he got on his plane to London, he'd regret leaving her behind.

She drew in a shaky breath, gathering her nerve. "What did you have in mind?"

CHAPTER ELEVEN

Charlotte strode toward Bearberry Brews as casually as she could, but her pulse raced. There was no mistaking Aidan's interest in her any longer. It was written all over his face and in his eyes. He might not have entertained romantic notions about her in London, or when he met her at the airport. Something had changed over the past few days, though, and she'd definitely felt a spark down on the beach. Not that things had sparked for her. Not seriously.

She had that part completely under control.

Ick. Her palms felt clammy, so she wiped them against the sides of her skirt.

She passed Sean as he exited the shop. He seemed in a hurry, checking his phone for the time. "Oh sorry," he said, squeezing past her. He called back to Misty and Lucas. "See ya tomorrow."

Charlotte stepped into the empty café and Lucas locked the door behind her. It was a little after six and they'd just closed up. "How was the walk?" he asked with a suspicious air.

"Fine. It was good."

Lucas's gray eyes narrowed and he just said, "Huh." Then he shook his head and walked away, mumbling something to himself as he entered the kitchen.

"Charlotte?" Misty punched a code into the register and shut it. "Did something…" She gasped then giggled. "Oh wow. Your nose is bright red."

Charlotte rubbed it self-consciously. "Is not." Although it did feel warm.

Misty's eyes widened. They were hazel like their mom's and rimmed with heavy eyeliner. "Oh my gosh," she whispered. "You and Aidan? What?"

"Shhh! Mom and Dad."

"They're gone," she replied.

"Lucas then."

"You're not enacting your plan?" Misty's eyebrows knitted together. "The evil woman one?"

Charlotte didn't like the way she'd phrased that. She wasn't being evil. Simply evening the score.

Misty called over her shoulder. "Nell!"

But Lucas appeared in the doorway instead. "She's in the office," he said, drying a coffee mug with a dish towel.

He turned around, and Misty jerked her chin in that direction. "I think this calls for a sisters' convo."

Charlotte sighed. She did not need her older and younger sisters telling her what to do. And she planned to tell them that in no uncertain terms. She and Misty met Nell in the hallway between the office and storeroom. Lucas had his back to them while unloading their industrial-size dishwasher.

"Did someone call me?" Nell asked. She had a pencil tucked behind one ear, poking through her auburn curls, and her purse strap slung over her shoulder.

"Yeah, we did." Misty latched onto her arm and tugged her into the storeroom. Charlotte too.

"*She* did," Charlotte said, glowering at Misty.

Nell stared at them blankly. "What's going on?"

Her gaze swept over Charlotte. "Uh-oh." She giggled and tapped the side of her nose.

Charlotte smirked. "Very funny."

"So," Nell said, growing animated. "You and Aidan took a walk and…?"

Misty jumped in. "My guess is that things went well." She didn't sound happy about it.

Nell frowned. "Wait. So you're not…" She covered her mouth with her hand then whispered, "Doing the evil woman thing?"

Charlotte clicked her tongue. "It's not so evil," she hissed. "All right? We just went for a walk on the beach. Took a trip down memory lane."

"Sounds a little romantic," Nell swooned.

"Well, it wasn't," Charlotte lied. "Far from it." Her gaze fell on Misty. "Oh hey. We saw some friends of yours. Cute family with a boy and a girl."

"The Jennings?"

"Not sure. The girl had a panda, though. Looked a lot like the one Lucas gave you."

She grinned. "That's them."

Charlotte paused, remembering. "Why does that kid call you 'Feeling the Wind Girl'?"

Misty's cheeks turned pink. "It's just a thing I do. Communing with nature."

Nell rolled her eyes, and Misty shoved her. "What? You commune now all the time," she teased. "With Grant."

Nell sighed. "True." She returned her attention to Charlotte. "A walk sounds harmless enough. It's not like you're dating him or anything."

"Um."

Misty's jaw dropped. "Are you?"

Charlotte winced. "We kind of have a tiny date tomorrow. No biggie."

"A date?" Nell's eyebrows arched. "Really?"

Misty crossed her arms. "But you're not actually going through with it? Trying to get him to fall for you so you can lower the boom?"

Nell frowned disapprovingly. "That's not very nice, Charlotte."

She blinked. "Seriously? After all he's done."

"He's done good things too," Nell countered.

Misty shook her head. "Did you learn *nothing* from what happened with Nell? She and Grant tried to outplay each other and it almost blew them apart."

"Almost. Not quite." Nell glanced at her engagement ring then at Charlotte. "But Misty's right. It was stupid to play games. You don't need to go there."

Charlotte set her hand on her hip, growing annoyed. "I'm not going anywhere, okay? Things between me and Aidan will never get serious. I don't intend to let them."

"Oh yeah?" Nell's eyebrows shot up. "What if you can't help yourself."

"Yeah," Misty giggled. "From helping yourself—to him."

"It's true," Nell said to Misty. "Charlotte's always had a weakness for great-looking guys."

"Stop."

"I'm serious, though," Misty said. "Aidan came here to do a good thing and won't be here that long. He might even lose his whole company to us. Why pile on one more thing?"

"I'm not going to pile," Charlotte said indignant-ly. "And he's not going to fall." She set her chin. "Neither am I. I don't think of him that way. But he might leave Majestic thinking a little more favorably of me and like he missed his one shot."

"For?" Nell asked.

Charlotte put on her haughty tone. "Marrying somebody perfect."

Misty groaned. "So it *is* about that."

"Knock-knock!" They all jumped. It was Lucas.

He cracked open the door. "Can I get in there for a sec? I need to grab some new mugs. A few of the ones coming out of the dishwasher looked worn or chipped."

The three of them scooted out of the storeroom and into the hallway, where Misty grabbed her denim jacket off a hook. "How much of that do you think he heard?"

"Don't know." Nell frowned. "Hopefully, not all of it."

Charlotte still wore her heavy cardigan sweater, and Nell was ready to go. Except for one thing. Charlotte reached out and pulled the pencil from behind her ear. "You forgot this," she said, handing it over.

Nell dropped it in her purse. "Uh, thanks."

As they headed toward the door, Misty whis-pered, "Charlotte? You're not really going to do it? Not actually going to lead poor Aidan on?"

Charlotte scoffed. "First off, Aidan is not poor. He's minted. Secondly, I won't be leading him any-where he doesn't willingly want to go."

• • •

Aidan woke up the next morning feeling energized. He didn't take off from work often but today looked like the perfect day for a break. The fact that he'd be spending much of it with Charlotte made the prospect of a breather even more enticing. He kept telling himself he wasn't interested in becoming involved with her but was also astute enough to know that he hadn't exactly behaved that way yesterday.

She hadn't seemed to mind their mild banter or his playful antics, either. She'd actually appeared to enjoy his company in a way. He'd definitely liked being with her and was eager to see her again. Just to spend time. Bask in that lyrical laugh of hers.

He stepped off the front porch of the B&B and into the misty morning dressed for his run in his sweat clothes and trainers. *Scratch that.* Running shoes. His lingo didn't matter so much and Charlotte was right. People basically understood him despite his Britishisms, which were not as pronounced as Trudy's. Still, he felt a bit out of his skin.

He'd lived here as a kid but had spent his formative teenage and adult years in the UK. While traveling for business, he'd never needed to adjust his language, because most folks he dealt with either spoke or easily understood the Queen's English, including his top execs in New York and LA. Being back in small-town Maine gave him pause, though. Made him want to blend in rather than stick out by appearing—or in this case sounding—too different.

Salty sea breezes ripped across the lawn,

testifying to the ocean not being far away. Burgeoning sunlight painted a haze across the sky and the ocean's sounds grew louder as he approached the whooshing and sighing of waves.

He'd planned to meet Lucas at the stone steps and go for an early run. Though Misty'd apparently run with Lucas during their intense courtship, he joked that he suspected running wasn't really her thing, because she'd been looking for opportunities to avoid it ever since. Not that it mattered to Lucas in the least.

Aidan liked Lucas and was glad about him and Misty pairing up.

Lucas waved from his spot on the sidewalk as he stretched out his arms and legs.

Aidan picked up his speed, joining him at the top of the stone staircase. The ocean tumbled and roared down below them, crashing against the beach in pummeling foam.

"Rough seas this morning," he said.

"Yeah," Lucas agreed. "Winter's coming and the ocean knows it."

Aidan laughed. "Got to get through fall first." He did a few stretches himself, then they headed down the steps, jogging as they went.

"And Fall Fest." Lucas winked jokingly. "How's that going?"

"The planning?"

"Yeah."

"Coming along."

They ran toward the ocean where the surface was flatter although a bit rocky. Aidan recalled walking barefoot here with Charlotte, and warmth spread through his chest. She'd looked really pretty with the wind sifting through her hair. And when he'd held her in his arms, truly beautiful with that bright red nose of hers showing off her subtle freckles. The same ones she'd had as a girl.

They headed north toward the wildlife refuge. Lucas's oceanfront cottage was a few miles beyond that. "Word is Charlotte's got your contest all sewn up," Lucas said. Both of them were in shape enough to carry on a conversation while they ran.

"Contest hasn't happened yet, mate."

Lucas laughed. "You don't mean to seriously risk losing your business?"

"Never going to come to that," Aidan said.

Lucas turned to him. "You sound awfully sure."

"I know Charlotte's cunning, but I wasn't born yesterday myself."

"True. You're what? Thirty?"

"Yeah," he answered. "Same as Nell."

The sun rose higher and the misty haze began to lift off the water.

"If I were you, I'd be a little careful around her."

"Who?" Aidan was taken aback. "Charlotte?"

Lucas stopped running, causing Aidan to stop too. "I probably shouldn't say this because—Misty. And the Delaneys. We're all very tight. But look. You're a nice guy, it seems. Heart's in the right place in helping them."

"Yes?"

Lucas hung his head and then looked up. "Just be careful, man."

Aidan had no clue what he was on about. "Of what?"

Lucas blew out a breath. "I overheard Charlotte and her sisters talking last night. After we closed the shop and after you and Charlotte went on your walk."

"I'm not sure I follow."

"You're just here for another week." His gray eyes spoke volumes. "I'd hate to see you getting hurt."

But how? Why?

"Charlotte's sudden *interest* in you"—Lucas made quotation marks with his hands—"might not be on the level."

Aidan took a sucker punch to the gut. So, all that flirty chit-chat yesterday? Her asking about his life? Pretending to be sorry about the adjustments he'd had to make after the move? *Which was in no way my doing.* His face burned hot. "Charlotte wants me to think she likes me, huh? So she can do what, exactly?"

Lucas winced. "Maybe make you see what it's like when the shoe is on the other foot?"

Aidan blew out a breath. Unbelievable. She'd felt... What? Rejected? So now she wanted a chance to reject him? "Dump me, you mean?"

"That's only assuming the two of you, you know."

"Get together?" Aidan crossed his arms. "Right. Hmm. I see."

Was Charlotte really that vindictive? What had he done other than try to make amends between their two families and businesses? Okay. Yeah. He could have let on about not going through with the marriage scheme earlier.

Maybe a small part of him had still been mad at

Charlotte and her sisters because of how they'd picked on him as a kid. He didn't know. In any case, concealing his true intent had probably been foolish and likely a bad move.

Too late to undo it now, though, and he'd made some very generous gestures.

"Lucas, why are you telling me this?"

He pursed his lips. "Because it's the right thing to do."

"And Misty? Will you tell her what you've told me?"

"I'm afraid I'll have to." He shrugged. "Misty and I don't keep secrets."

"Won't that raise holy hell among the sisters?"

Lucas held up both hands. "It might."

"Right."

Aidan considered the day he'd planned for Charlotte. He'd gotten them tickets to an oyster festival up the coast. If that went well, he'd thought about asking her to dinner and had even reserved a romantic table for two at Mariner's on a hopeful whim.

His jaw tensed. What an idiot he'd been.

He'd played right into her hands.

"Thanks, mate." Aidan slapped Lucas's shoulder. "Appreciate your telling me."

Lucas's forehead furrowed. "So, what do you plan to do? About Charlotte?"

"Nothing," he said. "Absolutely nothing. Things will come out all right." He'd make sure of it. Charlotte Delaney was not going to get the better of him.

He could let her think she was, though.

CHAPTER TWELVE

Charlotte tidied her small living room with its bay window overlooking the docks, picking up clippings from magazines she'd been using to create her latest project. She'd been up late last night, sitting on the floor and happily wielding her scissors while listening to eighties rock. She didn't know why she was drawn to that era. It was really her parents' generation, not hers. So she'd heard a lot of it growing up. Maybe that's why she liked it. It was comforting, like home.

The group of historic rowhouses lining her street once housed fishermen and their families. More recently, they'd been taken over by young couples or singles. Charlotte's red-brick structure was three stories tall, but the basement apartment below her was a separate rental. Her unit had only four rooms. A living room and eat-in kitchen downstairs with a bedroom and a bathroom up above. While the water view was nice from here, it was spectacular from her bedroom window, which framed the far-off lighthouse and tumultuous sea.

She heard a chugging sound on the street and stared outside. An old hippie van with psychedelic daisies on it pulled up to the curb, and she laughed at the old clunker, which had to be Crystal's. Aidan sat behind the wheel, navigating his way into the parallel parking space between two other vehicles.

Her heart pounded at the thought of spending the day with him. But that was only because he was easy to be around sometimes. When he decided to be agreeable. Plus, he was easy on the eyes. And smart. And funny.

She was *not* liking him in a romantic way. Just acknowledging some facts. Her task was to get him to like her, which should be a piece of cake if yesterday was any indication. It was eleven a.m. and they were headed to a nearby town for fresh oysters and beer. She wasn't huge on eating her oysters raw but did enjoy them in a chowder. She liked them fried, too, and of course loved her dad's homemade oyster stuffing at Thanksgiving. That was yum.

She stashed away her last bit of collage supplies and straightened the throw pillows on her teal-colored living room sofa and matching armchair. She had a small cabinet that doubled as a wine rack and liquor cabinet, and her retro record player sat on top of that, with her record albums stored in the hollow beneath. She didn't own a TV. It was easy enough to watch movies or shows on her computer.

Aidan rang her doorbell, and she answered.

"Good morning." He looked unbelievably handsome in a moss-green sweater, jeans, and boat shoes. Darn it. Did the man never have a bad day? He also wore a light windbreaker.

"Hi there," she said breezily. "Come on in."

He grinned. "Thanks." He surveyed the busy dock area before shutting the door, then glanced around her living room. "Cool place."

"Thanks. I like it." She hunted in the kitchen for her purse, then remembered she'd left it on her dresser. "I'll just be a minute," she said, heading toward her stairs. Her ceilings were tall, so the wooden steps were steep. "Gotta grab my purse."

"Might want to bring a jacket too. It's windy out there." He smiled. "This is the first time I've seen you out of those cowgirl boots."

She laughed, glancing down at her canvas shoes with rubber soles. "Yeah, thought these might be best for walking." She was also in jeans and a sweater, which had a maritime theme with horizontal navy and white stripes.

"Good call."

Charlotte went up to her bedroom and grabbed her purse, double-checking her reflection in the mirror. She looked all right. Almost pretty. But not because she was excited about going out with Aidan. She was simply having a good day. On bad days, she appeared incredibly washed out, no matter how hard she tried. At other times, she looked surprisingly good. There didn't seem to be any rhyme or reason. Maybe just pure luck or fate.

She returned a few minutes later to find Aidan examining her series of three collages over the sofa. "These are cool." He glanced over his shoulder. "Did you make them?"

She smiled proudly. "I did."

He set his hand on his chin. "What's the theme?"

In spite of herself, she liked that he'd asked. Weirdly, a lot of the guys she'd dated hadn't noticed her collages, and most hadn't known she'd made them. "Eighties rock bands."

"Nice." He turned around to study them again. "Want me to guess?"

She gestured with her hand. "Please."

"Okay." He pointed to the one in the middle with

lots of different vehicles. Race cars and convertibles. Old station wagons and Mini Coopers. Bunches and bunches of them in various bright colors pasted over each other with some pieces snipped and fitted together to create unique forms.

"This one is easy." He smiled. "The Cars."

"Very good."

He stepped closer to another matted and framed piece filled with travel images. Airplanes. Boats. Trains. Campers and tents. A winding path through the forest and a mountain trail. A vast ocean. "Hmm. This one has me stumped."

She laughed. "Journey."

"'Don't Stop Believing,'" he said.

"You like eighties music, too?" This surprised her, but maybe it shouldn't have. She had other friends her age who were into that time period. It was probably a nostalgia thing.

"I do." His gaze snagged on her record player. It was an old-fashioned one-box unit with built-in speakers. She'd inherited it from her mom. "Sweet. You still play vinyls?"

"Yeah."

"You're full of surprises, Charlotte," he said, and her nose felt hot.

She covered it with her hand and asked, "Last one?"

He studied the sandy slopes studded with sea oats interposed with images of dark and lighted corridors in houses, office buildings, and schools. "Oh, I think I've got it. Hall and Oats?" He looked so hopeful of being right she couldn't help but grin.

"Yep."

"Wow. These are fabulous. Do you have more?"

She shrugged. "Blondie and The Go-Go's are in the kitchen. I've got a few others upstairs."

He laughed warmly. "I love this about you." His gaze swept over her, and her pulse fluttered.

She checked the time on her phone, feeling self-conscious by his attention to her art. Having Aidan in her personal space felt—well, personal. His presence here made her a little nervous somehow. Like he was getting tiny glimpses into her soul. And she wasn't planning to let him get too close. Just close enough to develop a mild infatuation. So maybe it was okay that he was appreciating her creativity. Another point in her favor.

"Should we get going?" she said.

"Can I peek at Blondie and The Go-Go's first?"

She hesitated, and he pressed, "I'd really love to see them."

She laughed. "Sure." She set her phone down next to the record player and picked up her jacket, slipping it on. Whatever. He'd already seen the collages in the living room. She didn't intend to let him go upstairs. Like ever. Collages for Heart and Kiss hung over her bed. The Red Hot Chili Peppers were in the bathroom. She was working on Huey Lewis and the News next, but she hadn't decided where to hang it.

He ducked into the kitchen then came back out, and she nabbed her purse.

"You're seriously talented."

Her cheeks warmed. "It's a hobby."

"You know who would love your work?"

She took a guess. "Your record producer friend?"

He nodded. "Yeah, Tony." He seemed to have a

thought. "Would you mind if I snapped a photo or two?"

She hadn't really shared her work around and wasn't sure how comfortable she felt about it. "I can tell him it's for his eyes only," Aidan said, reading her face. "But if you'd rather I not."

"No, no. It's fine." She couldn't really see the harm. "He can even show Jill."

He shot her an admiring look. "You're very good with names."

"I don't miss much."

"I bet you don't," he said, holding open the front door.

· · ·

Charlotte gave Crystal's van a skeptical once-over. "Are you sure she's road-worthy?"

Aidan laughed. "Yeah. I just topped off the gas and oil and will check again before we head back."

"How far's the trip?"

"Navigation app says forty-five minutes."

"Not bad." She hoped it wouldn't be awkward being confined in a vehicle with him looking so sexy and smelling like summer rain. But she could be around a good-looking guy and not be attracted. Grant and Lucas were great-looking guys, and she'd never experienced a hint of attraction toward them. Which was fortunate, considering they were engaged to her sisters.

It was possible Aidan thought she looked good, too, although he hadn't said it. She bristled at his lapse. Most guys commented on how pretty she looked when they picked her up. But she and Aidan weren't *dating* dating. He'd just asked her out and she was going along—with the intention of making him like her.

So she'd better get busy.

"Thanks for the invitation. I can't remember the last time I went to an oyster festival."

They buckled their seat belts.

"Me either," he said. "Should be fun."

It took a few cranks with the key to get the van started. Finally, it gurgled and jolted to life, and Charlotte jumped. "Yikes!"

"Yeah, sorry." He grinned. "Groovy's got a personality of her own."

"Groovy?" Charlotte giggled. "You mean Crystal named her van?"

"She did."

Charlotte sighed. "She and Mr. Mulroney are a pair."

"Yeah, but somehow it works."

"Opposites can attract."

He pulled out of the parking spot and drove down the street, turning toward the highway. "We're not so opposite, you know."

"What?" From her view, they were very different. He was smug and difficult for starters.

"You like being in charge and I do too." He shrugged. "We're both also as sly as foxes."

"Ha!" That's what he thought. But she'd be outfoxing him today. She'd even go out with him again if that's what it took. As long as they didn't get physical, he couldn't claim she was leading him on. She was more like advertising. No. *Marketing* herself as the stellar potential wife he'd missed.

His lips twitched. "Great-looking too."

Wait. He was still listing his traits?

Charlotte rolled her eyes. "Someone has an ego."

He thoughtfully thumped the steering wheel. "Competitive. Smart. Creative thinkers." He flashed her a grin. "How am I doing?"

She shoved his arm. "If you're trying to compliment me," she said lightly, "you're really botching it." She straightened in her seat. "You might have said I looked nice today. Something like that." There. She'd said it. It was going to be hard to entice him if he kept ticking her off.

"You look nice today, Charlotte."

Okay. So this was going to be a long trip.

She drew in a breath then exhaled slowly. "So do you."

Thankfully, he changed the subject. She was tired of hearing him talk himself up.

"Tell me about Nell and Grant," he said. "How did they get together?"

"Oh that! It's a really fun story. I mean, fun now." She grimaced. "They had a couple of moments."

"Such as?"

"Nell had crushed on Grant forever. So when—" *You let us dive into that stupid bet headlong when you could have stopped it…*

She bit her lip when her blood boiled. Now was not the time to get angry. Not when getting even was better. She pushed her emotions aside.

"When we made our bet." She rolled her eyes like it was hilarious and no big deal. "You know the one."

"I sure do," he said in a singsong tone.

"Yeah. Well. Anyway. When the timeline hit, it sort of forced her hand."

"To go after him?"

"And boy did she ever—with gusto. Pretending to be a nature girl and everything."

"Nature doesn't sound like Nell."

Charlotte laughed. "It wasn't. But now that she's with Grant? Honestly, she's learning."

"Well, I'm glad that they worked out."

"Yeah. Me too. There were only a few bumps in the road."

They pulled onto the highway that skirted the ocean. He'd been right about the wind judging by the number of whitecaps out there. Still, the day was sunny and beautiful. Charlotte loved Maine. She was very relieved about not having to live in London for five years.

She crossed her arms.

With him.

Stay flirty, Charlotte. And pleasant.

Resist the urge to growl.

"And Lucas and Misty?" he asked.

"They're a sweet couple," she said. "So meant to be for so many years, only Misty didn't see it."

"No?"

"Fortunately, Lucas enlightened her. Gently and in the right way. Or maybe it was partially her, finally waking up to what a great guy he is."

"Lucas is a great guy," he agreed.

"You two becoming buds now or something?"

"Don't know about 'buds,' but we've hung out once or twice. Gone for a couple of runs."

"Oh yeah?"

"Including this morning." The weight of his words hung there.

Charlotte's stomach churned.

Oh no. Lucas wouldn't have said anything—even if he'd overheard.

Lucas was family.

Aidan laughed, but it sounded kind of forced. "He told me something funny."

Her pulse skittered. "What's that?"

"He said he heard you and your sisters talking."

Her heart just—stopped.

She couldn't breathe.

"Really?"

"He wasn't sure if he got it right, though."

She couldn't bear to look at him but had to. She stole a quick peek his way, and he turned just in time, meeting her gaze. "But he thinks…" His eyes twinkled. "You fancy me."

A huge breath burst from her lungs with an, "Oh! Well." Her whole face was hot and her nose was on fire. "Maybe? A little?" She lifted a shoulder then decided she'd better clarify. Otherwise she would be leading him on, and "fancy" sounded like it had romantic undertones. "As a friend."

"That's great. Because I like you too. As a mate." He grinned warmly. "So, you see, we don't always have to be at odds, you and I. We can get along."

Yes. What a stroke of luck!

Whatever Lucas had overheard, he'd totally gotten things wrong.

In a way that worked in her favor. *Whew!* Close call.

They drove the next several minutes in painful silence. She couldn't think of a word to say, and obviously neither could he. Eventually, he reached for the radio knob.

"Music?"

"Sure." She pushed back her hair and her palm came back sweaty. Gross.

There was a lot of crackling static at first, but then he found a classic rock station.

The ancient speakers belted out a familiar catchy tune.

Aidan grinned. "Blondie."

"Mm." Her heart thudded. Why did she have the feeling Aidan knew something he wasn't letting on about?

"Though technically 1978."

"You know your music," she said.

"Learned from my mum and dad."

"Guess your folks and mine listened to a lot of the same stuff."

"Makes sense," he said. "They were mates."

Yeah, before your dad sneakily cheated mine in business.

Charlotte bit her tongue. Aidan was doing his best to be polite. Plus, he was taking her to the oyster festival. She could at least act upbeat and not throw any negativity on the day.

She glanced out her window at the prettily rolling sea. The sky was bright blue and the weather was gorgeous. She should relax and have fun. Enjoy this little road trip.

If Aidan happened to like her even better after their outing, that would be a bonus. And it would make him think twice as hard about what he'd missed out on once he was back in London.

CHAPTER THIRTEEN

Aidan steered Crystal's van into a crowded parking area as Charlotte absorbed the view. A huge white tent was set up on a boardwalk fronting the sea. That whole section was cordoned off from traffic, and people milled about, basking in the sunny weather and holding clear plastic cups of foamy draft beer. Lots of them were dressed as pirates.

Charlotte laughed, happy for the diversion. She was done thinking about what Lucas might have overheard and said. Things were all right. Everything was cool. If they weren't, she would have heard from someone. Nell or, most likely, Misty. Misty and Lucas supposedly told each other everything, so the fact that her sisters hadn't contacted her was a positive sign.

Besides, Aidan looked happy and relaxed. Not antagonized in any way, and he certainly didn't appear angry with her. Just the opposite. He seemed like he was enjoying her company, and in a weird way she was enjoying his. Charlotte hadn't been to an oyster festival in ages, and this one looked like fun.

Aidan backed into a parking space and glanced out the van's front window. "Looks like a good time."

She scanned the crowd, noting all the pirate outfits. "I didn't know it was a costume party."

He pointed to a man walking by. "That guy's a

regular doppelganger for Dixie Bull."

"Who?"

He stared at her, aghast. "The dread pirate? Born in England in the seventeenth century and traded knives and beads for furs right here in Maine? After his ship got robbed, he turned to a life of crime, pirating and plundering settlements. He looted and burned Pemaquid after brazenly storming its harbor."

She was fascinated by these tidbits. "How do you know so much about pirates?"

"Loved learning about them as a lad. Especially the ones who tormented Maine."

"I'm not the only one with a hidden side," she teased playfully.

His lips twitched. "It's a hobby."

"What? Still?"

"Yeah. Love scuba diving and hunting for buried treasure."

"You do not."

His eyebrows arched. "Scuba dive or hunt?"

Now she wasn't sure.

"I can take you sometime if you'd like?" he said.

"Seriously?" That sounded amazingly exciting, even if he was joking. He didn't look like he was, though.

"Most of the dives I've been on have been around sunken Spanish galleons. Treasure's been long gone, but it's still great fun for a look-see."

"Guess you had to train up for that?"

"Lessons aren't hard," he said. "You go out with a certified instructor who walks you through it."

She was interested and impressed. "What was

your last dive?"

"Wasn't for treasure. It was in Australia. Great Barrier Reef."

"I hear that's fantastic." She'd never imagined viewing it from the ocean's depths, but now that he'd planted the idea in her head, it sounded very cool. If she became involved with him, maybe that was something they might do together in the future.

But she wasn't going to.

So they wouldn't.

Get a grip.

"You should talk to Grant and Jordan about that," she told him. "They both studied in Australia. Not sure if either of them ever dived."

"Good thought. I'll ask." He grabbed his wallet from the console and his phone. "So. Dread Pirate Dixie Bull? No?"

She shook her head. "The only 'dread pirate' I know is the Dread Pirate Roberts from *The Princess Bride*."

He chuckled. "Into eighties films too?"

She began naming some. "*Sixteen Candles*, *Breakfast Club—*"

"*Risky Business*," he said. "*When Harry Met Sally*."

She giggled. "*Dirty Dancing*."

"*Flashdance*."

He was good at this. Didn't miss a step.

"*Fatal Attraction*," she said.

He fake shivered. "Scared me off dating for years."

She smirked then sighed. "Loved *Steel Magnolias* and *Moonstruck*."

"We can't forget the greatest Christmas flick of all time."

She plugged her ears and chided, "Don't say it, don't say it, don't—"

He pulled her fingers from her ears and whispered, "*Die Hard*."

"Why is that such a *thing*?"

"Excellent film. A classic." He removed the key from the ignition. "So," he asked. "Ready to get this party started?"

"Yeah." Charlotte had to admit she was having a good time. No. A *great* time. Without meaning to. The good news was that he seemed to be having fun, too, and that's what she wanted.

Aidan smiled as more pirate types walked by. "We're definitely going to have to buy two of those hats."

• • •

Two hours later, Aidan sat with Charlotte at a wooden picnic table as they savored the sunshine and their beers. The day had warmed up, but they both still needed their jackets to shield them against the sharp winds that kept trying to steal their new pirate hats. The ocean tumbled over itself, kicking up foamy spray, and seagulls soared and squawked above them. The birds were probably hopeful of some morsels of food being left behind. But they kept their distance, remaining wary of the people.

Meanwhile, Aidan was on his guard concerning Charlotte. He was cautious and generally no pushover. Life had taught him to stand up for himself.

He'd toughened up in business, and, before that, in boarding school. Despite that, it was hard not to be charmed by her when her lips tipped up in a smile and she captured his gaze in a certain way.

But no.

He wouldn't think that.

She was cunning and conniving.

Out to skewer his emotions. And for what? Him doing the Delaneys a favor?

He'd hate to see her reaction if he'd committed an actual transgression.

"Hey!" Charlotte shouted and tamped down her hat when the brim lifted off her forehead.

He pressed down on his hat, too. "Hang onto yer hat, Lassie," he said in his best imitation pirate voice. "We won't be wantin' to lose ours."

She laughed, and his neck warmed. Making her laugh felt good. Even when he understood her twisted plan. If she'd not been setting him up only to let him down, it might have felt even better.

"True," she said. "But better than losing our heads to some unscrupulous pirates." Her tone held a hint of sass, which might have intrigued him in any other situation. Meaning one in which she wasn't trying to game him.

He leaned toward her. "Aye, but none of these others look too menacing to me."

Charlotte surveyed their surroundings and the various grown-ups and kids wearing pirate outfits. Some wore eyepatches and head bandanas. Others had fake plastic hook arms.

"You never know," she quipped. "Some people have a hidden side."

He was captivated for a moment by her stunning blue eyes that matched the color of the sky, then he told himself not to be foolish. It took more than a pretty face and a bit of flirtation to win him over. He required a certain degree of trustworthiness that she clearly didn't possess, and he wasn't looking for a girlfriend anyhow.

"Aye, and some of us are more dangerous than we look."

"You? Dangerous?" Her eyebrows arched. "Good try. But no. Don't think so."

She took a sip of her beer, and he let out a growly "Arggh," startling her.

The beer sloshed in her cup, nearly spilling over its edges. She set it down on the table, still hanging onto it, and smirked. "Very funny."

"That was a surprise attack," he said in a husky whisper.

"Well, you can try all you want, Aidan. But you're not surprising me." She swept her hair over her shoulders, and it fell down her back in a shimmering dark ribbon below her hat.

"No? Then how about the scuba diving?"

The breeze relented for a moment, and she let go of her beer to take a spoonful of her oyster chowder. "Yeah. There's that. So." She cracked a grin. "Gonna take me?"

She was definitely playing flirty now.

The minx.

"Didn't think you'd be interested?"

"Sounds a little exciting." Her eyes danced in the sunlight, but he ignored their dazzling appeal, focusing instead on her full and sensuous lips as she sipped from her spoon.

Wrong move. He cleared his throat and returned his attention to his food. He was eating his oysters raw on the half shell and had ordered a dozen. He squeezed a small packet of hot sauce onto the three he had remaining and speared one with his plastic fork.

"I guess we'll just have to see how things go." He popped the oyster into his mouth and swallowed it whole. "Mmm. Delicious."

Oysters were rumored to increase the libido, but there'd be no worries about anybody acting on that here.

She pulled a face. "I don't see how you can eat them like that."

"I'm not the only one," he said, glancing around at the other tables. Almost everyone here was eating their oysters just like he was because they were such delicacies when fresh. He decided to answer her question from before. "I'd be happy to take you scuba diving sometime." He grinned. "As a friend."

She smiled. "Of course as a friend. What else would it be?"

"Nothing at all," he said, trying not to imagine Charlotte in a bikini while she peeled off her wet suit. Now that would be a sight. A fairly tantalizing one. Heat coursed through his veins, and he took a deep drag of very cold beer.

He gazed at the ocean and had an unsettling vision of him and Charlotte on a yacht. He stood on the bridge behind her while she held the captain's wheel. His arms were wrapped around her waist. They both wore seafaring caps. She glanced over her shoulder, her eyes twinkling, and laughed, saying something about the ship having two captains. He went in for a kiss, his mouth—

"Aidan?"

"Hmm?" He stared down at his plate. Then up into Charlotte's eyes.

"Where *were* you just now?"

"Ahh, nowhere." He made a point of paying close attention to his remaining oyster, coating it in extra hot sauce. "Just thinking of work."

"What?" She frowned. "Now?"

He shrugged. "Yeah. Sorry."

"Well, I'm glad you take breaks," she said, finishing her chowder. "With the scuba diving and whatnot. Maybe soon you'll have lots more leisure time."

"With us co-running the company?" he asked without skipping a beat.

She lowered her eyebrows at him. "I meant with me running the whole company."

He shook his head. "In your dreams."

"I am winning that contest, Aidan."

He finished his beer. "You're welcome to try."

"I'm going to. Trust me."

Ahh, but he didn't trust her. Not one iota. "I guess we'll see how that goes too."

"Guess so."

The wind kicked up, and they both grabbed the rims of their hats.

"Cooler weather's coming," Charlotte said.

He inhaled deeply, enjoying the scent of the briny sea. "I always liked winters in Maine."

"Didn't mind the snow?"

"Nope." He grinned. "But I probably prefer autumn."

"Yeah," she said. "Fall's my favorite season, too. So invigorating with cooler breezes and changing leaves. Sweater weather."

The wind gusted again and he glanced at the beach. "Good day for kite flying."

She turned to watch a father with his young son. The man ran alongside his child, trying to help him launch his kite, which was shaped like a lobster. Finally they got the kite into the air and it got buffeted about by the wind, rising higher into the azure sky. The child's shouts of glee sailed toward them through the breeze.

"That's fun." She smiled warmly. "My sisters and I used to do that with our folks."

"Yeah," he said. "I remember. Sometimes they took me along."

Her eyes widened. "That's right!"

"My parents weren't into it so much." A familiar ache grew in his chest, but he shrugged it off.

"Well, it's good you got to come with us, then."

"Yeah. It was nice being a part of your little kite-flying band, even when some of our strings got tangled up in one another's."

"That seemed to happen a lot," she said with a laugh.

He chuckled, too. "Yeah."

"Misty was the champion knot untier," Charlotte remarked. "Even as a kid."

"She's always been very dexterous, hasn't she? Must be the artist in her." He studied Charlotte. "When's the last time you flew a kite?"

"Me? Gosh. It's been ages. Not since back then. No, wait. I guess we had Kite Day in elementary school, but that was always in March. So I was probably, hmm, eleven."

"That's a long time to go without flying a kite," he teased.

She shrugged. "It's not really my thing any longer."

"Why?" he joked. "Too much fun?"

"Hey!" She shoved his arm. "I like to have fun!"

"Yes. I'm getting that." He held her gaze, and she blushed.

"So, when was the last time *you* flew a kite?" she asked.

He folded his arms, thinking. "Probably right here in Maine, in Majestic."

She stared at the kid with his dad. The boy had the kite fully under his command now and had let out its string. It dipped and swooped high above the waves. "Well, maybe you should try it again sometime yourself."

"Me personally?" He shook his head. "Don't think so."

"Why not?"

"Unlike you, Charlotte, I don't like to have fun."

"You! Great big liar!" She reached out and yanked on the brim of his hat, and he laughed.

"I'm not having fun now, I'm not." He held his lips in a firm line, but still his mouth twitched.

"Yeah." Her eyes danced. "I can see that."

Heat flickered between them like the faintest candle flame.

Aidan's heart skipped a beat.

There was something about Charlotte. Something

unnerving and alluring.

But no. She wasn't the woman for him.

Because her flirtatious behavior was all a part of her ploy. Given his executive role and extreme wealth, his life had sadly been filled with duplicitous people. Others who only pretended to be interested in him, but who were really after their own gain. It pained him to believe that Charlotte was also in this category, but he was old enough to know the score. And to read the tea leaves, once they'd been presented to him so plainly by Bearberry Brew's café manager.

She stood awkwardly, gathering her cup and disposable chowder bowl. "Should we clean up?"

"Yeah, maybe so." He got up to help her clear the table.

They dropped their trash in a receptacle, then were hit by a sharp blast of wind. This one took Charlotte's hat and sent it tumbling down the boardwalk, weaving through passersby.

"Oh no!" she shouted, nabbing her purse and racing after it.

Aidan took off his hat, holding it in one hand, and ran after her.

Another gust picked Charlotte's pirate hat up and sent it over a low stone wall, landing it in the sand. They jumped over the wall in hot pursuit, but whipping gusts pushed it farther down the beach. Aidan ran faster, passing Charlotte and nabbing the errant hat. He shook it out, dislodging some sand, and carried it back to her, where she stood panting.

"Milady." He took a bow and handed over the hat. She grabbed it, but he didn't let it go. "I'm not your lady."

A voice in his head said, *not yet*.

But he had an inkling she could be, if he pursued her.

Which was 100 percent *not* on his agenda.

His eyebrows arched. "Never said that I wanted you to be."

She yanked the hat out of his hand. "Didn't have to."

Aidan's heart thudded. Had he been that transparent? He'd need to be much more careful around her. He couldn't let himself be drawn in by her fierce wit and captivating spirit. Or her gorgeous eyes. Pretending to be wowed was one thing, and a part of his plan. He was *not* going to fall for real.

"It's a fine thing we don't like each other, then," he said. "In a seriously romantic way."

Her nose turned bright red. "A blessing, yes."

"Because if we did"—he stepped closer, and she stared up at him—"who knows what could happen?"

There was daring in her eyes. A tangle of emotion too. "Who knows?"

He cupped her cheek with his hand, and her breath quickened. So did his. Every inch of him strained to hold her. To give her the walloping kiss she deserved and that he knew he was capable of.

But he'd never kiss a woman who didn't truly want him to, and Charlotte was only playing games here.

"That's why," he whispered, his mouth very close to hers, "we need to watch our step."

CHAPTER FOURTEEN

Charlotte tugged at the power crystal dangling from a leather strap around her neck. She valued its many attributes, but right now, she'd appreciate its calming properties most of all.

That exchange on the beach with Aidan had been too close.

What was she thinking?

A memory flashed of his swoony dark eyes and that lopsided grin.

Her skin flushed hot.

She'd been thinking of pressing her palms to that super sexy beard of his and bringing his mouth down to hers. That's what. His breath on her lips had been *so hot.* Her stomach fluttered and her hairline felt warm. Her whole back and neck too. Even her chest oozed with sweltering temperature flares.

"Want me to turn on the AC or something?" Aidan asked from behind the steering wheel. Neither of them had said much after that almost kiss other than that they should probably head back.

And her heart had shouted, *Yes, immediately!*

A tiny trickle ran down her cleavage beneath her bra and tank top.

Nooo. Was she sweating? She dug a tissue from her purse and dabbed at her forehead. Ooof. What was wrong with her? "I'm just a little warm."

It was probably from all that running after the pirate hat. She and Aidan had both laid their jackets on the back seat before leaving the festival because the run had gotten their endorphins going. Now she wished she'd stripped down a little more.

But not too much more.

No! She was not going there, not for real.

She was intentionally attracting Aidan just to show him what he'd missed... An unbelievably sweaty woman with overactive glands.

Okay. This was bad. She was a wreck.

She stole a peek at Aidan, and her nose almost hurt from its heat level. Were all of her pores expanding everywhere? She flipped open the vanity mirror then quickly flipped it shut. Oh great. Her face was the color of a very ripe tomato.

Aidan reached for the controls, but the AC dial came off in his hand. "Uh." He play-grimaced and set the dial on the console. "How about we crack some windows?"

"Better yet," she said. "I'll take off my sweater."

He nodded, and she proceeded to wriggle out of one sleeve beneath the crisscross confines of her seat belt. That was inconvenient. Her elbow was stuck mid-lift and jammed against the window.

"Need help there?" He attempted to tug at her other sweater sleeve, while driving, and she tugged back.

"No, no, keep your eyes on the road. I'm fine." But actually she wasn't. Now her other elbow was stuck. She grumbled, staring down at her seat belt. She could unhitch it briefly, but they were on the highway. It was doubtful this old clunker of a van had airbags.

"Tell you what," Aidan said, observing her

pretzel-like limb knot. "How about I pull over? I need to top off the oil anyway."

"Great idea!"

Fortunately, there was a station just ahead of them and on the right.

Aidan exited the van, and she undid her seat belt, yanking off her sweater, which was grossly damp in places. She checked her black tank top. Nooo. She'd pitted out! She rolled down her window with the old-fashioned hand crank, and a cool breeze filled the van.

Aidan opened the hood and smiled through the windshield. "Doing okay in there?"

She shoved her hands under her arms, covering the wet spots. "Uh-huh."

"Need to use the loo or anything?"

She shook her head.

He smiled again and opened the hood fully to tinker around with the oil.

With her now blocked from his view, she reached into the back seat and grabbed her jacket, shrugging it on. She could not let him see that tank top. It looked like she'd been at the gym, working out for *days* without showering. Ick.

He climbed back inside with a perplexed look. "I thought you were hot?"

She buckled her seat belt. "Much better now."

"Ah." He hadn't broken a sweat or perspired at all. He still looked as handsome as ever in that moss-green sweater of his. All calm, cool, and collected.

But he wasn't always that way.

On the beach, he'd brought the heat.

She grabbed her pirate hat off the floor and used

it to fan her face.

He pulled back onto the highway. "Hot again?"

"Um, no." She held the pirate hat out in front of her and turned it over, spinning it around in her hands. "Just admiring my gift." She smiled at him, because it had been a very sweet gesture. She hadn't expected him to pay for that on top of the festival tickets and two rounds of beers. "Thanks for this."

"My pleasure."

Wind buffeted into the car through her open window.

"You might want to roll that up a tad," he said. "When we get our speed up."

She nodded and stealthily fanned herself with the hat again when he was looking the other way. It was good she'd clarified about them just being friends, because she definitely couldn't let things get physical between them, like they'd almost been on the beach. Two times now! Counting their flirty walk yesterday.

She stole another peek his way, wondering if he was a decent kisser.

As a kid, he'd been the worst.

Then again, that had been her first kiss and probably his.

Didn't matter if he was a sex god anyway.

She'd had *friends with benefits* before and the relationships had never worked out. Things would be extra messy if she got involved with Aidan. He was so sure of himself about winning the contest, but she was just as sure he wouldn't. Which would be a big blow to his already substantial ego.

He had a trust fund to go back to in England, as well as, she guessed, an enormous estate. Not to mention those "flash cars" of his. Being unemployed, he'd have no reason to stick around Majestic. He probably wouldn't want to anyway. It wasn't like he had family here, and he'd been pretty clear about not being interested in finding a wife, any kind of wife, for the foreseeable future. Which was really great with her. Super. Totally fine.

Because she certainly wasn't going to marry him.

He'd obliterated all chances of that happening.

She checked the time on the round clock in the van, but its hands seemed stuck, reading ten thirty when it was the afternoon. From the position of the sun in the sky, it was maybe three or four o'clock. She set the hat on her lap and grabbed her purse, thinking she'd check her phone. It had been awfully silent lately. Generally, she heard from someone a couple of times each day and was nearly always in some kind of text chain with her sisters.

Wait. She dug through her purse, pushing aside her travel brush and wallet. Where…? She bit her lip. Beside the record player at home.

She'd been so distracted by Aidan admiring her collages, she'd forgotten to put it in her purse. But that was okay. She'd be home soon enough.

Aidan noticed her frown. "Lose something?"

"Just my phone." She sighed. "Must have left it at home. But it's fine. I'm sure I didn't miss anything."

• • •

They were halfway home when they passed the bill-board, and Charlotte had to bite her lip to keep from laughing at Aidan's reaction. He gawked up at her parents' sunny faces, standing outside the café, both holding Fall Fest cups. She'd taken a great pic of her folks, and the advertisement was epic.

Two For One Coffees at Fall Fest from Bearberry Brews!

Aidan blinked and kept driving. "When did that happen?"

"I guess while we were eating oysters." She couldn't help but sound pleased about it.

"On a Sunday?"

She smiled smugly. "I have friends in high places."

The billboard owner hadn't actually been thrilled about changing its advertising for the third time this month—from Grant's camp store ad to her one about Misty, then back again, and now to this one for Fall Fest—but Charlotte had put on her most persuasive spiel. The ad featuring her parents was for such a good cause! It would bring awareness to her family's café and the town. Great for local business!

Plus, she'd paid double.

On credit. But still.

A muscle in Aidan's jaw tensed. "Very clever of you to think big."

Maybe the reality was finally dawning on him that she had this contest sewn up. Her people? Her hometown? Her family café? There was no way he could compete with that. The cards were completely stacked against him.

"Thanks, Aidan."

"It's not over until it's over, you know."

She turned to him. "What's that mean?"

"The contest." He grinned. "There are still five more days before Fall Fest."

"I'm aware of the calendar." And the sooner September thirtieth got here the better, so she could take the big prize and say bye-bye.

"I wouldn't go counting me out already," he said. "I still have a trick or two up my sleeve."

She didn't doubt it. "You know what I say?"

He cut her a glance.

"Bring it."

He chuckled and irritation prickled through her. "I'm not so sure you could handle me *bringing* anything," he said.

She scoffed to dismiss the mental image of him bringing his heat on the beach. Best not to dwell on that at the moment. He'd just doused that memory in cold water, anyhow. "That just proves how little you know me."

"Seems I'm getting to know you better now, though, aren't I?" He shifted his hands on the steering wheel. "Which is why I'm quite certain you don't have what it takes to win."

She gaped at his gall. "Oh yeah? And what's that?"

He gave her an obnoxious grin. "My ingenuity."

Charlotte closed her eyes and counted to ten. How did he have this ability to drive her up the wall again and again? Thank goodness he'd be gone by week's end.

She forced a perky tone. "I guess we'll just have to see about that!"

At least this pseudo-date was almost over. Then it would just be a matter of getting through the next week. Which would be fine with both of them stay-ing busy.

Then, yay! Bearberry Coffee would be hers! She'd have saved her family business and her parents' home. And Aidan would land on his feet. He always seemed to, anyway. He was like a cat with ten lives, not nine. On top of that, he wasn't hurting for money.

Maybe he'd start a new company somewhere. As long as it didn't involve coffee, she didn't care. It would be rude of him to compete against his former company, but she wasn't sure she'd put anything past him. If he did, she'd deal with that too. She *was ready* for him to bring it. He didn't believe she could take it, but oh yes she could. He'd severely misjudged her, again.

A short time later, he pulled up to her place and parked the van. The dock area was bustling and the tables at the outdoor restaurants and pubs were full of people hanging out for a beer or an early supper. Now that she'd simmered down some, she conceded she'd actually enjoyed their outing. The first part of it, anyhow. Aidan had only blown it toward the end with his irritating assertions about him winning their contest. It was fine for him to feel confident, but he didn't have to act so smug about it.

She grabbed her purse and hat, wondering if she should ask him in, then decided maybe not. Why tempt fate and risk another too-close-for-comfort encounter? When the nice Aidan appeared, he was much tougher to resist than his infuriating evil twin. No. Far better to say goodbye here.

"Thanks a lot for the festival," she said. "I had fun."

His eyes shone when he grinned. "You know what? So did I." He surprised her by opening his door.

"Uh. Where are you going?" she asked, climbing from the van.

"I thought I'd walk you up."

"Oh." She blushed. "You don't need to do that, Aidan. Really."

She was still mildly fuming over his earlier comments, and also a little wary of herself after almost falling into his kisses on the beach. Conflicting emotions swam through her, warring with each other. But seriously. She was a grown-up. She could let him walk her to her front door without wrapping her arms around him and dragging him inside. She had that degree of control at least.

He glanced at the brick steps by the wrought-iron railing that led up to her front door. A few of the bricks had come loose, and one lay on the sidewalk, broken to bits. "Those stairs look a little dodgy."

She laughed. "Dodgy, huh?"

He shoved his hands in his pockets. "And anyhow. It's the gentlemanly thing to do."

She'd never figured him for much of a gentleman but decided not to say so. He did appear harmless enough standing there. Great-looking, sure, but that wasn't news.

She slung her purse strap over her shoulder while holding onto her hat. "Fine." She smiled, playing it cool. "If you insist."

Charlotte so totally had this. She was in complete control of the situation. Good. So why not allow this minor formality?

CHAPTER FIFTEEN

The moment they reached the top of the stairs, Charlotte regretted her decision. Because now she and Aidan were really close on the tiny stoop and he was…ooh, no, but yeah. Smelling like summer rain. While she probably smelled like a locker room. He didn't seem to notice. Thank goodness.

"Well then," he said. "I guess this is goodbye."

"Until tomorrow, yeah."

"Thanks for hanging out with me, Charlotte." His eyes twinkled and her heart beat faster.

"Thanks for the fun idea."

His eyebrows arched. "Guess I'll see you bright and early?"

"I'll be back to work first thing," she said, wishing he would *go, go, go.*

"Right. Me too." The longer they stood here, the more churned up she became by the warmth in his gaze and that crazy-cute grin of his.

It was time for him to turn and leave, but he didn't.

And she was not going to ask him in. Not. Not. Not.

If she couldn't keep herself from drooling over the guy on a public beach, she wasn't letting him in her living room. Or any other room in her house. It was weird how he made her feel so vulnerable in that way. Like she couldn't trust herself not to throw herself at his super-hot body. Because he drove her absolutely wild.

"Mind if I use the loo?"

She blinked, caught completely off guard. "What?"

"Your bathroom." He grimaced. "The beer."

She couldn't very well deny him that. That would be unkind. "Well, sure." She opened the door and let him in. "It's upstairs." At least guys were fast with that stuff, so he'd be in and out of here quickly. Then she could pour herself a big glass of wine and text her sisters.

She had to tell them about her day, which had been good in parts, but also really confusing. Nell always knew what to say and was good at analyzing things. Misty was her supportive cheerleader. And anyway, Charlotte was proud of herself for keeping things so above board with Aidan. For not giving into her hot guy lust for once.

So *there*. She did have a modicum of control. She was adulting! Yay!

She had a small mirror hanging over the entrance table, and her hair looked ghastly, all blown around by the wind. She grabbed her brush out of her purse and ran it through her hair then listened upstairs. The water was running like he was washing his hands.

Really quickly, she applied some more lipstick. Even though it didn't matter. She wasn't trying to look nice for him or anything. She just wanted his parting image of her to be presentable.

A door popped open in the upstairs hallway and he came back down the steps.

"Love the Red Hot Chili Peppers."

"Oh! Well. Thanks."

"All that color and steam."

She'd cut several photos and illustrations of peppers out of magazines—jalapenos, poblanos, and habaneros, where she'd been able to find them—and interposed those images with steampunk-like images of old railroad trains with smoke blowing out of their stacks. Steam-powered ocean liners too. The collage was one of her favorites.

"Yeah. Ha-ha."

"Flames too." Right. Some of those peppers were grilling.

"Yep."

"Quite a statement."

"It's, um, a band."

They seemed to be navigating closer to one another somehow, in barely discernable baby steps, each of them without even trying. Because suddenly he was right there, staring down at her with his swoony brown eyes under those very dark eyebrows and that swag of forward-falling hair.

"They say art is in the eye of the beholder." His voice was low and gravelly, sending delighted shivers through her. Charlotte rubbed her upper arms, mentally shaking them off.

"I think that's beauty," she said. "But anyway."

"Beauty, hmm. Yeah." He stared at her so intensely her heart thumped. His gaze swept over her in an appreciative way. "You're a very beautiful woman, Charlotte."

She nervously chewed her lip. "Thanks for saying so."

"Thanks for being you."

Her pulse quickened under his gaze.

He was looking at her like she was the most amazing creature on earth.

He made her feel desirable, captivating.

And—eep—she was beginning to desire and be captivated by him.

Her whole body warmed from her head down to her toes, and she was sure her nose was bright pink. "You're welcome," she said awkwardly. She swallowed hard but her mouth felt dry. "Well I guess you'd better—"

"Go," he said. "Now? Or like—"

Her breath hitched. "Not yet."

He gave a sultry grin. "All right."

Oh, no, no, no. Nooo.

But yeah. She was going to. She wanted to throw herself at the sexy guy and hang on tight. Run her hands over his seriously toned body and through his hair…across that beard. She went all tingly inside. A touch lightheaded with excitement, too.

"Charlotte?"

Her heart pounded so, so hard. "Hmm?"

His eyes sparkled knowingly. "Do you want me to…?"

Oh, what the heck.

She didn't know who moved first, but suddenly they had their arms wrapped around each other and his mouth was on hers. Or hers was on his. Whatever. He was solid and warm and ohhh, his kisses were heaven. He had her by the waist. No, the back. Arms. And her hands were everywhere. His fingers threaded into her hair, and she moaned.

Her phone dinged.

Not now.

She ignored it, then it dinged again.

He glanced toward her record player cabinet where the phone lay, but she latched onto that manly beard, cradling his face in her hands. Then he kissed her again, or she kissed him. Didn't matter. They were both in deep, and neither was complaining.

Tongues tangled, and he groaned.

Then he nibbled on her earlobe, her neck, her bottom lip.

Ohhhh. Where did he learn that?

No. She didn't want to know.

She whimpered and dragged him toward the sofa.

Her phone dinged again. Then again.

What the heck?

Bad timing.

He didn't seem to even hear it.

She kind of didn't, either. Not anymore.

He dropped down on the sofa and pulled her into his lap.

"Come here, you sexy siren, you." He started to peel back her jacket, but she tugged it closed, hiding her sweat-stained tank top.

"Uh. Why don't we leave that on?"

"Anything you like," he said, pulling her closer.

They kissed and kissed until her lips actually burned, but it was a nice burn. Delicious.

Warmth pooled in her belly, and her head spun.

Her and Aidan? No!

But yes. Yes. And *yes*.

Okay. This was good. He was good. Great. *Grand*.

But her stupid phone started ringing and ringing.

Totally blowing the mood.

Well. Not totally.

She was still pretty into it at the moment.

He paused in kissing her, stroking back her hair. "This isn't too much? You're okay?"

She found it adorably sweet that he'd asked. And also that he had cranberry-colored lipstick all over his face and neck. "Uh-oh."

His eyebrows arched. "What is it?"

She giggled softly. "My lipstick is all over you." She pulled a tissue from her jacket pocket and began cleaning him up.

"So, I'm a marked man," he growled in a super sexy way.

"You are marked." She kissed him on the lips. Her cell dinged again and she huffed. "Seriously?" She stared at the phone. "Maybe I should check. Something might be wrong. With Mom or Dad, or—" She slid off his lap and he scrambled to his feet.

"Right. You should do that." He ran his hands through his hair then straightened his sweater. He wore this dazed expression, like he didn't totally believe what had just happened. She almost didn't believe it herself. Maybe after she checked her phone, she'd offer him a drink or a cup of coffee and they could talk. Unpack it.

Her and Aidan making out like teenagers?

That was a lot to unpack.

She walked across the room and heard a *click*. What? He was at the front door already. "I…I think I'd better go."

"Right now?"

"Yes. For the best." His neck and face were pink.

What a sweetheart and a gentleman after all. She sighed. He didn't want to take advantage by risking having things go any further between them, so he was putting on the brakes. "All right then. But we probably should talk."

"Not so sure you'll be up for that." His comment made absolutely zero sense.

"Of course I will." Things were different now. They couldn't just pretend their make-out session hadn't happened. They'd need to sort things, even if they both agreed that it should never happen again.

But they wouldn't say that.

She giggled to herself. They'd had this huge breakthrough. Her skin still tingled all over. Her scorched lips too. She didn't know where they'd go from here, but it probably wouldn't be back to where they started. Aidan liked her. Really liked her. It was so flaming obvious.

Her nose warmed. She kind of *fancied* him, too.

"Okay then." She blew him a kiss. "See you tomorrow!" She held up her phone. "In the meantime, maybe text me?"

He stared at her phone like she held a grenade. "Uh, sure. See you, Charlotte." He shut the door and raced down the stairs. Through the bay window she saw him beat it toward the van and clamber inside.

Huh. Strange behavior. Maybe he'd embarrassed himself by tipping his hand and displaying his unfettered attraction. She bit her lip and squealed.

Aidan Strong was *totally* into her.

She stared at her phone and punched the button to light up the screen.

There were a gazillion text messages from her sisters.

And oodles of missed phone calls.

Her heart clenched. Maybe it *was* her mom or dad.

She phoned Misty, not wanting to bother with reading through everything if time was of the essence. Fear clawed at her gut. There'd been some kind of family emergency and she'd been recklessly making out with Aidan.

"Misty, hey. It's me. What's going on?"

"Where have you been? I've been trying to reach you all afternoon. So has Nell."

"With Aidan. Why?" Her imagination spiraled off in so many different worrisome directions. "What's wrong? Is it—?"

"He knows!" Time stood still. "Aidan knows that you're trying to play him just to dump him."

"What?" she asked shrilly.

"Lucas overheard us talking and told him." Misty sighed. "He didn't want either of you getting hurt."

The nerve of the man. Was that what he meant about him being dangerous? Then there was all that talk about both of them being as sly as foxes, and about how he didn't believe anyone could put much past her.

She fumed. He'd been making fun of her, all the while knowing what she was up to. Letting her think he was falling for her when he wasn't. It was all play-acting. She gasped and stared at the sofa.

Oh, that was very cold.

She frowned at that stupid pirate hat and took it to the kitchen and dumped it in the trash. The whole day had been a ploy to get her to like him more than he liked her while letting her think she had the upper hand.

Well, she was done.

Done with his lies and put-on kisses.

All she wanted to do now was win that contest so the despicable guy could leave town.

She couldn't wait to see him go.

"Charlotte? Are you still there?" Misty had been jabbering, but she hadn't heard a word she'd said. "I'm sorry. Really I am. I didn't find out about it until lunchtime when Lucas told me."

"It's okay," she told Misty. "It's not your fault."

"I hope you're not mad at Lucas?"

She wasn't 100 percent pleased, but she wasn't exactly mad at him either. They got along really well and he cared for all of the Delaneys. He never would have said anything to Aidan to intentionally hurt her. In his own way, he had to have believed that he was helping. "No." She set her chin. "It's fine."

"Wait. Are you still with him?"

Charlotte pursed her lips, seriously mad at herself for her major lapse in judgment. "Nope. He just left."

"Well, good." Misty sounded relieved. "At least I caught you in time, right? I mean it's only five o'clock. So. Nothing happened?"

Charlotte's heart pounded in her throat.

"Charlotte?"

CHAPTER SIXTEEN

Charlotte entered Bearberry Brews the next morning loaded for bear. No way was Aidan going to win that contest now. It would end "winner takes all," all right, with the Delaneys getting everything. She'd been up half the night devising a new plan and what she'd thought up was genius. She hoped her sisters would be just as excited by her new idea.

Misty and Nell were in the service area, setting up. The kitchen was dark, so it didn't look like anyone else was in yet. Which was okay. Their parents were overworked and worried about the business enough. She and her sisters had told them not to concern themselves over the coffee contest, the three girls would organize that with Charlotte at the helm. All they expected from their folks and Lucas was support in the way of supplying extra roasted beans, which they'd been more than happy to provide.

"Girls," Charlotte said, shutting the door behind her. "We're going to need to order more cups! And lids and napkins. Plus roast more coffee."

Nell blinked. "What? But I thought we'd prepared plenty?"

Misty twisted her lips. "And why are you holding that sheet?"

The folded queen-size top sheet in her arms was all pumpkin and harvest themed, part of a set she'd gotten on sale last winter. "I brought it for the office."

Misty and Nell stared at each other, then Misty spoke. "Why?"

"I might still have to work with him, but that doesn't mean I've got to look at him."

Nell shot her a scrutinizing look. "I thought you told Misty nothing happened."

"Right, nothing happened," Charlotte said. "But the point is he was playing me."

"Um." Nell pursed her lips. "Sort of like you were playing him?"

Charlotte shook her head at Nell. "Like you're one to talk."

"That's not fair," Misty said. She finished loading the register and shut the drawer. "Nell and Grant worked things out."

"But it wasn't easy," Nell added. "And we nearly didn't make it."

"Which is why"—Misty got a stubborn gleam in her eye—"we advised you not to go there with Aidan."

"The only place I went with Aidan was to an oyster festival. Besides that." Charlotte squared her shoulders. "My situation with him is nothing like Grant and Nell's." She stared at her oldest sister. "You wanted to make Grant fall in love with you."

"Only at first!" She frowned. "And then he ticked me off, and I didn't."

"Right! See? That's where I am with Aidan. I don't want him to actually fall for me. I just want to tempt him enough so he's sorry when he can't have me."

Nell's eyebrows arched. "So, how did that go? The *tempting*?"

Charlotte flushed hot. "It's not how you're making it sound. Okay?"

Nell crossed her arms. "Then nothing really happened?"

"No."

"He didn't kiss you?"

Charlotte laughed and rolled her eyes. "As if." It had been more of a mutual tackle. She really needed to get her hormones under control. But Aidan hadn't been completely blameless. He'd lost control of himself—and the situation—too. That's why she doubted Aidan would say anything about their brief amorous encounter to anyone. He liked presenting the impression of being in charge as opposed to a man who couldn't control his passions. Trouble was, Charlotte had no clue whether his ardor had been for real. In lots of ways, it had seemed authentic. But this was pull-the-rug-out-from-under-you Aidan here, and not some ordinary guy.

She set her purse and the sheet on a table. "What can I do?"

"Sounds like you need to get to work," Misty said.

"Right." Nell nodded. "But not in here." She pointed to the office.

"So," Misty said. "We're ordering more supplies and roasting more beans because—"

"We're going to sell more coffee," Charlotte said. Wasn't that obvious?

Nell shook out her curls. "There's a limited size to this town and not everyone loves coffee."

"True," Charlotte said slyly. "But they can give it as gifts."

"Well, okay." Nell licked her lips. "I can see a few folks buying a hot cup of joe for a friend, but not to the level you're—"

"I'm not talking hot brew."

Misty's ponytail swished sideways as she turned her head. "Cold?"

Charlotte bit her bottom lip, delighted with her idea. "Whole bean and ground."

Nell wrinkled up her forehead. "I'm not sure what you're saying?"

"Ooh!" Misty jumped in. "We're going to load cups with coffee to sell as gift items!"

Charlotte scanned their faces, hoping they'd be just as on board with her plan as she was. "What do you think?"

Nell grinned. "Very clever, Charlotte."

Misty agreed. "Nobody said the number of cups sold had to be brewed coffee, did they?"

Charlotte grinned. "Nope!"

"Misty, you're artsy," Nell said, after thinking this through. "Maybe you could make up cute little cups covered in cellophane tied with pretty fall-colored ribbons."

Misty's eyes lit up. "I love it."

"That's a great thought, you two," Charlotte said. She preened. "And a great way to sell extra coffees."

Nell nodded. "Even to non-coffee drinkers!"

Misty grinned from ear to ear. "Fun. I'll get on it." She turned to Charlotte. "I'm sure I can find what we need online. I know some cute shops on Etsy. Oh—maybe we can add pumpkin decorations!"

Nell grew animated. "I saw coffee stirrers once

that looked like pumpkins. They're the kind made from chocolate that melt in the coffee when you stir it in. Wouldn't that be cute to wrap in the cellophane with each gift?"

Charlotte squealed with joy. "This is going to be *amazing*. But, shhh! Nobody let Aidan in on our plan."

"Of course not," Nell said.

Charlotte pinned her gaze on Misty. "You can't tell Lucas."

"But—"

"Misty!" Charlotte said. "He might tell Aidan. Now that they're getting all buddy-buddy."

"They're not getting that buddy-buddy, and he wouldn't share that. Lucas wants us to win the contest as much as we do."

Charlotte frowned. "I suppose you're right. But, if you do mention it to Lucas, swear him to absolute secrecy."

"Swear me to secrecy about what?" Lucas asked, walking in the door.

Charlotte shot Misty a glance.

"Okay," Misty said. "I promise."

• • •

Aidan and Trudy walked into the office and nearly collided with the large bedsheet dividing the space.

"What's all this?" asked Trudy.

Aidan peeked around the corner of the sheet, which was suspended on clips at either end of the room. Charlotte sat in front of the window with her earbuds in, busily typing.

He cleared his throat and then made a louder sound, coughing into his hand.

Charlotte removed her earbuds and looked up. "Oh, hi," she said flatly. Her pretty eyes held a cool sheen, almost like she couldn't see him. But she was aware of his presence all right. She just didn't care to acknowledge him too strongly.

So...what? This was about last night?

That wasn't all on him. It took two to tango, and they'd both been guilty of dancing on the sofa. He motioned toward the sheet.

She shrugged. "Your side's over there."

Yeah, that's what he gathered. Trudy leaned toward him and whispered, "Is something going on?"

He addressed Charlotte, who was already typing again and pretending not to listen. Although she'd left her earbuds out. "Is this really necessary?"

She didn't look up. "I work better without distraction."

Seriously? Things were so bad she couldn't bear to look at him?

"Suit yourself." That was so like Charlotte to pin the blame on him. So, she was going to give him the cold shoulder, was she? As if everything had been his fault. As he recalled, she'd been a willing participant with those fiery hot kisses of hers.

Trudy's eyebrows arched. "Did something happen between you two?"

"Not to my knowledge," he lied. Trudy was his assistant, and yes, they got on, but she didn't need filling in on his love life. Which was technically non-existent, since he currently wasn't involved with anyone, and he wasn't starting now. With Charlotte.

Hell would freeze over first.

Aidan and Trudy took their seats, arranging their electronic devices and notepads on the table. Trudy also kept a special spiral notebook that included Aidan's daily calendar in print form. It served as a backup to the calendars on both of their phones.

Apart from a few emergency calls with the home office in London, this entire week had been reserved for Fall Fest planning. Aidan was lucky he had the flexibility to take this much time off to dedicate to a frivolous event that might not prove so frivolous if he lost the coffee contest to Charlotte. But he had ways of ensuring that wouldn't happen by staying one step ahead of her. Or at least by surpassing her efforts at every juncture.

He still had plenty of time to pull off his coup, but he needed an idea to top Charlotte's billboard advertisement. Something that would establish an even wider reach. There was just one billboard in this small town, apparently, and she'd already claimed it.

The billboard had a distinct disadvantage, though. It only caught the eye of travelers entering town from the north, and he wasn't sure how many outsiders would be attending this local fair. For townsfolk to see it, they'd actually need to leave Majestic and then re-enter. So no. While flashy, that billboard wasn't actually the greatest.

He needed something that would gain local attention. On a huge scale.

Meanwhile, he wanted to be sure they had enough cups, because he was going to outsell her. No question. Did Charlotte really think she could outsmart him? Maybe she was feeling some insecurity about that, given that he'd bested her yesterday? Outfoxed the fox who'd planned to outfox him.

"Can you give me a line on inventory?" he asked Trudy quietly. "Quite possible we'll need to step that up."

She nodded. "Best to step up quickly then—to secure everything by Friday."

"Right." It was Monday, so they didn't have much time.

She pushed back her chair and stood. "I think I've got our numbers, but let me take a count in the storeroom to double-check." She grabbed her notepad and a pen, taking them with her, as well as her phone, on which she'd opened a calculator app.

"Thanks." He found it mildly annoying that he no longer had that lovely view of the sandy slope and sea outside the window. If the room felt cramped before, now it was positively claustrophobic. Charlotte was doing this on purpose to try to punish him. Just like she'd devised that scheme to gain his interest merely to dump him. Well, he was 100 percent turned off to her now. Him falling for her? The concept was so ludicrous he wanted to laugh.

She was a handful to deal with even in the best of situations. When she was behaving like this, she made him want to pull his hair out, strand by strand.

He got up and walked around the sheet.

Charlotte stared at him. "You want something?"

"I think we need to talk."

"Maybe later, in private."

Aidan cocked his head. "Trudy's stepped out for a moment."

"Oh."

"Charlotte, about yesterday—"

"How could you, Aidan? Be so underhanded?"

"Me underhanded?" He turned up his palms. "You were setting me up for a fall!"

"Because you deserved it!"

"So that's how you play?" He paused, then pointedly asked, "Dirty?"

She flushed. "You went right down in the dirt with me."

"Look. I'm sorry." He raked a hand through his hair. "That's not how I meant for things to go."

"No? Then what were you hoping would happen? You lied to me about everything. The entire day was a fabrication."

"Hang on." He shook his head. "Not the whole day."

"It was low of you to pretend to like my art."

"Charlotte. I wasn't pretending."

She set her jaw. "And later?"

He pressed his hands to his chest. "No! Look. I didn't mean for any of that to happen. I'm guessing you didn't either."

"Maybe I did?" Sarcasm dripped from her words.

"Come on." He got that she was hurt and angry, but he was telling the truth. "It was an accident, okay? And I think both of us know it. Emotions sometimes run high between us and we got in over our heads."

She inhaled deeply. "I don't appreciate that level of trickery."

"It wasn't a trick!"

Trudy walked in the door then backed out of it.

"Oops. Sorry! I'll just—"

"It's fine, Trudy," Charlotte said. "Come on in." Which clearly meant she was done discussing things.

Well, fine. So was he. The impossible woman. He'd made his effort to apologize and she'd immediately shot him down. He didn't care to look at her any longer anyway. She got on his every last nerve. He grumbled and yanked out his chair, dropping down into it.

"You're not going to win the contest!" Charlotte called over the sheet.

Aidan laced his fingers together and held them against his chest. "We'll just see about that," he told Trudy.

The bedsheet design had pumpkin patches on it. Haystacks too. That's how it had been trying to get Charlotte to take a charitable view of his actions yesterday. Like hunting for a needle in a haystack. Pretty impossible. Particularly with her acting prickly.

Trudy's cell buzzed and she checked it. "So," she said. "Those supply numbers." She handed him some scribbled notes. "We'll likely need some more?"

"We'll definitely need some more." He'd been researching advertising ideas and, since he had the funds, the sky was the limit. Literally.

Trudy sent a few texts back and forth and typed notes on her computer. "Okay," she said, shutting her laptop. "I'm off!"

"What? So soon?"

She nodded. "I've got a line on more supplies, so I'd better chop-chop."

"Ahh, well. Great." He knew she'd be taking

Crystal's van. "Don't forget to top off the oil."

"And petrol." She nodded. "I won't." She seemed a bit distracted, pulling things together and shoving them in her bag. Her cheeks also looked a little pink.

"Are you okay?"

She smiled. "Oh yes. Fine."

"You were out late last night."

"Hmm."

"Missed you at breakfast."

"Decided to skip it," she said. "I slept in."

Which was why, he guessed, she came prancing down the stairs at the inn holding a travel cup of tea and saying, "Cheerio, let's go!" Aidan had been finishing his coffee in the dining room while reading the morning edition of *The Seaside Daily*.

"Trudy," Aidan said when she turned to go.

"Hmm?"

He was her boss and not her minder. Still, he worried she had something secretive going on and he felt a bit protective of her, in a brotherly way. But she was a grown woman. Her involvements were her call. That didn't mean he didn't care.

"Just mind your step," he said. "That's all."

"I will, boss. No worries!"

A short time later, Aidan decided he was ready for a break. He needed to stretch his legs and maybe grab a coffee. He stood and rounded the sheet the same time as Charlotte. They almost knocked heads.

"Whoa!" she shouted.

He jumped back. "Sorry." But he shouldn't be apologizing. Seriously. He'd done that already and she hadn't been gracious about it in the least. He waited for Charlotte to move out of his way but she didn't. He gestured toward the door.

Then she gestured, too, mimicking his action.

Aidan scowled. "Very funny."

"I'm not trying to be funny," she said. "I just don't want you behind me."

"Why not?"

"Because you're a backstabber."

He blinked. "Me?"

She gestured again, but he waited.

"Maybe I should be careful of you?"

Her eyes flashed but there was passion behind her glare. "You're the one who claimed to be dangerous."

"I was pretending to be a pirate, Charlotte. Come on."

"Yeah. Well." She stepped toward him. "You're not going to take the treasure this time."

He stepped toward her as well. "If you're talking about the contest, I believe I am."

She lifted her chin, giving him a full view of her beautiful mouth and kissable lips.

He shoved all memories of kissing her out of his mind. But that wasn't easy. The fierceness of her desire had been intoxicating. Unexpected. Most definitely unforgettable. But he needed to forget it.

Her eyebrows arched. "It will be a race to the finish."

His heart pounded. "You'd better buckle up. It's going to be a bumpy ride."

"For you maybe." She was close enough for him to smell her perfume and the light scent of her shampoo. Her gaze locked on his and for an instant he was swept away. Caught up in her current. But it was a riptide. Dragging him down and under and hurling him out to sea. Maybe this was going to be a bumpy ride for the two of them.

"Perhaps we should grant each other a wide berth," he said in clipped tones. "Until Fall Fest is over. Stay out of each other's way?"

She blinked like she'd been affronted.

As if his suggestion had been unreasonable. When by all accounts it made perfect sense. They always seemed to bring out the worst in each other, so why encourage it? It wasn't like they had a future here. Aidan couldn't wait to get the heck out of Majestic.

The less he saw of Charlotte Delaney after this week the better. He wasn't keen on speaking with her either. Or texting, or communicating by email. No, sir. He was done. They could co-run Bearberry Coffee by putting intermediaries in place.

"Great idea." Her words were calm and cool, but they burned like dry ice.

She narrowed her eyes and raised her defenses. He could almost hear those castle gates clanking shut, walling off her emotions.

Which was stellar.

He'd locked down his heart ages ago and then thrown away the key.

CHAPTER SEVENTEEN

The next evening, Charlotte and her sisters sat around Nell's dining room table, filling coffee cups with roasted beans and ground coffee. The aromas were almost overwhelming but still delicious. Nell's quaint cottage sat by a cranberry bog on a cliff overlooking the sea. It was dark out, so you couldn't see the ocean. You could hear it, though, thundering down below. Nell was proud of herself for owning her own home and rightly so. She was probably the most conservative with money among the three of them. Maybe it was the accountant in her.

"I think it's very cool you found all this at the craft shop," Nell said to Misty.

Misty had gone off on her lunch break to track down the supplies for their coffee cup kits. This was after she'd learned about the Etsy shipping delays. They couldn't afford to waste time with this project and had to get everything ready.

Fall-colored ribbons were laid out on the table along with sheets of cellophane. They decided to wrap the lids on the cups to keep each package intact and so they could add an enticing sweet. Some had chocolate stirrers included, others individually wrapped mini biscotti that Lucas's mom had sent over from her bakery. There were other treats too. The three of them had gone shopping at McIntyre's Market after work before coming back here, where they'd all shared a large pizza. The empty pizza box sat off to one side.

Charlotte displayed one of their finished specimens tied up in a pretty gold, brown, and orange bow. It held whole-bean berry-flavored coffee that had been measured out and was just enough to brew twelve cups. A mini package of candy corn was wrapped up with it.

"How cute is this?"

"Folks are going to go gaga for these gift cups," Nell told her.

"Yeah," Misty said. "They'll be selling like hot cakes. But not two for one, right?" She glanced at Charlotte.

Charlotte blew out a breath. "I can't bankrupt us completely. The two for one is just for the actual hot coffee per cup since that's relatively cheap on our end."

"Don't forget about that extra ten percent discount," Nell said. "Which is why it's good you thought this up. Selling the coffee kits will help keep us afloat so we don't go too deeply in the hole for offering the hot coffee as a loss leader."

Charlotte smiled, still proud of herself for the coffee kit concept. She really did have a knack for marketing. Who knew what she'd be able to do once she took the reins at Bearberry Coffee? Their brand was reliable but bland. With the right kind of promotional push and ingenuity, Bearberry Coffee could become even larger than it was. More innovative and exciting. Her adrenaline rushed at the thought of helping the company grow.

She'd never taken on a challenge that big, but she was determined to lean into it, not shy away from it.

Plus, she'd have the existing team in place to help her. She was changing nothing about the corporate structure until she got to know and understand it fully. She'd wait a year or two to assess things before making any revisions and would probably hire experts and consultants to obtain their valuable input. It would be wise of her to make more of an effort with Trudy in trying to establish a bond. Trudy's knowledge could prove invaluable in the future.

"So," Misty said casually, "when is that sheet in the office coming down?"

Never, as far as she was concerned. She'd been relieved not to have to stare at Aidan these past two days. It was much easier to focus when he wasn't sitting there distracting her with his good looks and annoying personality. When he'd said that thing about them keeping their distance from each other, she'd been steamed.

Naturally, they should keep a "wide berth." She didn't want Aidan anywhere near her over the next couple of days. Which was why the sheet divider worked wonders. The less she saw of Aidan Strong the better. It wasn't like she was imagining what he was doing on the other side of the office. She frankly didn't care.

Only one very small part of her was the slightest bit curious. Wondering if he was sitting over there, pining after her, and extremely sorry for all his injustices.

But no. That didn't sound like Aidan.

He'd probably flushed her from his brain already. Just like that.

The jerk.

"I think it's fine where it is," she said, snapping the lid on a cup.

"Well, I think it's in the way." Nell frowned. "I've got to work in there, too, you know."

"We just have three more days," Charlotte said. "And then it's Fall Fest!"

Nell smirked at Misty. "She's never gonna dish, is she?"

Misty shook her head. "Doubtful."

Charlotte set her hands on the table, palms down. "Guys! I'm right here."

"Honey," Nell said. Compassion flickered in her eyes. "You know you can tell us—"

"*Anything*," Misty emphasized.

"And we do know," Nell said, "that something's going on between you and Aidan. You two have been dancing around each other since yesterday. When you come into the service area, he goes the other way. You see him in the kitchen, you dash out the side door. It's almost like you've been ordered not to get within twenty feet of each other. Did you have a fight or something?"

"It must have to do with whatever happened during that oyster festival," Misty said to Nell in confiding tones.

"In that case, they both have something to be mad about. To be fair."

"Fine!" Charlotte blew out a breath and they stared at her. It was hard keeping stuff from her sisters. Besides that, she kind of needed their support. "If you must know." She buried her face in her hands and peeked through her fingers. "I had a lapse."

Nell twisted up her lips. "Define lapse."

Charlotte shrank back from the table. "We might have become, um."

"No way!" Misty said. "You didn't?"

Charlotte rolled her eyes. "Not like *that*, Misty. I wouldn't. It's just that Aidan, he and I—"

Nell got all excited. "Made out?"

Charlotte released a whoosh of air. "Yes." It was such a relief coming clean with her sisters, even though the truth was embarrassing to admit. "But it wasn't huge, huge." Okay, so yeah. It had gone on for a whole hour but they didn't need to know that. "I mean. Only kissing. Of course!"

Nell laid a hand on her arm. "We don't blame you," she said, her expression awash with caring. "He's a very nice-looking guy and you two have chemistry."

"We do. *Not*. Have. Chemistry." Charlotte hid her face in her hands and moaned. "Or maybe we do?"

Nell placed her hand on Charlotte's shoulder. "Oh, honey."

"So." Misty clicked her tongue. "Was he any good? Like some kind of great kisser?"

"Unfortunately," Charlotte wailed. "Yesss."

"Okay." Nell twisted a curly lock of reddish hair around her finger. "Maybe this isn't so bad. You and Aidan. Maybe there's a way to make things work."

"It is not working out between me and Aidan, okay?" Charlotte's heart ached in the very tender spot he'd trampled on. She'd played tough around him like it didn't matter and she didn't care. But deep inside, his words had stung plenty. The cool dismissal in his eyes had hurt even worse. "The man wants absolutely nothing to do with me anymore."

Nell gasped. "He said so?"

Charlotte nodded. "In so many words."

Misty and Nell stared at each other.

Misty approached the topic gently. "Did you guys ever talk about it? After the day?"

Charlotte sighed. "He tried to, but I just… couldn't." She whimpered. "He even apologized."

"For?" Misty asked.

"Pretty much all of it," Charlotte admitted. "He knew I was trying to play him, so he was just playing me back. He also said us getting physical was a mistake. Our emotions ran high. We both got in over our heads."

Misty's forehead furrowed. "Was he right?"

"I don't know." Charlotte sighed. "Maybe."

"What did you say?" Nell asked her. "Did you apologize, too?"

"Of course not." Charlotte blew out a breath. "For what?"

Her sisters raised their eyebrows at each other.

"I'm just saying." Nell tied another bow around a coffee cup. "Sounds like he made an effort."

Misty frowned. "And you didn't."

"What was I supposed to do? Say thanks for setting me up?"

"You set him up first," Nell said.

Misty pursed her lips. "Seems to me like it was mutual."

So, okay. Maybe they had a point. But it was too late now. Fall Fest was almost here, and Charlotte's goal was to win the coffee contest against Aidan. She didn't need to go mixing in personal complications on top of that. They didn't have to like each other, or even spend time together. And, after she won the contest, they wouldn't even have to work together as colleagues in the future. They'd have a whole ocean between them.

"You know what I think?" Nell said.

No. She didn't, but she was sure Nell would enlighten her, and then she did.

"I think you should apologize, too."

Charlotte's heart thumped.

Her eating crow?

Nope. Not happening.

Especially after the way Aidan had treated her.

"Yeah," Misty said. "Good idea."

Charlotte's jaw dropped. "What?"

"Think about it, Charlotte." Nell met her eyes. "The festival is still four days away. On Saturday and this is Tuesday. That's a long time for you and Aidan to be on 'not speaking' terms."

"It's not like that," Charlotte said. "Things aren't antagonistic."

"Yeah," Misty countered. "But they're not exactly pleasant now, either."

"True," Nell said. "The tension's so thick at the café you could cut it with a knife, and that's not good for anybody."

"Mom and Dad are starting to fret, too," Misty said, and Charlotte's stomach sank. That was the kicker. The last thing in the world she meant to do was cause more stress for her parents.

"What?"

"Don't act all innocent, Charlotte," Misty said. "They know you and Aidan are at odds. I mean, hello. Everybody's seen your sheet hanging up in the office, pretty clearly separating your work space from his."

Nell frowned. "It's true. Mom asked me what that was about, so I had to tell her you and Aidan were having a minor moment."

Misty leaped in. "That only made her worry that you were compromising the contest by pushing his buttons. Then she shared her fears with Dad and he got all uptight too. They were finally starting to relax and believe that maybe they wouldn't really lose the shop. That, one way or another, things would be okay. Now they think if you totally alienate Aidan, he might call the whole thing off. Decide not to give half his company to us after all."

Charlotte released a shaky breath. Making things harder for her parents was not at all what she'd intended. "Oh… I didn't know."

"Maybe not," Nell said gently. "But you might have guessed."

"Yeah." Charlotte felt like the biggest idiot on earth. "But Mom and Dad seriously don't have to worry. For all his faults, I don't believe Aidan would do that—rescind his initial offer. I think he's too proud to walk back on his wager with me as well."

"It's risky, though," Misty said. "You could be playing with fire."

Yeah, she'd played too close to Aidan's flames and she'd definitely gotten burned.

But her sisters had a point.

Maybe he was feeling a bit burned, too.

"At least it's not too late." Nell tied a bow around a coffee cup and smiled. "You still have time to make things up with Aidan."

Charlotte gasped. "What? Now?"

Nell nodded. "You remember that thing Mom and Dad used to say? Birds in their nest agree?"

"Yeah, but…" Charlotte bit her lip. "Aidan's not in our flock."

Misty locked on her gaze. "While he's there with us at Bearberry Brews, he's at least in our nest, and we need to keep harmony at the café, for Mom and Dad's sake if nothing else."

Charlotte sighed. Her stubborn head didn't want to listen. But, in her heart, she understood that her sisters were making sense.

She wasn't one for grand gestures, though.

Or mea culpas.

She'd never been great at apologies.

"You don't have to make a huge deal of it," Nell said, guiding her along. "Just tell him you're sorry, too."

Easier said than done.

Groveling wasn't her style.

"Yeah," Misty said. "Then the two of you can forgive each other and move on."

What Charlotte wanted to move on from was this discussion about her apologizing to Aidan. Okay. All right. Fine. Maybe she should do it. Because of her parents and in the interest of "harmony" at the café. Whatever.

But she wasn't going to do it tonight.

Charlotte grabbed a scoop and ladled beans into a cup, ready to talk about anything other than her and Aidan. "So," she asked Misty. "Heard from Mei-Lin lately?"

"Yes!" Her whole face lit up. "She's having the best time out on the ranch. Learning to horseback ride and everything."

Nell sighed. "Sounds romantic and dreamy, especially with a cowboy like Dusty."

They all giggled and agreed.

"How's she getting along with his family?" Nell asked next.

"Really well. He's got a lot of brothers with wives, and nieces and nephews."

"Sounds like a crew," Charlotte said. "When's she coming home?"

"Sunday."

"Too bad she'll miss Fall Fest," Nell said.

Misty shrugged. "Yeah, but I'll fill her in."

Nell glanced around the table. "I'm ready for a break. Prosecco, anyone?"

Charlotte didn't need to be asked twice.

• • •

Aidan slid onto a bar stool beside Lucas at Mariner's. "Cheers, mate. Thanks for your text."

Aidan was used to operating on his own and had no trouble hanging out solo during his various travels. Nonetheless he appreciated Lucas reaching out. He also appreciated that Lucas didn't immediately judge him for his interactions with Charlotte at the oyster festival and afterward. While he probably didn't know all of it, chances were Charlotte had filled Misty and Nell in somewhat and that Misty'd told him.

Lucas shrugged. "Anytime. Baching it tonight."

"Yeah?"

"Misty's hanging with her sisters." He stared into his beer. "They're working on a project."

"I'm glad they're all such good friends."

"Yeah," Lucas said. "It's nice when siblings are tight."

"How about you? Got any?"

"Ramon, yeah. Kid brother." Lucas puffed up his chest. "Going to Brown next year."

Aidan whistled. "Ivy League. That's cool."

Lucas smiled. "He earned it."

"I'm sure he did."

The bartender set down their beers and handed them each a menu. It was Clive's night off and he was attending a recorder performance at his kid's school. Clive and Aidan kept talking about getting together, and Aidan wanted to soon, while he was still in Majestic. The two of them had been friends back when they were kids, before Aidan moved away.

He and Lucas ordered pub sandwiches, then Aidan said, "Gotta be nice having a brother."

"It can be." Lucas smirked. "When he's not being a royal pain."

"Aww, come on. I bet he's a good kid." Seemed like he had to be if he was Lucas's brother and Lucas was a pretty chill guy. Aidan hadn't known him as a kid in Majestic because Lucas had attended a Catholic school early on.

Lucas took a belt of beer. "You're right. He is in general."

He didn't ask about Aidan's family because, by now, that was public record. Even if the Delaneys hadn't filled him in, Allison and Darcy had profiled Aidan in their earlier stories about him supposedly coming to Majestic to claim his bride. Aidan shook his head, amazed that the whole town had believed it. That the Delaney sisters had believed it too.

Aidan felt ashamed that Charlotte was right. He'd played a part in that faulty perception. Once he'd arrived in Majestic, though, it hadn't taken long for him to clear the air. In retrospect, he understood why Charlotte was so angry about how he'd made his pronouncement regarding there being no marriage. But it was a little too late to walk that back now.

He sipped from his mug while Lucas seemed to mull something over, evidently lost in happier thoughts.

After a bit, Lucas turned to him with raised eyebrows. "Things are looking interesting in the office these days," he said. "Very divided."

"Yeah." Aidan set down his beer. "The sheet was Charlotte's idea."

Lucas took a sip of beer. "I heard."

Aidan was tempted to ask what else he'd heard, but he wasn't going to put Lucas on the spot. Lucas probably regretted trying to warn him off from becoming involved with Charlotte, and had likely endured kickback from the sisters about it. "Look, mate, about what you told me before down on the beach—"

"I'd probably rather not talk about it." Lucas's forehead rose. "Anymore."

"I'm sorry if I got you in a pinch, though. With Misty and the others."

"Don't sweat it. Everything's cool." He took a drag of beer and set down his mug. "I am a little worried about this contest, though. To tell you the truth."

"The coffee selling contest? No need."

"Charlotte and her sisters are working extra hard to ensure they'll win."

"I'd expect no less," Aidan said.

Lucas's face creased with concern. "Have you thought this out? All your options? In the event you—" He pursed his lips.

"Lose?" asked Aidan. He took a few sips of beer. "I'm not so worried about that outcome."

"Maybe you should be."

"What's that mean?"

Their food arrived and they pushed aside their mugs.

Lucas frowned. "I'm afraid I can't answer that."

Aidan took a bite of his sandwich and chewed. The French fries were good and hot, and tasty too. "I do have a backup plan, if that's what you mean. I've got loads of savings and investments. Not going to walk out of this a poor man by any means."

Lucas heaved a breath. "That's good to know." He ate for a bit, too. "Not going to say it's happening— but, if you lose the company, what's your next move?"

This hit him like a sucker punch because he'd never actually foreseen that as a possibility. His gut clenched momentarily then he inhaled a deep breath. "I suppose I could do something different." He shrugged. "Start another company. My mate Tony's always joking I should go into business with him."

"What's Tony do?"

"Produce records."

"That's a big change."

"He wants me in on the distribution end. Maybe in marketing." He thought of Charlotte's collages. "Speaking of records and art." He took out his phone and showed Lucas the images. "Have you seen these collages of Charlotte's?" He'd sent them to Tony but hadn't heard back.

"Yeah. They're pretty cool." He looked closer at the photos. "The two in the kitchen are new."

"Since?"

Lucas finished his sandwich and wiped his mouth. "Since I helped Charlotte move into her new digs. She had another place on the same street but the landlord sold it, so she needed to relocate. Her sisters and I helped her with some of the heavy lifting. Ramon pitched in, too."

"Yeah? When was this?"

"About…?" He glanced at the ceiling. "A year or so ago."

"Did she have Red Hot Chili Peppers then?"

"Don't think so. I would have remembered that."

"Kiss? Heart?"

He shook his head then grinned. "Considering a career as an art dealer?"

"Not exactly. I'm just thinking Charlotte could do something with those collages if she wanted to."

Lucas shrugged. "Maybe she doesn't want to?"

"Maybe not. But she is super talented and seems to work fast."

Lucas leaned toward him. "Maybe she'll be putting all her energy into running Bearberry Coffee before too long."

Aidan didn't know about that. It could happen, but it would be a long shot for Charlotte to be the winner taking all.

"Maybe." He grinned. "But I don't think so."

Lucas frowned. "I just hope things work out for everybody. The Delaneys, their café. Charlotte." He met Aidan's gaze. "And you."

Aidan felt certain things would work out well for the Delaneys and the café. He was less sure about his rocky relationship with Charlotte. Considering her behavior these past two days, it was going to be rough seas until the fair and their contest. In a different universe where they'd gotten along, he might have been looking forward to a business partnership with her.

But the woman was impossible to deal with and as stubborn as a mule.

The type of person who could never admit she was wrong.

And that one little characteristic outweighed all her positive traits.

Aidan raised his mug in a toast, not aiming to bring Lucas down with his negativity. So he put on an upbeat face. "Here's to things working out."

Lucas clinked his mug. "Cheers!"

CHAPTER EIGHTEEN

The following morning at Bearberry Brews, Aidan stared at Trudy's laptop and the advertisement she was in the process of booking. He'd wanted to think broader than Charlotte's quaint billboard ad and, with Trudy's help, he'd arrived at an amazing solution. Aerial advertising campaigns were big along beaches in coastal towns.

Charlotte would never be able to top this. The sky was the limit indeed and this ad hit its mark. People from all over Majestic would see it everywhere. For the next three days in daylight hours.

It might even draw others from neighboring areas to the fair. Who didn't love a great deal on coffee? Other than non-coffee drinkers, and there wasn't a whole lot he could do about them, apart from offer tea. And his bet with Charlotte was all about selling the most cups of *coffee*.

"I think that's good." He grinned at Trudy. "Absolutely brilliant."

"And the copy?"

There was a large Bearberry Coffee logo showing a stylized BC on a paper coffee cup.

Then: We'll match the best price at Fall Fest!

Aidan rubbed his beard. "Maybe tweak it like so." He reached across to her keyboard and adjusted the template, changing "match" to "beat."

"Ooh, yes." She smiled approvingly. "I like it!"

"So whatever price Charlotte sets," he whispered,

"we can't be undercut."

Charlotte wasn't on her side of the sheet. She'd popped out for an errand. But he never knew when she might sneak back in and be listening. They'd not been letting each other in on the other's marketing plans for obvious reasons. He'd found out about her newsletter discount and the flyers around town and had stumbled across that billboard.

She only knew about his "Friends and Family Discount" as advertised in *The Seaside Daily*. She had no clue about his plans for airplane ads. By the time she learned about them it would be too late for her to book any of her own. The only game in town with airplane advertising required a deposit to be made forty-eight hours before campaign setup and nothing could be finalized without that money down first. So she'd be out of luck with the timing.

"Okay then," Trudy said, standing. "I'm off!" She stuffed her laptop into her bag, explaining, "The company wants the balance of the payment in cash to make this work. It's so last minute and we want this to start running tomorrow."

Aidan nodded. "Through Saturday. Don't forget. We'll want to keep it going all the way through Fall Fest."

She tapped her temple. "Mind's like a steel trap, boss."

That was true and he was glad.

"Um, Aidan." She hesitated with the sheet dangling behind her, partway blocking the door. "I know this might be bad timing, but do you think I could have tomorrow off?"

Tomorrow was Thursday. Two days before the fair.

Trudy flashed him a smile. "I won't do it unless we've got everything in order, I swear. I should be able to set the rest of the arrangements in place today. Then on Friday we'll be busy taking our counts and organizing stock so we can set up easily on Saturday."

"Yeah, Trudy, that's fine. I'm sure I can manage a whole day without you."

"Thanks, boss!" she said, bouncing out the door.

In a way, he'd been managing without her a lot lately. While she was still getting her work done, she'd been making herself rather scarce these past several days. Who knew what she'd been up to, but she seemed to be having a good time with it. Which was great.

Trudy worked hard and he'd almost never seen her let her hair down and have fun. She was all work, work, work normally. He just hoped she wouldn't be too let down when whatever she was involved with ended. He'd need her mind wholly back on business with him and Charlotte co-running the company.

Trudy was right. They were reasonably prepared for Fall Fest. Now with this new advertisement planned, doubly so. He also needed to confirm with Darcy and Allison, who'd offered to cover their coffee contest at the fair. That would be good publicity for both Bearberry Coffee and Bearberry Brews, regardless of who the winner was.

Meaning him.

He knew Charlotte would be disappointed after putting so much effort into their competition, but sometimes you win and sometimes you lose. She surely couldn't expect to win every single time. Nobody had that kind of great fortune, not even him.

Maybe it would be good for her to lose for once, learn to show some humility. Because if there was one thing Charlotte was *not*, it was humble. She wasn't very gracious, either. When he'd tried to make peace between them, she'd shot his efforts down with a cannonball.

He heard a sound behind the sheet and looked up from his tablet, where he'd been scanning through the day's headlines. Some of them were depressing and he was glad to have his mind on other things for a bit. Like a small seaside town, a fall festival, and the Delaneys. Not necessarily Charlotte. Though he did occasionally think about her. But only once in a while. Okay. Frankly, quite often, and probably more than he should. Because he'd been trying to figure her out like a challenging puzzle. Just when he thought he had her solved, he'd discover another piece that wouldn't fit.

Shadows moved behind the sheet and in front of the window. "Charlotte? Is that you?"

A small object peeked above the top of the sheet. It was shaped like a pointy triangle. Then more of the item emerged. No way, but it was. It was a kite stamped with a Jolly Roger pirate emblem on its front. He laughed out loud.

Charlotte lowered the kite and poked her head around the edge of the sheet.

"So." She pursed her lips. He could tell this was painful for her. Probably on the level of a root canal. "It's windy out." Her face burned bright red, particularly her nose. "I was thinking you might want to fly a kite?"

He crossed his arms. If this was her mode of apology it was fairly weak. She could probably do better than that. He'd made the effort on his part. Very earnestly.

"I'm afraid I haven't flown a kite in years."

She stood up straighter, holding the kite in front of her. "Exactly." She grinned. "That's why it's such a good idea! Look at you, working so hard." Her gaze swept his table and he covered his notes with his tablet. "Maybe you're due for a break?"

"With you?" he asked, determined not to make this easy on her. She'd been acting childish all week and her stringing up that sheet had been the last straw. He shook his head. "I'm afraid I don't fly kites with my enemies."

She blinked, appearing hurt. "We're not enemies."

"I wouldn't exactly say we're pals at the moment, either." He cocked his chin. "Pals are good to one another. Don't step on each other's toes."

She swallowed hard. "Okay, that part was an accident."

He studied the sheet then locked on her gaze. "Pals also know when to say they're sorry."

She blew out a breath, but he didn't look away.

He just sat there waiting.

But she held her ground.

Finally, she rolled her eyes.

She raised the kite up in front of her face and squeaked out, "Sorry."

"Uh, nope," he answered. "No dice. Not loud enough."

She lowered the kite and gritted her teeth. "Seriously?"

He nodded and cupped a hand behind his ear like he was straining to hear.

"Sorry," she said with more force.

His lips twitched. "I want the whole café to hear you."

She huffed and threw down the kite. "You are so not worth this."

He watched her, utterly fascinated, wondering what she'd do next… Storm off in a fit, or come back and woman up with a real apology?

She hit the threshold and spun around, her fists clenched at her sides. Then she shut her eyes and appeared to be counting. He'd seen her do that before. Maybe he'd gotten under her skin again? He chuckled to himself. Yeah. Probably so. He kept watching for the steam to pour out of her ears, but it didn't.

She opened her eyes and stomped toward him in her cowgirl boots and flouncy skirt. She picked the kite up off the floor on the way. "Fine." She set a hand on her hip, grasping the kite in the other, then threw back her head, shouting up at the ceiling, "I'm sorry!" It echoed off the walls and he grinned. She drew in a breath then said more quietly, "Okay?"

"You forgot to say my name."

"Grrr." She took one giant step toward him and popped him over the head with the kite. He ducked, absorbing the blow, which was minor considering the weapon. "Forget it," she said. "We're not going."

Ooh. She was so easy to tease, it was almost impossible not to tease her.

But maybe he'd gone too far.

He latched onto her sweater sleeve and she turned. "Why not?" he asked, gently releasing her.

She stood there breathing hard like a fiery dragon. A very formidable one with hypnotizing blue eyes.

"Because," she said evenly, "one of us might not make it off that beach alive."

Okay. So he *had* gone too far and now she was majorly incensed.

She had been trying to apologize in her own way. Which was a little subpar but heartfelt, he supposed.

"Hey." He softened his tone. "I'm sorry, too. Honestly. I didn't mean to wind you up."

She arched one eyebrow. "Really? Because that sounded very intentional to me."

He laid a hand across his chest. "I'm gutted that you'd think that of me."

"You're gutted?" She rolled her eyes. "That's rubbish," she said, tossing a Britishism back at him. It was a take-that verbal slap, but he didn't mind it. He probably deserved it, anyway.

He held up both hands. "We *are* a pair."

"No, we're not." She glanced at the sheet. "We're quite separate."

"About that?" He got to his feet. "When does it come down?"

She motioned grandly. "Be my guest, if you think you can stand working across from me."

He grinned and lobbed back her phrase. "*Bring it.*"

She smirked and tugged down the sheet, holding it by a snatch of fabric in its center. "You going to help me or what?"

He removed the clips on the other end. "I thought you'd never ask."

They held it out lengthwise between them, shaking it out. Then they doubled it horizontally before folding over again in a sequence of small squares while walking toward each other. Soon they were face to face.

"Nice seeing you again, Charlotte Delaney."

She locked on his gaze and his pulse pounded harder.

"Why, Aidan Strong." She smirked. "What a surprise!"

She was such a smart aleck and aggravating too. But there was a strange appeal in her aggravation.

He passed her his folded-up section of the sheet, and she aligned it with her portion before setting it down on the table.

Then she picked up the kite. "Ready to rock and roll?"

"I am, but first." He reached down in the bag under his desk and pulled her sweater out, handing it to her. "Trudy found this on the floor in the back of the van."

She pulled a face and snatched it away, dropping it onto her chair. "Sorry about that."

He recalled her taking it off when she'd become overheated after the oyster festival. His body temperature had gone up a notch, too. First on the beach when they'd nearly kissed, then back at her flat when she'd come on like a wildcat, driving him out of his mind with those white-hot kisses of hers.

"You might want to wear your jacket. It's windy outside."

He glanced down at her boots. "You're going to fly a kite in those?"

She shrugged. "I was thinking I might go barefoot." When she was out of those boots in a skirt, he saw more of her sexy legs. And Charlotte's legs were stellar.

He nodded. "I can work with that."

They passed through the kitchen with Charlotte carrying the kite and exited through the side door. Sean met them on his way in.

"Where were you?" Charlotte asked.

"Out on my break."

Charlotte stole a peek at Aidan. "With anyone in particular?"

"Not necessarily," Sean said. "No."

"You're sure?"

"Yeah, I'm sure." He frowned. "Look-it, Charlotte. You're not my mother. I get enough intrusive questions from Nell."

Charlotte raised her eyebrows at Aidan then answered Sean. "You're right. Sorry."

High winds buffeted against them the moment they stepped outdoors and Charlotte nearly lost hold of the kite.

"You weren't kidding," he said. "It's quite blustery."

She shook out the kite. "But a great day for this."

"Yeah." He wondered about something. "You suspect Sean and Trudy are seeing each other?"

"It's hard to say, but both seem to be gone a lot at the same time."

"But Trudy is working."

Charlotte laughed. "Sure."

Mary Beth passed them on their way toward the stone steps. She stopped them with a curious smile. "Well, hi, you two." She stared at Aidan, then at Charlotte, and finally at the kite. "Looks like you're off to have fun."

Aidan shifted on his feet. She'd texted him five times since they'd gone out for a bite at Mariner's, and he hadn't replied. He'd been too busy competing against—and becoming irritated by—Charlotte. "Ah, yeah." He gazed at the billowy clouds in the sky. "Great day for kite flying."

"I've been trying to reach you," Mary Beth said. "Haven't you gotten my messages?"

He sank his hands in his pockets. "Well, I… Um, sure! It's just that with the fair coming along and everything, it's been busy." He cleared his throat, looking for an escape. The beach wasn't far away. Just down the steps. He could make a break for it, but that would be rude.

"All work and no play." Mary Beth giggled and shoved his shoulder. When Charlotte playfully shoved him, he didn't mind it. It almost felt like a natural extension of the teasing banter they often shared. When Mary Beth touched him, though, it just felt wrong.

Charlotte's eyebrows knitted together and for a split second she appeared vexed.

She was jealous?

That really didn't seem like her. Then again, she had been staring at him from outside when he was at Mariner's with Mary Beth. Sneakily spying on him, some might think.

"Oh, don't worry about us," Charlotte said saucily. "Aidan and I have been playing *quite a lot* lately."

Mary Beth paled. "Oh?"

Charlotte smiled and waved the kite. "We went out to an oyster festival." She nudged him. "Didn't we, Aidan?"

"Oh, right. Right." Charlotte widened her eyes at him, urging him to play along. He got it. She wasn't jealous at all. She was helping him shake Mary Beth. "We did do, yes."

He casually draped an arm around Charlotte's shoulders, and Mary Beth did her best not to scowl. "So." She clicked her tongue. "You two are an item now? I mean *actually* together?"

"Well, I don't know about *together* together," Aidan said at the same time Charlotte chirped, "Yes!"

"But the papers said—"

Charlotte batted her eyelashes. "It's all brand new."

Mary Beth opened her mouth like she was about to make some pithy comment. Then she pursed her lips. "Never mind."

"I'm sorry, Mary Beth," Aidan said. "You're lovely."

"Sure I am." She raised her chin and strode away. "Just obviously not lovely enough for you."

Aidan removed his arm from around Charlotte's shoulders, and they stared at each other.

"Yikes," she said. "Mary Beth really comes on strong. Guess she has the hots for you."

"Thanks for the save there."

"Anytime." She shrugged. "You would have done the same for me."

The truth was he probably would have. "She's a nice person but—"

"I get it," Charlotte answered. "When it's there, it's there. When it's not, it's not."

They took the stone steps down to the beach.

"My thinking exactly," he said. "Some things can't be forced."

"No."

And others came on like a freight train. Like the weight of her full beauty hitting him just now as she stood on the beach, holding that kite, with wind whipping through her dark hair.

Aidan's heart pounded in his throat, which suddenly felt extra raw.

"Come on." She teasingly elbowed him. "Aren't you going to get out of those shoes?" She'd already wiggled out of one cowgirl boot and was working her way out of the other. But it appeared to be stuck as she attempted to balance on one foot while holding the railing with one hand and the kite with the other.

"Here," he said. "Allow me."

He set his grip around the heel of her boot and tugged.

"Oh!" She went off balance and fell backward, and he fell over the top of her, hitting the sand right above her, crouched on all fours. Fortunately, he didn't squash anything or land on top of her. She started laughing and couldn't stop.

"Some help!" she cackled, pushing up on his chest with her palms.

He laughed and sat back on his knees, pulling her up. "Yeah, sorry."

He stood and helped her the rest of the way up, landing her almost in his arms. He was so tempted to hold her like he'd done before.

But no. Not if she didn't want that.

She stepped away and grabbed the kite. "So," she began, her face all pink, "remember how this works?"

"Think so," he said, kicking off his shoes. The sand was gritty and cool but not uncomfortable.

"Let's head down this way." She pointed to the lighthouse. "Then we can work our way back here."

"Sounds like a plan."

What he didn't plan on was it being so darn difficult to launch this beastly kite. They kept trying to get it up by taking turns holding it and running.

The kite nose-dived into the sand time after time. Once, it even spiraled into an eddy, going for a brief swim.

Charlotte laughed as a blast of wind blew a few ebony locks across her lips. "We're not very good at this, are we?" she said, sweeping back her hair. He'd never known her to be a quitter, and he wasn't about to encourage her to give up now.

"Let's try one more time," he said. "You take the string and start out ahead of me. I'll run behind you, holding the kite, and only let it go when it catches the wind."

"Okay, but this is it." She laughed. "After this try, I'm toast."

She took hold of the string where it was wound tight and skipped ahead, allowing it to quickly unravel.

Aidan matched her pace from behind her, holding the kite high and into the wind.

And then—at last—magic happened.

The wind caught the kite with a big billow, sending it high above them, its Jolly Roger emblem blazing in the shimmering sunlight.

"Charlotte!" Aidan called. "Look!"

She peered over her shoulder and whooped with glee. "Ya-hoo! We did it! Yes!"

She laughed and ran along, moving faster and faster as the kite curtseyed and soared above the beach, every so often skimming the waves with brazen darts and jags.

He stopped and cupped his hands on either side of his mouth. "Nice job! Keep going!"

She peeked over her shoulder, and her grin took his breath away.

Then she spun back around and ran in happy zigzags down the shore, her bare feet kicking up sand and spray. Looking as happy as she'd been as a kid.

Wild. Unfettered. Free.

He was loving this. So hard.

But he was *not* falling in love with her—his heart thumped—was he?

CHAPTER NINETEEN

Charlotte laughed so much she could barely breathe. Aidan stood beside her, reeling in her kite with expert precision. There was only so much kite flying a woman could do in a day. But, wow, it had been exhilarating. Once she'd gotten started it had been hard to stop until she grew winded and couldn't run any farther.

"Well, that was amazing."

"You're a natural." He grinned, and the waning daylight cast a golden hue across his bearded face. From the look in his eyes, he'd had a blast, too. He wound the kite string tighter, bringing it down to earth. He leaped up and caught it by its frame as it fluttered toward the sand after bobbing briefly over the waves.

"I guess certain things come back to you," she said. "Like riding a bike."

"Never learned to ride a bike."

"That is such a lie," she teased. "I remember you getting a ten-speed for your birthday."

"True." He nodded. "Though I preferred my longboard." He pointed to the faint scar above his left eyebrow, and Charlotte recalled the accident he'd had while trying to pop wheelies using ramps down at the docks.

"That was you and Clive, right?" she said.

"Me and Clive. Yeah." He shook his head and laughed. "We got into trouble once in a while. It was always his idea."

"Sure it was," she said, not believing him. When they were kids, she'd always figured Aidan for being shy and awkward and maybe something of a goody-goody. She didn't realize that he'd had a mischievous side.

He held up his hand in pledge. "I wasn't the troublemaker."

"Hmm. If you say so." She laughed, because it took one to know one, and Charlotte strongly suspected Aidan had stirred quite a few pots in his day. He definitely seemed to enjoy making trouble now—with her.

The wind howled and she wrapped her arms around herself. Now that she'd stopped moving, her bare feet were chilled sinking in wet sand. Icy pinpricks skittered across her ankles and shot to her knees, causing gooseflesh to rise on her legs.

She shivered.

Aidan frowned. "Chilly?"

"I'll be all right."

He passed her the kite and removed his jacket. "Here," he said, holding it up so she could slide her free arm into a sleeve.

"Oh no, you don't have to—"

"It's fine, really. I want to."

She shifted the kite to her other hand, slipping his jacket on fully. Its warmth from his body heat enveloped her along with his summer rain scent. "Thank you."

He retrieved the kite so she could zip his jacket. "That's a nice look," he said. "A little roomy, but not bad."

Her nose warmed, the heat making it tickle, and she rubbed it.

She studied his pullover sweater and the evidence of a T-shirt underneath. "Are you sure you won't be cold now?"

"I'm tough enough to take it," he joked. "It's all those manly hormones of mine. They keep my thermostat running high."

"Ha!" She rolled her eyes. He had the weirdest sense of humor, but it made him charming in a way. Different from most guys she knew. Unique and funny. "I'll keep that in mind."

"Aye, ya'd better, lassie. Er things might be get dangerous." His imitation pirate brogue reminded her of the oyster festival and their wild kissing session afterward. Now she felt hot, instantly overheated in Aidan's jacket. She unzipped it partway.

"They did get dangerous," she said. "Good thing that cooler heads prevailed."

"I thought it was that slew of phone calls and text messages from your sisters that prevailed? Ding after ding and ring after ring?"

"You really have no shame," she said. "Do you?"

His eyes danced. "I'd say we're evenly matched in that department."

It pleased her that he considered her an equal in intellect and toughness. She'd never really met her match in a man before. He was interesting and different. That didn't mean she was falling for him, though. Just that they were getting along, and getting along was better than being at odds with each other. He was right.

They walked back toward the stone steps. It was silly to be disappointed, but she felt the tiniest bit let down that their time together was drawing to a close. She didn't often let herself go or behave in a carefree way. And for a few special hours today, she'd forgotten about all her routine worries. She was glad she'd thought of buying a kite. Offering that as an olive branch had worked out far better than humiliating herself with a straight-up apology.

"Did you and Clive keep up after you moved to England?" she asked, thinking of their former friendship. Aidan hadn't stayed in touch with her or her sisters.

Then again, none of them had made efforts to reach out to him, either. He'd been the kid of her parents' friends and business partners that she and Misty and Nell had been forced to spend time with when the two families got together for vacations and holidays.

"For a short time by computer chat, yeah," he said, answering her question about Clive. "But our lives soon became really different. He got into dating girls and such, and I got into boarding school."

She thought of how that was often portrayed in movies. "Was that awful or more like Hogwarts?"

He laughed. "The landscape was definitely dramatic and, yeah, sometimes gloomy. But there were no flying lessons involved, if that's what you mean."

She chuckled. "Now, that would have been cool."

His smile faded and he grew distant a moment. "My dad was traveling a lot, per usual, and Mum was busy with all her society teas, so I suppose it was easier to tuck me away."

She frowned because that sounded so sad. "It can be hard going away." Her heart twisted and a memory hit her with a jolt. But she'd been so young then. That was different.

"Wait." He turned to study her. "You went away to school?"

She shook her head. "Not until college. I did go to summer camp once."

He squinted at the horizon, evidently trying to imagine this. "Yeah? When was this?"

Charlotte pursed her lips, thinking. "It was the summer after you all moved to London."

"Overnight camp?"

She nodded and a chill ran through her. She huddled her arms around herself and Aidan gently touched her arm. "Hey? Are you all right?"

She glanced at his handsome profile. "It's silly, really. But I didn't have such a great time." She'd never told anyone this story. She'd never even confessed her misery to her sisters. Somehow, though, she felt comfortable sharing this with him. It was so long ago, and she'd been a kid. She knew he wouldn't judge her.

Concern etched into his features. "Did something happen?"

Charlotte blew out a breath. "Nothing terrible. I just got homesick. I mean really homesick. Tummy ache and everything."

"Psychosomatic?"

"Probably." She bit her bottom lip. "My best friend Margaret was supposed to come with me, but then she got the flu and couldn't go."

He rubbed his cheek. "So, your sisters didn't go, either?"

They kept ambling along at a comfortable pace. She could see the stone steps in the distance. "My sisters never wanted to go away. They were homebodies. I was always the 'brave one.'" She laughed sadly. "It was a whole heck of a lot easier being brave when I thought my bestie was going with me."

"Whatever happened to Margaret?"

"She and I went to different colleges. We eventually lost touch."

He stared down at his feet a moment. "Those things happen," he said, looking up. "It seems that you're close with your sisters, though."

She smiled. "I am."

They were really the best friends she had, and she loved them dearly. Like she did her whole family. And they admired her as the tough, take-charge one. Maybe that's why she'd never told any of them the story she was sharing with Aidan now. She'd never wanted to shatter that illusion.

He thought a moment before asking, "What was the name of this camp?"

"Camp Castaway."

He burst out laughing. "Was not."

"I swear it's true." She nudged him with her elbow, then giggled, relenting. "Okay, that wasn't *technically* the name. That's just what us campers called it."

He frowned, appearing pained for her. "So you had a totally miserable time."

"Oh no! I didn't."

Surprise washed over his face. "But I thought—?"

Charlotte set her chin. "That's when I learned to

be tougher than tough. The counselors wanted to call my parents, but I wouldn't let them. I mean, I couldn't disappoint my family. Or make them drive all the way back to New Hampshire after dropping me off. It was only for a week, and I'd *begged and begged* to go. So, I had to make the most of it. I turned myself into the cool girl, the fun and outgoing one." She squared her shoulders. "I was actually very popular."

He grinned at her. "I can definitely see it. Tie-dye leader. Archery captain…"

She nudged him. "Now stop." She laughed. "There were no such things."

"So it wasn't all bad, then?" It was his turn to nudge her, and her face heated. He was a lot easier to talk to than she'd imagined. And certainly less annoying than when they'd been kids.

Her stomach churned at the video reel in her head of her parents and Misty and Nell all walking away, their own little band, chatting happily together. And her being left behind. "No, it wasn't all bad. It made me independent." She forced a smile. "Resilient." She stared up at him. "Probably like boarding school did for you."

He shoved his hands in his pockets. "I got a fine education, anyway. Got me into Cambridge and all that." He turned to her. "Where did you wind up going to college?"

"University of Vermont."

"Like it?" he asked her.

"Liked being in Scotland more."

"Maybe you should have studied there the whole time."

"My parents would have freaked. They had a hard enough time when Nell went away and then me a year later. Misty was the only one who stayed home, but now it's her turn."

"That's so great for Misty," he said. "Pursuing her dreams."

"Everyone should do that, yeah."

"I agree." The warmth in his eyes seeped into her core, filling her soul with sunshine. Her emotions went all out of kilter when he stared at her that way. Like she was amazing and powerful enough to sweep him away.

She gazed out over the ocean, hiding her blush. "Maybe you should reconnect with Clive?" she said, turning back to him. Anything to keep them from talking about pursuing dreams. That made her think of fairytales and happily ever afters. Stories like those romance novels Nell and Mei-Lin read.

Charlotte was more into music than reading. She was also pretty skeptical about finding her own Prince Charming. That would mean relying on someone other than herself. That seemed risky. Charlotte preferred sure bets. That's why she'd focused on obtainable goals, like doing well in school and in business.

Aidan nodded and continued speaking about Clive. "He suggested going out for a beer or two." He chuckled. "When he's not serving them himself."

Charlotte smiled, glad to be talking about Clive and not the future, because all of a sudden her dreams were becoming less clear than before. "He's got three kids now, you know that?"

"Yeah. Guess his life has moved on in a pretty

different way." His smile warmed her heart. "You planning to have kids someday?"

His question threw her. Of course she'd thought about it in an abstract fashion. But that seemed so far down the road. She shrugged. "That's something I'll have to discuss with my husband, but I'm thinking yeah, that would be nice."

His eyes sparkled. "Yeah, I think that would be nice, too."

She guessed he would be a good dad, having learned from his own dad's mistakes. He seemed to have a caring side that he masked with his subtle sarcasm. He had a playful nature, too. Plus he was daring. Bold when he needed to be. She thought back to what he'd said about them not being so different. She'd scoffed at the notion at the time, but the more she was around him, the more she began to wonder if it was true.

Though she'd acted like she'd wanted to find a husband first to win that bet with her sisters, in her heart, she'd known that she wouldn't. That's why the fake marriage to Aidan had seemed so good. It would have allowed her to work on both businesses, Bearberry Brews and its parent corporation, Bearberry Coffee, without the distraction of a serious relationship. And you couldn't get more serious than becoming engaged to some random guy within thirty days.

Nell had known Grant in high school, and Misty and Lucas had a long history as friends, so their stories were different. Charlotte had never so much as fallen in love with a man, so attempting to rapid-fire marry one was out of the question. A pretend marriage seemed to fit, because she wouldn't have had to sacrifice anything emotionally.

She had worried a tad about Aidan being a grown-up goofball, or worse—an ogre. Someone who'd be impossible to work with. But now he didn't seem that way at all. Except for when he was teasing her with his quick-witted banter. Or attracting her with his sexy good looks and undeniably smooth moves. She relived his kisses on her sofa and her nose burned hot.

"Well," he said, when they reached the spot where they'd left their shoes. "I guess this is it then. Thanks for the fun time." They both sat on the steps and dusted the sand from their feet, and he slid on his loafers.

She put on her cowgirl boots, fighting the tug of emotion that said she didn't want their fun time together to end. "Aidan?"

"Hmm."

"Do you think… I mean, would you like to…?" Oh man, she was botching this.

His gaze washed over her and her heart fluttered.

"Grab a bite to eat?" he finished for her.

Yes. "If you've got the time?"

"Time is all I've got, Charlotte." Her heart melted when he looked in her eyes. "And I'm more than happy to share mine with you."

CHAPTER TWENTY

Charlotte and Aidan sat on a bench at the end of a long pier stretching into the ocean. He was close enough for her to feel his body heat beside her in the chill of the evening, but she didn't mind their proximity. Somehow it seemed natural and good. Waves crashed against the beach below them and winds circled around from all sides. They held packages of lobster rolls in their laps.

Aidan held up the twist-cap Chianti bottle. "Nice to get by without a corkscrew."

"I prefer the convenience," she said. It was nearly dark now with faint ribbons of light fading across the water. The Majestic lighthouse stood on an outcropping called Lookout Point, its blinking beacon radiating out to sea. "Not too cold for you here?" she asked him.

"It's perfect." He removed the cap and passed her the bottle. "No cups?"

She grinned and took a swig. "I prefer this convenience, too."

He laughed and took back the bottle when she handed it to him.

"Besides," she said, glancing around. "Cups? Where would we put them?"

"You're right. They'd get blown away."

But she was the one blown away by this moment. Her and Aidan on an impromptu date at one of her favorite spots in Majestic. She tried not to get ahead of herself and wonder what would happen when they said good night. Because she didn't want to kiss him again. That impulse she'd had on the beach after flying the kite had been a minor blip. She had things reined in now. She really did.

Okay, no. She didn't.

That's why they were here and not back at her place. She knew her limits.

They'd wedged the kite under the bench in such a way it was held there by its frame. Charlotte's house was so close by, they could have dropped it off there, and she could have grabbed her own jacket. But she hadn't wanted to break the spell they were under, basking in each other's company, like being together was the most natural thing in the world. She also favored being outdoors and in public. Since she didn't trust herself not to tackle Aidan to the sofa, based on how she was feeling. All churned up inside.

She wanted to believe her tangle of emotions was all about physical attraction, but in her heart, she wasn't sure. Something strange was happening, and she was liking him more and more. Not because of his looks, because he clearly had those, but because of something deeper. The way he made her feel appreciated and warm when they were getting along and sharing their stories. He didn't just listen, he heard her. Like he understood her on some intrinsic level. None of the guys she'd dated before had made her feel like that.

Aidan passed her the wine bottle. "So, what should we drink to?"

"Family?" She smiled but then her smile turned

into a frown when his gaze misted over. "I'm sorry, Aidan. You and your mom?"

He shrugged. "We get on all right. But we're not tight like you girls are with your folks. And my dad…" He sighed heavily. "Turned into someone I almost didn't know, honestly."

Charlotte spoke in caring tones. "He was gone a lot, huh?"

"He was gone *always*." Aidan looked away and out at the ocean. "Emotionally."

She took a small sip of wine and gave him the bottle. "Here."

"Thanks." He downed a swig.

"So, not to family then," she murmured.

"Oh, we can drink to yours." His eyes twinkled sadly. "I just don't think mine will be winning any accolades for family of the year. Present company included." He rested the wine bottle on his knee. "You know what they say about apples not falling far from the tree."

"Aidan," she said, getting where he was going with this and stopping him. "You are not your dad, okay? You're your own person."

He stared at her long and hard. "That's what I'd like to believe, but some days—"

She touched his arm and said sternly, "You are."

Charlotte hated he was going through this. Having the family she did, it was hard to relate. Yet she did have enough compassion to guess what it must feel like to him. Maybe she'd felt abandoned at Camp Castaway, but Aidan had been the real castaway over there in England. Off in a foreign land with no one he felt he could count on. That had to have been awfully hard.

"Why are you being so nice to me, Charlotte?" He peered into her eyes and her nose burned hot. She rubbed the side of it and grabbed back the bottle.

"I'm not being nice," she quipped. "I'm just calling it as I see it."

His eyebrows arched as she drank from the wine, then he took another sip too. He lifted the bottle cap in his other hand. "Had enough?"

"Yeah, thanks." She sighed, feeling like something had just happened between them. A moment of shared truths.

She had a hunch Aidan didn't talk much about his family, especially about his dad, and she could see where he was conflicted about him. She remembered Aidan's parents from when they were kids. Both being British, they'd seemed a little distant, but they'd been friendly enough and had really seemed to get along with her mom and dad. She guessed all that sudden wealth had changed them. Or maybe she hadn't been able to judge things so well since she was just a child.

Aidan recapped the bottle and set it down on a floorboard beside the bench. The mood had grown quiet between them, and she yearned to bring back their lively banter, sweep those gloomy storm clouds from his soul.

"You should try that lobster roll," she urged.

"Great idea," he said, sharing a smile.

His smile was a little melancholy, like a part of him was still back in London. He'd really come a long way, managing a global corporation on his own.

It occurred to Charlotte for the first time that his journey might have been a lonely one. He'd mentioned his friend Tony, but that was different from having family who had your back. Charlotte had never taken that for granted. She knew how lucky she was.

Aidan unwrapped his lobster roll and took a bite. "Hmm. Good."

She did the same. Yeah, it was fresh and tasty. Very basic, made with mayo and a little lemon juice on a white roll. But the flavor of the lobster was to die for. Its firm and juicy texture too.

"Harry's serves the best," she said, referring to the shack's name. "They've been in business for years."

"Funny. Don't remember them. Then again, my folks weren't much into seafood. Yours?"

"Oh yeah, they're big on it. All of us are. Well." She took another bite of her lobster roll and chewed. "Except for Nell. She's a little squeamish when it comes to things from the sea."

He smiled. "To each their own, I suppose."

"Yeah."

"Aidan," she said, braving it. "I know we got off on the wrong foot with everything about the marriage of convenience, but I am sorry about judging you so harshly." She'd gotten so many things about him really, really wrong, and it shamed her to admit it.

He arched one eyebrow. "You sure you're not just buttering me up again just to burn me?"

"Aidan. No! Come on." She giggled and pressed her shoulder against his. "Gosh."

She could never do that to him now. Not after getting to know him better and seeing who he was: an actual kind and caring person. Someone with a history that had helped shape him. A history she'd never fully pondered until today. It made her want to learn more about him and open her heart just a little. Because, seriously. How could she not?

"Well, I'm sorry too," he said. "About pretty much everything. Whatever I did or said to offend you. There's probably more that I haven't thought of but—"

She smiled at him. "How about we call a truce? For real this time?"

He smiled too. "That should make us co-running the business go much more smoothly."

Oh, but she'd still so much rather run it on her own. That would be simpler than sharing and having to negotiate over every turn. She frowned in a playful manner. "You're not backing out of our bet?"

"Far from it." He picked up the bottle of wine and offered her some more. She accepted it and took a sip. "Let's just say, I'm *very* prepared for Fall Fest."

She viewed him curiously. "Are you?"

"I am." He drank from the wine. "Trudy helped."

"Well, if you must know," she said, squaring her shoulders. "I'm very prepared myself. Nell and Misty helped me."

"That's great. I'd expect nothing less." His eyes shone like he thought he had this in the bag. But, boy, was he wrong.

She doubted very seriously he'd considered selling coffee to non-coffee drinkers the way she planned to do to increase her cup-sale count. The gift packages had all come out gorgeous. She and her sisters had made twelve dozen kits! Besides that, whatever price he charged per cup of hot coffee, she intended to charge less. Charlotte Delaney would not be undersold. No sirree. Neither would Bearberry Brews.

They finished eating and sagged back against the bench.

"I'm sure you're going to give it your best," she said. "But I don't want you to be too disappointed if it doesn't go the way you think." He stared at her in the looming shadows, and she continued kindly, "I just want you to be prepared, that's all." If he didn't have his trust fund to rely on, Charlotte might feel bad about winning all of Bearberry Coffee out from under him. But he was a capable man, resilient, in some ways like she was. He'd bounce back no problem.

He wrapped an arm around her shoulders. "Are you prepared, Charlotte?" His voice went husky and tingles shot through her. "For the fact that you might lose?"

"Oh, but I won't."

He leaned closer and her cheeks warmed. "So you're the captain who goes down with her ship?"

"My ship is not"—her voice shook because his mouth was so close—"going down." But she was sinking so, so fast. Consumed by his sultry stare. It made her want to let go and give in—to one delirious moment of pleasure.

"Neither is mine," he rasped.

His lips brushed over hers and heat swamped

through her.

"Aidan," she groaned, but then he kissed her again—so gently it felt like a warm wisp of wind at first. But silky smooth and so tender. So different from his passionate ardor last night.

Heat pooled in her belly. It was impossible to say which she liked better. Both of his approaches took her breath away.

He cupped her chin in his hand and traced her cheek with his thumb. "Win or lose." He kissed her lips and then her nose, the side of her neck. Electricity crackled through her. "I want you to know." His breath combed through hers. "I'll still respect you on Sunday."

She breathed out the words, "I'm not going to lose."

"Neither am I."

Then her world went topsy-turvy and she fell into his kiss.

• • •

After a while, the temperature dropped so low that even their hot kisses weren't enough to ward off the chill.

"We should probably call it a day," Charlotte said. Her cheeks were warm and her lips tingled. What Aidan did to her.

He smiled. "Yeah, it's getting nippy out." Wind riffled the kite wedged beneath their bench, threatening to steal it away. He grabbed it.

"Nice save!" She gathered their trash and the near empty wine bottle. "Want to take this back to the B&B?" she asked about the Chianti.

"No, it's all right. Why don't you take it home with you?"

"All right." She never argued with free wine. He'd bought that, but she'd sprung for the lobster rolls.

They passed others on the pier strolling along and more folks near the eateries at the dock area. "Charlotte," he said. "This was nice." His gaze washed over her. "The whole day has been nice. Thanks for the kite and the apology."

"Thanks for apologizing, too."

"You see there," he teased. "We can get along when we want to."

They more than got along in her mind. They were developing feelings for each other. Which was dangerous and exciting, and totally messed with her head. She didn't know how she'd handle falling for Aidan. If she did, what would that mean about their future? She *did* plan to win that coffee contest and take over his company. So she'd be occasionally traveling to London. She guessed they could see each other then, but would that be enough?

They reached her stoop and he walked her up the brick steps to her front door.

"You should probably keep the kite," he said, handing it to her. "Not sure about bringing it on a plane."

Her heart twisted at his hint that he was leaving. But of course he was, one way or another. She knew that.

She sighed. "You're probably right."

"Just set it aside," he suggested.

"For?"

He leaned toward her and gave her a kiss. "Another time."

Her heart pounded because she hoped there would be another fun time like today. It was just hard to predict when that would happen with him leaving Majestic so soon, on Sunday.

"I'll take very good care of it," she promised.

"I'm sure you will." He gave her a sweet peck on the lips. "Night, Charlotte."

"Good night." She slid her key in her door feeling like she was on cloud nine.

Maybe things could work out with Aidan somehow. Not this week, but eventually. Assuming they kept up and continued to get along as well as they had today. She sighed and walked inside to her dimly lit living room. Outside the bay window, she watched Aidan walk away.

If only she had a crystal ball and could tell what the future might bring.

Lots would be resolved on Saturday. After that, she'd just have to brace herself for whatever might happen next.

But—for tonight—she could dream of a fairytale life with the Dread Pirate Aidan far away in a castle across the sea.

CHAPTER TWENTY-ONE

Charlotte woke up the next morning still floating on air.

Aidan Strong was impossible and maddening—and *dreamy*.

So what if he thought he'd win their coffee contest? He wouldn't, then they'd have to deal with the fallout. Aidan didn't seem like he'd be a sore loser. He'd assured her he had plenty to go back to in London, including substantial financial support. So he'd be okay.

But would her heart?

His kisses had been so swoony on the pier last night, and she'd be lying if she said she didn't have the best time flying a kite with him. If she'd met someone like him sooner maybe she would have won that bet against her sisters about finding a husband first. Ironically, it took the real Aidan to beat her imagined horrible reality of him. He was so not the guy she'd expected.

He was talented, and cool, and funny. And so much more.

Charlotte traipsed down the stairs in her PJs as morning light spilled in through the bay window. Things were already busy at the docks, as they always were bright and early, with the clanking and chugging of fishing boats unmooring and heading out to sea. She loved her house and loved Majestic.

Thank goodness she wasn't moving to London

full-time for the next five years. The thought of being there with Aidan took some of the sting out of it now, but no. That marriage of convenience was completely off the table. At Aidan's insistence.

But that was fine. She didn't need to marry the guy—pretend-wise or otherwise. That didn't mean she couldn't enjoy being with him for a few more days. Her stomach knotted when she realized that once he left they could be severing their relationship for good. Assuming she won their contest like she believed she would, she'd own all of Bearberry Coffee and be fully in charge. Maybe there'd be a transition period when she'd deal with him some.

Then after that? He'd be off on his way to begin a new life.

A new life without her, more than likely.

Charlotte passed the living room wastebasket on her way to the kitchen. Not much sat inside it besides some old magazine clippings and the pirate hat from Aidan. She felt bad now about throwing it away. She reached into the bin and pulled it out, shaking magazine clippings from its brim. It really was a cute gift and so unexpected.

She popped it onto her head, thinking of their fun day at the oyster festival. Aidan had almost kissed her there, and the day before during their first walk on the beach, before they'd run into that family Misty knew. Her gaze fell on the sofa and she flushed. When they'd finally kissed in here, it had been well worth the wait. His tender kisses last night were mind-blowingly sweet compared to last Sunday's hungry passion. She'd probably hang onto the memory of both times forever. Charlotte had kissed a lot of guys, but she'd never known anyone to kiss like Aidan.

She went into the kitchen and switched on her coffeemaker, wondering how she was going to face him. Would seeing him this morning be awkward after they'd essentially had a date? They were still in competition against each other and he was leaving in three days. Her chest grew tight when she got that she was going to miss him. Probably a lot more than she wanted to, and definitely more than she'd expected.

Charlotte brought her hands to her chest when her heart ached. Panic gripped her and she sat down in a kitchen chair. How had she put herself in this position? She couldn't—wouldn't—let herself be left behind. And Aidan would leave her when he left Majestic. And, if not then, eventually for sure. It was ludicrous to believe they could keep up a relationship. Part of her had known that from the start. She hadn't even realized she'd let down her guard and let Aidan in.

She got up and poured herself some coffee, taking a sip.

She needed to snap out of it.

This entire arrangement with Aidan was about bettering circumstances for her parents and their business. Not about Charlotte finding her forever one. The whole notion was ridiculous. She didn't even believe in that. She was so not the mushy type. That was definitely Nell. Misty was a sweetheart, too. But not Charlotte. She liked to think of herself as tough as nails most days.

Which was why being around Aidan unnerved

her. He brought out her softer side, and she didn't like to show that often to anyone other than family. The people who knew and loved her best understood what she was all about, but she'd never let any of the guys she'd dated close enough to tell she had a tender heart that could be easily hurt. No. That part she kept to herself.

She was glad things had worked out for her sisters. But her and Aidan? Not happening.

Didn't matter that they had similar personalities and certain things in common, like their love of eighties music and movies. It was their differences that really counted. His life was in England now and hers was here. Plus, he drove her totally nuts most of the time. Except for when he took her in his arms and made her crazy with desire.

Oops. Not helping.

Even if Aidan desired her, he didn't want to become her boyfriend. When he arrived in Majestic, he'd made it very clear that he wasn't looking to get serious with anyone in the foreseeable future. And, since then, he hadn't said anything to indicate he'd changed his mind.

Which was stellar. She felt the same way.

She took another sip of coffee, deciding to text her sisters. She needed to stop thinking about Aidan and focus on winning that contest for the sake of her family and Bearberry Brews. She was practically ready and only had a few more things to get in order. Some of what she needed to do could be accomplished virtually. She had an interview with Darcy and Allison this afternoon, but there was no reason she couldn't work remotely this morning.

She pulled up the group chat with her sisters on her phone.

Charlotte: *Working from home this morning.*

Charlotte: *Be in after lunch.*

Misty: *What? Did something happen?*

Nell: *Honey, are you okay?*

She blew out a breath and replied.

Charlotte: *Yeah. Fine.*

Charlotte: *Just things to get done without distraction.*

Ten minutes later, Misty and Nell arrived on her doorstep.

Charlotte still hadn't gotten dressed.

"So. What's going on?" Nell asked, barreling through the door.

Misty was right behind her. "Wait! Is he here?"

Charlotte backed up and let them in. "Who?"

"Aidan," Misty whispered. She glanced at the stairs and Charlotte shook her head.

"Of course not."

Nell tugged on the brim of Charlotte's pirate hat. "That's cute. That from him?"

"Um, yeah. We got it at the festival."

Misty's eyes sparkled. "We heard that things are heating up between the two of you."

Nell chuckled, explaining, "Mary Beth came into the shop to pick up a coffee and drop off some gossip. Said something about you and Aidan being all coupley and flying a kite?"

Charlotte crossed her arms. "Yeah, well. So? You guys told me to apologize."

"What does that have to do with anything?" Misty yawned and covered her mouth.

Nell stared down the mug Charlotte held in her hand.

"Oh sure, sure," Charlotte said, getting the hint. "You all want coffee?"

"Yes, we want coffee," Nell said. "We also want the truth."

"Wait." Charlotte glanced over her shoulder as they followed her into the kitchen. "What about the café? Who's manning it? Why aren't the two of you there?"

"Lucas and Sean are handling things for now," Misty said.

Nell nodded. "We told them we had to run out for a minute and would be right back."

Charlotte's face heated. "I hope you didn't mention me."

Misty winced. "I might have whispered to Lucas that we were headed here to check on you, but don't worry. It's not like he's going to tell anyone."

"Was Aidan in yet?"

"No," Nell said. "Is that what you're avoiding?" Her eyebrows arched. "Seeing him?"

Misty shot Nell a look and squealed. "It's got to be. A lot more's happened than she's letting on."

"Eeep!" Nell whispered excitedly to Misty, although she *had to know* Charlotte was standing right there. "Do you think she'll spill?"

Charlotte avoided their eyes while pouring their coffees. "I'm not withholding anything, okay?" She handed them each a mug and they all sat at her table. "I've just been spending a lot of time around Aidan and thought it might be good to take a break so I could focus on wrapping up my plans for Fall Fest."

Misty leaned toward her. "Then is what Mary Beth said true? She claimed you and Aidan were acting like you were together."

Charlotte rolled her eyes. "Acting is the operative word. I was only helping Aidan because Mary Beth was making a play for him."

"Hmm." Nell set her chin. "After seeing them together at Mariner's, I'd believe that."

Negative emotion seethed through her. It felt a whole lot like jealousy. But Charlotte wasn't the jealous type. She hadn't liked the way Mary Beth had thrown herself all over Aidan at Mariner's, though. And she'd clearly tried to contact him afterward to meet back up.

"But he's not interested in her?" Misty asked. She tightened her ponytail band and grinned. "Because—"

Nell grinned, too. "He's interested in Charlotte!"

"No," Charlotte said. "It's not like that."

"Then why is your nose all red?" Misty said in teasing tones.

Nell giggled. "So it's mutual? You like him too?"

Charlotte sighed. "Okay. I like him. Who wouldn't? He's hot and smart, has a decent sense of humor."

"Look at her," Nell said to Misty. "She's smitten."

Charlotte rubbed her too-hot nose. "No. I'm. Not."

"Then why aren't you coming in this morning?" Misty asked her.

"Because." Charlotte cleared her throat. "I needed my—space."

"Did he crowd you?" Nell's hazel eyes sparkled.

Misty giggled. "In a good way?"

"*No*. We were out on the pier. In a public place! Okay?"

"Doing what?" Nell asked.

"Eating lobster rolls and drinking wine."

"Aww," Misty said. "That's sweet."

Nell clicked her tongue. "Sounds like a date to me."

"Well, it wasn't a date." Charlotte set down her coffee mug. How did her sisters always figure her out? "Okay, so maybe it was?" She hurried to add, "But it's not like we planned it. The whole day just kind of happened!"

"Sure," Misty said. "And that kite, what, fell out of the sky?"

"All right." Charlotte sighed. It was good to unburden her soul, and Nell and Misty were her best friends. "I did buy the kite as a gesture. We'd seen a dad and his kid flying a kite at the oyster festival and talked about how we used to do that when we were little."

"Oh yeah," Misty said. "I always got stuck untangling the knots in everybody's strings."

Nell smirked. "That's because you were good at it." She sipped from her coffee then asked Charlotte, "So you bought the kite and then what? Asked him to go fly it with you?"

"Sort of." Charlotte lifted a shoulder. "He wanted me to apologize first."

Nell hooted. "So *that's* what that was all about!"

Misty laughed as well. "We thought we heard you yelling *sorry*."

Charlotte buried her face in her hands. "Did any

customers hear me too?"

"Um." Nell bit her lip and glanced at Misty. "Only a few."

"But don't worry," Misty said. "They were our regulars." Meaning they were used to quirky stuff happening at the café.

"So," Nell said in a singsong voice. "How did the kite flying go?"

Charlotte's skin warmed. "Pretty wonderfully."

Misty grinned. "Really? Whoa."

"And after?" Nell prodded.

Charlotte whimpered. "Oh guys, I don't know what to do. I'm so confused about everything."

There was really only one way to become unconfused and Charlotte knew it. By sealing off her heart. Just like she'd done with all the other guys she'd dated before. She didn't know how she'd let Aidan pry it open, but he'd sneakily gotten in there somehow. At least a little part of the way. That didn't mean she couldn't shove him right back out again, though.

Nell placed a hand on Charlotte's arm as it rested on the table. "But you like him, yeah?" Her eyes twinkled. "A lot?"

Charlotte bit her lip. "Unfortunately." Her shoulders sagged under the weight of the truth. "I do." But at least it wasn't too late to stop it and rein herself in.

Misty sat up straighter. "Well, there's nothing unfortunate about that. This sounds like good news!"

"Yes," Nell said. Her face lit up. "Maybe you and Aidan will—"

"No," Charlotte cut in, because there was no way. No way she'd open her heart fully to Aidan just to let him break it. She was not as tough as everyone thought.

Misty finished the thought anyway. "Get together! Cool!" She frowned. "Except for the part about your coffee competition and that you might win his whole business."

Nell frowned too. "Yeah. Things could get awkward after that."

Misty met her eyes. "What are you going to do?"

"Honestly," Charlotte said. "I'm not sure."

"Well," Nell said, trying to put a good spin on it. "You've been involved with other guys before."

"Loads of guys," Misty said.

"Righto." Nell smiled warmly. "And that's never stopped you from bouncing back."

No, but those times had been a lot easier, since Charlotte hadn't been invested. She didn't think she was invested with Aidan, either. But it did kind of feel like she was standing in quicksand. In a very precarious position where things could change at any minute. Which was why she was working from home this morning, rather than going in to face the music. She needed some time to strengthen her resolve. And probably a whole pot of coffee.

"Charlotte?" Misty said softly. "Are you all right?"

Charlotte nodded. "Things will get sorted, one way or another."

Nell leaned toward her with a hug. "We love you, hon."

Misty hugged her from the other side. "Yeah.

Whatever you need."

She knew that and she was grateful, but she didn't believe either of her sisters could pull a rabbit out of a hat and make everything work out beautifully. Things were bound to get messy with Aidan. She should have guessed that from the start and protected her heart instead of caving in to his super-hot kisses and heart-melting grin.

Nell checked the clock over the stove. "We'd better get back." She shot Misty a glance.

"Yeah," Misty said. "So then, we'll see you later?"

They all stood and Charlotte walked them to the door. "I'll be in around two."

Nell gave her a tender smile. "Things will all work out as they should. You'll see."

• • •

By the time two p.m. came, Charlotte had become so engrossed in her work, she'd nearly forgotten all about Aidan. She wrote up a new "flash sale" edition of the "Bearberry News" newsletter that would go out first thing tomorrow morning. She mentioned media coverage of the coffee contest, urging customers to come out and support their local business while bringing along family and friends. She included pics of the cute gift packs she and her sisters had put together, saying those would be available too and had a long shelf life so could make great holiday gifts.

She planned to use the interviews with Allison and Darcy as additional promo opportunities and had dressed well in a pretty top and skirt for the occasion, in the event they took photos, and she guessed they would. She stroked her power crystal, centering her energy and feeling more balanced and in control. This was great! Things would be awesome, and she was going to win this contest.

She'd begun her short walk to the café when an annoying buzzing noise met her ears. It sounded like a low-flying airplane. She stared directly overhead at a cloudy gray sky. It was predicted to rain today and tomorrow, but would thankfully clear up by Saturday, the day of the fair. The noise overhead continued and she searched the coastal section of the town fronting the beach with its towering cliffs.

Wait. That was one of those advertising airplanes.

It sailed through the overcast sky at the point where the beach met the ocean, dragging a fluttering banner behind it. No way. But, yeah, he had! Argh. Aidan had created a brilliant eye-catching advertisement, flying high above Majestic for all to see. This far surpassed her billboard and tacked-up flyers on lampposts around town. How had he even thought of it?

And, naturally, it had cost money. Probably a lot more than Bearberry Brews could afford. She stomped back around and headed for her dilapidated brick staircase. Dodgy, right. The one who'd been "dodgy" here was Aidan with this sly advertising maneuver. She'd make a few phone calls and see if she couldn't get her own airplane advertising going too.

But, after several failed efforts and phone-call redirects, she realized it was too late. Fall Fest was the day after tomorrow and there was no way to book an aerial ad now. She growled and stared at the pirate hat on her kitchen table. Yeah, he was dangerous, all right. Dangerous and sneaky.

Charlotte drew in a deep breath and released it.

But there was no reason to panic. She had her coffee kits up her sleeve. She also planned to stay on top of Aidan's pricing at the fair and lower hers accordingly. So there. That was that. Things would be okay and she could handle this minor setback. It was only airplane advertising and not the end of the world.

She set her jaw.

Still, she conceded, it had been an amazing idea. She kicked herself for not thinking of it first.

CHAPTER TWENTY-TWO

Charlotte strode into the office at Bearberry Brews looking like hell on wheels. Very attractive hell on wheels in a nice skirt and blouse covered by a long cardigan sweater. She had on those kickin' cowgirl boots, too, which were obviously her favorites.

Aidan had grown fond of them too after nearly falling on top of Charlotte while trying to help her get them off. That had been a moment. And they'd had so many others. Last night at the pier, she'd been warm and tender, her willing mouth welcoming his. He'd even believed for a moment they might be developing feelings for each other.

A deep attraction, maybe even a hint of affection, based on mutual respect.

Right now, though, she looked like she wanted to bite him. He didn't know what had happened between their saying goodbye on her doorstep yesterday evening and today, but for the moment he was politely keeping his distance. And keeping his mouth shut about pretty much everything personal, unless she decided to broach the topic first.

"Charlotte," Aidan said with a hint of trepidation. "Morning."

Darcy stood and shook her hand. He'd left his trench coat unbuttoned but still had it on. "We've just finished up with Aidan here." He nodded at the stocky brunette with curly hair, who had a leopard print umbrella propped against her chair. "Allison and I got the full report on what he's got planned."

"Oh really?" Charlotte's eyebrows shot up. "Including sky-high advertising?" Her gaze bore into his. So there. She'd seen it. But she was bound to sooner or later. He couldn't tell if Charlotte was mad or envious of his brilliant scheme. Knowing her, it was likely the latter and that's what had her so wound up.

Allison tittered. "A very ingenious way to attract a crowd." She smiled at Charlotte. "Sounds like it's going to be a killer contest."

Charlotte set her chin. "Hmm. Yes. It will be neck and neck until the end. Totally worth your coverage."

"Anything to shine a light on local events," Darcy said.

"It's just a shame there's no love *brewing* between the two of you," Allison added, clearly proud of her play on words. "That would make this coffee contest even more intriguing."

"But like I told them, Charlotte." Aidan cleared his throat. "You and I are just colleagues and…" He hesitated on the word. "Friends."

Her cheeks held a faint blush, but she remained poised. "Exactly."

Just saying the word *friends* made him think of her in a different context. They'd gotten more than friendly on her sofa and at the pier. During their memorable walks on the beach, too. But she clearly wasn't letting on to Allison and Darcy. As far as they were concerned, the marriage of convenience had been called off and that was the end of it.

Aidan would never have wanted Charlotte like

that, under the false pretense of them faking their love for each other. Only on account of some prior business arrangement in order to help her family. She was head and shoulders above that demeaning situation and deserved more. Like a husband who cared for her because of her many great attributes. Her strength, her cunning, her intellect. Those characteristics only made her fierce beauty more brilliant.

Some guys might not have been able to take the heat of her razor-sharp wit or the scorching sensuality that ripped through her veins.

But he was not most men.

He wasn't overwhelmed by her intensity.

He was drawn to it.

Like a moth to a—mosquito zapper.

Ouch.

"So it's a friendly little competition then?" Darcy chortled. "Should be a very good show. I can't wait to see who wins. Our hometown hero, Bearberry Brews, or your corporate giant, Bearberry Coffee."

"I suppose it's a coin toss," he said, believing it wasn't. He had this contest sewn up.

Charlotte folded her arms and smiled at Aidan like she was ready for him to leave. "If you don't mind. Maybe we can have the office?"

"Of course."

Since Trudy was out and Charlotte hadn't been here, Darcy and Allison had positioned two of the folding chairs in front of Aidan's table to speak with him. He'd talked up his efforts, as well as Charlotte's, saying they'd each worked hard to prepare for this competition, and that both were determined to win.

He and Charlotte had agreed not to disclose the nature of the bet behind the contest or its very high stakes. That was between Aidan and Charlotte, and their two respective families. From earlier press reports, it was already public knowledge that Aidan had arrived here like a knight in shining armor prepared to give the Delaneys half of Bearberry Coffee with no strings attached. So nobody thought that element was under question at all.

He'd love to know what Charlotte was going to say to Allison and Darcy, but he suspected she didn't want him to be in on any information she shared. This story wouldn't hit print until Sunday morning, after the contest. Though online versions were likely to get posted by Darcy and Allison after the fair ended late Saturday afternoon.

Charlotte set her purse on her table and stared at the empty spot where her chair had been.

"Oh, sorry," Darcy said. "I moved that." He began to pick up his chair, but Aidan grabbed his own chair first, carrying it over to Charlotte.

"Here you go. You can have mine." He grinned at her and she grinned back, but her smile looked strained. Put on for present company. She wasn't the only one out of sorts from their interactions last night. His emotions had been thrown for a loop too.

On his way back to the Majestic B&B he'd walked right past the building two times! He'd been in such a daze, questioning what he'd done and why he'd done it. Charlotte was alluring, sure. And beautiful and a spitfire—who could very well burn him if he wasn't watchful. She'd already attempted to trick him once, so he knew he should be cautious around her. And yet, last night, it hadn't seemed like she was pretending at all. The most stunning thing was, neither was he.

Which honestly made for a big mess. She was out to win this contest, but he had every confidence he was going to beat her, then have to go back to London and partner with her day after day. And that might not be so bad if he didn't find himself helplessly falling for her. Against his better judgment and every ounce of willpower he tried to exert to fight it.

He set his chair down behind Charlotte's table and she sat in it without giving him a glance. "Thanks."

Then Allison and Darcy lugged their folding chairs over to position them facing her.

Aidan shoved his hands in his pockets. "Right." He clearly wasn't wanted here. Nor did he intend to stay. "I'm on my way."

He did feel like he needed to talk to Charlotte later, though. Alone.

There were certain things they needed to clear up before Fall Fest.

Like what on earth was going on between them.

Maybe she could shed some light, because this was the most unusual situation he'd ever been in. Trying not to fall for the woman you were supposed to be in a canceled arranged marriage with, who was also your family's former archenemy, and now your direct foe in a heated coffee contest. He couldn't even think all that through without his head pounding.

"I'll just be out there," he said, and walked through the door.

• • •

"Where's Trudy today?" Misty asked as she rang up Aidan's coffee order a few minutes later.

"She took the day off." Sean was working behind the counter, whipping up a tall hot beverage with foam. He passed the customer their coffee then spoke quietly to Nell. "Okay if I head out now?"

She checked the time on her phone then glanced around the café. They were experiencing their mid-afternoon lull. "I think that's fine," she said. "Did you talk to Lucas?"

"Yeah." Sean shrugged. "He said it was okay."

"Sean?" Aidan asked a few minutes later when Sean walked by the table where he'd sat. "Are you meeting someone?"

Sean appeared incredibly called out. "Um. Yeah. Maybe."

Aidan's eyebrows rose. "Someone from England maybe?"

"England?" Sean's face drew a total blank.

Or maybe not.

"Never mind," Aidan said. "Sorry."

Misty and Nell both shot him looks and shrugged. Trudy had been gone all day and Sean was just leaving. The only other guy he'd seen her flirting with was—

Hang on. Jordan? But wouldn't Jordan have let on to Grant, and then Grant to Nell?

He left his coffee cup on his table and walked up to the counter. No one was standing there at the moment and only a handful of customers occupied other tables and chairs in the cozy café.

"So, Nell?" he asked quietly. "About Grant?"

"Yeah?" She cocked her chin, and long curls

framed her face. "What about him?"

"Has he, you know, said anything lately about Jordan?"

"Jordan?" She pursed her lips then said, "No, I don't think so." She frowned. "Is something wrong?"

"Not wrong, no." He shrugged. "I've just been wondering what Trudy's been up to."

Nell giggled, seeming excited by the idea. "And you think it might concern Jordan?"

Aidan held up both hands. "Let's not go starting any rumors, because honestly I'm not sure. It's just a hunch."

"Hmm," she said, like she was thinking about it. Later, he saw her go and whisper something to Misty.

Misty gasped. "Oh wow. Maybe? They did really hit it off."

It seemed to take forever for Charlotte to finish her interview with Allison and Darcy. Especially since Aidan was working up the nerve to ask her out to dinner. If they were going to discuss their personal situation, they should do it properly, over a good meal with wine. The nicest restaurant in town was supposedly Mariner's. They had a fancy dining room upstairs above the bar with great views of the shoreline.

If she said yes, that would be a good sign that she was interested in an open and honest conversation. If she said no, though, he'd know at once that there was no reason for any of that. With a few short days left before their contest, she'd prefer to keep her mind strictly on business, and her mouth off of his.

Which was fine. No problem.

He checked the time on his phone. What was she

going on about to that blogger and reporter, anyway? Sharing state secrets? Normally, he wasn't anxious about asking a woman out. But this felt different. Like he was taking a huge risk somehow, simply by bringing it up.

He looked over his schedule for next week in London on his phone. Read through the day's headlines in all the major papers online. Checked in with the home office. Played a game of Sudoku. Got a second cup of coffee, and then a third, deciding he'd better stop.

He stared out the window at the sea. Noticed Misty spent a lot of time texting. Spied Nell knitting what looked like a pair of baby booties behind the counter.

Wait. What?

He decided Lucas acted a lot more serious at work than off the job. Grasped that Mr. and Mrs. Delaney actually did very little to run the shop beyond designing and roasting new varieties of coffee.

Finally, Allison and Darcy exited together through the café's front door, telling him goodbye and thanks again. He got up to stretch his legs and they were stiff from sitting for so long. Okay. He ran a hand through his hair. It was time to confront Charlotte.

He walked back to the office, passing Lucas and the Delaneys working in the kitchen. They'd produced mounds and mounds of twelve-ounce bags of coffee beans in heavenly-scented flavors and were in the process of loading up more. He gauged they'd been making extra for the fair. Tomorrow would be busy with coffee grinding and sorting supplies.

Trudy had secured already ground coffee from

their suppliers to skip that last-minute step. Although Bearberry Brews' coffee might taste fresher being newly ground, it would take a true coffee connoisseur to tell the difference.

That's what he was banking on: Fall Fest attendees being swayed by the bottom line. Why pay more for a cup of joe with a berry-something nuance when they could purchase a stable and reliable brand for a fraction of the price?

He and Trudy had piled a whole lot of stuff in that storeroom and it would all need to be gotten out and organized. He was grateful for Mr. and Mrs. Delaney's generosity in providing them with a ground zero from which to operate.

He entered the office where Charlotte was in the process of collapsing her folding table. She'd already closed a couple of the folding chairs and leaned them against the wall. He went to help her, clicking the table legs into their brackets. "Putting things away already?"

She checked the fading daylight outside the window. "Getting close to five o'clock. I've done all I've got to do here today."

"And tomorrow?"

"Tomorrow's all about organizing. My planning's all wrapped up. How about yours?"

"Done, too." He righted the table, picking it up by its side. "Where does this go?"

"Normally in the storeroom."

"Ah." But he knew there wasn't an inch of space left in there.

"We can just lean it against a wall in here for now," she said. "We'll be using both of these tables for our booths at the fair."

"Right." He helped her finish packing up, be-cause—basically—there was nothing else he could do today, either. Saturday was the day of their show-down, and both of them were pulling out all stops to win. It rattled him that he didn't have a precise plan for what would happen between the two of them afterward, because he always had a schedule and Trudy kept him on it.

The only thing was Trudy hadn't exactly been around lately, and she helped organize his profes-sional pursuits, not his personal conquests. Not that Charlotte Delaney was a conquest. He didn't think of her that way. Sometimes, though, he questioned whether that was how she thought of him. Maybe he was completely naive and yesterday she'd been play-ing him again. He had to find out about the kite flying and all the rest of it. Assure himself that she'd been on the level.

Otherwise he'd been the earth's biggest fool.

"Charlotte?"

"Yeah?" She stood up taller on her cowgirl boots to stare at him.

"About yesterday." She waited and he cleared his throat, suddenly feeling all of fourteen. "That was nice, is all."

Color warmed her cheeks. "I thought so, too."

"So you're not—mad? About the airplane ad?"

She sighed. "I'm only mad at myself." Her lips twitched. "For not thinking of it first."

"I told you I had plans," he teased, hoping to bring back their playful banter. It was much easier to be around her when they were verbally sparring than when an uncomfortable silence persisted between them.

"I know." She set a hand on her hip, looking saucy. "And I said I have them, too."

"Is that what you were discussing with Darcy and Allison all that time? Your strategy?"

She chuckled. "There's only so much I'm willing to give away. Even to them."

"So tonight?" He ran a hand through his hair, feeling dangerously exposed. Like he was opening himself up for big trouble, but Charlotte Delaney was the kind of trouble he wanted. "Are you free?"

"I might be." Her eyes sparkled. "Why?"

"I was thinking, well." He crossed his arms. "That it might be good for us to, um. Discuss things."

"Things?"

"Apart from Fall Fest."

Her nose went slightly pink. "I see."

Get on with it, man. Don't be a wuss.

He cleared his throat. "I've never been upstairs at Mariner's, have you?"

She hesitated before responding. "Their dining room is very nice."

His neck warmed because he wanted this so badly. Which put him at a disadvantage. He understood that. But he needed the chance to clear the air with Charlotte and tell her that—no matter where they went from here—their time together had meant something.

So, he pushed himself toward that cliff. "Want to go?"

CHAPTER TWENTY-THREE

When Charlotte arrived at Mariner's, Aidan was sitting at a table for two by a window with a view of the night sky and the darkened sea. The illuminated lighthouse at Lookout Point hugged its cliffside perch, and, beyond that, the dock area shimmered with twinkling lights. A fine mist cloaked the water as a heavy fog rolled in. Light rain pitter-pattered against the windowpanes, creating tiny streaks that looked like tears. She'd left her damp raincoat and closed umbrella in the coat room at the top of the stairs.

He stood to greet her. "Charlotte." His eyes sparkled. "You look nice."

At last. He'd said it.

"Thanks. So do you."

And she had made an effort tonight. Since Aidan was leaving in another couple of days—most likely forever—she wanted to leave him with a positive lasting impression. She'd tried on three different outfits, settling on a form-fitting red dress with a wide belt, and had broken out of her mold and slipped on spiky black heels. She'd worn her hair in a loose twist in the back with a few strands framing her face. The look was a little sexy, but this very much felt like a date.

Mariner's upstairs?

Definitely.

She didn't completely know what he wanted to

talk about, but she figured the conversation would touch on the shift in their personal relationship. Since she was still making sense of things herself, she wasn't looking forward to discussing it. Still, she understood it was the mature thing to do.

He held back her chair and she sat, admiring the same navy suit he'd had on when he'd arrived at the airport. It looked like he'd gotten it laundered and pressed. His crisp white button-down shirt too. He'd left that open at the collar and wore no tie.

Aidan looked like a dream in a sweater and jeans. All dressed up, though, he was a knockout. She'd love to see him in a tux. He'd kill it.

She scooted in her chair, and he joined her at the table.

A small LED candle flickered between them and a single rose stood in a bud vase.

"You weren't kidding," he said, glancing around. "This is a nice place." The other tables were filled by couples. A few held a pair of couples dining out together.

"Yeah." She smiled. "It's a little more upscale than the bar."

The noise from downstairs filtered up to them. Laughter and the clanking of dishes. The occasional clinking of mugs. That was mostly overcome by the instrumental jazz music piped in on the restaurant's speakers. Charlotte recognized a tune or two. It wasn't what she normally listened to, but she appreciated it as mood music for setting a particular ambiance.

A waiter appeared and filled their water glasses. "What are we drinking tonight?"

Aidan's eyebrows rose. "Your call," he said to Charlotte.

"I'd love some wine."

Aidan turned to their server. "Do you have a list?"

"Right there, below your menus on the table, sir."

"Ah." Aidan picked it up and studied it. "Thanks."

For an instant, Charlotte could almost believe they were a regular couple who'd been together for a while. Anyone seeing them here would think so. They fit together so seamlessly, like they'd done this a million times. But they hadn't, and the flirty friendship between them would be ending soon. Better to cool things off now before getting in any deeper.

Aidan looked up from the wine list. "Red or white?"

Normally, she liked to look after herself. But it was nice to be pampered once in a while. "Depends on what we're eating?"

"What's good?" he asked the waiter, who proceeded to list their specials. One item in particular, a Chateaubriand for two, caught her attention. It was a very tender beef roast served with house-made scalloped potatoes and a mushroom and shallot gravy. They offered a salad or roasted asparagus on the side.

"Okay," Charlotte murmured. "That sounds amazing."

Then the waiter named the price and she bit her lip.

"Get what you want," Aidan said. "This one's on me."

"No, Aidan. Really."

"Indulge me." He grinned and her pulse fluttered. He still had that effect on her, but she couldn't give in. She'd gotten a lot more clear-headed about things this morning.

"All right."

"We'll take the Chateaubriand," he told their server. They both decided on a salad, then Aidan asked, "So, what do you think, a red wine?"

She grinned. "Perfect."

When their waiter left, she said to Aidan, "You seriously should have let me split the tab." She couldn't resist teasing him. "I mean, after Saturday, you could be out of a job." Though she tried to make light of it, her gut twisted. He'd also be out of her life, more than likely, and that outcome was probably for the best.

"Or." He toasted her with her water glass. "We could be in business together."

"Ha-ha. We'll see." Her nerves skittered at the thought. She never should have spent so much of last night thinking about fairytale castles, dread pirates, and what ifs. None of her romantic relationships had ever lasted, so why would things with Aidan be different?

If he walked first, it would be devastating having to co-run the company with him afterward. And, if she left him, things would be awkward and uncomfortable between them to say the least. She'd never been the kind to buddy up with her exes and didn't imagine that changing in London. No.

What she imagined was running Bearberry Coffee entirely by herself.

The waiter returned with a wine bottle and

uncorked it once he'd displayed the label. He glanced from one to the other and Aidan motioned with his hand. "Charlotte? Will you do the honors?"

"Of course," she said, sampling the wine and granting it her approval.

The waiter filled both their glasses and left the bottle on the table.

"You're very good at posh manners," Aidan said when it was just the two of them.

"Shocking." She grinned. "So are you."

"They beat it into me in boarding school."

She tossed her cloth napkin at him and he caught it.

"You are such a big tease!"

He laughed and handed her napkin back to her. "Can be, but I wasn't joking this time."

"Seriously?" She took a sip of wine, savoring its hints of cherry and chocolate. And, oh yeah. Its crisp peppery finish.

"The headmistress used to line us boys up at the table and make us practice, practice, practice. Using the right fork, spoon, and so on."

She laughed. "We call that finishing school over here."

He smirked. "Well, anyway. It was all part of the package." He drank from his wineglass and studied her. "I remember your parents insisting on table manners."

"Yeah, but they were pretty basic. Don't chew with your mouth full, that kind of thing."

He laughed.

"We definitely didn't use multiple spoons in my house."

His eyebrows arched. "So. How did you learn?"

She thought of her adventures in Scotland and then of some of the different men she'd dated. A few of them had been wealthy and had taken her to fancy places, but she wasn't going to say anything about that to Aidan. Somehow that just felt wrong. "I picked things up. Around."

He frowned thoughtfully. "You come off as very worldly for being from Majestic."

She returned the volley. "I could say the same of you."

He grimaced. "Sorry. Didn't mean to insult your hometown."

"It's your hometown, too," she said. "Was, anyway."

"Yeah." He glanced out the window. "I'd almost forgotten so many things about it. A lot of it is the same." His gaze fell on her. "But then a lot of it isn't."

"Times change," she quipped. "People don't."

"And some people just get better." He stared at her so intently her heart thumped.

"Aidan." She licked her lips. "About the contest."

"Yes?"

"I just wanted to say that—whatever happens—I hope it will be all right. Between us, I mean." The last thing she wanted was Aidan holding a grudge against her for winning. She'd also want him to go on and lead a happy life. Her chin trembled when she realized that meant without her. But that was okay. Really fine. Just what she wanted.

His eyebrows rose. "Why wouldn't it be?"

"Some things are bound to change," she said.

He reached out and took her hand. "Maybe they'll change for the better," he said, "but not in the way you're expecting?"

It was hard to see how. She tried to pull her hand away, but he hung onto it. "Whatever happens, I don't want you to think that I'll regret this. Regret any of our time together. Not flying that kite with you on the beach, or eating lobster rolls on the pier, or going to that oyster festival." He locked on her gaze. "None of it, Charlotte. I mean it." He pursed his lips. "I hope you don't regret any of it, either."

"I don't," she answered honestly, even though her heart ached. She relaxed her hand in his grip, allowing herself to enjoy the warmth of his touch for a brief moment. It was a scary emotion, being open and vulnerable. No wonder she'd shied away from it before. Also, exactly why she should back off from it now. She couldn't let herself get duped into thinking they could make a romantic partnership work. Or a business one, either. Hopefully, they wouldn't have to.

"I understand you're going to do your best to win on Saturday," he said, "but it might also be good to prepare yourself for the possibility that you might not."

She tugged her hand away. "In that case, you should prepare yourself, too."

"What I'm prepared for is to divide the company fairly as I intended. I'm sure your lawyer told you the agreement is very equitable."

Her family's attorney had in fact said that. She'd also said if Charlotte could possibly get the "winner takes all" arrangement then she should go for it.

Splitting the assets would be one thing and probably make everyone more comfortable. But if she won everything, her parents would be set for life.

They could retire now and never have to work again. They were weary. She saw it in their faces. They put on a brave front but had already put in some very hard years running the café. It was time for them to take a break. Have fun for once, instead of worrying about keeping their coffee shop afloat while supplying their daughters with employment.

If Charlotte could give them that, it would be the biggest gift of all.

Complete financial freedom.

Plus, she'd buy Misty a car so she could get back and forth from Providence to Majestic, *and* make sure Nell and Grant had a small nest egg for that baby they were already talking about making as soon as they got married.

"And if you lose?" She leaned toward him. "And go back to London? What then?"

He drew in a breath and released it. "Answer me one thing. Why do you want to win this contest so badly? It can't only be about things you want to do for your family. And it can't only be about pride." His expression softened. "Is there nothing in there you want for yourself?"

"There's nothing I want—other than the chance to run a major corporation." Her nose burned hot because that felt like a lie. But it wasn't. She was good just the way she was. "I think I'll do a bang-up job of it, too."

"Look, Charlotte. We're talking in circles again about Fall Fest and are clearly at cross purposes.

You're convinced of one thing, and I'm certain of something else. I don't think we can resolve anything tonight. That's going to have to be settled on Saturday." He sighed. "If I lose, I'll honor the agreement we made."

He stared at her with a hint of wistfulness. "Then I suppose we'll see what happens from there. But, if you want to talk about it —" He reached for her hand, but she removed it from the table.

"I don't." She set her chin and blinked back the heat in her eyes. Her whole involvement with Aidan had been a mistake from the start. While she didn't regret spending time with him, she was sorry she hadn't guarded her emotions. There was no good way for things to end now. Her head was already a complicated mess, and it wasn't even Saturday yet.

She lifted her wineglass. "Here's to Fall Fest. May the best man or woman win."

He clinked her glass with his but worry masked his eyes. "Cheers."

Their waiter arrived with their salads and topped off their wine.

"This looks lovely," Aidan said, turning his attention to their food.

"Hmm. Delicious. So," she began, forcing bright tones. She was ready to talk about *anything but* Fall Fest and Aidan leaving for England afterward. "What's up with Trudy? Misty and Nell say you think she might be seeing someone?"

He seemed relieved to have a new topic of conversation as well. "She's definitely seeing someone." He chuckled. "I just can't say who. At first I thought it was Sean."

"But no?"

The waiter cleared their salad plates and returned with their entrees, which smelled fantastic. But her stomach had soured. The last thing she felt like doing was eating, but still, she made an effort to try. She thanked the waiter, who bowed and made himself scarce.

"Not so sure," Aidan said. "I asked Sean about it, but he seemed clueless."

Charlotte shrugged. "Misty says maybe Jordan?"

Aidan paused in cutting his meat, lifting his knife. "That would be my guess."

Charlotte was sure her beef was superbly prepared. Somehow, though, it tasted like shoe leather. "Jordan's going to be a pretty sad guy then," she said. "When Trudy leaves town."

"She might be a little heartbroken herself." He frowned. "But I hope not."

Charlotte frowned, too. "I hope things work out for her and whoever."

"I'll drink to that." Aidan picked up his wine. "Oh, by the way, I sent those pics of your collages to Tony."

"Oh yeah?"

He grinned. "He said they're fabulous. Exhibit-worthy."

Charlotte blushed. "I don't know about that."

"He was serious, though. He knows several gallery owners. Said if you're ever in London—" He pursed his lips. "Sorry. Didn't mean to bring England back up."

"It's okay," she said. "I'm flattered about Tony." She sipped from her wineglass, trying to imagine seeing her work hanging in a gallery somewhere. Then she envisioned being there with Aidan, and him looking so proud of her. The image shook her. That was a fantasy for certain. She put it immediately out of her head. "But I'm not sure I'm that good."

"Don't underestimate yourself, Charlotte. You're a very talented artist." He noticed she'd barely touched her meal. "How's your beef?"

"Really good," she said, forcing herself to take a bite.

She was okay. She'd be okay. She'd only had a weak moment last night, as people sometimes do when taking a mental leap into a reality that could never materialize. What mattered most was her family and all the amazing things she'd be able to do for them after she took over Bearberry Coffee.

"The dessert menu looks pretty good," he said, indicating the cart getting rolled by their table. It held all sorts of delicacies from tiramisu to crème brûlée and chocolate torte.

"Yum." She smiled. "Sure does." She decided to get over her self-pity party and try the pumpkin spice mousse pie with a graham cracker crust. He made a show of enjoying his dessert, too, and they both carried on pleasantly, ignoring the fact that this could be their last dinner together. Their last outing together. Depending on how everything worked out.

They grabbed their coats from the coat room and walked down the stairs. The crowded bar area hummed with conversation and laughter.

"Aidan!" Clive called from behind the bar. He made a motion by his ear like he was talking on his phone and Aidan nodded, waving good night.

"Are you going out with Clive then?" she asked as they stepped outdoors.

"Yeah," Aidan said. "He mentioned tomorrow evening. We're supposed to get in touch."

So that was that, then. Aidan had already made plans for tomorrow, so they wouldn't have another date night, which was absolutely for the best. Maybe she'd text Nell and Misty and they could do a girls' sleepover? They hadn't done that in forever, and right now would be a good time.

"That's great," she said. "Have fun catching up."

They paused on the sidewalk and the light rain grew heavier. Charlotte opened her umbrella, shielding them both. "Thanks for the dinner. It was really good."

"You're welcome." He tried to read her eyes like he could tell that something was wrong. Or maybe she was just projecting because she felt so rotten inside.

The rain came down harder, pelting the umbrella.

"I guess I'd better run!" she said above the noise.

"Yeah. Me too." He leaned toward her and gave her a kiss. One tender peck on the lips. "Good night, Charlotte," he said, and her heart broke just as surely as if he'd said goodbye.

He put up the hood on his raincoat and rounded the corner, heading for the B&B, while she hurried along toward the docks, tilting her umbrella against the heavy winds.

Wait. Was that Crystal's van?

She stared across the gloomy street and under a burnt-out streetlamp. It was the beat-up Volkswagen with big daisy stickers, all right. Impossible to miss. Two figures were inside it, apparently making out in the back seat, because the glass was all fogged up. Charlotte smiled and shook her head, grateful for a lighthearted moment. So Trudy *was* seeing someone. She was not about to knock on one of those van windows to determine who.

She started walking faster and the rain came down harder, creating puddles in the cobblestone street. By the time she reached her front door she was drenched, but she didn't care. What had started as a fairytale date had ended on such a down note, she almost wanted to cry.

But she wouldn't cry about Aidan.

Not now. Not ever.

Even when she did her best, she couldn't control every single thing in the universe. Whatever was meant to happen—after the festival—was going to happen, and she'd deal. In the meantime, she was going to summarily beat Aidan in that coffee competition.

She let herself into her townhouse and cranked up the music.

She'd change into her PJs and stay up all night being creative, if that's what it took to keep her mind off of other things. Like Sunday morning, and how she'd be feeling without Aidan.

CHAPTER TWENTY-FOUR

The next day there was chaos at Bearberry Brews. When Aidan and Trudy arrived first thing it appeared that half the objects in the storeroom had been deposited in the hallway and the kitchen. Packaged coffee cups and lids littered the top of Nell's desk in the office, too. It was hard to walk in there with all the clutter of coffee urns and decorations. There was a cute fall-themed banner saying "Bearberry Brews" and all sorts of ribbons and streamers. Balloons and packages of small twinkly lights as well.

Trudy gaped at Aidan. "Nobody said we had to dress up our booth."

He frowned. "A little late for that now."

"Maybe I can run out and—"

He latched onto her elbow before she could escape again. "It's fine." He met her eyes. "I need you right here."

She nodded, glancing around. "Where do we start?"

He noticed some Bearberry Coffee cups nested beneath a package of Bearberry Brews ones. "As a first step, sorting some of this stuff out."

In the background, he heard Charlotte grumbling, "Seriously, Sean? You just dumped everything together?"

"Hey, look-it," he said. "A cup's a cup, right? I grouped them."

Trudy sighed and set her hands on her hips.

Charlotte appeared in the doorway. "Sorry about the mega mess."

"Charlotte!" Misty called. "Could use your help out here!"

Charlotte blew out a breath. "On top of all this, we're swamped today."

He wondered if there were extra people in town because his airplane ad had drawn attention to the fair. "Increased business is good, yeah?"

Charlotte locked on his gaze, appearing flustered. Her hair had halfway fallen out of its ponytail band and her green apron was askew. "Normally, yeah. But today of all days!" She threw up her hands and laughed. "Sorry. Can you guys—?"

"Sure, sure," Aidan said. As long as he and Trudy were sorting through things it made sense to create two piles. He was happy to help Charlotte, who was clearly overwhelmed. He'd never seen her off-kilter. She'd even kept her cool during last night's difficult conversation. He was glad that he'd taken her to dinner and that he'd said what he had. Because he didn't regret a moment of the time he'd spent with Charlotte. He was beginning to worry he'd miss her, though, if the contest worked out the way she wanted.ed.

Charlotte had so many complicated layers, and he felt like he'd only scratched the surface. Neither of them had been able to talk about what might happen beyond tomorrow's contest. He supposed the contemplation of certain outcomes was too painful. Admittedly for him and—by the sorrow in her eyes when she'd said good night—probably also for her.

He'd agreed to meet Clive at the Dockside to-night. Lucas was joining them. He was glad about reconnecting with Clive, and Lucas was beginning to feel more and more like a friend. Going back to London was going to be harder than he'd originally thought when he'd first landed here over a week ago. Leaving Charlotte behind was going to be the hardest part of all. It was impossible to know what terms they'd be on at the time.

Up until recently, he'd believed with his whole heart that giving her half the business was beyond fair in making amends for the damage his dad had caused. But, after learning about her more personal goals for helping members of her family, he'd begun to think differently.

But it was game-on now and they were almost to the festival. Fall Fest was tomorrow and his objective was to win. He was still confident he would. Only now he didn't feel quite as happy about it.

Trudy had begun dragging urns across the room to make way for a big rolling cart. "How about if we stack some of the heavier stuff on this?" she said. "That way, we can more easily move it to the front door when we set up in the morning."

"Brilliant, Trudy! Is there a second cart?"

"I believe so, buried in the back of the store-room."

"Let's dig it out then. We can use one for our heavy stuff, and the other for theirs."

Mr. and Mrs. Delaney entered the office. "We want to help."

Lucas arrived next. "Me too. Put me to work!"

The hours flew by with them only taking a short

break for lunch. Charlotte and her sisters came back to pitch in when they could, and Lucas ducked out on occasion to check on the roaster.

There were also periods of shrill whining from the coffee grinder as berry-scented smells permeated the shop. It was one big operation, but somehow all of them worked in tandem, despite the fact that they'd be competing against each other in the morning.

Aidan and Charlotte had barely said two words to each other, but maybe that had been for the best. They'd cleared the air as much as they could last night. At this point, time was simply ticking down until their contest began and then ended, delivering their resolution.

Bearberry Brews had closed an hour ago, and they'd all hustled to shift their supplies out front. The shop would be closed entirely tomorrow since the whole street would be cordoned off for the festival. Aidan glanced around the café where its tables had been pushed aside to make way for the rolling carts and collapsible tables and other items ready to be hauled out the door. They had outdoor extension cords for the urns so they could brew the coffee at their tables, enticing customers with their delectable scents.

The Delaneys had armed themselves with gallon-size jugs of water so they could refill the urns without having to come into the shop. Once Trudy had spotted the cache of water jugs in the storeroom, she'd asked what they were about and had then procured a huge number of them for Bearberry Coffee too.

"Well," Lucas said. "I think we can call it a day!" Sweat beaded his forehead, and the rest of them were a mess too.

"Yes," Mr. Delaney said. "Great teamwork."

Mrs. Delaney smiled at the group. "Thanks, everyone!"

As they were leaving, Aidan passed Charlotte on the sidewalk.

"Charlotte."

She'd been walking with her sisters but stopped so they could walk ahead. "Yeah?"

She was tired and sweaty, but he'd never seen her looking more beautiful.

"Good luck tomorrow." He shifted on his feet. "That's all."

She wrinkled up her forehead like she was puzzling him out.

At last, she smiled. "Thanks, Aidan. You too."

Then she turned and walked away with her sisters, casting a lonely shadow across his soul. It felt like a part of him was walking away with her. But that was ridiculous. He and Charlotte weren't together. Likely never would be.

Lucas came out the door next. "So." He grinned. "See you in a few?"

Aidan forced a smile. "Yeah. Sounds good."

• • •

Charlotte, Misty, and Nell sat on their sleeping bags in Nell's living room with pillows propped behind their backs against the sofa. Nell was the only one of them with a house, so they'd decided to hold their sleepover party here. She and her sisters all wore comfy T-shirts and stretch pants.

Nell's cottage wasn't huge, but the living room was large enough to hold a decent amount of furniture, including their late grandmother's piano, which Nell had inherited. Nell was musical like Misty and played when the mood struck her. Charlotte had sung in an acapella group in college but had not done much with music since. Apart from singing along to her old vinyl records, which she still liked to do when no one was around to listen.

They'd been eating chicken parmigiana, enjoying the hearty meal and each other's company while watching a movie. It had been far too long since they'd had overnight girls' time like this, and it was always so fun. Nell had baked brownies and Misty'd brought some delicious-looking and smelling cinnamon rolls from Lucas's mom's bakery for breakfast.

They were halfway through a rom-com and sitting in birth order without meaning to, with Charlotte in the middle. It was weird how that sometimes happened without them planning it.

Nell paused the movie and stood. "Let me go grab us more wine." She reached for Misty's and Charlotte's empty plates. "Here, let me take those."

"You don't have to baby us, Nell," Misty said. But she passed Nell her empty dish anyway.

"I know." Nell smiled. "But I like being a mother."

Charlotte giggled. "So that's what all those baby booties are about."

Nell gasped. "What?"

"Come on, Nell!" Misty grinned from ear to ear.

"We've seen you sneakily knitting at work."

"Ooh, look at this." Charlotte rolled over past Nell's empty spot and grabbed something out of her knitting basket.

"Look, Misty! It's an itty-bitty sweater that looks like the matching ones Nell and Grant have!" She laid it against her chest, flattening it out. It really was adorable with teeny tiny buttons and everything. Then Charlotte yanked something else out of the basket. "And a matching baby hat!"

Nell's face glowed pink, showcasing her array of freckles. "Just planning for the future."

Charlotte and Misty goggled at her stomach and Nell looked down.

"Not that close of a future! Gee!"

Misty glanced at Nell's wineglass. "Right."

Charlotte just said, "Whew!"

"Will you two stop?" Nell rolled her eyes and scooted out of the room. "Don't talk about me! I'll be right back." When she was in the kitchen, she called, "Brownies, anyone?"

"Later!" Misty and Charlotte answered together.

Nell returned with the wine bottle.

"Your chicken parmigiana was delicious as always," she told Charlotte. "How in the world did you have time to make it?"

Charlotte shrugged and held out her glass so Nell could fill it. "Didn't. I pulled it from the freezer."

"I need to do that more," Nell said. "Learn to cook ahead."

Misty cackled. "You'll be cooking for a crowd judging by all that baby stuff you're knitting."

"Very funny, Misty." Nell took her seat on her

sleeping bag, getting comfortable. "What about you and Lucas? Have you talked about starting a family?"

"In the way distant future," Misty said. "I've got to get through school first, and he wants to launch his business, the new book café."

Charlotte frowned. Sean was supposed to be training up to fill in as manager for Lucas after Lucas left Bearberry Brews, but he didn't exactly seem to have his eye on the ball most days. "What do you guys think about Sean?"

"He's—okay," Nell said diplomatically. "Seems to try hard, when he's trying."

Misty clicked her tongue. "That's just the point. His heart doesn't seem to be in it."

"Maybe he still wants to be a star in Nashville?" Charlotte ventured.

"Well. I guess dreams can sometimes come true." Misty sighed because she used to date him, so she knew all about his dreams.

"Mine sure have," Nell said, flashing her engagement ring.

Misty settled back against her pillows with her wine and stared up at Charlotte. "What's going on with you and Aidan? Really?"

Charlotte took a sip of wine, trying to sound casual. "We went out to Mariner's."

Nell propped herself up on her elbows, taking care not to disturb the wine bottle she'd set on the floor beside her. "What? When?"

"Last night."

Nell's eyebrows arched. "And?"

"Pretty much nothing."

"Wait," Misty said. "The two of you didn't discuss it? This wild chemistry you've got with each other?"

"Wild what?"

"Seriously, Charlotte." Nell shook her head. "It's not like Misty and I don't have eyes."

"And ears!" Misty piped in.

Charlotte's nose felt hot. "Okay. So I do. I mean I have…arggh!" She folded her face in her hands. "I don't know."

"You told us yesterday that you thought you liked him," Misty said.

Nell nodded. "That the two of you had some sort of romantic lobster-roll-eating date out on the pier."

"And then he takes you to Mariner's." Misty tapped her chin. "It's all adding up." Her face brightened. "He's head over heels for you, Charlotte!"

Charlotte grimaced. "I'm…not so sure about that."

Nell flipped back her hair, pushing it past her shoulders. "Then why did he go to all that trouble, hmm?"

"I think he wanted to talk."

"Talk is cheap," Misty pointed out. "Mariner's is not."

"Not the restaurant part upstairs," Nell agreed. "That's true."

"So," Misty said. "What did you talk about? At Mariner's?"

As much as she loved them, it was uncomfortable admitting her feelings even to her sisters. So she latched onto other details. "We talked about Sean."

"What?" Nell looked totally perplexed. "Why him?"

"About him maybe being involved with Trudy."

Misty laughed. "Yeah. Aidan said something to us about that. But maybe it's not Sean. Maybe Jordan?"

Nell frowned. "It's weird he'd take you to a really fancy dinner just to discuss that."

"No. He mentioned my collages too."

This piqued their interest.

"What do you mean?" Nell asked.

"He's got a record producer friend in London who has gallery contacts, I guess. Aidan sent this friend a few pics of my work and this friend thought it was good." She squealed. "Maybe even museum worthy?"

"Wow! Charlotte!" Misty yelped. "That's fantastic!"

"Yeah, but." Charlotte bit her lip. "Like that's going to happen."

"Why won't it?" Nell asked.

Charlotte settled back against the sofa and bent up her knees, resting her wineglass on one of them. "That would involve me being in London and probably creating more work, and I think I'm going to have my hands full as it is."

"Running all of Bearberry Coffee." Nell clinked her glass.

"Yeah."

Misty smiled. "You're my hero, Charlotte."

"What? Me?"

"Yeah. You," Misty answered. "Look at you. So brave. You're never afraid of anything."

"She's right," Nell said. "You're the toughest one of the three of us. You must know that inside. That's why you were going to sacrifice yourself to Aidan."

"Not so much of a sacrifice now, is it!" Misty hooted, then a pall fell over the room when Charlotte's chin trembled. Her eyes grew hot and she wiped back a warm trickle on her cheek.

"Honey?" Nell asked softly. "What is it?"

"Sorry, Char." Misty looked like she wanted to weep herself. "I was just fooling around. I didn't mean—"

"It's okay." Charlotte sniffed. She'd told herself she wasn't going to do this. Cry over Aidan. And she wasn't starting now. She drew in deep calming breaths and stroked her power crystal. After a few minutes she opened her eyes, feeling less shaky. "I'm okay. Really."

Nell gave a pouty frown like her heart was breaking for her. "You've really come to care for him, huh?"

Charlotte nodded. "I know it's stupid."

"It. Is. *Not*. Stupid to have feelings," Misty told her. "We can't always help where those come from. Sometimes they just—surprise us. Yeah?"

"But you don't think," Nell tiptoed into it, peering at Charlotte, "he feels the same?"

"It's hard to say."

"Well then he's a doofus, isn't he?" Misty scowled.

Nell gave her the side-eye. "Misty's right, though, sweetie. If Aidan doesn't get what a prize you are, then it's his loss."

But she wasn't sure if that was it completely. Her gut told her that Aidan did value and care for her, maybe a whole lot more than he'd let on. But there

were circumstances standing between them that
might not get easily resolved. Charlotte stared at her
protective baby sister and then at her caring older
one, understanding they had her back and always
would. "Thanks, girls."

Nell touched her arm. "You still want to win that
contest, though?"

"You bet I do," Charlotte said.

"Then we're going to help you." Misty threw her
arm around Charlotte's shoulder, tugging her in for
a hug. "Okay?"

Nobody asked her anything else about Aidan, or
about what might happen after the fair. They got
that this was a sensitive subject and that she didn't
want to talk about it. Both had worried looks on
their faces, though, like they were wishing they could
figure out what to do or say to help her. But this
wasn't something that Misty or Nell could fix.
Charlotte was going to have to deal with it on her
own.

"All righty!" Nell said, lifting the remote. "Should
we go back to our movie?"

Misty held her wineglass high. "I think we
should!"

Nell restarted the film and Charlotte pretended
to laugh and cheer along with the others, but in her
heart, she was sobbing. They were watching *The
Princess Bride* and every time she saw Wesley as the
Dread Pirate Roberts, she thought of Aidan…and it
hurt.

When Nell brought out the brownies, she asked,
"So what do you say? Should we watch one more
or—"

"Definitely one more!" Charlotte said. "How about something newer?"

"What?" Misty teased. "I thought you were an eighties girl?"

"I am," she said. "But not so much in the mood tonight."

Neither of them read anything into that, and Charlotte was glad. She was also glad when they settled on a new chick flick on Netflix that none of them had seen before.

"Let's do it!" Charlotte said, holding her glass out for a refill.

"Uh, Charlotte," Nell said. "You do know we're getting up early? Very early?"

Yeah. But she wanted to sleep well tonight.

CHAPTER TWENTY-FIVE

Misty's phone alarm went off, blaring out trumpet music.

"What the heck?" Nell sat bolt upright.

Charlotte dragged a pillow over her face and moaned. Wait. She knew that tune. She peeked out into the sunlit room, staring at Misty, who grappled for her phone on the coffee table while still lying on her stomach in her sleeping bag.

"You're kidding me. Is that 'The Bare Necessities' from *The Jungle Book*?"

Misty finally found the button and turned it off. "Yeah," she said groggily. "It's our favorite song."

"What?" Nell blinked. "You and Lucas?"

Charlotte tugged the pillow back over her eyes. Why was the lighting in here so bright all of a sudden? "I don't even want to know."

Misty shoved her. "It's something special between us, okay? It's the first thing Lucas played for me on the trumpet."

"Hang on," Nell said. She was obviously more awake than the rest of them because she sounded perky and everything. "I didn't know Lucas played the trumpet."

"There's a lot you guys don't know about Lucas," Misty teased. "I don't tell you *everything*." Her sleeping bag rustled then she gasped. "Charlotte!" She yanked away the pillow. Cruel. Charlotte squinted at her as her head pounded. Misty held up her phone, looking all wild-eyed with her heavy eyeliner smeared. "Get up! We're late."

Nell checked her phone. "It's already seven o'clock? *Mist-y*, we told you to set your alarm for six!" She scrambled to her feet and Misty scooted out of her sleeping bag.

"Sorry." Misty grimaced. "Had a little wine."

She wasn't the only one. Charlotte moaned and held her temples. They throbbed.

Misty shot her a look then glanced at Nell. "Acetaminophen."

"Righto!" She scuttled into the kitchen and switched on her coffeemaker. She returned with meds for Charlotte and a glass of OJ.

Charlotte stared at the glass and grimaced.

"Just drink it," Nell said sternly.

Misty peered down at her leggings. "I was going to go home and change."

"Yeah," Charlotte said. "Me too."

"No time," Nell instructed. "We'll have to go straight to the café. Mom and Dad are probably already wondering where we are. Fall Fest starts at nine and we wanted to have our booth ready by eight thirty. We promised we'd be there at six thirty to start setting up."

"I didn't even bring a jacket," Charlotte complained. "I knew we'd be hanging out all cozy indoors."

Misty frowned. "Same."

"No worries." Nell grinned. "I've got plenty of sweaters." She observed Charlotte's and Misty's sluggish states. "Chop-chop, everyone, as Trudy would say! I'm betting Aidan and Trudy are already there."

This spurred Charlotte into action. She leaped to her feet and took the pills from Nell, slugging them down with the OJ. "Okay. Let me grab a quick shower." At least she'd brought her toothbrush...but no makeup.

"Use anything you want in the bathroom," Nell said.

"I keep eyeliner in my purse!" Misty called after her because she knew Nell didn't wear it.

Charlotte nodded and hurried away as Misty rolled up their sleeping bags and Nell carried empty wineglasses and brownie plates into the kitchen.

She could *not* lose this contest to Aidan.

She didn't plan to, either. Today she was going to sell beaucoup coffee from Bearberry Brews— Oh, the coffee cup kits! They'd kept them hidden here so Trudy and Aidan wouldn't stumble upon them at the café. She reached the bathroom and spun around, racing back to her sisters.

"The coffee—"

"On it!" Nell said, lugging a huge box of them out of the kitchen.

• • •

They got to Bearberry Brews twenty-five minutes later, which wasn't bad considering the drive. "You're almost an hour late," their mom said, tacking up the banner above their booth.

"Yeah, sorry!" Nell said, winded. "We had a little hold-up."

Their dad stood beside their mom, blowing up a red balloon, his cheeks all puffed out and nearly the same color. He nodded in greeting while Sean stepped past him, setting water jugs down on the sidewalk. Lucas's arms were loaded with bags of aromatic ground coffee.

Sean and Lucas had hoisted out their tent, setting it up to provide their tables with shade. They had two product display tables forming a U with the checkout table in back. One held three giant coffee urns. Two would brew regular berry-flavored coffees and one decaf. Cups and lids were to be stacked right there, along with napkin dispensers and other supplies. The opposite table, also perpendicular to the checkout one, was where Nell set down her first heavy box of coffee kits. Misty set hers down next, and then Charlotte did the same.

"Aren't these cute?" Their mom picked up a kit to examine it closely. "Ohh, and look, Bob," she said to her husband. "It comes with a mini scone!"

He finished tying off his balloon. "What a top-notch idea. Will those count as cup sales?"

"You bet they will!" Misty grinned, her ponytail bouncing behind her as she set another box of kits on the table.

Lucas leaned over and gave her a kiss. "Morning, sweetness."

She got all starry-eyed. "Hi."

So much for them not being coupley.

"Cute hat," he said, noticing it matched her sweater. "Is that one of Nell's?"

"Yeah." Misty gave him a lovesick grin, and Charlotte turned away because she seriously couldn't take it. With her luck, Grant would show up next so he and Nell could moon over each other. Yay that they were happy but ugh—this really wasn't the place or time.

She scanned the milling crowd, but she didn't spy Grant among the others. Vendors busied themselves organizing their wares. There were farm stands selling fall produce, jellies, pickles, and jams. Artists offering ceramics, framed prints, and hand-carved wooden items like bowls, cutting boards, and walking sticks.

Lucas's mom was there at the booth for the bakery she managed called Dolphin Donuts. Charlotte sent her a wave and she smiled and waved back. Her bakery's cinnamon rolls were legendary. She and her sisters had crammed some of them down for breakfast on their way here. Another person she didn't see around was Aidan.

"Where are Aidan and Trudy?" she asked her folks.

"Up there on the corner right at the start of the fair," her dad said. "They apparently got this idea that they could catch more business with people first coming in." His blue eyes twinkled. "But our regular customers will know where we are. Right here in front of our shop, where we are every year. At our little end of the street."

Charlotte's stomach tightened.

That had been a crafty move on Aidan's part.

But all he had was coffee. Not coffee kits.

Plus his booth was bound to look pretty basic compared to theirs.

Her mom handed her a box of lights. "Charlotte, we need to get busy, hon."

"Oh right! Sure. Sorry."

She unpacked the box and Nell took the other end of the string of lights. They draped it across the front of the tent, taping it up as they went to the underside of the small overhang with the heavy-duty tape Lucas handed them. "Is Grant around?"

"He'll be here," Nell said. "He and Jordan led an overnight summit climb last night. Some sort of sunrise adventure. They should be back by lunchtime, or shortly after."

Charlotte nodded and they finished their work. "I'll go grab another extension cord for the lights."

"Super." Nell smiled. "I'll start making coffee."

Misty commandeered the cash drawer, getting that all set up for the day. Though she normally ran the register at the café, today was Charlotte's turn to play cashier.

She didn't want Aidan trying to wheedle her win out from under her based on some technicality, saying that she—personally—hadn't sold the coffees.

The air hummed with excitement as people around them chatted and laughed, shouting orders to others assisting them. A cool breeze ripped off the ocean, fluttering their banner that read Bearberry Brews. It was very cute with acorns and pumpkins on it. Fall leaves too. And, of course, their stenciled logo showing a black bear up on its hind legs grabbing for low-hanging fruit on a mythical tree that grew both berries and coffee beans.

Charlotte did up another button on her sweater. The look wasn't bad. It just wasn't her. The fit was a bit bulky for her liking, but the piece was warm and beautifully made of blue, brown, and gold yarn. Nell was really talented and spent tons of time knitting. It was her number one hobby apart from playing Scrabble.

Scratch that. Spending time with Grant was now number one. Knitting and Scrabble tied for second place. Reading romance novels came in third.

Charlotte chuckled because she was so matchy-matchy with her sisters. Sort of like she'd been as a kid, when her mom had sometimes dressed the three of them alike. She and Misty and Nell had to look like triplets in their similar sweaters and hats. Since her hair was still damp from her nanosecond shower, she was grateful for the extra layers.

"Charlotte," Nell said. She had the lid off a coffee urn and ladled coffee grounds into its basket. "Can you grab those creamer carafes from the fridge in the kitchen?"

"Yeah." Charlotte peered down the street. Curiosity was killing her about what Aidan's booth looked like. Probably all plain with set-up tables and urns. Fairgoers would likely pass it by without giving it a second look. "Be back in a sec!"

"Wait," Misty said. She held a batch of bills in her hands. "Where are you going?"

"To check out the competition."

Charlotte strode toward the corner, weaving through groups of people working on their booths. Some were done out nicely, but none were as pretty as the one belonging to Bearberry Brews.

She stopped abruptly, staring at Aidan.

What in the world was all that psychedelic stuff in his booth?

And *what* was he doing?

Hanging love beads from his tent?

Trudy held an oblong lava lamp in her hands, turning it upside down and then right side up again, its gooey purple center bubbling up and down — waxing long and then growing bulbous. She wore white go-go boots and a short sleeveless shift with geometric patterns on it. The white cap on her head matched her knee-high boots.

"What is this, boss?" A flashing neon sign behind her said "groovy." The whole booth was an ode to the sixties with a peace sign flag draped from the checkout table. Smiley face and daisy decorations were everywhere, even pasted on the coffee urns. She hoped those weren't loaners. That tacky glue would never come off.

"Just put it on the table," he said, his eyes on his work.

He looked up and saw Charlotte. "Oh, hi, Charlotte." He smiled at her outfit. "Nice knits."

She walked right up to him and lifted his looped necklace in her fingers. It was made from lots of little plastic balls. "Where did you get this?"

He grinned. "Courtesy of Crystal."

Everything clicked. She dropped the necklace, goggling at her surroundings. This was too much. These decorations weren't fall-like. They were more like fallbacks. Or throwbacks really. Going back years and years.

"Morning, Charlotte!" Trudy said. She giggled and held up the lava lamp. "Ever seen one of these?"

"Um. Yeah." Okay. So they'd decorated. And gone supremely overboard. "Where did Crystal get all this stuff?"

"She said she had it in boxes," Aidan answered.

Trudy nodded. "This morning we were lamenting over breakfast about how we hadn't thought to doll up our booth, and Crystal said no problem, she had us covered."

Boy did she ever. The groovy sign cycled through an array of flashing rainbow colors. Charlotte's eyes bugged out. "Oh wow. Uh-huh. What a display!"

Aidan tied back a section of the dangling beads to give his tent an entering-a-den effect. "Eye-catching, isn't it?"

"It's certainly something."

Her heart pounded. This wild-looking booth was sure to draw attention, out of curiosity if nothing else. Then once people were here, they'd buy coffee. She craned her neck to try to peek behind Trudy. A whiteboard had been erected on the checkout table and 3D-looking letters spelled out: Friends and Family Discount 60%

Sixty? Ha-ha. For the 1960s. So cute and *not* funny.

She quickly did the math.

Sixty percent off was better than her two-for-one offer with the extra ten percent off coupon. Coffee normally sold for three dollars a cup at Fall Fest. So her two-for-one offer meant each cup was only a dollar fifty. With the ten percent coupon applied to the three dollars, the total price was two seventy or a dollar thirty-five per cup. Aidan's sixty percent discount topped that! Sixty percent off a three-dollar cup was a dollar eighty. So he was selling his at only a dollar twenty a cup—beating her out by fifteen cents a pop!

Her face burned hot.

She'd just have to lower her price then.

Two for one at two fifty! Which was two twenty-five with the ten percent off, or a dollar twelve per cup, give or take. She was sure customers would favor her parents' hometown brand over Aidan's bland corporate slush. Especially at that price. Plus, she had their coffee kits.

Hmm. She might think of lowering the price on those too. Trying two for one as well but at the three-dollar price point for the kits. Two fifty without the coupon for hot coffee. Forget the coupon! Everyone got the extra ten percent discount. That way she'd always be undercutting Aidan no matter what.

Yes. She had a plan.

"You wanted something?" His light brown gaze washed over her, and she summoned her reserves. She was not going to think about him being handsome, or nice, or interesting today.

No. Today was about one thing only.

Their coffee competition at Fall Fest.

"I just wanted to wish you luck, you and Trudy." He started to smile, but then she said, "You're going to need it."

She scurried back to her booth before he could devise some quick comeback.

She ran into Allison and Darcy on the way.

"We were just at your booth looking for you. Saw Nell and Misty." Allison smiled, surveying Charlotte's outfit. "Didn't get the memo about this being hat and sweater day." Allison wore a turtleneck and jeans so wasn't exactly decked out herself.

"Yes. Well." Charlotte grinned. "Solidarity."

"Your booth's coming along." Darcy nodded. "Very festive."

Allison held up her phone. "Snapped some pics but would love to catch you during the action."

"Sure. Stop by whenever you'd like." Charlotte decided to boast. "I expect I'll be too busy to chat." She shrugged. "But seeing as how we covered our bases yesterday."

"Right," Darcy said. "We're counting on that. Super huge crowds at your booth and Aidan's. We'll photo document the crowd and select the best pics to post with our pieces." He wore a digital camera on a long strap around his neck. It had an attached long lens. "We'll run your interview alongside Aidan's. So readers can see how you each predicted things would go."

"Versus the *actual* outcome." Allison leaned toward her. "It's very exciting with you both so sure of the win."

Charlotte tried not to roll her eyes. Maybe she should be grateful for another slow news day in Majestic. "How are you positioning this on your blog?" Since Allison mostly covered romance, this contest was out of her purview.

Allison tapped her chin. "You and Aidan were rumored to have a romance—once. Or at least a marriage of convenience planned. So, this is a what-ever-happens-next story. Showing that even when dreams fall apart, people can still be friends."

Charlotte frowned. "Marrying Aidan was never my dream."

"Maybe not," Darcy interceded. "But the entire town knows you were willing to do it."

Yeah, and she would never live that down. Apparently.

"And now you two can compete amicably," Allison said. "Like grown-ups!"

Charlotte's grin felt tight at the corners. "Sure."

Darcy flipped shut his small notebook with a spiral binder and tucked it in his coat pocket. He always wore that trench coat it seemed, even when the sky was clear. "Well. We're off to check on Aidan and see what he's up to with his booth."

"Not expecting much there," Allison said. "He told us yesterday he didn't know anything about decorations, so he hadn't been prepared for that."

Charlotte decided not to fill them in on Aidan's sixties booth. They'd see that for themselves soon enough. She realized she'd been gone a while and hurried back to her station.

Nell frowned. "The creamers?"

Charlotte slapped her forehead. "Be right back."

"Hurry," Misty said, arranging napkin dispensers. "It's almost time."

. . .

The fair started with a bang and folks lined up, hankering for their familiar brand.

"Ooh, two for one," one woman said. "What a deal!"

"That hippie fella's got sixty percent off," her husband told her. "Maybe we should go and take a look."

"My offer's better," Charlotte assured them. She shared the math and the woman grinned at her husband. "Look at her, Wilbur. She's a regular human calculator."

"I'll say." He grinned. "We'll take two for one then."

The woman's face brightened. "Oh! And two of your little kits. They're darling."

Charlotte accepted their money, making change. Then she handed them two cups. "Help yourself to the coffee and pick out any two kits you'd like. Need a bag?"

"No, thanks." The woman patted the canvas bag hanging from her shoulder. "We're good."

Things picked up even more as word of mouth spread about their coffee kits.

"Things are going really great," Misty whispered, walking past her. She'd brought more ground coffee out of the shop as they'd already gone through several bags. Sean arrived next with more jugs of water.

"Yeah." Nell grinned, returning with a rinsed-out urn. "I can't wait to see our numbers."

Charlotte nodded but she didn't have time to take inventory. Their booth was suddenly slammed. She spotted Allison and Darcy in the background. Allison snapped pics on her phone while Darcy used his digital camera.

"Oh, this is so exciting!" her mom crooned. "Look!" She pointed at Allison and Darcy. "We're making the news."

Such as it was. Charlotte decided not to burst her parents' happy bubble. They appeared ecstatic. Like floating on air.

"Yes, Grace." Her dad patted her mom's arm. "I told you our hometown people would turn out."

"I can't imagine if we win it." She clasped her hands together. "All of Bearberry Coffee. Wouldn't that be cool?"

Her dad put his arms around her mom's shoulders. "Really lovely, my love." He fondly kissed her cheek. "But shh. That's our little secret for now."

Nothing like pressure. As if Charlotte didn't put enough of it on herself. But her folks didn't mean it that way. They were just excited because victory loomed on the horizon. She was going to snatch that brass ring for her parents, and her whole family. She was in this to win.

Darcy shot her a thumbs-up while Allison stared at her phone. Well, that was sweet. Charlotte hadn't known Darcy had a favorite horse in this race. Maybe *The Seaside Daily* would grant her more favorable coverage in that case. Although Allison was bound to write a positive story, too, after Charlotte's win.

Nell came up to the checkout table beside her, standing with her back to the crowd. "When I'm done setting up this pot," she whispered, "I'll sneak down and check on Aidan."

"Great idea," Misty said, having overheard her. "I'll come with you."

They cagily avoided Darcy and Allison by walking behind several vendor booths. When they dashed back later, both had yanked off their hats.

"He's doing sixty-six percent off now!" Misty hissed quietly.

"What?" Charlotte's heart stopped. Then it started again. She processed another customer while doing the new math in her head. "That's basically a dollar a cup," she grumbled. "A dollar and two cents."

Someone in her line tapped another customer on the shoulder. "I hear the guy with the groovy sign has lowered his price to beat theirs."

"That's Bearberry Coffee, yeah? With the airplane ad? I saw that yesterday."

The woman nodded.

A group of people turned away and Charlotte panicked.

"Wait!" she shouted. "Don't go!"

Nell's forehead wrinkled when she frowned. "Can we go that low?"

"We'll have to," Charlotte said quietly. "But we're going to make the calculations easier on our customers." She grabbed the propped-up chalkboard near her cash drawer where they had their prices listed. She erased their previous pricing and wrote:

Fall Fest's Best!

$1.00 per cup

Nell gasped. "Coffee kits too?"

Charlotte nodded. "All of it."

"What if someone brings the discount coupon from the newsletter?" Misty asked her.

"Then we'll sell it to them for ninety cents." She glanced at Nell and Misty. "Go spread the word, girls, and maybe carry around a few of our coffee kits as demos."

Charlotte searched for Allison and Darcy to fill them in, but figured they were on the opposite end of the street, covering Aidan and his burgeoning line.

"I think there's a sandwich sign in the

storeroom," Misty said. "I can write up a promo on it real quick. Might help if I wore that around."

"Great idea," Charlotte said. "Go. Go. Just don't go anywhere near Aidan—or Trudy. But if you see Allison and Darcy, talk up our new price. Big time."

Nell's eyes blazed like she was on a mission. "Righto."

CHAPTER TWENTY-SIX

Aidan stared at Trudy as he rang up a customer. "She's doing what?"

"Selling these ingenious coffee kits," Trudy whispered. "And only for a dollar!" She produced one and set it on the table. He grabbed it, shoving it out of his customer's view. What was Trudy doing? Advertising for Charlotte?

"Thank you. Help yourself right over there." He smiled at his customer and stole a peek under the table at the cup he held. It was the most stunning little package he'd ever seen and included a melting chocolate coffee stirrer resembling an acorn.

"Where did you get this?" he quietly asked Trudy.

"I bought it off another customer leaving their booth. Paid double for it."

"Smart thinking." Smart thinking of Charlotte, too. So she was selling these in addition to hot coffees. And since the packages were essentially cups—of coffee. He set his chin.

He couldn't help but admire the move, as sly as it was.

"What about the hot coffee they're selling?" he asked Trudy. "How much?"

"Also a dollar." She removed her white cap and ran a hand through her wavy blond hair. "Buyers are flocking to them. Non-coffee drinkers too."

"Hmm, yeah. Sneaky of her."

"She's very good at this," Trudy said admiringly.

"She'll be an asset at Bearberry Coffee."

He had no doubt of that. "Okay then. We'll just have to lower our price even further."

"What?"

He grabbed the whiteboard and wiped it clean with a cloth. "Two for a Dollar," he said, writing that in.

"If you say so, boss."

The crowd thinned for a moment near the apple pie stand, and he spied Nell and Misty. Both still wore their complementary sweaters, but they'd removed their hats. Misty had some kind of sandwich sign hanging from her shoulders with words printed on the front and back. Nell carried coffee kit samples.

Trudy spotted them, too. "There's Nell and Misty!"

"Hmm. Yes. Working the crowd."

Allison and Darcy caught up with them and they shared what appeared to be exciting news because Allison and Darcy reacted favorably. But then they looked up.

An airplane buzzed overhead and a group of folks pointed to the sky.

Misty and Nell's eyes were glued to the heavens as well.

Trudy grinned. "It's our ad!"

A bright yellow biplane roared by, dragging a fluttering banner behind it, showing their company logo and their ad copy: We'll beat the best price at Fall Fest!

"Good." Aidan checked his watch. "It's about time. They were supposed to start this morning, not after one." But that was okay. The ad had been running for the past few days and was visible all over town, plus for a few miles beyond Majestic up and down the coast.

More people chattered and looked up at the sky, watching the plane drag its wavering banner behind it, following the shoreline.

The aerial ad seemed to work wonders. Before long, Aidan's booth swarmed with business again. Customers complimented him on the airplane promo, saying they might not have known about his great deal otherwise.

Darcy and Allison scuttled over, Darcy's trench coat flapping open like khaki-colored wings.

"Great going with that airplane ad." Allison winked at Aidan and he got a funny feeling. He didn't think that she was flirting exactly. Word was she was dating Darcy. Still. Her appraisal was a bit too admiring for his comfort.

"Thanks." He gave her a quick glance, speaking to his customer while returning her change. He really was very busy, and Darcy and Allison were getting in the way. Trudy scrambled to refill coffee urns with water and fresh grounds so he couldn't count on her to run interference.

Darcy grinned. "When you explained the airplane ad to us yesterday, I didn't quite have the vision. Seeing it in person, though. That's something else. Very sharp and appealing."

Allison's shimmering brown eyes matched her dark hair. She lifted her phone and snapped a pic of Aidan before taking another and another. She mashed her thumb down on the button, holding her phone every which way. Vertically, horizontally, angled slightly to one side.

Darcy nudged her and she stopped.

"Oh! Sorry! Just wanted to be sure to get a good shot."

Aidan greeted the next people in line. He recognized them as Sean's parents, owners of McIntyre's Market. They wore heavy fisherman's sweaters and had chubby cheeks and gray hair. "I'm a little surprised to see you, but thanks for your business."

Mr. McIntyre lowered his voice. "Just don't say a word to Sean now."

Mrs. McIntyre's eyes twinkled. "Your prices are just too good to beat."

"Love the decor, too," Mr. McIntyre declared. "It's far out!"

"Ha-ha, yeah." He took their payment, which was right on the money.

Darcy surveyed the growing line, surmising it wouldn't let up anytime soon. "Well, keep slogging away at it," he said. "We'll know the results by the end of the day."

Allison crossed her fingers. "We're pulling for you."

Darcy turned to her. "We're not supposed to take sides."

"I'm not," Allison said. "Totally impartial." Then when Darcy wasn't looking she winked at Aidan. She was really into this contest. Maybe her romance blog was flagging now that Misty's and Nell's stories had been told. There wasn't a lot of love breaking out in Majestic at the moment, apparently.

Allison had fished around for a story about him

and Charlotte. But they'd both blown her off, claiming to be friends. And they were friends—with kissing benefits. Although that had only happened a couple of times, those memories had been seared into his brain.

So had some others.

He could probably recall every conversation they'd had in detail. And he'd never forget the sheer joy on Charlotte's face when she'd been flying that kite. Aidan's heart throbbed dully. But when he'd tried to discuss their relationship at Mariner's, she'd been unwilling to talk about it. Maybe because she'd believed they wouldn't have much of a relationship for too much longer. She'd been that sure of her win and of taking over his company.

Trudy tsked when Allison and Darcy walked away. "She was certainly eyeing you up."

"Was not," he said. Although he had felt like meat at a butcher shop counter.

"I can't fault the women in Majestic for their taste," Trudy joked. "First Mary Beth. Now Allison."

"Stop."

She rolled her eyes. "Before her, Charlotte."

Aidan's face steamed. "Charlotte? No. What makes you say that?"

"I've seen you two, Aidan. At Bearberry Brews and around town. You think that sheet up in the office wasn't some kind of sexy hint?"

"Sexy? Uh. No."

"It was a sheet, boss. From a *bed*."

"With pumpkins and acorns all over it, yeah." Aidan cleared his throat. "Charlotte only put it there so she wouldn't have to look at me."

"And think about you." Trudy gave a knowing nod. "The girl has got it bad."

"She does not."

"Oh, I think she does." She met his eyes. "Charlotte fancies you."

As if.

But what if she did? For real?

Would they stand a chance?

Could they find a way?

The idea of them winding up together seemed so far off, abstract.

Unattainable.

But…what if it wasn't?

Doubt clawed at him, settling like a lead weight in his gut. He'd never really opened himself up to a woman before. Not completely. He wasn't even sure if he knew how. When he'd told Charlotte that boarding school had toughened him up, he'd meant it. He'd learned he didn't need anyone else's affection to get by, least of all his parents'.

Aidan was good at emotional distancing. That skill would come in handy with him and Charlotte co-running the company. He could work with her without falling for her. Trudy was wrong about Charlotte. Dead wrong. If she cared about him in that way, he'd have known it by now. She would have given him some sort of sign when he'd mentioned the future. Instead of wanting to discuss it, she'd basically pulled away.

He saw Grant stroll by and waved.

Grant waved back. Jordan was with him.

Trudy's eyes shone. "Maybe I should go check on Misty and Nell and see what Misty's got on that sandwich board of hers." Aidan suspected she was much more interested in checking on Jordan.

"Fine, but don't be gone long. I need you here."

She nodded, then Aidan said, "Can you check the urns before you go? Be sure they're topped off?"

A little while later, Darcy and Allison stopped by again, saying business was rocking at Bearberry Brews, and part of him wanted to be glad. Happy for Charlotte that things were working out for her and she was selling tons of coffee. As twisted as that seemed. He did feel bad about his father taking advantage of Mr. Delaney and wanted to fix things. But having Charlotte win the entire corporation wasn't the right answer.

His heart pounded.

Was it?

Trudy chit-chatted with the pair while she worked and Aidan decided to take a short break. He'd duck into Bearberry Brews to grab his lunch from the refrigerator there. Crystal had packed him and Trudy sandwiches, wishing them luck. She was new in town, so not very well acquainted with the Delaneys.

Mr. Mulroney was fond of the Delaney girls and at first wanted Charlotte to win the coffee contest. Once Aidan explained it would be a win-win either way for Charlotte, Mr. Mulroney had said something about it sounding like a healthy competition. He didn't see the harm in Crystal loaning them some of her hippie stuff.

Aidan made his way through the crowd, smiling down at kids who'd had their faces painted in animal motifs. One looked like a cat. Another a squirrel. A third had acorns and autumn leaves painted on her cheeks. Couples walked dogs and people carried brimming canvas bags full of purchases, some clutching fresh-cut bouquets of flowers.

Sunlight warmed the street between the rows of booths on either side, and a cool breeze lifted off the ocean as seagulls called above. People sipped from paper beverage cups, pausing to admire artwork and handmade wares. The scent of fresh-popped popcorn filled the air, along with the spicy aroma of hot apple cider and—as he drew closer—berry-flavored coffee.

The Delaneys' booth was jam-packed with the line backing up into the street. He stole a glimpse of Charlotte smiling at a customer. Her dark hair caught a wave of light, glistening in the sun. She was absolutely stunning. So beautiful and in her element.

Her parents stood beside her, and her dad had his arm around her mom. He leaned over and tenderly kissed her cheek. Lucas helped Misty remove her sandwich board when she returned for a break. Nell set her coffee kits on the table and leaped into Grant's open arms when he appeared.

It was a portrait of family.

His heart twisted.

The kind of family Aidan wished he had.

He stepped into the café and out of everyone's view.

Black-and-white photos of scenes around Majestic hung on its walls and shadows trailed across the floor with the interior lights turned off. Even with the furniture moved around and completely empty, it felt homey. It was a home, he realized. A home of sorts for the Delaneys.

He peered back out the front window at their crowded booth on the street. They shared a close bond. Charlotte and her sisters, and their parents. Soon Lucas and Grant would join their clan. Lucky blokes. He wondered about him and Charlotte. Would they ever have a chance?

He thought of her face when he'd seen her outside. She'd had that determined look in her eyes and had appeared so radiant. Glowing. It was her competitive spirit. Her drive. One of the things that he loved about her.

Warmth spread through his chest.

Loved?

He raked his hands through his hair.

Fine. He couldn't deny it any longer.

He was head over heels for the woman.

Gobsmacked by her brains and beauty.

How had this happened? *When* had it happened? When he'd tugged her into the waves on the beach? When he'd bought her that goofy pirate hat? When he'd kissed her on the pier? It was impossible to say. It had more or less snuck up on him. He rubbed the side of his neck. That dastardly little feeling.

Aidan frowned.

Now, what was he going to do with it? Especially if Charlotte didn't feel the same? Waves of conflicting emotions crashed through him, then peace flooded his veins.

Whether or not she returned his feelings, that was beside the point. The point was he needed to ensure he did right by everybody. Not just by Charlotte, but also by her family.

He knew exactly what Charlotte wanted because

she'd told him very clearly. She wanted to run 100 percent of Bearberry Coffee, and she wanted to run it without him. And maybe that was for the best. He'd only be in her way. Him with his unrequited feelings that would ultimately do her more harm than good. Who was he fooling to think he was nowhere like his dad? His lack of close relationships, excepting Tony and Jill, proved otherwise.

He couldn't give Charlotte the kind of love a woman like her deserved. Not the whole-hearted sort that Grant gushed toward Nell and Lucas showered on Misty. Part of him would always be holding back, because if Aidan let that part of himself go, he wouldn't know who he was anymore. Shielding that inner part of himself kept him strong, assertive. Able to remain in control. If he gave away the secret key to his heart, he'd crumble. Then he'd be of no use to anybody. Least of all himself.

He returned to his booth where Trudy had put everything in order.

"I brought you your lunch," he said, handing her a white paper bag.

"Excellent, thanks."

"Trudy?"

"Hmm?"

"Why don't you take a break for a while? I think Nell and Misty have knocked off for a bit anyway. I can handle things here."

"Are you sure?" If a face could register a happy dance, it was hers. "Splendid. Thanks!" She departed through the roaming crowd. "Won't be gone long!"

• • •

Two hours later, Aidan checked the sky. Afternoon clouds rolled in, partly blocking the sun. Waves crashed against the beach down below them. His booth had a clear view of those old stone steps. The ones he and Charlotte had taken to go on their walk that first day and then kite flying after that, the day Charlotte had issued her surprising apology.

He laughed out loud, finally getting it.

That's when he'd totally fallen for her. It was when he'd first seen the top of that pirate kite peeking over that sheet in the office. He'd known immediately what she was up to but had decided to antagonize her. Make her draw out her apology. She'd been adorably perturbed with him then, like she had so many times before.

He shook his head.

She was without a doubt the most remarkably interesting woman he'd ever met. She was also fiercely loyal and loved her family. There was a lot to admire in that. There was a lot to admire about her. She was fun, and sexy, and smart, and free-spirited. Gifted in so many ways.

Aidan smiled at a customer who had a question.

"Your airplane ad says you've got the best coffee price, yeah?"

"That's right."

"Well, Bearberry Brews is down to fifty cents a cup now. So." He shrugged. "Can you beat that?"

Aidan pursed his lips. There was one way to beat that for sure. A way to give Charlotte her heart's desire and guarantee she won this contest. Certainty coursed through him. He was a wealthy guy. He didn't need Bearberry Coffee. But the Delaneys?

Yeah, maybe they did. Then Mr. and Mrs. Delaney could retire, finally get to tour Ireland. And Charlotte could get Misty that car. Something nice for the baby Grant and Nell would have coming someday, too.

His heart beat harder when he knew what he should do.

It was really so simple and the second set of paperwork had been prepared. He could help with the transition and then, if Charlotte wanted him to bow out, he would. In fact, that would probably be better. He could give the Delaneys what his dad should have given them twenty years ago. He wanted her to be happy. He wanted all of them to be happy. The Delaneys had been through enough. It was time for the tables to turn.

"I believe I can beat that," Aidan told the guy, who'd been patiently waiting for his reply. He picked up the whiteboard and erased the price, inserting a new message:

Free to a good home.

Let the sunshine in!

The customer's jaw dropped. "You're serious? No charge?"

Aidan handed over a coffee cup. "Help yourself."

It didn't take long for Aidan to deplete his entire inventory.

Trudy still hadn't returned, and he needed to talk to her about getting arrangements in order. Maybe she could stay behind a day or two to help execute the paperwork. For his part, he felt like going home. But first, he wanted to speak with Charlotte—one last time.

He closed up his cashbox and carried it with him, searching for Trudy in the crowd.

There was one of those photo booths up ahead. The kind you put coins into and that produced a roll of black-and-white pictures. You sat on a stool behind a closed curtain while the camera snapped shots. For the life of him, those looked like Trudy's white go-go boots under the curtain. Another pair of legs in jeans was also there.

He strode up to the photo booth and stopped.

He couldn't very well intrude.

The curtain flew open, and Trudy was sitting on Jordan's lap.

She held a printed reel of photos, and she and Jordan were kissing in all of them.

"Hi, boss!"

Her face was bright red and Jordan seemed embarrassed too. He shifted Trudy to her feet and off his lap. "Uh. Hey, Aidan." He and Trudy exited the photo booth and a group of teenage girls clamored inside, giggling as they went.

Aidan shoved his hands in his pockets, feeling awkward too. What Trudy did was her business, but now he knew who she'd been doing it with all this time. Proof positive.

"I—was just looking for you."

She spotted his cashbox. "What's happening? Why aren't you manning the booth?"

He grinned. "We're all sold out."

"Sold out?" Her jaw dropped. "How?"

"You got a minute?"

She glanced at Jordan. "Sure."

A diamond sparkled on her left hand. It was really huge and glittery.

Whoa. Her and Jordan…engaged?

She grinned and flashed her ring. "It's true. And new!"

Jordan placed an arm around her. "And official."

"But when? How?"

"He's been teaching me all about America." Trudy beamed. "And I love it. And"—she shot Jordan a dreamy gaze—"I love him."

"Wow, okay." Aidan shifted on his feet. "That happened fast."

Jordan shrugged happily. "When you know, you know."

"So, Trudy?"

Her eyebrows arched.

"You're planning to—"

"Move here! That's right," she said. "Just as soon as I can manage, and we've made the transition to you hiring a new assistant in London. Of course, if you'd still like me working over here, I'd be more than glad to accommodate. Maybe I can help out the Delaneys and Charlotte?"

Actually. That was an excellent plan.

Darcy and Allison appeared with cameras ready.

"I hear an engagement's in the offing?" Allison said with a big grin. She was obviously really glad to finally be covering a romantic story. And this one was juicy. Insta-love between strangers from different continents across the Atlantic.

"It is," Jordan said. "We're planning to announce it in *The Seaside Daily* soon."

Allison grinned. "Talk about making my day."

"Yeah," Darcy concurred. "What a fun local scoop."

While they were busy talking, Aidan slipped away.

. . .

Business couldn't have been better at Charlotte's booth. They'd sold gobs and gobs of coffee. Coffee kits too. Sean had to keep racing back into the storeroom to grab more cups, and Misty and Nell kept up with the urns.

"Looks like you just sold your last coffee kit," Lucas said.

Charlotte stared at the table, seeing it was true. Wow! They were cleaned out.

Misty'd snuck down to check on Aidan, but no way could he be doing this well. Cutting their price to fifty cents a cup had been a genius move. She'd no longer turn a profit, but that wasn't her main goal. Winning this contest was, while not going into the red financially. Nell sat behind her, running some numbers on her spreadsheet. "Charlotte," she said. "This is amazing. We're still in the black, but barely."

That was great because she didn't want to cause her parents' struggling business to fall into a further deficit. Once she took over Bearberry Coffee as a whole, she'd set everything right. Pay off their bank loan *and* their house. Her body buzzed with energy. She could feel it. She was going to win this. Then Aidan— No. She refused to think about him. She'd deal with those emotions after the fair. And after they'd executed their agreement.

Her emotions were so murky, anyway, they were hard to sort out. Yes, she was drawn to him. Attracted. Okay. Highly attracted. But other things came first before her personal happiness. Like her parents' peace of mind for the rest of their days. Aidan also left her feeling scared and vulnerable, putting her in a position of weakness, and Charlotte did not like appearing weak in the least. Feeling weak was even worse. She needed to stay strong and at the top of her game if she was going to run Bearberry Coffee.

Misty came scuttling back toward her, her face pale, like she'd witnessed a train wreck. Charlotte's heart clenched.

"Charlotte, I'm sorry." Her eyes grew huge and weepy. "He's completely sold out."

Her head spun. "What?" She checked the time on her phone. But the fair wasn't even over yet. It was just after four o'clock and Fall Fest went until five.

Misty's chin trembled. "He and Trudy are gone, but their booth is still there. There were no cups on the table. Nada. I checked the urns, but they were unplugged and empty. The cashbox is missing too."

Charlotte's mind whirled. He *sold out*? Won the contest? How? By charging twenty-five cents a cup? Ten? Heat burned in her eyes.

Aidan had to have tricked her somehow. Pulled something underhanded. But no. That didn't sound right. She gripped her power crystal necklace. She hadn't lost everything. She still had fifty percent of Bearberry Coffee. But then all this work had been for nothing.

Her stomach flip-flopped.

She'd wanted this so badly for her family.

Charlotte glanced at her parents, who were laughing and chatting with Lucas and Grant, and her heart ached at the thought of disappointing them. Sean talked on his cell phone a distance away from the group. He grinned to beat all get-out and fist-pumped in the air. At least someone had gotten good news today.

Misty touched her arm. "Charlotte?"

More customers had lined up to pay, but she couldn't do this. She had to find Aidan. She stood and her legs wobbled. "I, uh, need a minute, okay?"

"Sure, sure." Misty slid into her chair and picked up cashiering in an instant. "That will be one fifty," she said to the lady who'd bought three coffees for herself and her friends. "Thanks! Have a great day!"

Charlotte walked off in a daze and Nell hurried to catch up with her. "Sweetie? Are you all right?"

"I am." Charlotte set her jaw. "I just don't understand it. We seemed to be outselling him an hour ago. Hand over fist."

Nell looked deeply into her eyes. "Listen to me. It's going to be fine. Fifty percent is better than nothing, and nothing is what we had before. Best part?" Her eyebrows arched. "Now, nobody has to marry Aidan."

Charlotte's heart twisted. "Right." She would have to work with him, though, and that could prove awkward. Given how she'd been feeling these past few days. Like she was teetering on the edge of falling in love with the guy. But that was before she'd been kicked in the gut.

She wouldn't rest until she learned how he'd beat her. Was it that airplane ad? Some super-low price he'd offered? What? Charlotte weaved through the crowd, which was thinning due to the late afternoon hour. Finally, she spotted him at his booth, disassembling things. He looked up when he saw her coming.

"Aidan." She gestured to his empty tables. "What's going on?"

He folded the flaps on the lava lamp's box. "I'm all out of coffee."

"I see that."

"That was quite a contest," he said. "Neck and neck till the very end."

"Yeah, but…" She pursed her lips. "Looks like you've won it."

"No, Charlotte," he said softly. "You have."

His words washed over her in a warm wave, and yet they made no sense. "What?"

Aidan's eyes sparkled dimly. "I believe you've won the contest. We can run the numbers if you'd like, but I'm very sure you outsold me at coffee."

"But how?"

"I stopped selling my coffee more than an hour ago. I wound up giving it away."

Her heart pounded. "Why?"

"Because I realized something, Charlotte. You were right about what you said. Fifty percent just isn't good enough. You and your family? You deserve it all."

She gasped. "All of Bearberry Coffee?"

"I trust you'll learn what to do with it and that you'll treat it with care. No matter what you think of my father, he took pains to build a solid company. All that I ask is that you honor his legacy, as tainted as it is, because, well." He swallowed hard. "It's my legacy too."

She didn't get this. "So, you're what? Just giving

up? Walking away?"

Leaving me?

Her lungs seized up and for an instant she couldn't breathe. Her heart pounded in her throat and her palms went clammy.

"You've won the contest fair and square." He nodded. "Congratulations."

She went all lightheaded and her stomach churned, like at any moment she was going to throw up. This wasn't a fair contest if he threw it, but now he had, and he was abandoning her.

"Aidan. I don't know." She drew in a shaky breath. "This doesn't feel right."

"But it's everything you wanted."

No, not everything.

The realization hit her like a lightning bolt slamming down from the sky. She didn't just want the corporation, she wanted *him*. She tried to speak, but the words caught in her throat.

"Don't worry about the transition," he said. "I'll make sure it goes smoothly. If you'd rather manage things from here than from London, that can be arranged. And here's a newsflash." He grinned. "Trudy will be staying in Majestic to help you."

"Trudy?" Her head spun. "What?"

He ran a hand through his hair. "She's fallen for Jordan. Believe it or not, they're engaged."

Charlotte's jaw dropped. "Engaged? As in to be married?"

Aidan shook his head. "I know." His eyes sparkled. "Talk about rash."

"Who does that?"

He crossed his arms. "Beats me." His face was a

warm ray of sunshine, but deep inside she only felt rain. Heavy, drowning rain. A downpour, filling her soul to the brim with excruciating sadness.

"In any case." He inhaled deeply. "Trudy's all filled in. She's staying on next week to see the paperwork through. She and Jordan will work things out once she's closed down her position in London." He shifted on his feet. "You and I should be able to tackle the handoff remotely. I'll introduce you by video conference to my team."

Hurt burned through her. This was what she wanted. What she'd thought she'd wanted, so badly. The victory rang hollow, though. "Remotely. I see."

"That way, you can stay right here with your family."

"Yeah," she murmured, still getting her head around it. He'd given her his entire company. No strings.

He peered into her eyes. "You are happy about this?"

Her heart thumped. "Yes."

"Because if I've gotten it wrong?" His voice grew rough. "In any way?"

But this wasn't all up to her. Thunder rumbled in her soul. There was only one reason he wouldn't speak up. He didn't feel it, too. She stood up taller in her boots, determined to handle this with grace and style. She'd dealt with disappointment before. She'd survive this.

"No. It's perfect, thanks."

"Charlotte?" He stared deeply into her eyes, longingly it seemed.

She held her breath, grasping at straws. Clinging

to a small shred of hope.

Please, say it. Tell me you don't want to go—you don't want to leave me behind.

He smiled, but his smile said goodbye. "I'm going to miss you, is all."

Her heart shattered to bits. "I'll miss you, too."

Her eyes grew hot, but she was not going to cry for Aidan. No. Like Nell said, it was his loss.

She saw Allison and Darcy coming and turned away, walking back toward the café. The last thing she wanted to do was talk to either of them. Let them get the story from Aidan, if he wanted to share.

There he went. Pulling the rug out from under her—again. And she'd had absolutely nothing to say about it. She should be happy about winning Bearberry Coffee, and she was. She just wasn't thrilled with the way it had happened, or about Aidan breaking her heart.

CHAPTER TWENTY-SEVEN

Charlotte turned off the light in the storeroom and shut the door. It had taken them less time to pack things up than to put them out this morning. It helped that they'd sold most of their inventory. Aidan had disappeared with Crystal's van shortly after he and Charlotte had talked and had been ferrying things back to the B&B in shifts. Like Crystal's sixties decorations and any loaners and surplus supplies that Trudy would return to their associate vendors on Monday.

This was so surreal. She'd won Bearberry Coffee, all of it. She should be ecstatic. Instead, she felt in a fog. Nothing was clear anymore. Her emotions were all churned up. Every ounce of her ached. Her too-hot eyes. Her rocky stomach. Her sore and tender heart.

Misty slid into her denim jacket in the hallway. "Talk about a wild day."

Lucas stood beside her. "Amazing how it worked out, yeah." He shook his head. "I had a feeling about Aidan."

"Oh yeah?" Charlotte asked. "What kind of feeling?"

Lucas shrugged. "That he's not a bad guy."

No. He was a great guy. Surprisingly selfless in the end. But he didn't want Charlotte. He wanted her to have his company, though. That was no small consolation. It was huge.

Grant was hanging around, waiting on Nell.

"I can't believe it about Jordan and Trudy," Charlotte told him.

"Wait." Nell paused in putting on her coat. It was the puffy kind with a big fuchsia collar made of feathers. Charlotte wouldn't be caught dead in it. Misty, either. But Nell could pull it off. "What's happening with Jordan and Trudy?" She glanced at Grant, who shrugged.

"Wow. This must be hot off the press then," Charlotte said. "They're engaged."

"*What?*" Nell shrieked. "Already? How super!"

Grant rubbed the side of his neck. "I mean, Jordan might have mentioned he was going through with it, but I didn't think today. They've been spending tons of time together and I knew he was in pretty deep."

Misty grinned. "Well, I think it's cool."

"Yeah," Lucas said. "Me too."

They all got ready to go and Misty paused, looking around. "Everybody heard about Sean, right?"

Lucas smiled. "Now we know why he's been so distracted and where he's been."

"Right," Misty said. "Great for him!"

Charlotte blinked. "Okay. I missed this."

"Charlotte," Nell said. "He's been doing virtual auditions online — with Nashville! Some music studio over there wants to give him a listen in person."

"Seriously? Whoa."

"I know." Misty chuckled. "He's talked about this forever and finally followed through. I'm honestly really proud of him."

"Yeah," Lucas said. "Me too. Only now I'll have

to scout about for a new replacement manager."

"Possibly," Misty corrected. "It's not a done deal."

Grant crossed his fingers. "Let's hope for Sean's sake it works out. How cool would that be? All of us knowing a celebrity."

They chattered as they shut the rest of the place down. Charlotte's parents had gone home more than an hour ago, floating on a happy bubble after Charlotte had shared the news about them being able to retire and travel, if they wanted. In any case, they were going to be taken care of financially for the rest of their days.

Grant held open the alley door and Charlotte followed Nell into the chilly cold. "This is awesome news on all fronts," he said. "Maybe we should call Jordan and Trudy and go out and celebrate? Sean, too."

Misty's face lit up. "Great idea."

But Charlotte felt like she'd done enough celebrating last night at Nell's place.

"You all go on ahead," she said. "I'm beat after today."

"It doesn't seem like you should be alone tonight," Nell told her.

"I'll be all right. I could probably use the downtime. I'm meeting Trudy at the bank on Monday and want to spend tomorrow getting organized."

Lucas punched buttons on his phone. "I'll reach out to Aidan. Bet he'd like to come." His phone dinged a few seconds later and he frowned. "Or maybe not."

"What?" Grant asked him.

Lucas looked up. "He's changed his flight for tomorrow and is leaving super early."

Charlotte fought the heat in her eyes and the twisting burn in her heart.

Leaving.

Of course he was.

. . .

Aidan left the inn and zipped up his jacket, heading for the beach. He needed a walk to clear his head and sort through all that had happened these past ten days in Majestic.

Lonely shadows painted the cobblestone street, accentuating the gloominess in his soul. As he rounded the corner, Saturday night sounds hummed up from the dock area from its restaurants and bars. Charlotte's townhouse was down that way, but he doubted she was home. Likely out with her sisters, celebrating. Lucas had texted about a group of them going out and had been nice enough to ask him along. But Aidan hadn't felt like doing anything cheery tonight.

He approached the stone steps, glancing down the street at Mariner's. Doing a lively business tonight, judging by the bar scene through its big front window. The upstairs windows were darker and candlelight flickered on tables. Charlotte had looked beautiful during their dinner date together, but—even then—something about her had changed. When he'd seen her on the beach flying that kite, she'd been a bright, bold butterfly. So effervescent and free. But at Mariner's, she'd folded those pretty wings back into that cocoon of hers, shutting him out.

He descended the steps to the beach, which was mostly deserted. A group of teenagers passed him on their way up the steps. Then an older couple appeared. He was stunned to recognize them as Mr. and Mrs. Delaney. They had their trouser legs rolled up and strolled hand in hand, walking barefoot toward the steps.

"Aidan, son?" Mr. Delaney said, squinting at him in the moonlight. "Is that you?"

Mrs. Delaney trained her flashlight on his eyes and Aidan blinked. "It *is* him." She lowered the flashlight in her hand. "Oh, sorry!"

Aidan nodded at them. "Mr. and Mrs. Delaney."

Mrs. Delaney met his eyes. "We heard you were leaving tomorrow." She frowned. "Why so soon?"

"Exactly." Mr. Delaney smiled. "No need to rush. We'd wanted to have you over to dinner as a thank-you."

Mrs. Delaney tittered. "Although no amount of pot roast could be enough." She beamed at him. "Aidan, what you did today was remarkable. Thank you."

Mr. Delaney's forehead creased. "Above and beyond the call, son. We wouldn't blame you for thinking twice about it." Anxiety showed in his tone.

Aidan rushed to put him at ease. "Don't worry, Mr. Delaney. My mind's made up. I've already signed my portion of the paperwork. Charlotte will sign hers on Monday."

"She's a headstrong girl, our Charlotte." Mr. Delaney's blue eyes sparkled and for an instant they looked so much like Charlotte's.

Mrs. Delaney nodded. "Stubborn as an ox sometimes."

"She's good-hearted, though," Mr. Delaney said. "Very sweet at her core."

Aidan shifted on his feet, uncomfortable they were telling him this. "Yes, she's very special."

Mrs. Delaney switched off her flashlight when the ambient light from the streetlamps up above them flooded their faces. "The two of you seemed to be getting along for a time."

Mr. Delaney leaned toward him and whispered, "We saw you flying kites from the café's window."

Aidan's neck warmed. "Who else saw?"

Mrs. Delaney giggled. "Just the two of us." She glanced at her husband. "We used to do that, too, but it's been a while."

Aidan smiled at her. "Yes, I remember."

Mr. Delaney snapped his fingers. "That's right. You always came with us when we took the girls."

Aidan rubbed his chin. "Those were good times."

"Not all good times have to end." Mr. Delaney patted his shoulder. "You sure you won't stay in Majestic just a few more days?"

"No, sir. I've got things to get back to in London."

Mrs. Delaney cocked her head. "You'll have to come back and visit us, then."

Aidan wasn't so sure he could do that. He felt like this chapter was closing.

"Will we see you tomorrow?" Mrs. Delaney asked.

"Don't think so. My flight leaves early."

Mr. Delaney held out his hand. "In that case, safe travels."

Aidan shook Mr. Delaney's thick hand then Mrs. Delaney hugged his shoulders. "Give my best to your mom."

"Will do." Aidan sank his hands in his pockets as they climbed the steps, once again holding hands. All those years together and they were still obviously in love. Now that was an inspiration.

He removed his shoes, deciding to walk away from the lighthouse this time. Going back in that direction would remind him of Charlotte, as if her parents hadn't reminded him enough. They'd clearly been hinting about something regarding their middle daughter, he just wasn't sure what. Nobody had to tell him she was headstrong. He'd experienced that enough. He supposed he was stubborn, too. That seemed to be just one more thing he and Charlotte had in common.

His shoulders sank as he drew near the water, strolling across wet sand. The soles of his feet chilled, reminding him of the silly game he'd played with Charlotte while tugging her into the waves. He'd been so desperate to kiss her then, just like he'd been at the oyster festival. By the time they'd gotten back to her place, he'd been out of his mind to take her in his arms. Then, finally, he had.

He didn't believe that chemistry was all that existed between them. In his gut, he intuited they shared much more. Ambition. Creativity. Passion. A sense of duty to their families, as different as those families were. Aidan glanced over his shoulder at the stone steps that were now far behind him. The Delaneys were a great family, and his was what it was. He knew his mum loved him in her own way, and—intellectually—he figured his dad must have cared for him on some level as well. It had just been awfully hard not feeling it.

Aidan was glad he'd given all of Bearberry Coffee to Charlotte. It was the right thing to do. Him leaving here tomorrow was also the right thing. There'd been that moment at the festival when he and Charlotte had said goodbye, and he'd wondered if she might say something about the two of them. Let on—even the tiniest bit—that she cared. If she'd given him any sort of sign, maybe he'd have been tempted to try forging a real relationship with her.

But it was obviously for the best that she hadn't. Traveling for a job was one thing. Being emotionally unavailable was so much worse. Aidan's heart thumped at the fear he'd turned out like his father. Even if Charlotte somehow miraculously cared for him, she was bound to want more than he could provide. She must have sensed this. That's why she'd put on the brakes during their dinner conversation at Mariner's. She'd already known what it had taken Aidan too long to figure out. Heat prickled the back of his eyes, making them burn hot. That the two of them had no future.

The wind whipped up, nipping Aidan's face. He blinked and dragged his palms across his cheeks. They were damp… Was he crying? He was mostly a Brit now and definitely not a weeper. What was happening to him?

He sniffed and turned toward the sea, welcoming the ocean's sharp breeze and pulling himself together. He hadn't become emotional like this since he'd been first sent off to boarding school, and it made no sense for him to fall apart now. He'd come to Maine with a very specific agenda, and he'd more than delivered, making full amends for his dad's previous wrongs. Now his work here was done and it was time to go home.

His gaze panned the white-tipped waves glistening in the moonlight. Way over there—across the sea—his home was waiting in London. Although, somehow, he already felt homesick for Majestic— and for Charlotte most of all.

• • •

Charlotte sat at her kitchen table, working on *The Princess Bride* collage she'd started Thursday night. She was too wound up to do anything besides clip and paste. She didn't even need any music. She was in the zone.

This was so much better than going out with the others to celebrate. Her heart hadn't felt like celebrating her achievement. As amazing as it was, she felt like it had been handed to her, not that she'd earned it. That was the precise kind of arrangement she'd been trying to avoid with Aidan when she'd suggested their "winner takes all" coffee contest. She'd never wanted herself—or her family—to be a charity case.

Now, Aidan was leaving in the morning and he hadn't even said a proper goodbye. Saying "so long" at the festival didn't count. They'd been in a public place, and there were a few things that needed to be said just between the two of them.

Shame coursed through her. Yeah, she'd blown a

chance to do that at Mariner's. Aidan had wanted to talk about the future, but she hadn't been open to it. Maybe because, in her mind, her heart had already slammed that door shut, walling itself off again as it always did when she sensed she and some guy were becoming too close.

If Aidan were more like Wesley from *The Princess Bride*, maybe he would have pursued her. Fought off six-fingered men and giants to prove his true love. Charlotte stared down at the letters she'd cut out for "true love" and that she intended to add to her collage.

That was a laugh because Aidan didn't love her. They'd only kissed a couple of times and had gone out and had fun. They'd also competed against each other very fiercely, until he'd run that white flag up his ship's mast, throwing in the towel.

She glanced toward her living room and out her bay window, wondering what he was doing at the moment. Maybe he was thinking of her. Her heart wrenched. Or maybe he wasn't. Since he'd moved his flight up, he was clearly eager to get out of town. But why would he be in a rush to go if it wasn't on account of her?

She'd gone back and forth so many times, wanting to believe Aidan really cared for her, and then convincing herself he didn't. He could have spoken up at Fall Fest, or even earlier at Mariner's, but he hadn't. Charlotte's face warmed because she didn't know what she would have told him if he had. She also owned the guilty truth that she could have spoken up, too, and didn't.

Charlotte sighed, wondering if fairytales were

still possible. Maybe Aidan would surprise her? Send her a text or knock on her door? Both Nell and Misty had found their own princes who'd made grand gestures in wooing them. But it was silly to make that comparison, because Aidan wasn't the grand gesture type.

Wait.

She rubbed her nose when it burned hot. What about him giving her all of Bearberry Coffee? You really couldn't get any grander than that. What if he hadn't been trying to trip her up by pulling the rug out from under her? Maybe he'd wanted to do something for her and her family out of kindness. In restitution, sure. But, possibly, also out of love?

Her heart thumped and then it beat harder.

No. That was too big a reach. She was reading too much into it. Ceding the entire corporation to the Delaneys had been about making things right with her family and not about her personally. She'd not been that great an influence on Aidan. He didn't even know her.

Charlotte's eyes brimmed with heat, but she held back her tears.

She grabbed another magazine and thumbed through it, searching for the bridal image she'd seen earlier. She'd create a gold crown from yellow-colored cut-outs and add that to the veil on the bride's head. This collage was going to be the very best. Lively and fun. Her heart ached. It would also probably remind her of Aidan every single day.

She checked the text messages on her phone, but nothing new had come through. Her sisters and their guys were all out partying, along with Jordan and

Trudy. Who knew about those two? While their courtship had seemed short, so had Nell's with Grant and Misty's with Lucas. Although, in those cases, the couples had shared a certain history.

Trudy and Jordan getting together seemed pretty abrupt, but, apparently, both of them had known they were meant for each other the instant they met. She definitely hadn't felt that with Aidan. She'd been irritated with him more than anything, and with good cause. He'd had a lot of nerve showing up in Majestic and telling her he'd never want to marry her. She definitely hadn't wanted to marry him then—or now.

He was such an annoying guy. Even when he'd stopped being annoying, that had annoyed her, because his niceness had been unpredictable. Then, when he'd become more reliably nice, he'd turned into the most frustrating person of all, because— probably without meaning to—he'd made her want to like him. The next thing she knew, she really liked him. Then she got that scare-the-daylights-out-of-you fear that she was falling for the guy.

Which was ridiculous.

She should have never let herself—or her heart—go there.

A lump welled in her throat, leaving it tender and raw. She took a sip of water and it hurt going down, like it had to slosh its way past huge knots of emotion.

She'd worried about becoming more deeply involved with Aidan, and making things worse, but she wasn't sure how she could feel any more terrible than she did right now. Like, maybe she'd finally met a guy she could talk to—and laugh with. Someone she could run down the beach with flying kites. Someone who could send her to the moon with his kisses and sprinkle her world with stardust when he smiled. Someone who *got her*, and who wasn't afraid of her strength for once. The kind of man who could really make her happy, and someone she'd want to make happy, too.

She checked her phone again, but there still weren't any new messages, and it was getting late. Charlotte's eyes burned hot, but she willed herself not to cry. She'd told herself she wouldn't cry for Aidan, and anyway, what was the point of doing that here and now?

He'd evidently made up his mind and was going back to London tomorrow.

She drew in a deep, shuddering breath, her whole body aching.

This was what she *hadn't* wanted happening.

She wrapped her arms around herself when her heart clenched.

She felt dizzy, sick.

Abandoned.

Ooh. She grabbed the edge of her table, bracing herself on her arms. Her stomach roiled and bile rose in her throat. Nooo! Her skin flushed hot and her insides revolted.

She raced upstairs to the bathroom—making it just in time.

CHAPTER TWENTY-EIGHT

Charlotte woke up the next morning well before dawn. She'd barely slept a wink, tossing and turning. It had taken a while for her stomach to calm down, but the sparkling water with lemon and crackers had eventually helped. She couldn't believe she'd let herself get so tied up in knots over Aidan. If he was leaving, he was leaving. There was nothing she could do.

She checked the clock on her nightstand. Only five!

She rolled onto her side, attempting to go back to sleep. He was probably up now. Maybe even headed to the airport. If not yet, she was betting soon.

Charlotte flipped over onto her stomach, feeling grumpy with him—and herself. She'd gotten herself so worked up she'd become physically ill. Over Aidan? Seriously? He wasn't worth it. If he was, he would have come here last night, or texted her at least. Something, anything. Even an email.

But no.

She grumbled and flipped over again, holding onto her pillow. Last night she was sad, but now she was angry. What kind of guy just gets on a plane to London without clearing the air? Aidan. That's who. He had to have felt the pull between them, the deep longing and attraction. The caring, maybe even love. She had *not* been imagining it. She'd been right in the beginning, when she'd accused him of being a chicken.

The sound echoed in her brain.

Balk, balk, balk, balk. Balk, balk, balk, balk!

Charlotte sat up in her bed and gasped, alarm bells ringing in her head.

You're the chicken, Charlotte.

She gritted her teeth. Nuh-uh. No way.

"I am not the chicken!" she shouted up at her ceiling.

Her heart clenched so hard it felt like a great big fist was around it. Ow.

Or maybe I am.

But what was she supposed to do? Race out there and declare her love for Aidan? Not in a million years, thank you very much. If he refused to do that for her, she for sure wasn't going to confess that to him. Besides that, it was probably too late.

Charlotte switched on the light on her nightstand, tired of trying to fall back to sleep, which was not happening. She groused and grabbed the sweatshirt hanging over the back of her chair. She'd worn leggings and a tank top to bed and the air was chilly this morning, seeping in through the slightly cracked window.

The sound of the waves generally lulled her to sleep, then the clanking of the fishing boats woke her up. This morning, she'd even beaten the fisherfolk in rising early. She splashed cold water on her face and brushed her teeth before loping downstairs, desperate for her coffee.

When she reached the living room, she stopped.

She'd been so tired when she'd finally gone to bed, she'd accidentally left a lamp on. Its glow cast a bright beam of light across her collage. She'd propped it up on the sofa and one set of letters jumped out at her.

They spelled: *True Love*.

In *The Princess Bride*, that's what had been worth living and dying for.

Last night, she'd made herself so sick from nerves, she'd felt like she was dying. In the early light of day, Charlotte suddenly wondered if she'd ever really let herself live. Boldly, by taking those big chances. The hard ones that turned your gut inside out and made you sweat bullets. The difficult choices that made you literally sick with worry because you were putting yourself out there and laying yourself on the line. Opening your heart to risk, and possibly devastation. She didn't know for a fact that Aidan didn't love her. She'd left it all on him to come forward first. What if he'd been just like she was? Afraid of taking that major leap?

Wait. No. But yeah.

Charlotte held her head and groaned. Oh. My. Gosh! He'd been so totally right. She and he were two of a kind. Too stubborn and proud to admit what was going on between them. For fear of what? Failing? Not being loved back? Not being able to love the other fully enough? Well, she was not being loved now, was she? Not sitting here trying to pretend that her heart wasn't breaking into two ghastly pieces.

No.

Charlotte mentally kicked herself, staring at her collage. Though she'd been in denial, her heart had sensed this all along. She'd been waiting on Aidan to

be her Dread Pirate Roberts and scale castle walls
for her, playing the hero.

Charlotte covered her mouth in shock.

Aidan wasn't the famed dread pirate.

Hello! *She* was.

He'd already made a huge sacrifice for her and
her family. Now it was her time to step up and make
a daring move. If she didn't try now, she'd never
know what might have been, and leading that kind
of life would be worse than dying.

Charlotte checked the time on her phone.

Oh no. If he hadn't gone already, he'd be leaving
any minute. She had to hurry!

. . .

Aidan took a final look around the Majestic B&B.
This was it, then. Time to head back to London. He
felt like he was in a stupor, as if all this was surreal.
His whole life was changing, but he was oddly de-
tached from it. Maybe this was how his dad had
always gotten by—on autopilot.

Crystal handed him a travel cup of coffee. "Your
car should be here any minute."

He smiled at her. "Thanks for arranging it."

Trudy hurried down the stairs in her robe and
slippers. "Aidan! Hang on."

He was going to miss having her in London once
she moved here. Then again, he'd no longer be at
Bearberry Coffee, so he'd be leaving lots of folks
behind.

"I can't believe you'd push off without a proper
hug." She held out her arms, and he hugged her for

the first time since they'd begun working together. It would have seemed unprofessional before. Now, it was more like saying so long to a friend. He'd known and trusted Trudy for a lot of years.

"Thanks for cleaning up here and, you know." He lifted his backpack, slinging it over his shoulder. "Helping Charlotte with the transition."

His gut churned. As right a move as ceding his company to Charlotte was, something about the handoff still felt wrong. But he'd been over the paperwork—again and again—several times last night, and everything appeared in order. What wasn't completely in order was his heart. He'd fallen for her harder than he'd allowed himself to understand. His imminent departure from Majestic caused him to confront it.

Trudy smiled brightly. "I'll see you back in London," she said. "There'll be stuff to see through on that end."

"I'll want to help all I can." He frowned. "Without being in anybody's way."

"And you and Charlotte?"

Aidan glanced at Crystal, who ducked away. "Have a safe flight now!" she said, heading for the kitchen.

"Thanks, Crystal. For everything." He'd already thanked Mr. Mulroney last night. He returned his gaze to Trudy, who stood there waiting. "I'm afraid there is no me and Charlotte."

She blinked. "But I thought—"

"We got along," he said. "Had a laugh." He'd never tell his soon-to-be former assistant the truth. He'd fallen head over heels for a woman who didn't return his feelings. But that was okay. She was an amazing woman who would find her way forward. One day, with the right guy.

A haunting voice in his heart said, *that man could be you.*

But he knew that was impossible. They'd said their goodbyes at Fall Fest. It was time for him to move on. He was tough and capable. But he was no Dread Pirate Roberts. Not the sort to wear his heart on his billowing shirt sleeve while wielding a flash sword, and Charlotte was no Princess Buttercup. She was light years away from being a damsel in distress. She was an independent woman who could probably have any man she wanted.

"In any case." He glanced at the front door. "It's off to new horizons for me."

Trudy eyed him sadly. "Where will those be?"

He sighed, actually having no idea. "I suppose I can write my own ticket."

She braced his arms and said warmly, "Let's do keep in touch." She cocked her head. "After."

After Charlotte owned Bearberry Coffee, she meant, and Aidan was out of the picture.

"No worries," he said. "We will." A car horn sounded outside. "That would be my ride."

He opened the inn's front door, and a fresh blast of autumn greeted his senses. The rush of salty air, the quiet rustle of leaves, the lulling tune of the sea. Majestic, Maine, made its own kind of music. He remembered that from when he was a boy.

He recalled lots of other things, too. Like what it was like being a part of the Delaneys' inner circle, and hanging out with those girls, even when they teased him. He secretly hadn't minded because he'd liked fitting in with their crowd. He'd liked being around Charlotte best of all. She'd chided him and challenged him and had never been afraid to tell him how she felt.

Until now?

He stared at the car at the curb, his heart beating harder.

Charlotte had always been proud—and stubborn, her folks were right. Maybe even too stubborn to admit she'd also fallen for him? Aidan raked a hand through his hair. That seemed like such a stretch. And yet. What if it wasn't?

Trudy poked her head out the door. "Is everything okay?"

He turned from where he stood on the porch. "Not sure."

His driver grew impatient, lightly tooting his horn, and Aidan held up one hand.

Being pressured to go only made him want to dig in his heels.

Stay.

With Charlotte.

His dad had doggedly looked out for his company, but he'd never defended the people he supposedly cared for. He'd been far too distracted to even pay attention half the time. But Aidan wasn't his father. He was attentive and careful. He minded other people's feelings, yet he'd been neglecting his own. He'd also been stupidly oblivious to Charlotte's.

Oh, how he hoped.

He passed Trudy his paper coffee cup. "Would

you mind holding this?"

"Sure, but—"

The driver tapped his wrist like he was wearing a watch, and Aidan scowled. "And also cancel the car."

"What?"

Aidan passed his backpack to Trudy, who took it along with his coffee cup, her mouth hanging open. "Boss?" she asked, as he strode down the steps and into the burgeoning daylight. "Where are you going?"

"I forgot something!" he called over his shoulder. *I'm my own man.*

He started walking faster and faster, until he broke into a jog, and then a sprint. Running with all his might toward the dock area and Charlotte's place.

· · ·

Charlotte dashed to the coffee table and scooped up her pirate hat, setting it on her head. Then she raced for the door. Her cowgirl boots were beside it. She wiggled those on and grabbed her keys. Her gut wrenched and she brought a hand to her belly.

But no, she could do this. Push past her fear.

It's now or never.

She chose now!

It was dark out with streetlamps lighting her way. She tore down the sidewalk and across cobblestones. The clanking began at the docks. Time was wasting. She could *not* let Aidan get away. Charlotte sprinted uphill, hanging onto her pirate hat. She was nearly to the street housing the Majestic B&B. Charlotte rounded the corner, nearly colliding with Aidan.

"Charlotte!" He braced her arms with his hands, sounding out of breath. His eyes shone in the early light of dawn and his face went red beneath his beard.

Her heart pounded. It wasn't too late!

"Aidan." She huffed and puffed, staring up at him below the brim of her hat.

He shot her a curious look. "You're out awfully early."

"I know." She wheezed then caught her breath. "I was coming to find you."

"Now, that's something." He relaxed his hold on her arms but didn't let go, and she was glad. She didn't totally trust her legs to support her. Her knees shook and her whole body trembled. "I was coming to find *you*."

"You were?" She licked her lips, terrified of the task ahead and delighted he'd wanted to see her. Maybe he wanted to officially say goodbye? But not until he heard her. "I thought you were on your way to the airport?"

"I'm not going to the airport, Charlotte." His gaze poured into her, blanketing her soul in warmth. "Not today."

"Aidan, I—"

He brought a finger to her lips and said tenderly, "Me first."

Emotion crashed over her like warring ocean waves. She hoped it was good news, whatever he had to say. *Please, please, please. Please.*

He gently released his grip. "I wasn't being completely honest yesterday." His husky words combed through the wind. "I could have told you how I feel, but I didn't." He raked a hand through his hair. "Maybe because I hadn't pieced it all together myself until last night. And maybe." He pursed his lips. "The rest of it finally came together for me this morning."

He stared deeply into her eyes. "I've fallen for you, Charlotte Delaney. Truly. Madly. Desperately. And I was gutted when I thought you didn't feel the same. I was also afraid," he blinked and briefly looked away, "that I was too much like my dad. Someone who could never give his heart fully."

"Aidan, no." She blushed because she didn't believe that of him.

He smiled down at her. "But you were right and I was wrong. I'm my own man. I also don't have to be my father to learn from the mistakes he made, and one of his biggest was not showing his family he cared. But, Charlotte," he said. "That's not me."

Understanding bloomed in her heart. "No," she said softly.

His gaze swept over her pirate hat and her nose burned hot. "It's not me, either, Aidan." Her pulse pounded in her throat and she gripped her power crystal. "I know that now. Know that—" Her stomach tensed but she released a calming breath. "There are some things worth fighting for. Worth living and dying for."

His handsome grin rivaled the most majestic sunrise. "True love," he said huskily.

"Yeah." Charlotte smiled, her lips trembling. "I made this collage."

He stepped closer. "Oh yeah?"

She nodded. "It's about *The Princess Bride*."

He chuckled warmly. "Branching out into movies now?"

"I am branching out." She gathered her courage. "In lots of ways."

"That's awesome."

Nerves skittered through her, but she had to stay strong. Maybe the best way to do that was by admitting her weakness. Aidan seemed to know she was on the brink of a confession.

"Whatever it is, Charlotte," he said gently. "I'm here."

"Aidan." Her chin wobbled and her eyes grew hot. "I'm afraid."

His forehead wrinkled. "Of—me?"

"No, not of you." A tear leaked from her eye. "Of losing you."

Aidan brought his arms around her. "You're not going to lose me, Charlotte."

Every fiber of her being wanted to believe that was true.

He lowered his mouth to hers and sweetly kissed her. "I'm not going anywhere," he rasped softly. He reached up and stroked back her tear with his thumb.

"You say that now." Her chin trembled.

He tipped up her chin, holding it in his hand. He scanned her eyes. "I mean that forever."

"How can you be so sure?"

"I can't," he said hoarsely. "But I can do my damnedest to work toward our future."

Our future. Her heart danced at the sound of that.

"Aidan," she said. His hand slid into her hair, cradling the nape of her neck. "I don't want all of Bearberry Coffee. I want to share it with you."

"Sorry, darling." His eyes twinkled. "No dice. You won it from me, fair and square."

She shoved his shoulder. "First off, that wasn't fair—or square. You threw the contest."

"Hmm, yeah." He lightly smirked. "Like you did the one about marrying me?"

"Now, stop." She blushed, but already her heart felt lighter. "I mean it, though," she persisted. "About the company."

He held her closer. "The paperwork has already been signed."

"On your end," she reminded him.

He pulled back to gaze at her. "I want you to still sign it on yours." His summer rain scent washed over her and she grew a little breathy.

"Then what?"

"I don't know." He shrugged. "Maybe you can hire me?"

"Hire?" Her mouth fell open, then she closed it.

"That could be a little sexy." His eyes held a devilish gleam. "Me working for you."

She giggled, her tension easing. "Oh, Aidan."

He lifted one eyebrow. "I'm serious, though."

She sassily cocked her head. "All right. I'll consider it."

He tugged on the brim of her hat. "Love this."

"Oh yeah?" She removed it from her head. "Well, here's a little newsflash." Charlotte dropped down on her knees, right there on the sidewalk. The morning foot traffic on Kittery Street had just started with the McIntyres approaching their market, and the paper carrier tossing out the newest edition of *The Seaside Daily*.

"Um, Charlotte?" He peered up and down the street. "What are you doing?"

"I'm making my pronouncement, you big knuck-lehead!"

He laughed, but a million sunrises were written in his eyes. A million sunsets, too. And suddenly Charlotte could envision spending them all with Aidan. From the corner of her eye, she saw some fisherfolk heading for the dock who'd paused to stop and stare. She thought she spied her parents at the end of the street, too. But none of that mattered.

She stared up at her one true love. "Aidan Strong," she said bravely. She raised her voice above the ocean's roar. "I want to be that person for you. The one that you can count on. The one that you can laugh with. Fly kites with! I want to be your lover and friend. No matter how hard things get, or what it takes to settle our differences." She boldly shouted louder, sending her words winging up to the heavens. "I'm ready to scale castle walls for you! Fight giants and pirates! Win at any battle of wits!"

A grin spread across his face. "You'd do all that for me? Fight giants?"

"Six-fingered men, too!" she said, making another reference to the movie.

His laughter filled her soul, chasing out her fear of falling. Because, the truth was, she'd already taken that dive. She pressed her pirate hat to her chest. "Aidan Strong," she said. "I want to be your Dread Pirate Charlotte, if you'll pretty please be my Prince

Buttercup?" Her heart pounded in her throat as she stared up at him, waiting. Maybe she'd made a wrong move. "I mean." She winced. "This is the twenty-first century?"

He latched onto her hands and tugged her to her feet as her pirate hat spiraled into the road. "So, Trudy was right," he teased. "You *do* fancy me." She couldn't believe he was ribbing her now. But yeah, he was, and she still loved him for it because she loved him. That's all there was to it.

"I more than *fancy* you, Aidan." Her pulse fluttered. "I've fallen for you very hard."

"It's funny how alike we are, because I've fallen for you, too." He reached down into the road and picked up her hat, tamping it down firmly on her head. He smiled from ear to ear. "So. You're going to be my Dread Pirate Charlotte?"

She laughed, loving the sound of him saying that. "Aye, laddie. If you'll have me."

"I'll have you all right," he said in a sexy growl. He tugged her into his embrace, his warmth enveloping her in the early morning chill. But then he grew tender, cradling her cheek with his palm. The look in his eyes was so caring, it heated her through and through. "I'd be utterly lost without you. I hope you know that."

Her breath hitched. "I don't want you to be lost."

"Then bring me home, Charlotte Delaney. Rescue me."

Vaguely, in the background, Charlotte was aware of happy laughter, strangers' sighs, and others saying, *aww, isn't that sweet*. She wrapped her arms around him as applause broke out up and down Kittery

Street. Aidan's mouth grew nearer, and she was captured by his spell. Knowing that he had her, and that he'd meant what he'd said. Aidan wouldn't leave her, and even if someday he somehow did, being with him would have been worth the risk.

"I'm not going to leave you, Charlotte." His husky breath warmed her lips. "Not now." He gave her a sweet peck on the lips. "Not ever." He kissed her again and she swooned. "Not as long as I can help it."

"Wait!" Misty's voice echoed in her ears. "Is that Charlotte?"

"It *is* Charlotte." That was Nell's happy gasp. "With Aidan!"

The chatter around them faded away when his mouth met hers, and Charlotte's heart soared.

Higher than the highest kite.

Dancing through the cloud-dotted sky.

Far beyond the cliffs of Majestic.

And over the tumbling sea.

EPILOGUE

Aidan and Charlotte sat on the bench at the end of the pier with a full view of the lighthouse at Lookout Point and the sea. Both held lobster roll packages in their laps. Aidan uncapped the wine and passed it to Charlotte. "Happy date-aversary, Dread Pirate Charlotte."

She laughed and took the bottle, loving him so much. A shiny engagement diamond sparkled on her left hand next to her wedding band. "To you, too, Prince Buttercup."

Ten years ago today he'd taken her to that oyster festival, and the rest — as they say — was history. A very happy history for sure. Once they'd gotten over those few minor speedbumps.

She took a sip of wine and so did he before setting the bottle on a board by his feet. They'd talked about it, admitting they'd first fallen in love with each other on their kite-flying outing. She'd never been able to let herself go like that with any man before. Feel so free-spirited and alive, but also protected. Safe in the knowledge that he wouldn't let her down. He was her safety net and she was his. They no longer had fears of falling. They'd joined hands and taken the plunge together, and the ride had been amazing the whole way down.

Three kids and a demanding dual-career later,

they were still as head over heels for each other as they'd been during that long-ago day at Fall Fest.

Aidan sat back against the bench and draped his arm around her shoulders. "I'm glad you decided to marry me for real." His eyes twinkled in the fading light. It was early evening and autumn, their favorite time of year. "I was thrilled when you finally asked me."

She smiled. "I was thrilled when you said yes."

They'd spent their first two years together ferrying back and forth between Majestic and London, while effectively merging their companies. Bearberry Coffee now offered a berry-infused line, and their joint marketing acumen had helped both businesses grow. The café was doing well and Nell still worked there as its accountant, while Grant managed his camp store. Nell and Grant had two kids, a boy and a girl, and Misty and Lucas had a new baby girl. Lucas's book café thrived and Misty ran her freelance design business from home.

One year after the merger, Charlotte's parents retired for good after going temporarily part-time. They'd taken a celebratory trip to Ireland, where their dad still had family. He hadn't been back home or able to see many of them for years, and their mom had never visited Ireland at all, making the journey extra special.

Trudy was still with Jordan, who worked with Grant, leading all sorts of rugged adventures, and when she could, Trudy went along. Trudy had become interested in café management and had stepped down from her corporate role to take Lucas's place overseeing Bearberry Brews. She'd brought on a stellar staff of new hires to replace those that had gone on to other things, and Charlotte and Aidan helped out when they could while running their global business remotely in partnership with their London team.

Once they'd learned that Charlotte was expecting their first child, she and Aidan had decided that Majestic was where they'd like to raise their family. Aidan's mom visited often and had taught their girls all about tea party manners. Violet, six, Mia, four, and Abigail, two, were spending tonight with Charlotte's parents, so she and Aidan could have couple time.

Charlotte unwrapped her lobster roll and took a bite. It was just as delicious as always.

"You'll never believe who I heard on the radio today," Aidan said, also enjoying his food.

Charlotte stared at him. "No."

"Yeah, Sean." He grinned. "Pretty amazing."

Charlotte laughed, so happy for Sean, who now lived in Nashville and was a big country music star. "Pretty amazing he married Mary Beth." She sighed. "I love it when things work out."

Aidan's eyes glimmered warmly. "Yeah. Me too." He inhaled the ocean air, his expression serene. "Three girls, Charlotte. Three girls." His eyebrows arched. "Can you believe it?"

She laughed. "I know."

"Do you suppose they'll be as much trouble as you, Misty, and Nell?"

She lightly shoved his chest. "We were never any trouble."

He laughed. "No. Never."

"I know one thing," she said. "They're going to love each other lots."

His smile warmed her heart. "They already do."

They sat there savoring the cool ocean breeze and their wine. The sound of fishing boats mooring at the docks, and the chatter of patrons at outdoor restaurants. The silhouette of the rising moon over the water.

"So. Tony called." He dropped it in casually but her heart pounded. She'd completed several collage series by now and Tony had been trying to get her a show for practically the past decade. Bless him. He and Jill were so cool. Both had become very good friends.

"And?"

"And." He gave her a lopsided grin and her pulse fluttered. "He's got you a gig, Charlotte. Your first art opening."

"What?" Her heart leaped with joy. "That's so exciting!"

"He wants us to come over in November with the girls so you can meet the gallery owner. It's a posh place, very high visibility."

While she'd initially been unsure about publicly displaying her art, once Tony had pursued it, she'd realized how fun it would be to share her work. It was a little daunting, sure, and nerve-wracking, because not everyone was going to love it. But Aidan did. So did her family. She had Tony and Jill's support, too. She finally felt ready to test her wings with the world.

Aidan hugged her. "What do you say? Interested?"

"You bet I am." She grinned, unable to imagine

any life better than this.

Then he held her closer.

"Oh wait," he said, pulling back. "I almost forgot." He patted his jacket pocket and took something out. It looked like a jewelry box.

"Aidan? What?"

"Ten years is epic," he said.

"But we haven't been married ten years." Their wedding had come after Nell's then Misty's, each of them being married a year apart.

"Doesn't matter. This is our date-aversary." His eyes twinkled. "Besides that, I saw this and thought of you."

He handed her the box and she flipped it open. The most gorgeous necklace rested inside. It was pure gold and shaped like a kite with a pretty diamond in its center. Charlotte gasped and covered her mouth. "A kite! How pretty!"

He lightly squeezed her shoulder. "I know you have your crystal." His gaze washed over her and heat warmed her eyes. "But just so you know. You still take my breath away just like you did that very first day when I saw you running down the beach with your Jolly Roger."

A tear leaked from her eye. "I swore I wouldn't do this." She dried her cheek with her napkin. "Cry for you."

He held her chin. "You're not crying for me, you're just showing your heart." He kissed her. "And what a beautiful heart it is."

She smiled. "Thanks, Aidan."

He took the necklace from its box, holding it from its delicate gold chain. "Want to try it on?" She held up her hair so he could close its clasp behind her. The pretty piece of jewelry draped from her neck, landing on the front of her sweater.

"It's gorgeous." She sighed. "Thank you."

"I love you, Charlotte." Things never got old with him, they only got better. It was hard to imagine loving him any more than she did today, but she'd thought that every day for the past ten years.

"I love you, too."

He threaded his fingers through her hair. "So," he said in a sexy growl, "the girls are at your parents' house…" His lips brushed over hers. "What say we head back home and make out on the sofa?"

She kissed him sweetly, her heart so full.

"You've got yourself a deal."

ACKNOWLEDGMENTS

I'd like to thank the many folks who made this book possible, starting with my agent, Jill Marsal, for helping me secure this fun series. Special thanks to editor Heather Howland for acquiring the Majestic Maine trilogy in the first place and to editor Lydia Sharp for her excellent input in shaping my initial manuscript for *Last Bride Standing* into its much finer form today.

Much appreciation as well to Chief Executive Officer and Publisher Liz Pelletier, Associate Publisher and Marketing Director Jessica Turner, Editorial Director Stacy Abrams, Senior Production Editor Curtis Svehlak, Relationship Manager Heather Riccio, Publicity Manager Riki Cleveland, Social Media Manager Meredith Johnson, Contracts Manager Aida Wright, and Subsidiary Rights and Finance Director Katie Clapsadl for their valuable contributions, and a deep bow of gratitude to Art Director Bree Archer for her absolutely beautiful cover. Additional kudos to copyeditor Julia Knapman for an outstanding job, with gratitude to any others who worked on this book, but that I've neglected to name here.

Heartfelt thanks to my sweet husband and family for seeing me through another set of deadlines, and, most importantly, *thank you all* for selecting Charlotte and Aidan's story, *Last Bride Standing*, with which to fill your precious hours. I hope you had a great time in Majestic, and enjoyed cheering on Nell, Misty, and Charlotte as they raced toward their HEAs. I really loved getting to know the Delaneys, and I hope you did, too.

Some towns have a magic all their own in this enchanting new series

Her
Unexpected
Match

USA TODAY BESTSELLING AUTHOR
LACEY BAKER

Travel writer Allie Sparks has one goal: to find the story that will save her career. So here she is, visiting her bestie on picturesque Crescent Island—with sun-warmed beaches, the briny smell of the ocean, and rumors of a secret astrologer-matchmaker who guarantees love. Of course, Allie doesn't believe in *any* of that stuff. If anything, she'll prove it's a total scam.

Ryan Parker believes in love—just not right now. He's focused on expanding his family's barbeque business, finding investors, and keeping his too-big Great Dane puppy from jumping on everyone, including his sister's pretty, whiskey-eyed best friend. Besides, falling for a tourist is definitely *not* in his astrological forecast.

Allie is doing everything she can to resist the charm of the town and its beauty, not to mention her attraction to Ryan. But there's a lot more happening on Crescent Island than anyone knows...and when her story goes to print, this tiny, close-knit town might never be the same.